"*Running Scared* offers titillating mind games."
—Romance Novel News

continued

Finding the Lost

"Exerts much the same appeal as Christine Feehan's Carpathian series, what with tortured heroes, the necessity of finding love or facing a fate worse than death, hot lovemaking, and danger-filled adventure." —*Booklist*

"A terrific grim thriller with the romantic subplot playing a strong supporting role. The cast is powerful, as the audience will feel every emotion that Andra feels, from fear for her sister to fear for her falling in love. *Finding the Lost* is a dark tale, as Shannon K. Butcher paints a forbidding, gloomy landscape in which an ancient war between humanity's guardians and their nasty adversaries heats up in Nebraska." —Alternative Worlds

"A very entertaining read . . . the ending was a great cliff-hanger and I can't wait to read the next book in this series. . . . A fast-paced story with great action scenes and lots of hot romance." —The Book Lush

"Butcher's paranormal reality is dark and gritty in this second Sentinel Wars installment. What makes this story so gripping [are] the seamlessly delivered hard-hitting action and wrenching emotions. Butcher is a major talent in the making." —*Romantic Times*

"Terrific . . . powerful." —*Midwest Book Review*

Burning Alive

"Starts off with nonstop action. Readers will race through the pages . . . a promising start for a new voice in urban fantasy/paranormal romance. I look forward to the next installment." —A Romance Review (5 Roses)

NOVELS OF THE SENTINEL WARS

BLOOD HUNT

THE SENTINEL WARS

SHANNON K. BUTCHER

A SIGNET BOOK

SIGNET
Published by New American Library, a division of
Penguin Group (USA) Inc., 375 Hudson Street,
New York, New York 10014, USA
Penguin Group (Canada), 90 Eglinton Avenue East, Suite 700, Toronto,
Ontario M4P 2Y3, Canada (a division of Pearson Penguin Canada Inc.)
Penguin Books Ltd., 80 Strand, London WC2R 0RL, England
Penguin Ireland, 25 St. Stephen's Green, Dublin 2,
Ireland (a division of Penguin Books Ltd.)
Penguin Group (Australia), 250 Camberwell Road, Camberwell, Victoria 3124,
Australia (a division of Pearson Australia Group Pty. Ltd.)
Penguin Books India Pvt. Ltd., 11 Community Centre, Panchsheel Park,
New Delhi - 110 017, India
Penguin Group (NZ), 67 Apollo Drive, Rosedale, Auckland 0632,
New Zealand (a division of Pearson New Zealand Ltd.)
Penguin Books (South Africa) (Pty.) Ltd., 24 Sturdee Avenue,
Rosebank, Johannesburg 2196, South Africa

Penguin Books Ltd., Registered Offices:
80 Strand, London WC2R 0RL, England

First published by Signet, an imprint of New American Library,
a division of Penguin Group (USA) Inc.

First Printing, August 2011
10 9 8 7 6 5 4 3 2 1

For Nephele Tempest.
Thanks for believing in my work and
always having my back.

Character List

Drake Asher: Theronai warrior, bonded to Helen Day

Briant Athar: Sanguinar

Connal Athar: Sanguinar

Logan Athar: Sanguinar, blood hunter

Aurora: Athanasian servant

Cain Aylward: Theronai warrior, Sibyl's protector

Angus Brinn: Theronai warrior, bonded to Gilda

Gilda Brinn: the Gray Lady, Theronai, bonded to Angus

Maura Brinn: Theronai, Sibyl's twin sister

Sibyl Brinn: Theronai, Maura's twin sister

Canaranth: Synestryn, Zillah's second-in-command

Meghan Clark: blooded human

Helen Day: the Scarlet Lady, Theronai, bonded to Drake Asher

Eron: Athanasian prince

Neal Etan: Theronai warrior

Madoc Gage: Theronai warrior, bonded to Nika Madison

John Hawthorne: blooded human

Mabel Hennesy: blooded human

Lexi Johns: the Jade Lady, Theronai, bonded to Zach Talon

Nicholas Laith: Theronai warrior

Liam Lann: Theronai warrior

Samuel Larsten: Theronai warrior

Thea Lewis: human woman living at Dabyr

Tynan Leygh: Sanguinar

Lucien: Athanasian prince

Andra Madison: the Sapphire Lady, Theronai, bonded to Paul Sloane, sister to Nika and Tori

Nika Madison: the White Lady, Theronai, bonded to Madoc Gage, sister to Andra and Tori

Victoria (Tori) Madison: Theronai, sister to Andra and Nika

Torr Maston: Theronai warrior

Jake Morrow: human, member of the Defenders of Humanity

Blake Norman: human, Grace Norman's stepbrother

Grace Norman: blooded human, Gerai

Jackie Patton: Theronai, daughter of Lucien

Andreas Phelan: Slayer, leader of the Slayers

Joseph Rayd: Theronai warrior, leader of the Sentinels

Viviana Rowan: the Bronze Lady, Theronai, bonded to Neal Etan

Cole Shepherd: blooded human

Alexander Siah: Sanguinar

Paul Sloane: Theronai warrior, bonded to Andra Madison

Carmen Taite: blooded human, Gerai, cousin to Vance and Slade Taite

Slade Taite: blooded human, Gerai, cousin to Carmen, brother to Vance

Vance Taite: blooded human, Gerai, cousin to Carmen, brother to Slade

Zach Talon: Theronai warrior, bonded to Lexi Johns

Iain Terra: Theronai warrior

Morgan Valens: Theronai warrior

Zillah: Synestryn lord

BLOOD
HUNT

Chapter 1

W*hen death comes for you, it will not be gentle.*
    Logan hadn't truly understood Sibyl's prophecy of his death until this moment. But now that he was staring into its jaws, he realized what she had meant.

A Synestryn demon crouched behind a run-down three-story building, its eyes glowing a bright, feral green. It was huge, making the Dumpster beside it look like a milk crate. Heavy muscles bulged in its limbs, quivering in anticipation of the kill. Its breath billowed from all four of its nostrils, creating pale plumes of steam in the cold night air. Bright moonlight gleamed across its skin, reflected off the viscous, poisonous fluid that leaked from its pores.

Logan had never seen anything like it before, but the human, Steve, groaning in pain on the pockmarked asphalt near the demon's feet, was testament to the power of its poison.

The man's wife, Pam, stood pressed against the cold brick, staring in horror at her husband. Her pregnant belly protruded from her slim body, promising the hope of a new generation.

Logan could not let anything happen to that child.

Steve was still moving, but if Logan didn't do something soon, he wasn't going to survive. Not that there was much Logan could do. After days without feeding he was weak, his powers now dwindled to the point he barely had the ability to walk upright.

Hunger churned inside him, demanding that he seek out the blood he needed, but there was no time to feed. No time to gather his strength. No time to call for help.

If this couple and their child—a child he'd worked so hard to see created—were killed, many of his people would starve. Logan could not allow that to happen.

The nameless creature lunged for Logan, bounding up from the pavement in a powerful leap so fast it made the thing look like a streak of moonlight.

Logan pitched his body to the left, hoping to avoid the attack. His shoulder slammed into a brick wall. Pain lanced across his back and down his spine. He slid to the dirty ground before he could catch himself.

The demon careened into a loading dock door, busting through it like tissue paper. The metal screamed as it gave way. Corrugated strips flew into the darkness of the run-down building, leaving behind a giant gaping hole.

A blow like that had to have stunned the demon, or even knocked it out.

Logan needed to carry Steve away from this place, and he knew the man's wife would follow. He'd made it only a few yards when he saw the feral green glow of two large eyes within the gaping hole in the doorway.

A sickening sense of defeat churned in his empty belly. Not only was the Synestryn still on its feet, but Logan now knew he was completely outclassed. If barreling through that metal door didn't slow the thing down, there was nothing Logan, as weak as he was, could do to stop it.

The demon lumbered through the opening, angling itself for another attack.

Steve pushed himself to his knees. He wavered there, next to a frozen mud puddle, between a discarded mattress and a rotting wooden pallet. His skin was roughened by goose bumps. With every passing second, poison went deeper into his system.

Time to grab the couple and run. Leave the Synestryn for someone else. It wasn't his place to destroy the demon. That was best left to those who were stronger than he.

Which currently included ninety percent of the planet's occupants, no doubt.

Logan shoved himself to his feet and sprinted across the slick pavement toward Steve. The tread of his boots slipped over the remnants of dirty snow left from the last storm, but he managed to stay upright and close the distance.

Behind him, the demon snorted out a heavy breath.

Logan spun around to face the thing, putting his body squarely between it and the pregnant woman.

"Please," whispered the woman in a voice trembling with fear. "Save him."

"Go," ordered Logan. "Run. I'll protect him."

"I'm not leaving him."

"Think of your child."

"I am. He needs his father."

There was no more time to argue. The demon charged.

The woman let out a frightened whimper. The heartbeat of the baby boy inside her sped up, as if sensing the danger it could not see.

That child deserved to live. If this demon got hold of the mother, both she and the baby would die because of the blood flowing through their veins.

The injustice made outrage unfurl in Logan's body, spreading dark wings of anger. That demon was not going to take the child—not while Logan still drew breath.

Claws extended from Logan's fingertips and his fangs lengthened. His natural weapons were nothing compared to the wicked blades the Theronai usually carried, but he refused to go down without a fight.

In the back of his mind, a hysterical part of him giggled at the notion of defeating such a creature. At his full strength he'd have a chance, but he was far from that—so far he couldn't even remember what it felt like not to be weak and hungry and cold.

But he had anger on his side, and it fueled him now, giving strength to his wasted limbs.

With a burst of speed, Logan charged the oncoming monster. He leaped to the top of a trash can and propelled himself over the thing's shoulder. His claws dug deep into the demon's slippery flesh, making it howl. Slick, mucuslike poison collected under his fingernails.

Logan straddled the demon's back, trying to choke it with his legs. One wide paw batted at him, its talons raking across his forearm.

Pain sliced up Logan's arm. Poison entered his system.

His first instinct was to shove the last of his dwindling reserves of power into creating an antidote, but there was no time for that. He had to kill the Synestryn before the poison incapacitated him, or being poisoned would be the least of his problems. And Steve's.

The creature headed for the cavelike shelter of the building, carrying Logan along for the ride. As they shoved through the opening, jagged metal sliced his skin, tearing a cry of pain from his lungs.

Logan fished beneath his coat for the dagger he kept hidden there. He stabbed it into the top of the creature's head, hoping to skewer its brain. Its skull was too thick and the blade slid to the side.

The cut to its scalp was deep, making the beast roar in pain. It reached back, grabbed Logan by the head, and whipped him off.

Logan was slammed against the concrete floor. Or maybe it was a wall. His vision was full of bright lights, so it was hard to tell. All he knew was pain and a foggy weakness that kept him pinned to the ground.

A deep vibration beneath him told him that the demon wasn't finished yet. It was still on its feet and it was getting closer.

Steve was growing weaker by the second. He pushed himself to his feet, and the effort left him panting.

Pam was by his side in an instant, her precious face staring up at him in worry. "We need to get you to a hospital."

"You know that won't help," he told her. As one of the Gerai, he knew enough about the Synestryn to realize that there was nothing a human doctor could do for him. "I need Logan."

His wife's face paled as she realized what he meant to do. "You can't. You can't go in there."

"I don't have a choice. I'll die without his help. And he'll die without mine."

"No," whispered Pam. Tears flowed down her cheeks. "You can't go in there. Please."

A wave of weakness shook Steve, telling him he was running out of time. "Go. Someplace public. Well lit. I need to know you and the baby are safe."

"I won't leave you."

"There's no time to argue. You're going. But I won't be long. Promise." The vow settled over him, comforting him. He kissed her mouth, praying it wouldn't be the last time. "Go, love. For our baby. Go."

She nodded. Sniffed.

Steve gently pushed Pam away. She stared at him, her expression a mix of fear and love. "Don't you dare die."

Steve hid his weakness the best that he could as he bent down and picked up a discarded section of two-by-four. It wasn't much of a weapon, but he'd find a way to make it work.

He'd promised to be quick, and he'd never once broken a promise to his sweet Pam.

The color of suffering was a dark, sickly yellow, and Hope Serrien knew she'd see it on a night like tonight.

A cold front had swept down over the city, slaying any hope that spring was coming soon. Power lines glistened with a layer of ice, and icicles dripped from street signs. The sidewalk under her feet was slick, but even that couldn't keep her indoors tonight. A night like this brought death to those who had no place to escape the cold.

And cold wasn't the only enemy on the streets. There were things out here. Dark, evil things. People were going missing, and Hope feared they hadn't simply moved on to warmer climes.

Sister Olive was a middle-aged woman who ran the homeless shelter where Hope volunteered. She'd insisted that Hope stay indoors tonight, but the nun had never truly felt the frigid desperation of having no place to go. She'd always had a warm, safe place where she knew she belonged.

Not everyone was so lucky.

Hope shifted the canvas bag on her shoulder and walked faster. She always carried sandwiches and blankets in case she ran into those in need—those who refused to come to the shelter. With any luck, they'd all have better sense than to be stubborn on a night like this.

She scanned the street, paying close attention to the dark crevices between buildings and inside recessed doorways. That glowing, yellow aura of suffering was not hard to miss.

Or maybe Hope had just had a lot of practice at spotting it.

If Sister Olive knew how Hope found people in need—if she knew Hope could see auras—the nun would probably have her committed. Good thing that wasn't something that came up in normal conversation. Hope wasn't sure she could lie to a nun.

A flicker of unease made Hope pull her coat closed more tightly around her neck. She'd seen things at night—things she knew couldn't be real. Dark, monstrous things that slinked between shadows, hiding from sight. Their auras were black. Silent. She couldn't read them, which made her question whether the monsters even truly existed outside her imagination.

She probably should have brought one of the men along with her to ward off any problems. But how would she explain to her escort how she knew where to go? It was better to do this alone and keep her secrets. Fitting in among normal people was hard enough when she *didn't* draw attention to her ability.

Hope forced herself to head toward the one place she hadn't yet searched for those missing souls. She hated getting near the run-down Tyler building—it brought up too much pain and confusion, too many bad memories. She'd promised herself that tonight she'd put her ridiculous fears aside and look for her friends there.

The three-story brick structure rose up into the night sky. The lighting here hadn't been maintained, leaving deep pools of darkness to hover about the building like an aura of decay.

A heavy thud and a screech of wrenching metal rose up from behind the structure.

There was definitely someone back there. Or some-*thing*.

Images of those dark creatures flickered in her mind. Her muscles locked up in fear, and for a moment, she stood frozen to the pavement.

The real danger out here tonight was the cold, not monsters, and the longer people were left to suffer in it, the more dangerous it became.

Hope forced her legs to move. Her first steps were slow and shuffling, as if her own body was working against her. Then slowly, she picked up speed, shoving all thoughts of monsters from her mind.

As she crept down the alley that led to the back of the building, she heard more noises she couldn't quite identify. There was a grunt of pain and the rattle of wood tumbling about. Once, she almost thought she heard a woman's voice, but she couldn't be sure. The only woman she knew who was too stubborn to come in out of the cold was her friend Rory.

Hope cleared the corner, and the first thing she saw was the gaping hole where the overhead door had been ripped open and partially off its track. The metal looked like it had been punched in with a giant fist, leaving jagged shards behind.

From inside the opening, Hope saw a brief flash of color—the sickly yellow of suffering.

Rory.

Desperate fear washed over her, making her lurch forward through the ragged opening. It was too dark inside to see, so she fished inside her satchel for the flashlight she always carried.

A feral growl of rage rose up from her left. It wasn't a human sound. Not even close.

Primal fear surged through her, and she had to fight the need to curl into the smallest space possible so she could hide.

Her search for the flashlight became frantic, her gloves hindering her as she fished around in her bag.

She located the hard, heavy cylinder, only to have it slip from her grasp.

Heavy, pounding steps shook the floor. A woman cried out in fear somewhere to Hope's right.

She grasped onto the flashlight and powered it on as she ripped it from the bag. The beam of light bobbed around, catching motes of dust as it passed.

Hope aimed it toward the sound of torment. The light bounced off something huge and shiny. Something pulsing with muscle, and moving so fast she couldn't keep the light trained on it.

Its aura was black nothingness.

Panic gripped her tight. She needed more light to ward off the thing. Something as hideous as that would hate the light. She felt it on an instinctive level, as if she'd been taught how to protect herself from the monster.

Hope swung the light around to the employee entrance next to the pulverized overhead door, hoping there would be a switch nearby. Surely, whoever came in through that door would need to have access to lights, right?

The beam of light shook in her grasp, vibrating with the trembling of her hands as she searched. It seemed to take forever, but as she neared the door, she saw a series of switches.

She sprinted over the dusty floor, praying that the power here was still on—that whoever was trying to sell this place had left the lights on for potential buyers.

Hope shoved all four switches up at once. There was a muted thunk, then an electric buzz. Light poured down over the room, and while many of the bulbs were burned out, it seemed as bright as the surface of the sun compared to a moment ago.

She blinked her eyes and turned, forcing herself to look at what her flashlight had touched.

The room was large and open. Lines that had been painted on the floor to outline separate areas were now covered in dust. A stack of wooden pallets had toppled, and the dust from their fall had not yet settled.

Across the room was a giant, hulking creature poised over someone she couldn't quite see. All she could tell was that they were surrounded by that yellow aura of hunger and suffering she'd come to know so well on the streets.

The beast's head swiveled toward her, the movement sinuous and fluid. Its green eyes fixed on her, and she swore they flared brighter for a brief moment.

An unnatural fear rose up inside Hope, screaming for her to run. She knew what this thing was. She didn't know its name or where it came from, but she knew that it wanted her blood.

A roar filled her ears as a distant memory tried to surface. Her head spun and she clutched the wall behind her to stay on her feet.

Please, God. Not now.

As much as Hope wanted to remember her past, she wouldn't survive the distraction. She fought off the memory, mourning its loss even before it passed.

The beast snorted out a heavy breath, sending four curls of steam into the cold air. Its mouth opened, revealing sharp, wicked teeth.

Hope was sure the thing wore a sinister grin.

"Run!" shouted a man.

She couldn't see him, but it was his aura that peeked out from behind the monster. It pulsed with a flare of bright blue courage, and a second later, the monster roared as if it had been struck.

Now that its attention was no longer focused on Hope, her knees unlocked and started working again. She needed to find help. Fast.

She turned to do just that, when she caught a glimpse of an aura peeking out from behind the toppled pile of pallets.

Hope rushed over and found a man lying unconscious on the floor. One side of his face had darkened with a bruise, and in his loose grip was a board covered in the same shiny stuff that coated the monster's skin.

His aura was faint, the colors flickering like the flames of a dying fire.

He wasn't going to make it if she didn't do something.

Across the room, a crash sounded as the fight wore on. Hope didn't waste time figuring out who was winning. It was going to take all her strength to get this man out of harm's way. Just in case it was the monster who won.

She shoved the pallet pinning him down off his legs. His jeans were dark with blood.

Hope patted his face, hoping to wake him. His eyes fluttered open, but she doubted his ability to focus. His pupils were huge and a cold sweat covered his brow. "Logan. I need Logan. Poison. He can fix it."

Hope didn't know how he knew that, but she doubted he'd waste his breath lying.

Her gaze slid across the room to the fight. The man battling that beast must be Logan. She had to help him. She had no idea how to defeat the monster, but she'd seen a length of metal pipe back near the door, and she wasn't afraid to use it.

*   *   *

Logan looked up from the floor where he landed. The spots cleared just in time for him to see the demon's giant, slimy foot hurling toward his head.

Logan rolled aside, dodging at the last instant. Chips of concrete flew into his face, stinging as they hit. He smelled his blood a moment before he felt the hot trickle of it sliding down his cheek.

The creature's foot was raised, poised for another attack. Logan's body shook with weakness, so cold he could barely feel his limbs. Only the dull throb of pain managed to get through the growing numbness of his body.

He was running out of time. Soon, the poison would incapacitate him, making him an easy meal.

There was no way Logan was walking away from this alive. The child had to be his first priority. He just needed to buy Pam enough time to escape. If her child survived, he could one day save others of Logan's race.

The thought brought him a sliver of solace.

It was time to pull out all the stops. He gathered up a bit of power and burst from the ground, shoving his dagger deep into the demon's groin. The beast howled. Black blood spurted from the wound.

Logan shoved the blade sideways to slice open a large wound before jerking it out. He stumbled backward as the demon clutched at its wound, trying to stop the flow of blood. Not that it would do any good. That blow was fatal. It was just a question of how long it would take the demon to bleed out and whether Logan would survive until it did.

It thrashed around, spraying blood across the floor in a black arc. One giant fist lashed out at Logan, knocking him back into a wall. Pain radiated out from his spine, but at least now he was out of the way of more blows.

The demon's eyes flared bright green as they fixed on him. He saw a streak of movement, heard a battle cry. A woman ran across the floor, wielding a pipe like a sword.

Logan screamed for her to stop, but he was weak and

out of breath. All he managed to get out was a growl of warning too low to reach her.

She slammed the pipe into the demon's leg. It roared in anger and turned around to face the new threat.

She hit it again and jumped back out of its reach. It took an awkward step toward her and slipped on its own blood. It toppled to the ground, nearly crushing the woman beneath it. She got out of the way just in time, backing up until she hit a large wooden crate.

Black blood pooled under the demon. Its tongue swept out to lap up its own blood in a vain attempt to heal itself. But it was too late for that. It was bleeding too fast.

Finally, with a last shuddering breath, the demon died.

There wasn't time to revel in the kill or celebrate their victory. Logan staggered away to where Steve had landed, so he could rid the man of poison. He'd just made it to Steve's side when his legs simply gave out.

The longer he waited to finish this, the more likely it was that the scent of his blood would draw other Synestryn to him.

Steve, his family, and the mystery woman needed to be long gone before that happened.

Logan closed his eyes and concentrated on manufacturing an antidote to the poison within his veins. It was slow, and every bit of energy he used had to be dragged out of the deepest recesses of his body. Each spark of power slowed his heart. His breathing became shallow, and he was so cold that his breath no longer misted in the frigid air.

By the time he was finished, he was blind, shivering uncontrollably, and could barely move. Even his own head was too heavy to support.

He couldn't draw the antidote from his veins as he normally would have done. There was no syringe and no time. Instead, he closed his mouth over Steve's and forced the antidote through his saliva glands and into the human's mouth.

Moments later, Steve moved. The movement was weak at first, then grew as the man's strength returned.

"You need blood," said Steve.

"Not yours. Poison."

"I'll find help." Like a rag doll, he moved where Steve pushed him, too weary to even speak and tell him not to bother. There wasn't time.

Cold sank into his body—a bone-deep cold he knew would never leave him. His breathing began to falter and his heart's rhythm stuttered as it slowed.

Pain and cold surrounded him as death came for him. And as Sibyl had said, it was not going to be gentle with Logan. It was going to scrape every last breath from his lungs and wring every last beat from his heart, forcing him to endure every second of pain and cold and hunger. He would find no peace in oblivion.

There was still so much work to do and now he was leaving his brothers to do it all alone. But selfishly, that was not his last thought. His last thought was how much he wished for one single moment of warmth before he died.

Chapter 2

Hope stared in shock at the scene that played out before her. One moment that poisoned man had been at death's door, and the next, he was on his feet, heading straight for Hope. All from a kiss from Logan—a man too beautiful for words.

Logan lay still and pale, his face a work of art even in his suffering. And he was suffering. His aura did not lie. It was the color of bile—of pain and sickness—streaked with the bright red of pain, tainted with black shards of hopelessness.

His face was gaunt, with stark shadows under his cheekbones. Dark hair fell over his wide forehead, highlighting the striking paleness of his skin. Blue tinged his full lips and she fought the urge to warm them with her own.

Hope was still staring in shock as the poisoned man came toward her. His movements were a bit shaky, but purpose filled his every stride. "You have to help him. He needs your blood."

A spike of fear struck her as she realized she knew nothing about these men or what they wanted. The mention of blood had her mind reeling, going through all the ritualistic killings she'd heard of over the years, the whispers of what might have befallen those who'd gone missing. The things humans would do to one another were sickening.

Hope backed away, but the stranger caught her arm.

"Please help him. He's dying and needs blood. I have to find my wife."

"I'll call for an ambulance."

"I know this is a lot to accept, but look over there." He pointed to the sagging corpse of the monster. "That thing is real, as are a lot of other things in this world. Right now, you need to accept that fact and save a dying man."

"I don't understand."

The man's mouth tightened in anxious frustration. "Go to him. Tell him you offer to help him. He'll do the rest."

That made no sense. "Stop it," she said, jerking her arm out of his grasp.

Love brighter than any she'd ever seen coursed through his aura, twining with fear. "I need to find my wife. She's out there alone, pregnant and scared out of her mind."

His wife was a lucky woman. Hope had never known a man who loved as deeply as this one did.

He stared down at her, worry twisting his face. "If I could help Logan myself, I would, but I was poisoned. He saved my life. Please. Please save his."

With that, the man turned and left to find his wife, disappearing through the opening in the metal door in an awkward, hurried sprint.

Hope looked down at Logan. His aura had shrunk. The colors dimmed. He had only a few minutes left to live.

She glanced over at the dead monster. He'd killed it. He'd apparently saved that man from poison somehow.

There were a lot of holes in Hope's memories—things she would never know about herself. But there was one thing she knew for a fact: People who would willingly sacrifice themselves for another were rare in this world. She could not stand by and do nothing while one of them died.

She fell to her knees beside his body, ripping the

gloves from her fingers so she could check for a pulse and make sure he was still breathing.

His leather coat hung open along his front, letting the cold sink into his body. If she didn't do something, she feared he wouldn't survive until an ambulance arrived.

Hope stripped out of her coat and covered his torso with it, praying the heat clinging to the quilted fabric would be enough to see him through. Immediately, the frigid air slid through her sweatshirt, its icy fingers stealing away her warmth.

She ignored the chill and jerked a blanket from her bag, sending a stack of sandwiches flying. She tucked that around him as well to keep him warm while help arrived.

With one hand, she pulled her cell phone from her back pocket, while feeling for his pulse with the other hand. It was faint, but there.

"Hold on," she whispered to the stranger. "Help is on the way."

She'd just dialed 9 when the man's eyes fluttered open. They were a pale, silvery gray—so light that they seemed to almost glow in the darkness. She'd never seen eyes like his before. The color was mesmerizing, luring her to stare and keep staring.

Hope was sucked in by his gaze for a moment before she remembered what she was doing. "You need to hold on. I'm calling for an ambulance now. I'm going to help you."

She moved to finish dialing. The phone was knocked from her hand and went flying across the concrete.

He'd moved so fast she hadn't seen his hand strike out until it was too late. Shock streaked through her, and by the time she'd processed what he'd done, he'd grabbed a fistful of her hair and jerked her head to the side.

His eyes fixed on her throat, and she was sure she saw light spilling from them.

Fear cut off her scream. Her body seized up. All she could do was stare at him and wait for him to release her.

"I'm sorry," he growled, letting out a rough, animal sound.

He became a blur of movement and enveloped her body in a crushing hug. He smelled of snow and desperation. His aura changed, pulsing with surges of bright blue victory. She felt the chill of his lips; then a sharp pain stabbed her neck. A moment later, a heavy, languid feeling fell over her, pinning her in place.

She couldn't move. She couldn't fight. And somewhere, a whispering presence in her mind told her she didn't even want to try.

As his grip on her tightened and the ravenous tugging at her throat intensified, Hope just let go and drifted within his grasp.

He grew warmer. Or maybe she was getting colder. She couldn't tell.

Pain that had been with her only moments ago turned to pleasure. Her body swelled with it, expanding with light and color. Tingling waves of warmth shivered through her limbs and pooled in her belly. A giggle bubbled within her, but she was too weak to let it out.

That pleasure grew until even the memory of pain was distant and inconsequential. All that mattered was drifting inside this cushion of comfort and purpose.

Whoever he was, whatever he was doing to her, Hope knew in her soul that he'd awakened something within her that would never again be lulled to sleep.

Power roared in the woman's blood, stronger than any he'd ever tasted. Including the blood of the powerful Theronai Helen. Logan drank it down as survival instincts took over. He was heedless of his prey, gripping her tight so she couldn't fight or flee.

He needed her, and he wasn't going to let her go.

Weakness fell away as power seethed inside him, stretching his cells. Her blood was rich, purer than any he'd ever tasted. He couldn't get enough. Each sucking gulp filled him more, driving away the pain of hunger and biting cold.

Warmth suffused him, making him giddy with relief. His cock stirred for the first time in centuries, shocking him. But even that shock could not penetrate the joyous feeling of no longer being hungry.

Her heart fluttered, struggling to pump blood that was not there. Her breathing faltered, and her hands fell limp at her sides. A quiet sound of pleasure spilled from her mouth.

It was that sound that saved her life.

Logan finally overcame the drunken high her blood gave him enough to realize he was killing her.

Anger at his carelessness swept through him as he willed the puncture wounds on her neck to close and ripped his mouth away from her skin. She lay limp and helpless in his grasp. Too pale. Too weak.

Her honey-colored hair splayed across the sleeve of his black coat. Her eyes slid open, and in them he saw betrayal.

Logan didn't understand why she'd look at him that way until he realized what she'd tried to do here tonight. She wore no coat against the cold, but there was one her size draped over his lap. A blanket lay crumpled between them. Individually wrapped sandwiches sat a few feet away, discarded on the floor.

He suddenly remembered her words, her sweet voice reassuring him that an ambulance was on the way.

She'd come to him, offering help, and he'd nearly killed her.

Guilt bore down on Logan, driving away the intoxicating haze of finally being full after so many years of hunger. Only seconds had passed, but even those had pushed her closer to death.

She needed fluids. Human blood. He didn't dare risk giving her his own for fear the shock to her system would kill her, or that some trace of poison lingered there. And even if his blood didn't kill her, he couldn't risk leaving her drugged by the narcotic effects his blood could cause.

She needed her memories of tonight purged so they could not draw Synestryn to her, but she was too weak for that. He'd have to find her later, after the humans had restored her health. After he had checked and made sure that Steve, Pam, and their child were safe.

Logan gathered up her body and rose to his feet. Muscles that had been withered for decades flexed, strong and solid in his limbs. The leather of his coat creaked against the stretch of his biceps. He reveled in that power—in feeling whole and strong, as he was meant to be.

There was a hospital not far from here. He ran toward it, his body gliding smoothly over the frozen ground. Buildings blurred past him as he moved. Wind tore at his face, but could not penetrate the warmth she'd given him.

Buoyant elation rose inside him, celebrating his survival. The woman in his arms was responsible for that, and he was not going to let her gift cause her death.

Logan would save her, and then when he did, he was going to find a way to repay her. He'd see to it that she was protected and cared for for the rest of her life.

The fact that she was heavily blooded, and therefore a perfect candidate for Project Lullaby, was only going to make that easier.

Logan cleared the emergency room doors and spotted the nurse behind the desk. She was young and plump, with a harried expression on her face and a name tag that read BARB. In one single instant, Barb's gaze moved over Logan's rescuer and dismissed her as unimportant. Beneath her notice.

"What drugs is she on?" asked the nurse as Logan approached.

Annoyance rose to the surface, tightening Logan's mouth. He refused to waste time arguing with Barb. Instead, he stared into her eyes and grabbed a hold of her mind.

Her face went slack and she swayed on her feet for a moment. Logan stilled her thoughts of disdain for Hope and replaced them with something else. He wove within her mind a series of emotional responses to events that never happened, implanting fleeting memories of Barb and Hope laughing and crying together. He borrowed from thoughts of Barb's sister, and connected them to Hope, creating a temporary, artificial connection.

"You love this woman like a sister, don't you?" asked Logan.

Pain creased Barb's face and tears filled her eyes as Logan let go of her mind. "Oh God. What happened to her?"

Logan filled his voice with compulsion, refusing to leave Hope's care to chance. "She needs a blood transfusion. Fluids. Immediately. Move!"

"Get a gurney!" shouted Barb.

Behind the desk, people scurried to obey.

Logan laid the woman on the clean white sheets. In the bright fluorescent lighting, he could see how beautiful she was. Her features were elegant, with high arching eyebrows and smooth, flawless skin. Her bone structure was model perfect, exquisite in its symmetry. Even now, with death hovering nearby, she had a regal beauty few humans possessed.

It was going to be a long time before he stopped seeing her face every time he closed his eyes. Even longer before he stopped seeing that look of betrayal shining in her gaze.

Logan turned and left her in the capable hands of her own people.

He'd done what he could. It was time to go and plan her place within Project Lullaby. His brother Tynan would help him decide where she would best belong—where she'd be happiest. They'd decide which man would be strong enough to ensure the continuation of her amazing bloodline.

The thought of putting her into the hands of another man gave him pause, but he assured himself it was only an aftereffect of taking so much of her blood. He felt connected. As if she were now part of him.

And he liked it.

That alone was warning enough for Logan to back away. He couldn't become personally entangled in the life of a human woman. Their roles were set. Immovable.

She would be paired with a human male who would make her happy—one who would complement the power flowing in her veins, rather than dilute it. They'd bring children into the world who could save Logan's race from starvation. She was a source of power. Food. It was as simple as that.

It wasn't nearly enough.

Logan fought the urge to slip back into the emergency room to check on her. The less time he spent with her, the better. He couldn't grow any more attached than he already was. It was time to hand her off to Tynan and get back to the mystery that had brought him here.

He still had yet to find the address that had been written in blood on his bathroom mirror a few days ago, along with the message *You have not been forgotten. You are not alone.*

Between the women and children who'd been rescued from the Synestryn, and the deaths of Angus and Gilda, Dabyr had been in an uproar. His presence there had been necessary to help people stay calm and positive. Grief and fear were enemies Project Lullaby could scarcely afford.

Tonight had been his first chance to seek out the address. He'd gotten close, but the frantic call for help from Steve had distracted him. And then the woman had distracted him even more.

It was time for Logan to get back to the job at hand. He needed to find the reason for the mysterious message on his mirror and make sure it posed no threat to his race.

With any luck at all, he'd find a man with the same vibrant power in his blood that Logan's lovely rescuer possessed. Tynan would pair her up and in a few years, her children would help save his people.

A pang of longing stabbed at him as he left the hospital and went back out into the cold. There were so many things he wanted that could never be. The woman who'd saved him tonight had served only to remind him of the things he could never have.

As he dialed Tynan's cell phone, he realized that he didn't even know her name.

And it was best that way.

Chapter 3

The flare of power that Krag had felt for a brief instant was gone now. All that was left was a faint ghost of energy fading as the seconds passed. Usually when he felt the presence of a blooded human, it was a gradual thing that grew as they came closer to him.

But not tonight. That flash of power had roared into his senses as if it had been plunked down out of nowhere. And it had vanished just as quickly.

The flash had come from downtown, several miles away. Perhaps a plane had landed and taken off with a blooded passenger aboard. If so, the human was already gone and out of his reach. Time to move on. Unless it happened again.

Krag settled back in his throne, surveying his worshippers. Both human and Synestryn alike, they gathered around him, eager to do his bidding.

Except for one.

"Bring her out," he ordered, his voice booming off the cement walls of his home.

This defunct manufacturing facility had been easy to convert into a fortress. What few windows there were high in the walls had been blacked out with paint, keeping out the deadly light of the sun. The main space was large, with several smaller rooms that had once been offices. Krag had those converted into his sleeping quarters, leaving room for his women on the floor surrounding his bed.

It was truly too bad that one of those women had defied him so openly. She was pretty. Young. Full of life, her blood more powerful than most.

But like a cancer, she had to be cut out before she could spread her rebellion to the others.

Two burly human men dragged her before him. Her clothing was torn and dirty. Her dyed hair hung in wild tangles around her face. The glaring pink of her shoes seemed to mock him, declaring to all that she held no respect for his position.

Her hands were bound in front of her. No doubt a consequence of the angry red claw marks she'd left on one of the men's cheeks. She was gagged, but there were no tears in her eyes as he would have hoped. No remorse. Only the glowing anger of her rebellious nature and promised retribution.

He was going to enjoy breaking her.

"Remove the gag," he ordered.

The men hastened to obey. As soon as the dirty fabric cleared her mouth, she spat on the ground at Krag's feet.

"Kneel."

Her guards shoved her down so hard he could hear her bones hit the concrete.

Krag smiled. "Have you considered my offer?"

"I'd rather fuck a rotting pig corpse than let you touch me."

Anger flared for an instant before he controlled it. He smoothed his features to regal stillness. "Throw her down below. I'm certain there is at least one rotting pig down there for her amusement."

She screamed, but it wasn't a cry of fear. Not this woman. Her scream was of feral outrage. Of angry defiance.

The men picked her up by her arms and hauled her out of his sight. The flooded section below housed some of the less advanced members of his race. They would make quick work of her. And when they were done, he'd mount her skull on the wall as a reminder to the others not to question his authority.

Before her screams faded, Krag beckoned one of the obedient women forward. She shivered in ecstasy at being chosen, as was proper, before crawling to his feet.

He patted his lap, inviting her to jump up like a pampered pet. As soon as he had her settled there, her naked body trembling, he jerked her head to the side and bit deep.

Her blood was weak, but once he'd taken it all, he felt better. Stronger.

Krag shoved her corpse to the floor, then motioned for her to be taken away. Let the lesser Synestryn feast on her flesh and bones. He had no more use for her.

Hope opened her eyes, already knowing that Logan was gone. She couldn't feel his presence or that consuming pleasure he'd given her.

Fear wove through her for a moment, but she wasn't sure if it was fear of the man, or fear caused by the fact she knew he was gone.

A plump, dark-haired nurse hovered over Hope. She couldn't remember the woman, but the way she was looking at Hope with tears in her eyes made her wonder if she shouldn't.

"You're awake. How are you feeling?"

Hope blinked a few times to make sure that blurry vision wasn't making her see concern that wasn't real. "Do I know you?"

"I'm Barb," she said, her tone of expectation telling Hope she *should* know the woman.

Was her memory getting worse? Was she losing more chunks of time? Hope pushed herself up in a panic and looked around, hoping it would clear her head.

She was surrounded by a striped curtain. Beyond that curtain, she could hear voices and the low moans of a man in pain. Disinfectant laced the stale air. A machine beeped insistently in the background. An IV bag hung above her, feeding fluids into the back of her hand.

A hospital. That's where she was.

Hope didn't know how she got here. The last thing she remembered was Logan. He'd grabbed her and . . . bitten her neck.

Her hand flew to the spot, feeling only smooth, whole skin.

"What is it, honey?" asked Barb.

"Do you see anything? Any marks on my neck?"

Barb leaned forward and brushed Hope's hair away. "It's a little red. Does it hurt?"

"No." Her skin tingled, and there was a throbbing warmth, but that was all. "Who brought me in?"

Barb frowned as if trying to remember. "A man. Tall. Dark hair. Do you know him?"

That description could be almost anyone. Or it could have been Logan. Either way the answer was the same. "No."

"The doctor will be in to see you soon. We couldn't find any injuries. Do you know what happened?"

Hope shook her head. What she thought had happened couldn't have. It wasn't possible. Either the stranger had bitten her and left marks, or he hadn't bitten her at all. Those were the only options.

Weren't they?

A wave of dizziness slid over her, and she shut her eyes to let it pass.

The smells of the hospital assaulted her nose, dragging from her memories of the last time she'd been here—the night Sister Olive had found her in the empty Tyler building and brought her here, insisting she get checked out. Hope had no injuries then, either. Nothing that explained her amnesia. She hadn't known her name or how old she was. Hope still didn't know. No one had claimed her. The only thing that had been in her possession was a wooden amulet clutched in her fist. The name Hope Serrien was burned into it.

She didn't even know if that was her real name.

That had been a decade ago and Hope still had no answers. All she had was a nagging sense of duty—that there was some vital task only she could complete. Every day that went by that didn't reveal her task left her feeling more restless and defeated.

There was something inside her—some forgotten knowledge she could almost put her finger on. It was there, evading her grasp, but she knew it was there. When Logan had been holding her, she'd almost been able to remember why she was here.

"I need to go," said Hope.

Barb shook her head. "Not until we know what happened. It's not safe."

Hope had to find him. She had to find Logan and figure out what he knew. Maybe he knew who she was. *What* she was.

"I'm leaving. Bring me whatever paperwork you need me to sign, but do it fast. I won't wait."

Whoever Logan was, Hope didn't want him to get far. She was going to find him. And then she was going to force him to give her the answers she needed. One way or another.

Logan met Steve and Pam in their apartment. They were fine. All three of them. Logan called Joseph—the leader of the Theronai—and asked him to send someone to guard them so they could rest. He then did what he could to remove the memory of tonight from their minds. He didn't want them to worry—didn't want the memory to draw more demons to them.

Tomorrow the couple would go to Dabyr, where they'd be safe. After tonight's attack, living in the city was no longer an option for them. If Logan hadn't been so close, if the GPS gadget on his cell phone hadn't made it possible for Steve's call to go to the closest Sentinel— namely Logan —things would have turned out very different tonight. It served only to display just how fragile their progress truly was.

As Logan got back in his van, the blond woman's face danced in his head. It was strange to no longer feel weak and hungry. Even walking inside Steve's formidable mind had been easy. There was no effort. No strain.

The power in that woman's blood was amazing. Too bad Logan knew he had to share.

Out of habit, he turned on the engine to get some heat before he realized he wasn't cold. Still.

Normally, the flush of feeding would have faded by now, leaving him chilled to the bone. For some reason, this time was different.

Logan dialed Tynan's cell phone. "We need to meet."

"Why?"

"I have blood to share."

"A new source?" The weariness in Tynan's voice worried Logan.

"Yes. A young woman. Her blood is strong. It's possible she may even be a Theronai."

"Are you sure?"

"No. Her blood is different from theirs—unlike any I've had before."

"We'll need to find her a suitable mate as soon as possible. Is she currently attached to a male?"

Logan hadn't even considered that possibility, but as soon as he did, anger stirred inside him. "I don't know."

"Find out. If she is, find out if her mate is suitably blooded."

"And if not?" asked Logan.

"Remove him from her life."

Her face appeared in Logan's mind, as vivid and clear as if she were sitting next to him. She had a sweet face. Kind, amber eyes the color of autumn sunset. Not only was she lovely, she was obviously caring as well. Why else would she have stayed to help him at great risk to her own life?

"I won't do that," said Logan. "I won't hurt her."

"We both know she'll be happier paired with a mate of our choosing."

"Who's to say that's true? It's not something we can

prove, simply something we tell ourselves to relieve the guilt of what we must do."

Tynan's voice hardened. "All of our matches are happy ones. We make sure of that."

"What if we're wrong, just this one time? I can't let that happen."

"Then I'll send someone who can. Where are you?"

Logan debated not telling him. Only the knowledge that their race couldn't afford any animosity held his rebellion. "Promise me you'll be the one to come and see to her. I don't want to entrust her to anyone else."

"Why?" asked Tynan, his skepticism clear.

"Her blood is too pure to risk."

"Are you certain there's not more to it than that?"

"Like what?" asked Logan.

"Do you have feelings for the woman?"

"Of course not. No more than is reasonable."

"You can't become involved with her," said Tynan. "None of us can. If she's human, we need her to breed. If she's Theronai, she's off-limits."

"I do not need you to tell me the facts."

"You're not detached enough. Without detachment our goals will become confused."

Anger made Logan's voice sharp. "I'm perfectly clear about our goals."

"And what might those be, Logan?"

"The same as yours. Survival of our race. We'll pair her with an acceptable mate and all will be well."

"If she's human, do you want to bed her first? Get her out of your system? That can be arranged."

Said in such a cold, clinical tone, the idea made Logan sneer. "Don't be ridiculous. Of course I don't."

"As you wish. I'll come, sample her blood myself as soon as I can get away, and we'll see her happily settled."

Do you want to bed her first?

The question haunted Logan, putting into his head a possibility that should not exist. He hadn't wanted a woman in centuries. He'd been too hungry, too weak for his body to respond in any sexual way. Until tonight.

He wasn't weak now. Thanks to her blood, there was a stirring of something he'd thought long dead—an interest that went beyond survival. Holding her, feeding from her, had aroused him. Made him hard.

He wanted her. There was no denying it, but that didn't mean he'd act on that desire.

"Come soon," said Logan. "I don't know how long they'll keep her at the hospital. She was too weak for me to remove her memories, so that must still be done."

"You won't lose her. Her blood is yours now."

Which meant he'd be able to find her if he chose to do so. Always.

Already the temptation to do just that was something he had to actively resist. "I have one quick errand to run, and then I'll be off. I can't stay and help you."

"You mean you won't stay," said Tynan.

"As you say."

Logan hung up the phone and drove toward the address that had been written in blood on his bathroom mirror. As he passed through the frozen streets, his mind filled with thoughts of what might await him. Would it be a home filled with people who could feed his race? The location of a gateway into Athanasia they could access? Even a group of humans willing to help them without all the coercion and lies would have been a welcome sight.

When he pulled up in front of the run-down building where he'd fought earlier tonight, and read the address, his excitement died.

This place, this Tyler building, did not house the savior of his race. It was simply an empty structure, void of hope. Worse yet, it was entirely possible that it had been a trap—that the creature he'd fought tonight had been sent here to wait for his arrival and had caught Steve's and Pam's scents as they'd passed by earlier.

Logan's throat burned with anger as he stared at the

run-down building. Power raged inside him, tempting him to raze the thing to the ground.

He could do it. He had enough strength now.

But if he did, he'd waste all the power she'd given him. He couldn't do that, no matter how angry he became. Self-control was as vital to his people's survival as blood. All the Sanguinar knew that, and those who didn't had died. Or been killed.

Logan wasn't always proud of the choices he'd had to make over the years, but he was still standing, as were many of his kind. Without those unpleasant choices, the Sanguinar would have been long extinct. And if that happened, it would be only a matter of time before the Theronai and Slayers fell as well, and the human race was left with no protectors.

The ends justified the means. It had to. After all the things Logan had done, it simply had to.

Chapter 4

Hope couldn't sleep. As tired as she was, every time she closed her eyes, she saw Logan's face. Beautiful. Suffering. Powerful.

She wished she didn't know his name. Somehow, knowing made him seem more real. Without that scrap of information, it would have been easy to pretend that everything that had happened tonight was a figment of her imagination.

Heaven knew her mind wasn't exactly a fortress. Whatever had stripped her life's memories away had left its scars. She saw things that couldn't possibly exist. Felt things that could not be real.

And right now, she was sure she could feel Logan's presence nearby, moving about the city. There was a warmth emanating from him, like sunlight on her skin.

Part of her willed him to come closer so she could bask in that warmth, while the saner part of her wished he'd just go away—so far she couldn't feel a thing.

Hope rolled onto her side, facing him. "You're not real," she whispered into the darkness of her bedroom.

Somehow, saying it out loud only made it worse. *Something* had happened tonight that put her in the hospital, and if she couldn't even trust herself enough to believe what she saw, then she was much worse off than she thought.

* * *

Something was wrong with Sibyl. Cain knew it. She hadn't come out of her room since her parents' deaths two weeks ago. She'd hardly spoken to him except to tell him she was fine and to ask him to bring her some of her mother's clothes.

Everyone mourned differently, and the distance that had been between Sibyl and her mother was no doubt adding to the pain of grief now. Perhaps Gilda's clothes gave Sibyl some kind of comfort. Cain deeply hoped so.

At least she'd been eating. The trays of food he'd left at her door were always returned empty. If not for that, Cain's fatherly instincts would have kicked in and he'd have removed her from her room by force.

So far, it hadn't come to that.

Cain retrieved the empty tray and rapped softly on her door. "Sibyl."

"I'm sleeping."

No, she wasn't. He could tell from her voice she was wide-awake. Cain had been watching over her for centuries and she couldn't fool him with such a bad lie.

"You need to come out. We need to talk."

"Talking changes nothing." Her voice sounded odd and deep, as if she were sick, only she never got sick. She had to have been crying.

"You're wrong. You of all people should know how powerful words can be."

When Sibyl was eight, she'd promised her mother she'd never grow up. And she hadn't. Centuries later, she was still trapped in the body of a child.

"Go away. Please."

Cain sighed. He was a patient man. He'd give her more time. Just not too much. Staying locked away in her room like this wasn't healthy. He loved her too much to let her destroy herself with grief.

"I'll be back in a couple of hours," he promised. "We'll talk then."

And if not then, he'd keep at her until she relented.

Little Sibyl was nothing if not stubborn, and it was Cain's job to see to it that she didn't suffer because of the inherited streak.

One way or another, she was coming out of that room and facing reality. And when she did, Cain would be there for her as he always had been.

Sibyl held her breath until she heard Cain's heavy steps fade as he moved down the hall.

She almost asked him to bring her more food, but she feared he'd figure out that something was wrong. Terribly wrong.

Sibyl tugged on the sleeve of Gilda's gown, trying to hide her wrists. They were all wrong. Bony. Too long. Everything about her new body was wrong.

She took a lurching step forward, tripping on her own feet. As she caught herself against the dresser, she knocked over the trinkets that sat atop it. A small crystal box shattered against the floor.

Her feet were bare. She had nothing that would fit them anymore. If she stepped wrong, she was sure she'd cut herself.

And she was sure she'd step wrong. Her body was no longer her own. It was this odd, alien thing that kept thwarting her every move. And the hunger was nearly unbearable.

The only thing that dulled it was the thought of her parents lying crushed under all that stone.

Cain hadn't told her that part, but he hadn't needed to. Sibyl had known it would happen all along. She'd known they'd die. That her sister, Maura, would be the cause of it. She'd seen all that in her visions. And she'd mourned for them a long time ago.

What she hadn't seen was herself, this gangly body and the loss of her ability.

The future was no longer her domain. She couldn't see it. Couldn't gift it to others. It stretched out, bleak and unknown, as if she were some normal person.

Without her ability, that's exactly what she was. Normal. Nothing special.

Sibyl couldn't even reach Maura anymore. Not even through the doll.

For the first time in her life, she was truly alone. Truly afraid.

"You look like you've been run over by a truck," said Jodi. Her blond hair was pulled up in a ponytail that stuck out through the back of a KC Royals baseball cap. Giant silver hearts swung from her earlobes.

"Gee, thanks," said Hope.

The workroom of the studio was Jodi's territory. She framed and matted all of Hope's portraits and photographs, and the woman had an eye for the job. What had started as a friendship forged during a business management class had bloomed into a growing business for both of them. Hope snapped the pictures, Jodi took them and created art.

Morning light streamed in, glinting off the tools lined up on Jodi's workbench. The walls in here were covered in beautiful pieces—little instances of people's lives that would live on for as long as the ink and paper lasted. Memories that could not be erased.

Hope's friend, roommate, and coworker ran her blade down the mat, making a perfect cut. "I call 'em like I see 'em. No one's going to want their picture taken by a woman who can't even keep her eyes open. You should call it quits and take a nap."

"I only have one more appointment today. I'll manage."

Jodi grinned, waggling her pale eyebrows. "So, where were you last night? Or should I say this morning?"

"You wouldn't believe me if I told you."

"Try me."

Hope considered blurting out the truth. Sadly, she couldn't think of a way to say it without using the word *vampire*, so she resisted the urge. "I met this guy and lost track of time."

"Uh-huh," said Jodi, her tone disbelieving. "One has a tendency to lose track of time when one is macking on some hot guy. He was hot, right?"

Logan's face flashed in her mind, all perfect symmetry and stark angles. Just the thought had her fingers itching for her camera. She could take a great photo of him. Except she wasn't sure vampires could even be photographed. Or that he was even real.

It had taken all morning, but she had convinced herself that last night's events were nothing more than a bizarre dream. There was no horrible monster. No beautiful Logan. All those events were simply something her mind had constructed to combat her fear of going near the Tyler building where she'd been found a decade ago.

"Hello. Hope. Are you in there?" asked Jodi, waving her hand in front of Hope's face. The large silver heart ring she wore caught the morning light and left little spots floating in Hope's vision.

"Sorry. I'm just tired."

Jodi took Hope by the arm and led her out of the workroom toward the stairway that led to their shared apartment upstairs. "Go to bed, girl. I'll wake you up as soon as your one o'clock gets here."

Maybe she was right. Maybe a nap would clear her head and rid her of the last remnants of a man who couldn't possibly exist.

Madoc stepped into Joseph's office unannounced. His black hair was a mess, as if he'd just gotten out of bed. "There's a naked man at the front gate. He's a Slayer."

Shock raced through Joseph, silencing him for a moment. Why would their enemy be at the gate? Was it some kind of trick? Custom dictated that a party offering to negotiate would show up naked as proof they were unarmed, but after so many years of the stagnant war between them, why would the Slayers want to negotiate anything? "What does he want?"

"He asked to talk to you. Do I let him in or do I kill

him?" Madoc's blunt features were expressionless, as if he truly didn't care which of those alternatives Joseph picked.

"Is he alone?"

"No. There are some men sitting in their vehicles at the main road. The only person at his side is one very pissed-off woman."

A woman? If one of the Slayers had found a female Theronai, would they have stuck to the old laws and brought her here? It wasn't likely, but it was possible, and with all the women popping up lately, Joseph refused to take any chances. "Let him and the woman in, but only them. Make them walk. No vehicles past the gate. Alert the men to be ready for trouble. Meet me at the front doors."

Madoc nodded and left.

Joseph combed his fingers through his hair and straightened his clothes. It wouldn't do his people any good to show up looking like the insomniac he was.

He hurried from his office, his mind spinning with possibilities. By the time he wound his way through the building, a dozen men were waiting for him at the front doors. They were all armed and their faces were grim.

He addressed them, looking each one in the eyes. "I don't want any trouble. Keep your swords sheathed unless I order otherwise. If this is a trick, we'll make sure it's the last of its kind."

Joseph was satisfied they'd listen. For now. He stepped forward and opened the wide double doors.

The man standing there was Andreas Phelan and he was, indeed, naked. He was nearly as tall as Joseph, with brown hair and tawny eyes. The tops of his ears were slightly pointed, proof that the Slayer blood in him was strong. His body had the sleek, high-performance muscles of an athlete. Joseph had met him once before when he'd had to sentence one of his own men to death. He truly hoped these circumstances were more cheerful.

Judging by the angry, thrashing woman over his shoulder, this visit would be interesting if nothing else.

Andreas set her down, holding her steady until she gained her balance. She had been wrapped tightly in a sheet and gagged with a strip of tape over her mouth. Her sunny blond hair was a tangled mess. Her face was red, and her eyes burned a pale golden yellow that promised retribution.

"Thank you for receiving us," he said, inclining his head briefly at Joseph. "This is my sister, Lyka, who has promised to behave."

The last part had clearly been said as a warning to his sister.

"Why are you here?"

Andreas lifted his hands away from his body and turned in a slow circle. "As you can see I'm unarmed. Lyka is as well, though I understand if you would like to remove the sheet and verify that for yourself."

She glared at him and a furious yell filtered through her gag.

"I don't dare arm her when she's this angry at me," said Andreas.

Joseph looked at Madoc. "Can you ask Nika to come down and check her for weapons?"

Madoc lifted his phone from his belt and made the call.

"I'll do it," offered Morgan Valens.

Joseph gave him a hard stare before he realized it was jealousy that had caused it. He didn't want any of the men looking at her naked body, though he guessed it was simply a reaction to her vulnerability. "No. You won't."

"I request that we be allowed into your home so that we can talk," said Andreas.

"What about?"

"A truce between our people," said Andreas.

Truce? Joseph felt the men behind him shift uncomfortably, and he himself scanned the area, looking for signs of a trap.

Andreas's mouth tightened in irritation. "I understand that you're skeptical, but I swear to you this is no trick. Do you really think I'd bring my sister along if I'd intended to attack?"

"She's gagged. Perhaps she's not your sister at all."

Andreas reached over to the woman and carefully worked the corner of the tape up. "Ready?" he asked, with a hint of apology in his tone.

She grunted, her nostrils flaring.

The Slayer ripped the tape free, wincing as he did so, as if the act hurt him, too. He pulled a wad of cloth from her mouth and nearly had his fingers bitten for his effort.

"You bastard!" she shouted. "It was bad enough you had to drag me here, but throwing me over your shoulder and making me look at your naked ass was going over the line. Do you want me to vomit?"

"You refused to come willingly," said Andreas in a weary tone, as if it was an old argument.

"This is a fool's errand. The Theronai will never agree to a truce. Their thirst for vengeance is too great. You've signed our death warrants."

Joseph held up his hands to stop her tirade. "Hold on a minute. No one is killing anyone yet. Tell me who you are."

"Lyka Phelan."

"My sister," said Andreas.

"Half sister," she corrected.

Nika walked up to the group. She'd gained a bit of weight over the last couple of weeks, filling out the gaunt hollows under her cheeks and giving her pale skin a bit of color. Her white hair hung straight, swaying about her chin to frame her face. Her bright blue eyes were on Madoc, and though she said no words aloud, Joseph was sure she'd asked him what this was all about.

The mental link the pair had was beyond anything Joseph had ever witnessed. They'd been together for only a couple of weeks, and in that time, they'd become a well-oiled killing machine. Madoc and Nika could now take down an entire nest by themselves, though it left a hell of a mess behind.

Nika went to the woman, reached up, and placed her hand on her head. Lyka flinched, as if Nika's hand was cold.

Nika turned to Joseph. "She has no weapons, but wishes she had one, so she could use it on this man." She pointed to Andreas.

Joseph looked at the Slayer. "Just like you said."

"May we come inside?" Andreas asked.

What the hell. It wasn't like a naked Slayer and his sister showed up on their doorstep every day. "We'll go to one of the cabins in back. We had a little incident with some explosives last year, so I'm a bit cautious."

"Suits me," said Andreas. "We're playing by the rules, all nice and civilized. Right, Lyka?"

Lyka growled at her brother.

"Someone fetch this man some pants," ordered Joseph.

"I'd appreciate something to wear, too," said Lyka.

The fact that she was naked under that sheet was not lost on Joseph. He found himself staring, trying to discern her shape. All he got was caterpillar.

"I'll find her something of Andra's that will fit," offered Nika. "They're about the same size."

Andreas picked up his sister in his arms and said, "Lead the way."

Joseph walked around Dabyr to one of the vacant cabins near the lake. Four of his men guarded his back, but he'd dismissed the others, knowing that there was a lot of bad blood between the two races.

It had been years since the last confrontation, but Theronai lived a long time, and he didn't know any of his men who hadn't lost someone due to violence initiated by the Slayers.

As leader, he had to put aside his own prejudices and focus on the present. He wouldn't think about the friends he'd lost at the hands of the Slayers. At least not right now.

If things turned ugly . . .

Joseph opened the door and flipped on the light. This cabin had been prepared for disuse, and the furniture was covered with white drop cloths. He motioned toward a small couch for his guests to sit.

Andreas set his sister down and then donned the pair of borrowed jeans, unselfconscious about his nudity. Lyka was still wrapped up in the sheet, and Joseph was keenly aware of hers.

"Mind if I get dressed?" she asked Joseph, her tone caustic and belligerent.

Joseph nodded his head toward the small bathroom behind him. "Feel free. Morgan, untape her."

The Theronai flashed a bright smile. "My pleasure."

Lyka lifted her chin to look up at him. "I may be unarmed, but that doesn't mean I won't find a way to hurt you."

Morgan laughed.

"Behave, Lyka," scolded her brother. "Show some honor."

"If he has his way, I'll be showing a hell of a lot more than honor. I'd really rather not put myself on display to our enemy."

"Enough," said Andreas. His voice was low, but the menace threaded through his tone was enough to make Joseph's hand twitch toward his sword.

Lyka pressed her lips closed and stood there while Morgan ripped the tape from the sheet.

Joseph wanted to watch him open such a lovely package, but he knew better than to leer. "You wanted to talk. Let's talk."

Lyka gripped the now loose sheet, and went into the bathroom where Nika had dropped a set of borrowed clothing.

Andreas pulled in a breath, like he was preparing to do something distasteful. "I've only recently come into power over the Slayers. Until I was privy to the information our previous leader had, I had no clue how bad things truly were."

"What things?"

"My people are dying—not by the hands of the Synestryn, but by their own decisions. We've bred with humans for so many generations that only a few of us still have the power of our ancestors."

"You're weak, so now you want to end the war? Is that it?"

"No. We're weak, and because of that, we're no longer as effective at fighting the Synestryn as we once were. They're getting stronger every year. Their numbers are growing. You know as well as I do that if we don't do something, we're going to lose everything." He leaned forward, his tawny eyes fixing on Joseph. "I was born into this war. I've even done harm to your people in my youth, but I see now that it can't continue. We can't keep fighting each other if we're to have any chance of beating back the demons."

"So why not just go on as we are, ignoring each other? It's been years since I wasted any assets on your people."

"I believe that things are changing. We're at a crossroads. If we don't join together, I fear that the war with the Synestryn is already lost and we just don't know it yet."

"What do you mean?"

"I mean I've seen things. I've followed huge hoards of Synestryn in the night, watching them. They're migrating."

"To where?"

"Here. They're closing in around you, filling the caves that riddle this area."

Joseph had seen proof of that as well, though not as up close as Andreas claimed to have seen. From the corner of his eye, he saw his men shift uncomfortably. Of all the men he had under his command, Madoc had been out fighting the most. He'd nearly run himself into the ground searching out every last living creature that had fed on Nika's blood.

Joseph turned to Madoc. "What do you think?"

Madoc frowned and crossed his thick arms over his chest as he shifted closer to Nika. "I think it would be a dumb-ass move to trust him. This is out of the blue. We don't know a thing about him."

Andreas nodded, not seeming angry. "I understand your lack of trust. That's why Lyka's here."

She walked out of the bathroom, wearing a pair of loose sweats and a T-shirt. Joseph's eyes skimmed her body, taking in the athletic curves he could detect beneath the clothes. Her hair was a million shades of yellow and gold and a total mess. It poufed around her face, like a mane.

Joseph found it cute.

Something in him loosened up as he watched her, like the pressure behind his eyes had been vented. A headache he'd had so long he'd stopped noticing it faded.

"Lyka has agreed to stay here under your authority as proof of my good intentions."

Lyka snorted. "I think *agreed* is a bit of a stretch. You didn't exactly give me much of a choice."

Joseph stared at Andreas in disbelief. "You're giving me your sister as a hostage?"

"I believe that the only way to save my people is to resort to the old ways. I'm abiding by the customs of my ancestors. Lyka's the perfect choice, because while she makes me want to scream and strangle her scrawny neck sometimes, there is no one on this planet I love more."

Tears pooled in Lyka's eyes and she turned away, blinking them back.

"You've got an odd way of showing it," said Joseph. "What makes you think I won't just kill her the moment your back is turned?"

"You're a smart man, a man of honor. If you weren't, you wouldn't have brought me your brother-in-arms when his soul died."

Just the memory of giving Chris's life over to Andreas was enough to make Joseph's gut clench in grief. "It was necessary."

"It proves you do what you must. As do I. You know as well as I do that all the Sentinels are nearing extinction. We have to do something, and I've decided to take the first step."

"What will you want from us?" asked Joseph.

"Nothing I'm not willing to give myself. I'd like to share intelligence and plan a strategy that has a hope of beating the Synestryn back."

"You said your people are weak. What good are they in a fight?"

"Not all of us are weak. My family's bloodline has been protected, as have a few others. I admit that most of our people will need protection, but I've heard you're used to that—that dozens of humans live here."

Joseph refused to confirm it. He trusted Andreas to a point, but until it was necessary to share information, he wasn't going to offer anything.

"How many?" asked Joseph. "How many of your people can fight?"

"I'll give you all the details you want as soon as I have your promise for peace."

Any promise Joseph offered would be binding, so he had to be careful what he said. "I will agree to a temporary truce—long enough to discuss this with my people and the Sanguinar. If things are as you say, then we'll consider something more binding."

"I need more than that. I need your promise not to attack my people."

"I've given you all I can for now. You can accept that or not. Your choice."

Andreas's jaw clenched, but he gave a curt nod. "May we stay while you decide? Or would you rather we get a hotel room in town?"

Joseph looked to Madoc. "Would you please get our guests settled in one of the suites? Make sure they're comfortable." And carefully watched. Joseph knew Madoc would do that without being asked. The man wasn't exactly the most trusting, especially with his wife under the same roof.

"Come with me," said Madoc.

They all left. Joseph hung back for a moment, staying in the cabin alone. He hoped like hell this wasn't a trick, because truth was, things were getting worse by the day. Without a united front, their chances of fending off the Synestryn before they could overrun Earth were slim.

On the other hand, if what Andreas said was true, then chances of fending off the Synestryn *with* the help of the Slayers weren't any better.

Chapter 5

Hope made it through the rest of her day and hurried over to the homeless shelter where she volunteered. There were still a few minutes before the dinner rush started, and Hope had fled to the rooftop to soak up what was left of the sun.

Sister Olive came into the rooftop greenhouse where Hope lounged. It was her favorite spot, all warm and sunny, especially on a day like today. As cold as it was outside, the sun was shining bright, making a sun worshiper like Hope groan in delight.

"I thought I'd find you up here," said Sister Olive. She was in her sixties, dressed in faded, plain street clothes rather than a habit. Her iron gray hair was pulled back in a tight bun at her nape, and her eyes were the same color as the sky above her head.

"Did you need me?" asked Hope.

Sister Olive shook her head and went about tending her plants. "No, I just wanted to see if you were okay. You look tired."

The scents of tomato plants and herbs filled the greenhouse, calming Hope's frayed nerves. "I had a late night."

Concern drew Sister Olive's overgrown brows together. "I hope there was no trouble."

Hope didn't want to worry her. Sister Olive was the closest thing to a mother Hope had. She'd taken Hope in when no one else claimed her, given her enough education to get her GED, and helped her start her photography business. And while Hope would never make big bucks, her work helped fill some of the void her lack of memory had left behind by creating lasting memories for others.

"Nothing I can't handle," she said, praying it was the truth.

"You went out looking for people again, didn't you?"

Hope couldn't lie to a nun. "Someone has to."

"You need to leave that to the police. You're going to get hurt if you go sticking your nose where it doesn't belong. I know there are gaps in your education, but I thought I'd at least taught you that much."

"I'm being careful," said Hope. "Besides, the police can't do much. They're already stretched thin as it is. There aren't resources for them to devote much time to looking for a handful of people they aren't even convinced are really missing."

"We've talked about this. People move on. They don't always say good-bye."

Hope filled a plastic watering can and hefted it up onto the bench beside Sister Olive. "I know that, but I have a bad feeling."

"So do I. I'm worried you're going to get hurt doing something you're not even remotely equipped to do."

"I have eyes. I can look for people as well as anyone else."

Sister Olive's mouth turned down at the edges as she stared over her glasses at Hope. "My fear is that you'll actually find out what's happened to them. The hard way."

"So you do believe I'm right. There is something bad going on."

Sister Olive stripped off her glove and cupped Hope's cheek. "What I believe is that I wouldn't survive if anything happened to you. You, child, are part of my heart. I knew from the moment I found you that you were special."

Hope soaked up the older woman's words like thirsty

plants soaked up water, and then sent up a prayer of thanks that this woman had been the one who'd found her all those years ago. "You say that about everyone."

"Well, you're especially special. God has plans for you. I can feel it."

Hope covered the woman's hand, knowing she'd never meet another soul as sweet as Sister Olive. "For all we know His plan is for me to find what's happening and stop it."

"Is that what you think?"

"I don't know. What I do know is that I can't stand by and do nothing. We've lost four regulars in as many months. And it's been a week since I saw Rory."

"That young woman with all the piercings and the pink hair?"

Hope nodded. "That's the one. She didn't come in every day, but she was here at least a couple times a week."

"She was probably just passing through. It happens all the time."

"She's been around for more than a year. How is that passing through?" asked Hope. "Don't I have a responsibility to look for her?"

Sister Olive sighed, pulled off the other glove, and set them on the workbench. "A shepherdess guarding her sheep. I guess I shouldn't complain about that now, should I?"

"I'll be careful," she promised Sister Olive.

"You do that. This place needs you. I need you." She dusted off her hands. "Speaking of which, I need to go and check on dinner. We'll have a big crowd tonight."

"I'll be down to help in a minute."

Sister Olive patted her shoulder. "You take your time. I know how much you miss the sun, and we don't have much of it this time of year. Enjoy it while it lasts."

Sister Olive left. Hope stripped out of her sweatshirt and let the sun soak into her skin. The tank top she wore was thin, allowing the delicious heat to slide over her.

The smell of basil and soil filled her nose, calming her

nerves. Everything was fine. She'd find Rory tonight and give her hell for scaring her like that.

Hope lounged there, soaking up the warmth until the sun disappeared behind the surrounding buildings. She felt better now that she'd had some time to herself. She hadn't once thought of Logan while she was here. Or that monster.

All was well in her world once again. She was safe, strong, and ready to finish off her duties for the day.

The dinner rush went by fast. Hope packed her bag full of sandwiches and blankets and was ready to hit the streets in search of Rory.

She stopped at the door, turning back to duck into the kitchen. She found the biggest, sharpest knife she could and added it to her bag. Just in case.

Iain slid his blade from the dead Synestryn and searched the tunnel for more. He'd come here to this nest to find the one kind of demon none of his Theronai brothers could fight: Synestryn with the faces of children.

Even though Iain's soul was long dead, he could still remember what it had felt like to have one. He knew that there had been a time when the thought of slaying such a creature would have turned his stomach. But no longer.

He stared down at the dead abomination. It may have had the face of a child, but that was where the resemblance ended. It was fast, with six spindly, claw-tipped legs. It had been able to cling to the ceiling of the cave before propelling itself toward Iain for the kill.

He held up his sleeve, looking through the holes that thing's teeth had left in his leather jacket—teeth strong enough to bite through the magical wards meant to protect him.

No, that thing was no more an innocent child than he was. But if he was the only one of his kind who could see that, then so be it. Everyone needed a reason to get up in the morning. Killing baby demons was his.

He'd push through the rest of this system of tunnels tonight, then head for the next one. Same ol', same ol'.

Ava's guards heard the commotion coming from down the corridor, and for the first time in what seemed like decades, she was left alone.

The chittering speech of the insectlike monsters who had held her captive grew louder, as it always did when they called more of their own kind.

She didn't have much time, and she was going to use every second of it to get herself out of this place.

The rough rock tunnels that were a maze to her when she'd first been brought here were now easy to navigate. Unfortunately, the only way out was down the tunnel, the way her guards had gone.

Fear had been a part of her for so long she almost failed to recognize a difference in the pounding of her heart as her bare feet slapped against the dirt floor. Little rocks dug into her skin, but she didn't slow for fear she'd miss her one chance for escape.

Her lungs burned from the unusual exertion, and she had to hold her round belly so it didn't feel like it was going to be ripped from her body with every hurried step. The weight of her pregnancy slowed her down too much, but that was probably what her guards had counted on.

Ava cleared a corner and nearly ran headlong into combat. She skidded to a halt, grabbing the wall of the cave to steady herself.

One man stood in the center of a thick ring of monsters—both the ones who guarded her as well as the smaller, feral ones that looked human from the neck up.

Ava knew better than to be fooled.

The man's sword moved almost too fast to see, and everywhere it passed, monsters fell. Black blood splattered over his clear face shield, but it didn't seem to slow him down. His powerful body moved with a mesmerizing grace and Ava had to jerk herself away from staring.

The dry skittering of more monsters grew louder, coming from her left.

They were going to see her and lock her up again. She couldn't let that happen. She couldn't have her baby in this place.

Ava pressed herself into a shadowy crevice, hoping her protruding belly wouldn't give her away. She held her breath, prayed her pounding heart would quiet itself, and squeezed her eyes shut.

They came so close to her she could feel a breeze from their bodies as they passed. Not one of them slowed. They all headed straight for the fight.

Ava didn't stick around to see whether the man won. There was nothing she could do to help him, anyway. The best thing she could do was run and hope that she and her baby got out of this hellhole alive.

Logan called Tynan as soon as he woke. "Where are you?" he asked.

"Dabyr."

"We were supposed to meet."

"I know. I wasn't able to get away."

"Why not?"

"Grace. She took a turn for the worse."

A pang of grief burst inside Logan's chest. He'd grown fond of the human. She was kind. Giving. A few days ago, she'd donned a magical device that transferred her health and vitality to a Theronai who had been paralyzed. The artifact worked, and Torr was now on his feet once again, but Grace's sacrifice had been great. The Sanguinar had done what they could, but no one expected her to live.

"How is Torr?" asked Logan.

"Desolate. Angry. He makes demands on me that are not possible."

"How long does she have?"

"Days at most. I told Torr I was leaving tonight, that I had work that must be done."

Logan doubted the man took that news well. "Are you safe?"

"His people have contained him so he won't hurt me when I go."

"When will you arrive?"

"It will be a few hours. I'll call you when I'm close. But I won't be able to stay away long, so have the woman ready to go."

"Ready?"

"Wring a promise from her to gain her cooperation. We're running out of time. These matches are taking too much time."

"They take as long as they take."

"Briant did some calculations. If we don't double our pace, sixty percent of our race will be dead within the next twenty years."

That news sent shock winging through Logan. He'd known things were grim, but he'd had no idea how bad they'd gotten. He'd thrived on a steady diet of hope and hard work, and it seemed cruel now that his efforts weren't good enough.

"Did you hear me, Logan?"

His voice cracked with the defeat that crushed his chest. "I did."

"Work faster, brother. We need her on our side. Now." Tynan hung up.

Logan ran his fingers through his hair in frustration. All that work and it wasn't even truly paying off.

How many lives had he altered? How many people had he tricked or coerced into doing his bidding? He'd lied. He'd even gone as far as entering the minds of his subjects to convince them to help.

They'd all done it willingly. Or so they thought.

Sure, those people were happy, but it wasn't because of their own choices. It was all Logan's doing. Artificial.

And the sad part was, he was prepared to do it again tonight. With the woman who had saved his life.

She had saved him, and now he was going to turn her life upside down.

The thought turned his stomach, but he knew better than to let his emotions sway him. Logically, it was the only course of action. If his race died, there would be no one to heal the Theronai or Slayers. They would fall to injury and poison. Their numbers would shrink until they, too, became extinct. Synestryn demons would overrun Earth. Countless people would die screaming in pain—food for the Synestryn. Better to sacrifice a few to artificial happiness than to allow the fall of mankind.

At least that's what he told himself as he set out to do what he knew he must. This was war, whether the humans knew it or not. And in war, there were sacrifices.

He just wished that the woman who'd saved his life didn't have to be one of them.

Hope saw no sign of Rory or any of the missing men as she searched the streets. None of the people she'd come to know had seen Rory. She hadn't been to the local convenience stores or any of the other shelters in town. It was as if she'd just vanished.

The police weren't concerned. Rory lived on the streets. They assured her that people like Rory moved around. And without a last name, Hope couldn't even file a proper missing person's report. The best they could do was take down her contact information and let her know if anyone matching Rory's description turned up in jail. Or in a morgue.

With that image firmly in Hope's vivid imagination, she gathered her courage to go back to the building she hated so much—the one she was certain had somehow eaten her past.

Not that a building could do such a thing. But it stood there, mocking her, taunting the edges of her mind with memories she could almost grasp. Like a fleck in her vision, as soon as she turned to look at it, it darted away, slipping out of reach.

Hope clutched a flashlight in her gloved hand and marched around the Tyler building to the back where the overhead door had been busted out. Someone had screwed a sheet of plywood over the opening to keep trespassers out.

She peered through the small window of the employee entrance, shining her flashlight inside. There was no giant monster corpse lying there, only an oily stain on the concrete. The only other proof of the battle was the fallen stack of pallets and the scuff marks in the dust coating the floor.

Hope twisted the doorknob. Locked. Of course.

She felt a subtle heat caress her nape a moment before she heard a low, cultured voice. "It's awfully cold to be out alone on a night like this."

Hope whirled around, lifting her flashlight to strike.

Logan stood there, ten feet away, well out of range. His arms were crossed over his wide chest, and his pale eyes narrowed in speculation.

Her heart pounded so hard she was sure he could hear it. "What are you doing here?" she asked.

"Looking for you." He stared up at the building. "I didn't think I'd find you here. Not after last night."

Last night. When he'd killed the monster and done ... something to her. She could still feel his lips on her throat, moving as if kissing her.

Hope's hand strayed to the spot and one side of Logan's mouth lifted in amusement.

"So you do remember," he said as he took a step forward. It had been only one step, but somehow, he was within reach, so close she could touch.

He was so beautiful. Wickedly so. The kind of man that made a woman's mind grind to a halt and her body go languid with need. His aura was bright, almost blinding, swirling with colors she'd never seen before. She didn't know how to interpret it, but it hardly mattered so long as she could keep staring at the movement of rainbows dancing around him.

The sensuous curve of his mouth promised delight. The sharp angle of his jaw and his high cheekbones cast loving shadows across his face and throat. They drew her gaze in, daring her to reach out a hand and touch. Even his silky, dark hair called to her, begging her to slide her fingers close to his scalp and drag his mouth where she wanted it most. She wasn't even entirely sure where that was, though she could imagine the fun she'd have finding out.

Not that she was going to do any of that. She wasn't. But a girl could dream, and Logan was definitely the stuff of dreams. "My memory isn't exactly trustworthy. I've learned not to pay any attention to it."

That news made an inky black brow lift in question. "I've always adored memories."

His eyes brightened, seeming to glow from within for a split second. His aura shifted, pulsing with an infrared flush of desire. Hope felt herself lean forward, trying to get closer.

Logan reached out and drew one finger from her forehead, down her temple, over her cheek, and onto her neck. A heated shiver swept through her as his finger made contact with the spot his mouth had been last night. "I'd like you to share yours with me."

"Share?" she asked, her voice barely there. Her chest was tight with longing, leaving little room for air.

Not that she needed it. She didn't need anything except the sight of this man and the feel of his fingers on her skin. It made her insane, but there was no help for that now.

"I only want a quick peek. Just a glimpse of the woman you are."

His hand slid around her neck, curling at her nape. He pulled her close, bowing his head until his forehead rested against hers.

He smelled of sunlight on snow—cold and clean. But the warmth of his skin seemed to burn into hers.

This wasn't right. There was something odd about him, and she needed to put some space between them in order to clear her senses and figure out what it was.

She shifted her weight to take a step back and was suddenly jerked against his torso, his arm wrapped around her, his hand splayed low on her hip. The hold was possessive. His grip demanding.

"Just relax," he whispered, and she was sure she could feel it in her mind as well as hear it in her ears. "I won't hurt you."

There was a hot pressure behind her eyes—not painful, but not right. It didn't belong. She instinctively fought the invasion, which seemed only to make it worse.

"Let go, lovely. Let me inside."

His words made heat flare in her belly. She pulled in a gasping breath. This wasn't right. It felt good, but it wasn't right.

Hope had no chance of breaking his grip. His body felt like hot steel against her front, his arms hard metal bands. And he smelled so good. She kept dragging his scent into her lungs, letting it become a part of her. She was losing herself in this man, slipping away.

With a surge of willpower, Hope gritted her teeth and shoved against that pressure in her head. "No!" she shouted, pushing him away.

Logan flew backward, slamming into the pavement.

Shock held Hope immobile as the realization of what she'd done set in. Her whole body trembled with fear and fatigue. A headache screamed behind her eyes. Her breath came out in harsh, uneven gasps, billowing in the cold air.

He pushed gracefully to his feet, his eyes never leaving her. "What are you?"

Not who. *What.*

Hope had always known she wasn't normal. The best guess of the doctors had placed her in her late teens or early twenties the night her life began. There were no records of her birth. No parents. No friends. Not a single person had come forward when her photo had been plastered all over TV and newspapers. No one claimed her. Except Sister Olive.

And now, nearly a decade later, Logan was voicing her deepest fears. No one had claimed her because no one knew her. It was as if she'd been plunked down, out of nowhere. An alien.

Or worse.

She'd always pretended she was normal. Her memory loss was a head injury no doctor could find on any CAT scan or MRI. She'd built a life for herself—a home for herself—based around a fundamental, flimsy lie: Hope was human.

Between Logan's question and the powerful outburst she'd just displayed, Hope's house of cards was beginning to fall.

"Leave me alone," she said, her words lacking the strength she'd intended to give them.

Logan dusted off his jeans and shook his head. "Not on your life. I need you."

Hope scoffed at that, letting out a laugh of derision she couldn't contain. "I bet you do." She nodded down at the bulge in his jeans—the one she'd been trying to avoid acknowledging.

"Would my erection be less offensive if I told you that's the first time that's happened to me in a long, long time?"

"You're such a flatterer. And a liar."

"Sometimes," he admitted, "but not now."

"I need to go. Do not follow me." She turned to walk away, determined to search the inside of that blasted memory-stealing building despite how freaked-out she was now.

Logan took hold of her arm and his living heat slid through her coat into her skin. "I'm sorry. I can't let you go. I need you. My people need you."

"The bullshit just keeps getting deeper." She tried to jerk out of his grasp, hoping for another burst of strength, but his hold stayed firm.

He stepped forward until his body was pressed against her back. Instantly, she wished for a longer coat—one that would mask the thick press of his erection against her ass and the languid warmth it caused to pool in her belly.

His arm snaked around her, sliding under her sweater until his fingers curled along her ribs. They were so warm. So gentle.

Never before had she allowed a stranger to touch her like this. She had no idea why she was now.

Hope felt his breath flutter across the top of her ear. "Please don't run. I promise I won't hurt you."

A comforting weight descended over her, but she knew it was a trick. Some kind of magic trick he was playing on her screwed-up mind.

"Five minutes. Please give me five minutes."

"To do what?" She could think of too many things a man like him could do with that amount of time. Her heart pounded hard at the idea, and a burst of need exploded in her chest.

He let go of her and caressed his way up her arm, over her shoulder, and up her throat until his hand settled along the side of her face. "I want to see your memories. Learn who you are."

"How is that even possible?"

"How was it possible you were able to cast me to the ground with more strength than a man twice your size?"

He had a point. "Why? Why do you want to see my memories?"

"I think we can help each other."

"How?"

"So many questions. It would take less time to show you than to explain. Aren't you curious?"

She was. That was the problem. She'd wanted to know the answer to so many questions for so long that even the merest hope of learning the truth called to her. What if he wasn't lying? What if he could see her memories and tell her once and for all if she was human or something else?

Hope nodded, feeling the heat of his fingers slide along her face. "Okay. Take a peek, but I swear that if you try anything funny, I'll beat your head in with my flashlight."

Chapter 6

She was a violent thing, but Logan discovered that it aroused him. Like everything else about her.

He truly shouldn't have allowed himself to get this close, to let the soft swell of her ass cradle his swollen cock. The appendage had a mind of its own, jerking and pulsing against her as if it could get closer.

She was meant for someone else. He had to remember that.

Logan had spent years ignoring hunger. This was simply one more type of hunger he would learn to ignore. Quickly.

Before she changed her mind, Logan pressed his advantage and swooped into her thoughts. She didn't fight him this time. In fact, he felt himself being pulled in, welcomed as if he belonged here.

He started with her most recent thoughts and memories. Tonight.

She was afraid of him. Attracted to him. He saw himself through her eyes and there was an odd sort of colorful halo surrounding him. He'd never seen anything like it before, but she was so used to it, her easy acceptance made him skim over that detail.

She was looking for someone. A friend. Logan could see the young woman's face clearly. Pretty. Dark eyes. Blond hair that had once been dyed pink, growing out to hide her face.

Logan tucked that away, and moved back along her

memories, seeing a stream of nameless people sliding through her life. Some of them she knew well. Others were strangers. She seemed to care for all of them, worry for them.

He moved back to her memories of last night, knowing he needed to remove all traces of the Synestryn she'd seen. That memory could lure others to her, putting her at risk. It had to be cleaned from her thoughts for her own safety.

Logan found the memories from last night. He saw himself battle the demon, and felt her fear as she'd watched. She'd seen him as courageous and noble. It was such an odd thing to witness that he lingered there for a moment, reveling in her perception of him. To her, he was a hero. He'd saved Steve's life.

Of course, she didn't know that he'd done it for his own selfish purposes. He needed Steve to survive. His people needed Steve. There was nothing noble at all about what he'd done last night. It was all cold, practical logic.

And yet, witnessing how she felt about the event gave him pause. He liked how she saw him. He found himself hesitating when he knew he had to rid her of the memory.

But if he did, how would she see him then? Would she remain in his arms, pliant and cooperative? Or would she become mistrustful and bolt the moment she got the opportunity?

That was not something Logan could allow. No matter how much he liked playing the part of a noble hero, her memories of the demon had to be erased.

Like a surgeon extracting a tumor, he found the edges of that memory, preparing to cut it out. The seams between when she showed up and saw the demon, and the time she woke up in the hospital had to be knit together in a way that would not leave her curious. The less he removed, the easier it would be for her, but if he left too much, she might poke at the memory until holes formed and the events came rushing back to her.

He found what he thought was the optimal balance and began to extract those memories to take them into himself.

It didn't work. No matter how hard he tugged, the memories remained fixed in place. If he tried any harder, he'd hurt her, and that was simply not something he could tolerate.

This kind of thing rarely happened, but he had heard of it. Sadly, that left him with only one option: He had to blur what was there.

His skills with this kind of work were far less advanced. He had to leave the majority of the memory intact, while hazing over that which would draw Synestryn to her.

Slowly, Logan began layering a fog over the creature, covering it every moment of her memory. It took several iterations, but when he was done, all that was left was a black, shadowy spot in her vision, as if she'd never been able to clearly see the thing that had attacked.

Logan wasn't sure how well his work would hold. He'd have to check on it again later to ensure that nothing had come unraveled. Which meant he had to stay by her side, at least for a little while.

Time had no meaning while he worked, but they were out in the open and he needed to finish his task before it became dangerous.

He moved back in time, watching her body change and thin with adolescence. He wanted to see her parents so he could help uncover the mystery of her powerful bloodline, but he didn't get far before his consciousness rammed into something. A wall. A barrier of some kind. He pushed against it, and felt an answering moan of pain coming from the woman he held in his arms.

It was too strong for him to break through without hurting her. Logan wasn't willing to do that. At least not now. He couldn't afford to ruin her newborn trust.

He moved within the stream of her memories, weaving through them until right before he hit that barrier.

She was young. Cold. Afraid. Naked and shivering in an alley as she hugged herself. The world around her was strange, the building looming over her larger than anything she'd ever seen before. Through her eyes he saw her staring down at a chunk of wood. It had been rounded and sanded until it was as smooth as a river pebble. A thin leather strip woven through a roughly drilled hole. Burned into the wood was the name Hope Serrien.

Her name.

Why would that be? Why would someone strip her of her belongings and memories and leave her this one token of her identity?

Logan had no idea. What he did know was that it was no coincidence that the address scrawled in blood across his mirror was the same one where Hope's memories ceased. The same one where the demon he'd killed last night had emerged. The same one where they stood now, pressed together, their minds connected.

This place held some kind of significance. Logan didn't know what it was, but he was going to find out. And in the meantime, he had something to occupy his thoughts: finding Hope a suitable mate.

He removed himself from her mind, but couldn't bring himself to ease away from her body. He held her, sharing warmth as the cold wind whipped around them.

"Hope Serrien," he said, feeling her name roll from his tongue.

"What did you see?"

"Your life. Your memories. Where they began. Here, in this place."

She turned inside his arms, facing him. Her eyes were filled with a shame he couldn't understand. "Do you know who I am?"

"I know no more than you do."

"You must. The things you can do . . ."

The desperation in her voice called to him. He ached to wipe it away and replace it with pleasure. A woman like her deserved nothing less. The way she cared for others was rare—a gift to be treasured.

"I may be able to help. Given enough time."

"Time?" She sounded distant, almost distracted, as she stared at his mouth. She licked her lips.

The urge to bend down and kiss her was almost more than he could fight. Logan's body tensed with the effort, his muscles clamping down to hold him in check. "Come with me. I have someone I'd like you to meet."

He wasn't sure who that man would be yet, but he'd figure that out once he'd secured her agreement. Perhaps putting a name to the man who would belong to her would help him remember his place.

He was a matchmaker—a tool. Nothing more. Certainly not someone who should be thinking about how well Hope fit in his arms, or how her scent went to his head, driving away all rational thought.

Before things got out of hand and he did something irrevocable, Logan gently separated them and took a long step back. Cold air sucked her heat from his skin and he mourned the loss.

Hope blinked a couple of times as if the move had helped clear her head. "I can't go anywhere with you."

"Why not?"

"People are missing. And even if they weren't, I have a job to do."

"I'll help you find your friends. I'm quite good at hunting people." Her face paled, and he realized his wording had been indelicate. "I mean *finding* people."

She had the loveliest amber-colored eyes. They reminded him of sunlight streaming through autumn leaves—sunlight he could see but never feel against his skin. In the moonlight, her hair was a paler gold, the color of honey. Shadows lay against her cheek like a lover's caress, and the uncertainty in her gaze made him want to hold her close.

But what she needed right now was not his touch. She

needed reassurance that he could help. That he was harmless.

Logan knew without a doubt the latter was a lie. He was more predator than man, scheming to get his way whenever necessary. And if he had to do so again now to gain her cooperation, so be it.

He forced a kind smile to curve his lips. "We'll find your friends, and then you can come with me as repayment."

"Is that how you live your life?" she asked. "Counting the cost of your service to others so the debt can be repaid? I'm not sure I can accept the help of someone like that."

He looked at her in confusion, unsure of what he'd said to upset her. "It only seems fair that if I help you, you would offer me something in return."

"Fair. I see." She bent and picked up her flashlight from where it had fallen out of her grasp. The beam fell across his eyes, ruining his vision for a moment. "Thanks for your offer, but no thanks. I'll find Rory and the others on my own."

It took Logan a moment to regain his mental balance. Usually when he offered his aid, people accepted. He couldn't remember the last time he'd been turned down. "What?"

"You heard me. I'll figure it out on my own."

"But . . . why? I'm offering to help."

"For a price."

"So?"

She shone her flashlight along the brick wall and began to walk. Away from him. "So, I'm not the kind of person who is willing to strike a deal with an asshole. I lived on the streets long enough to know that it will only get me in trouble."

She'd lived on the streets? He'd sped through her memories so fast, he must have missed that part of her life. The news that she'd suffered like that made something fierce and dangerous rise up inside Logan. His claws began to extend, and he had to take several deep breaths through his nose to keep his fangs from showing.

He shoved his hands in the pockets of his trench coat and followed her. "Where do you live now?"

"None of your business."

"Are you afraid of me?"

She stopped and turned to face him. Her feet were braced apart, and her grip on the sturdy Maglite tightened. "Should I be?"

Logan truly didn't know what to say. He meant her no harm, but the lengths he was willing to go to ensure her participation in Project Lullaby would frighten most humans.

He settled for the ever-present lie. "No. Of course not."

She stared at him, her amber gaze unwavering. "I saw what you did to that . . . monster. Didn't I?"

The fact that she remembered enough of it to know it had been a monster proved just how inept he'd been at masking the memory. "I have no idea what you saw."

"Are you saying you didn't kill it?"

"No."

"Then what are you saying?"

"Perceptions are tricky things. People see the same thing differently."

"And how do you see me?" she asked. "As some sort of gullible girl to be sucked in by a hot, mysterious guy?"

The idea that she found him "hot" held more than a little appeal to him. But that wasn't what he needed from her, and it wasn't what she'd asked.

He studied her, enjoying the path from the snow boots on her feet, up her slim legs, over the curve of her hips, past the puffy jacket that hid too much, and on to her lovely face. Every inch of the journey delighted him, and made him think of how she might look divested of all her trappings. Including her angry glare. "You're alone. Vulnerable. Afraid."

She glanced at the erection he couldn't seem to rid himself of. Her lips tightened in disgust. "And that excites you?"

She was slipping away from him, growing cold, shoving so much mental distance between them that Logan would never be able to bridge the gap. Normally, women were much easier to deal with than Hope was. Normally, they stumbled over themselves, enthralled by his looks, offering him anything he asked for and some things he didn't. While she may have liked his appearance, she was far from enthralled.

"No. Your beauty excites me."

She let out a derisive snort. "Good-bye, Logan." She walked away, searching for something along the wall.

Logan hurried to catch up. He had to mend things with her, but every time he opened his mouth, he seemed to muck things up. "Your past intrigues me."

She glanced over her shoulder. "What do you know of my past?"

"Not as much as I'd like to."

"That makes two of us."

"I could help you with that. I could help you break through that wall."

"And what would that cost me? Wait, let me guess. All I have to do is sleep with you."

Her words made lovely images explode in his mind. Long, tanned limbs draped in shadow. Her slender fingers gliding over his naked skin. The sweet curve of her breasts. His cock buried inside her while he fed from her beautiful neck.

All powerful, compelling daydreams. All completely out of the question.

Logan cleared his throat so he could speak. "I offer my services as a gift. Free of charge."

She stopped and turned, and as her gaze fell upon him once again, he felt satisfied and somehow more complete.

A slight smile played at her lips. "I see you're a fast learner."

Her eyes slid down his body. Logan shifted, closing his coat to hide the inconvenient effect she had on his body. "The swiftest. I assure you."

"Why? Why would you help me?"

"Most people would ask how, not why."

"Most people would trust whatever words came out of that lovely mouth of yours, no doubt."

So she did find him appealing. He smiled. "You've learned my secret."

"So now you have to kill me?"

"Hardly. I'd give my life for yours."

A blond eyebrow twitched upward. "Laying it on a bit thick, aren't you?"

"It's the truth. I need you. My people need you. Whatever it takes to gain your cooperation, I'll do."

"Ah, so this is about what *you* want."

"I mean only to remove any barrier that stands in the way of your acceptance of my proposal."

"What proposal is that?"

The truth seemed to be making more progress than manipulation did, so Logan decided to give it a try. The novel approach felt clumsy to him, but he was an adaptable creature. "There's a man I'd like you to meet."

She laughed, the sound echoing off the brick building. "You're doing all of this to set me up on a blind date?"

She didn't seem worried by the notion. Only amused. "What if I am?"

Hope shook her head. Moonlight slid over the silky strands. "You're wasting your time. I don't date. I'm too busy."

"Finding lost friends?"

"Among other things."

"I will help you."

"I already told you I didn't want your help. I'm not interested in partnering with any man who has to be paid off to do the right thing."

"What if I told you that what I'm asking of you *is* the

right thing? And that I seek only to further the greater good?"

Disbelief filled her tone. "By setting me up on a blind date?"

He was getting caught in the language, his meaning becoming diluted because of the words. It would be so much simpler if he could convey his wishes to her directly—send his thoughts into hers so she understood them without the barrier of communication.

Logan stepped forward, reaching toward her.

Hope stumbled back, raising the flashlight as a weapon. "Stay where you are. You're not getting more of my blood."

"You remember that?" Which meant her mind was powerful indeed. No wonder her mental barrier was so formidable. Chances were she'd erected it herself in an effort to forget some painful past best left uncovered.

If it hadn't been for Logan's need to know her origins, he would have decided then and there to let that barrier stand.

But he did need to know. She may have siblings. Children. If so, he needed to find them.

Her gloved hand strayed to her neck. Her voice became distant, vibrating with a subtle trace of fear. "I wasn't sure until just now. I thought it might have been a dream."

"I apologize if I hurt or frightened you."

She took a long step back. Her face had gone ashen and he could hear her pulse speed.

His mouth began to water, but he ignored it. He'd fed well from her. He was still strong. Still full. He didn't need any more of her blood. It was merely a want, and one he wouldn't indulge. Not only was she likely to still be weak from what he'd taken; if he fed from her now, she'd never trust him.

"Are you a vampire?" she asked.

Logan detested the term, and he felt his mouth twist with a sneer. "No."

"You killed that monster. You took my blood. If you're not a vampire, then what are you?"

"Anxious to help you find your friend."

"So you can drink her blood."

He pinned her with a stare, gliding forward. "Would that bother you? To see my lips at another woman's throat?"

Fear vanished from her features and was replaced with indignation. "Hardly. Get over yourself."

"Would you like to stand out here in the cold and continue to talk, or would you rather find your friend?"

"Rory. Her name is Rory."

He nodded his acknowledgment. "Tell me about her. Where did you last see her?"

"At the convenience store on the corner. I tried to get her to come sleep at the shelter where I work and she refused. As always. She said she'd rather sleep here, in this building, where there were no prying eyes."

"Was she paranoid?"

"Maybe. Would it matter to you if she was crazy?"

"There's a woman I know named Nika. Everyone thought she was crazy, too. As it turned out, she simply saw things the rest of us could not. Since then, I've become more conservative in making judgment calls about such things."

Hope's body went still. "What kinds of things did she see?"

"Why? Do you see things? Did your friend?"

"No," she answered too quickly. "I just mean you hear stories about people seeing odd things. You know. Ghosts. Vampires."

She was baiting him. Logan refused to take it. "As far as I know, such things do not exist. Though there are other things that do. Far worse things."

"Like what?"

"I could spend a week of nights listing the nightmares that lurk in the dark. I fear, however, we do not have that kind of time. Rory is still lost."

Hope nodded. "Right. You're right. We need to focus. Ghost stories will wait."

"What was your plan for locating her?"

"I was looking for a way inside. This is the only place where I know she stayed that I haven't searched."

"Have you notified the human police?"

She frowned. "Is there any other kind?"

He realized his mistake too late. "I only mean the ones who care. The good cops."

"No. That's not what you meant. I don't want to slow us down, but I'll have you know I'm making a list of questions."

Good. That meant she was planning to be with him long enough to ask questions. "As you please."

"The answer is yes, I did report her missing. The police did what they could, which wasn't much. Which is why I'm out here, trying to break into private property."

"Allow me," he said, heading back to the boarded-up overhead door.

As strong as he was now, thanks to Hope's blood, all he had to do was shove his foot against the wood. The force of his kick ripped the screws holding the wood loose, sending the board clattering onto the concrete floor inside.

"How did you . . . ?"

"I work out," he lied.

While she was still staring in shock, Logan stepped through the opening. He channeled power to his senses, gathering information and seeking out threats. The poisonous Synestryn that had nearly killed him last night had chosen this place for a reason. For all he knew, there might be more demons lurking inside.

Chapter 7

The only reason Tori had not yet slit her own wrists was the promise of revenge. It burned inside her, churning and roiling in her belly until she couldn't think of anything else.

The Synestryn lord Zillah was going to die. She wasn't sure how yet, but every one of the hundreds of painful possibilities was appealing in its own way.

He'd stolen her when she was little. Caged her. Fed her his blood. Raped her. Forced her to bear his spawn—all dead. Like his soul.

It didn't matter how many times she tortured him or killed him, it would never be enough. Her hunger for his agony would never be sated. Her thirst for his suffering never quenched.

She could feel his presence burning in her blood. His blood.

Beneath her pale skin, she could see the black of his essence pulsing inside her. The healers here had tried to get rid of it, but it had only made them sick.

She made them sick.

The door to her room opened and panic ripped through her. She held her breath, peering out from under the bed where she lay. Big, booted feet crossed the carpet.

"Tori?"

Andra's voice. Her sister.

"What?"

"I brought you something. Can you come out?"

Andra wouldn't go away until she'd given her whatever it was. It was faster to let her do what she wanted and get it over with.

Tori wriggled out from under the far side of the bed. She stood, pressing herself into the corner.

Light from the hall spilled inside, burning Tori's eyes. After so many years of living in blackness, light burned. Especially sunlight.

For so many years, she'd dreamt of seeing the sun again, and now it brought only pain.

That was one more sin Zillah had to pay for.

"You don't have to sleep under there, baby," said Andra, her voice soft, like she was talking to a child.

She was shielding something on a tray with her hand. A searing glow poured over Andra's face and body.

Tori closed her eyes. "This room is too big." It loomed around her, like the open jaws of a giant monster. One wrong move and those jaws would clamp shut, trapping her inside.

"We'll figure something out. So you're more comfortable."

"Why are you here?" asked Tori, hoping her sister would hurry up and leave.

"I brought you something."

Andra moved her hand and the flare of fire stabbed Tori's eyes. She hissed in pain, falling to a crouch to cover her head so she wouldn't get burned.

There was a sound of heavy breathing, then the smell of smoke. Her sister's voice was filled with guilt. "I'm sorry, baby. I didn't mean to scare you."

Tori didn't answer. There was nothing she could say to make it better. For either of them.

"I knew you wouldn't want a bunch of people around, but I wanted to do something."

Now that the fire was gone, Tori looked up. Andra held something Tori recognized but could not name. It was sweet. She remembered that much. Mom used to make them in the dreams she had before the caves.

Andra offered it. The tiny, pink torch stuck out from the top, sending a tendril of smoke into the air between them. "It's a cupcake."

Cupcake. Yes. That was the word.

Tori took it. Her fingers sank into it until she lightened her grip. The sweet smell of it turned her stomach, but she hid that from her sister. She thought it might hurt Andra's feelings.

"You don't have to eat it now if you don't want to. I just wanted to do something," said Andra.

"Why?"

Her sister reached out to touch her, but Tori flinched away. She couldn't stop herself.

Andra's hand fell to her side and sadness covered her. Even her hair looked sad. "Today is your birthday, baby. Don't you remember? You're eighteen."

Shock stilled Tori's heart for a moment. That had to be wrong. She had been in those caves forever. Not just ten years.

Andra let out a sad sigh and rose to her feet. "Is there anything I can do? Anything I can get you?"

"No," said Tori automatically. She didn't like it when people were around. It was easier to think when she was alone under the bed. Safe.

Andra nodded. As she left the room, she said, "Happy birthday, Tori," then shut the door.

Tori stared at the cupcake for a long time. She opened the bottom drawer of the little cabinet beside her bed and set the cupcake inside. She might need it later, if she got hungry, and she didn't want anyone to see it and take it away.

It was her cupcake. She'd kill anyone who tried to take it.

Andra managed to shut the door before the tears started to fall. Her baby sister was home, but she wasn't okay. Whatever the Synestryn had done to her had destroyed her. Their blood still flowed in her veins.

Tynan said she was dangerous. To others as well as herself. He wanted to put her in a magically prolonged sleep until they could figure out how to filter her blood.

If they could figure out how. So far, everyone had failed.

Maybe he was right. Andra had hoped that with time and love, Tori would heal, but that was looking less and less likely as each day passed.

Her husband Paul's comforting presence slid through the luceria that linked them together. He was in a meeting with Joseph, but he was never far from her mind.

He was worried what Tori might do.

Andra wasn't. If she had to, she'd restrain her sister. She refused to fear her. Tori needed help, not to be shunned.

The real fear wasn't what Tori would do to others; it was what she'd do to herself.

Maybe Tynan was right. Maybe it was time to put Tori to sleep. Just for a while.

Hope stepped through the hole Logan had opened in the overhead door. Leather stretched over his broad back. She was sure the first time she'd seen him, he'd been thinner. Gaunt. But now he was packed with lean, athletic muscle. So much so his coat barely fit. She wanted to run her hands over him to see if it was real or just one more trick her mind had played on her. Of course, the thought of touching him made her hands shake and something hot and excited fluttered in her stomach.

She had to forcibly drag her gaze away from his back and focus on what they were doing.

The building was quiet. Dust floated in the beam of her flashlight. The scent of lumber and musty animals filled her nose. There was barely any ambient light sliding in from the windows. Several of them had been boarded up, and those that weren't were filthy with age and neglect.

"What is this place?" asked Logan.

"The Tyler building. They built custom furniture here years ago. It's been for sale for as long as I can remember."

He glanced over his shoulder, his pale eyes brilliant in the dark. "How did you lose your memory?"

She didn't want to talk about this. Not with him. Not with anyone. "I don't know. That's the thing with amnesia. You can't remember."

"Were you wounded?"

"I don't know," she repeated, shoving the words out from between gritted teeth so he'd take a hint.

"As you wish," he said. "Tell me about your friend. Why are you looking here for her?"

"She lives on the streets. She'd stay here sometimes, along with a lot of other people. It's a good place to get out of the cold and snow."

"How do you know her?"

"Sometimes she comes to the homeless shelter where I volunteer. Picks up a quick meal."

"Are you sure she's missing? Could it be that she's moved on?"

Hope sighed, gathering her patience. It wasn't his fault he was asking the same questions she'd already answered a hundred times. "I'd like to think she would have said something to me. She knows I worry."

"Do you worry about all the people you know?"

"Yes, but not like Rory. She was young. Too young to be out here alone. She told me she was twenty-five, but she looked sixteen."

"A runaway?"

"Probably. She's tough. Rebellious. That's enough to tell me she isn't new to the streets."

They passed through a doorway that led to a stairwell. Logan went up. "Is she a prostitute?"

"Maybe. I don't ask. Does it matter?"

Logan shrugged. His leather jacket creaked. "Not to me."

A tension riding along Hope's neck loosened at his words. He wasn't the type of man to instantly write off another because of mistakes they'd made or the things they were driven to do for the sake of survival. That was refreshing. And unexpected.

It gave her the courage to let him in on her fears. "Have you ever had a bad feeling? One that wouldn't go away?"

"Constantly."

"No. I mean something that had no basis in logic or fact, but you were sure was true, anyway?"

He stopped on a landing and gave her a steady look. "The notion is not a foreign one, no. Do you have a feeling like that?"

Hope nodded, avoiding his gaze. "Yeah. About Rory. She was running from something. I'm afraid that that something might have caught up with her."

Logan laid a comforting hand on her shoulder. She could feel the warmth of his touch sink through the puffy layers of her quilted jacket and into her skin.

"What makes you think she was running?"

"She moved around a lot. Never slept in the same place two nights in a row. Most people develop patterns. She had none that I could tell."

"How long have you known her?"

"About a year."

"That's a long time for someone like that to stay in one place."

"Yeah. I thought so, too. I asked her about it once and she said she was looking for someone. She wouldn't say who."

Logan's eyes narrowed in speculation. "Did she happen to have a ring-shaped birthmark that you're aware of?"

Hope was taken aback by the odd question. "No. Why?"

"Do you?"

"What?"

His gaze grew intense, brightening a bit in the gloom of the stairwell. "Do you have a ring-shaped birthmark?"

"Why do you want to know?"

"It would explain a lot."

"How? All you're doing is confusing me."

His hand slid down her arm until he grasped her fingers. Her leather gloves warmed to his touch, and she wished she hadn't put them on now. The need to feel his skin on hers was suddenly an overwhelming, consuming thing.

He took a small step toward her, closing the space between them. "I would very much like it if you'd answer my question."

"Tell me why first."

"That mark is important. It's proof of a certain . . . genetic predisposition that identifies its bearer as a rare treasure."

"Like some kind of blood donor or something?"

A small smile stretched his mouth, making him heart-stoppingly beautiful. "Indeed. Do you wear it?"

Hope shook her head, feeling a stab of disappointment. The way he said it—that rare treasure bit—made it sound romantic and special.

What she wouldn't give to be a good kind of special, instead of a brain-damaged, head-case kind of special.

"No. Sorry."

He squeezed her hand before letting it go. "No worries. It simply means we still have a mystery to solve."

"Mystery?"

"The location of your missing friend, of course," he said, though she was certain that he'd meant something else entirely.

"Right. We should get moving. I don't like being here. Gives me the willies."

"We can't have that, now, can we?" He turned and headed up the stairs, exiting the door onto the third floor. "I don't suppose you have anything with Rory's blood on it, do you?"

"Her blood?"

He nodded as he scanned the large open area sprinkled with wooden platforms she guessed were workbenches.

"If I had some, I'd be able to locate her easily."

"How?" asked Hope.

He ignored her question and headed toward the far end of the room where several bare mattresses sat. "This looks like a place one would sleep, does it not?"

"How could you find her with her blood?"

Logan gave her a panty-melting grin. "There are some things even your sweet face cannot coax out of me."

The veiled compliment slid through her, warming her down to her toes. Staring at that smile, she forgot what she wanted to know or why it mattered. His male beauty filled her head and made a pool of longing swell deep in her belly.

She stood there, staring, watching his pale eyes slide over her body. That sunshine-warm feeling he gave off blasted her front, making her nipples bead up against a shiver of need.

He pulled in a deep breath through his nose and his hands fisted at his sides. "When you look at me like that, I forget who I am."

"Like what?"

"Like you want me. Like you wouldn't care if I tossed you down on one of those dirty mattresses and took my pleasure with you."

Would she care? If it meant she could get his hands on her bare skin, sliding over her. Or maybe even get his mouth on her neck again and feel that hot tugging at her throat.

The memory of what he'd done to her bloomed in her mind, only this time, there was no fear, only that languid pleasure of his mouth on her, his tongue swirling over her skin.

Her hand fluttered to that spot, feeling an answering

warmth glowing there so bright she was sure he could see it.

A low hiss rose from him and his eyes flared bright, spilling light across her chest. "You should not tempt me."

Her voice shook with need as she answered. "I'm not doing anything."

"I am not a man," he said, making it sound like a warning.

"Then what are you?"

"Dangerous. Hungry."

"Then let me feed you." She'd meant food, but the way his gaze shot to her neck made her realize the other interpretations her words might have.

"You're too giving for your own good. I will use that against you. Eventually."

"But not now?"

"Alas, no."

"Why warn me?" she asked.

He shook his head, and when he spoke, she was sure she saw a white flash of fangs in his mouth. "I have no idea. You're a weakness I can't seem to understand. It's best we complete our task and go our separate ways before I do something irrevocable."

He turned, striding toward the mattresses, clearly ending the conversation.

Hope stood where she was, shaking. Now that he was farther away, she could feel her body returning to normal. Her pulse slowed, as did her breathing. The dots of sweat that had formed along her hairline evaporated into the cold night air. Her abdomen relaxed and that flush of heat dissipated from her skin.

Whoever he was, *what*ever he was, Logan was potent. Intoxicating. Hope had always abstained from drugs and alcohol, worried that such things had contributed to her amnesia. She'd never even been tempted. But Logan was a different matter entirely. She wanted him. More than she'd ever wanted a man before in her life.

It wasn't right. She sensed that there was some reason he kept his distance.

Perhaps he was married.

The thought shriveled something small and hopeful in her heart. She'd never poach. Not even for a man as beautiful as Logan. It was best they kept their distance and stayed professional. She wouldn't turn away his help to find Rory—she couldn't do that to her friend—but she could keep things light. Stay detached.

With that decision made, Hope felt better. Stronger. She pulled in a deep breath and went to Logan's side where he was staring down at the floor.

Silvery light spilled out over the dusty mattress. It was coming from Logan's eyes.

He appeared to be in some kind of trance, his focus beyond the floor. His face was lax and his breathing slow and even.

A moment later, he blinked several times and crouched next to the mattress. "Someone was killed here."

"How can you tell?"

He gave the mattress a hard shove and it slid over the floorboards, leaving a trail in the dust. There was a dark, irregular stain on the wood, several feet across. Hope shone her flashlight on it and saw the rusty brown of dried blood.

"Is that what I think it is?" she asked.

"Blood. And whomever it belonged to couldn't have survived that kind of loss."

Hope didn't ask him if he was sure. She guessed he knew what he was talking about in this area of expertise.

"It looks old," she said, trying to convince herself it was true. It had been only a few days since she'd seen Rory. It couldn't be hers.

"A couple of days at most."

Worry tightened Hope's throat. "How can you tell?"

"The smell. She was healthy at the time of her death."

"She?"

"It's a woman's blood," he said.

"You can't know that from the way it smells."

He stood suddenly, his eyes darting to the far side of the room. He grabbed her arm and pushed her behind him. "Someone's here. Stay silent. I'll shield us from sight."

She had no idea what he meant, but a second later, she felt a stirring of something around them. It brushed her cheek, but felt nothing like wind. The fine hair along her arms lifted as a silvery light slid up from the ground in a cylinder.

It surrounded them both, pulsing and fluttering with what looked like bits of glitter. The effect was oddly like being trapped inside a snow globe.

Hope didn't dare ask how he'd done it. She worried her voice would give them away.

What if it was the killer coming back?

A door on the far side of the room opened and Hope saw the faintest edge of an aura slip through a moment before a man entered the room. From this distance, with sparkling flecks blocking her vision, she couldn't see him clearly, but his aura was familiar.

Faded with time and bent with age, the halo of color surrounded the man, gliding along as his constant companion. Red streaks of pain slid through swaths of cool green acceptance. Pale golden strokes of happiness hovered behind him, and ahead of him was calm, fearless, brilliant hope. Sections of color were simply missing, as if his aura was too old and weary to fill in the gaps.

Hope had seen this before. It was the aura of the elderly—of those who were ready to go to meet their maker.

The man shuffled forward, a paper sack clenched in his gnarled hand. His plaid coat hung open, showing off baggy clothes beneath. He lifted his head, giving her a glimpse of his face.

"It's Charlie," she whispered close to Logan's ear. "I know him. He's harmless."

The glittering column dissipated, taking with it the odd tingling energy that had created it.

"Hello, Charlie," said Logan in a low, calm voice.

The man stopped in his tracks, clutching his sack to his chest. "Who's there?"

Hope stepped forward so he could see her clearly, shining the flashlight on her face. "It's me. Hope Serrien."

The man sagged in relief. "Hell, girl. You nearly scared me out of my skin."

"Sorry. What are you doing here?"

"The shelter was crowded. I couldn't take it tonight, so I thought I'd slip up here for a bit. Who's the fella?"

Logan ignored his question. "There's blood on the floor. Do you know how it got there?"

Charlie's rheumy eyes narrowed. "Son, you'd best leave that alone if you know what's good for you."

That sounded suspiciously like he did know.

Hope crossed the space, hurrying to his side. "Was it Rory? Was she here?"

"You're a sweet girl. No good can come of you poking your nose into things. Understand?"

"No," she said. "I don't. If Rory was killed here, you would have reported it, right?"

Charlie turned around as if to leave. "The less I see, the safer I am. You, too."

Hope took his arm, feeling his bones easily through the layers of clothing. "You have to tell me. I won't make you talk to the police. I'll do it myself."

Charlie shook his shaggy head. "Girl, there's nothing the police can do to fix some things. What happened here is one of them. You'd best leave it be. Walk away."

"Perhaps I can help," said Logan.

Charlie looked him up and down, wearing a dismissive expression. "If so, I'll eat my hat."

"You're afraid. Understandably so. But I assure you

that if there is some kind of creature lurking here, I'm more capable of dispatching it than any policeman would be."

"That so?" asked Charlie.

"It is."

"What makes you think it's some kind of creature?"

Logan's chest expanded with a frustrated breath, but it didn't come out in a sigh. "I killed one here last night. Typically, these things congregate in nests. When you see one, there are more lurking nearby."

"Like cockroaches."

"Precisely."

"Guess I need to find myself a new place to sleep, then."

Hope couldn't let him get away. Not until she knew the truth. "Please, Charlie. At least tell me if it was Rory. I have to know what happened to her."

The old man paused, his thin lips mashing together in hesitation. "I didn't see who it was. By the time I got here, her head was already gone. There were things feeding on her, though. And they weren't no rats."

An image of Rory's lifeless body being gnawed away by animals flashed in Hope's mind, horrifying her. She choked back a cry of anguish, pressing the back of her hand against her mouth. It took several deep breaths to gather herself enough to speak.

"Her shoes," asked Hope. "Were they pink high-tops?"

Hope had found a pair in a donations box and given them to Rory. Since the other woman had dyed her hair the same color, Hope was sure she'd like them. And lace-up shoes like that were good. They were harder for someone else to steal when you were sleeping. She figured Rory needed every advantage she could get.

Charlie frowned as if trying to remember. "I don't think so. I think I would have remembered a thing like that."

Hope sagged in relief. Logan's hand caught her elbow and held her steady. He gave her a worried look and studied her face.

"I'm fine," she told him. "That couldn't have been Rory."

Logan nodded and turned his attention to Charlie. He reached into his pocket and pulled out a money clip stuffed with cash. He peeled off a couple hundred dollars and handed it to Charlie. "Thank you for your service."

Charlie eyed the money in suspicion. "I didn't do nothin'."

"It's not safe here. Buy a room. Get warm."

"He's right," said Hope. "You can't stay here."

Charlie hesitantly reached for the money. Logan grabbed his hand and held on, covering the other man's hand in both of his.

That odd tingling feeling slid through the air again, only this time there were no glittery flecks surrounding them. Pale silvery light flared for a split second—so fast Hope couldn't locate the source of it.

Charlie's aura changed. Some of the gaps filled in, and a few of the red streaks of pain dissipated. From the corner of her eye, she saw those streaks appear in Logan's aura for a moment before fading away, as if he'd somehow absorbed them.

Charlie stumbled back.

Logan surged forward, steadying the old man before he could fall. "Careful."

"What did you do?" asked Charlie, his eyes wide with accusation.

Logan frowned in confusion. "Do?"

Charlie shoved the money in his pocket and wiped his hand on his pants. He looked at Hope. "Go home, girl. I don't know what that man is, but I sure as hell know it ain't right."

Hope glanced at Logan, who was the picture of innocence.

Charlie left, standing straighter, his shuffling gait more steady and swift than she'd ever seen it. The stairwell door shut behind him.

"What did you do to him?" she asked.

"I don't know what you mean," said Logan. But he was paler than he had been, which seemed impossible. And his aura was smaller. Dimmer. As if whatever he'd done had cost him something.

Hope had never seen anything like it before.

"You helped him somehow," she insisted.

"And what makes you say that?"

She was trapped now. She couldn't very well tell him she could see auras. She'd never told anyone. "I could tell."

"How?" he pressed.

"Woman's intuition."

His gaze narrowed as he scrutinized her. "Did you know I can smell it when you lie?"

"That's ridiculous."

"Is it?" he asked. "After all you've seen, *that's* the thing that you find ridiculous?"

He had a point—one she was not going to look at very closely.

He intrigued her. The more time she spent with him, the more she wanted to know about him, the more she wanted to unravel the mystery he presented.

"Okay," she heard herself say before she realized what she was doing. "I'll go on that blind date."

"In exchange for . . . ?"

"Nothing. You gave Charlie a gift and I want to repay your kindness. But I can't be distracted by dating until I find out what happened to those missing people, what happened to Rory. Help me if you like. Or don't. That's your choice."

"I'll help you," he said. "And then you'll help me. Do you promise?"

"I already said I would. We don't have to bargain."

"Indulge me. Give me your word."

Hope sighed. The man had some odd ideas, but if he could track blood, he was going to be more useful than the police could ever hope to be. "Fine. I promise."

As the words left her mouth, a weight descended on her, like someone had doused her under a waterfall. She gasped in shock and actually looked up to see if something had fallen.

A satisfied smile lifted his mouth. "Lovely. A bargain is struck."

Hope didn't know exactly what she'd gotten herself into, but she was pretty sure it was binding. And somehow, the idea of being with Logan long enough for their "bargain" to play out didn't bother her nearly as much as it probably should have.

"Can we just get moving?" she asked. "It's a big building and I want to make sure Rory's not in here somewhere."

Logan gave her a small bow. "As you wish."

Logan had done it. He'd wrung a promise from Hope and now she was bound to it.

Sadly, he didn't feel like celebrating his victory. Instead, he scolded himself for his lack of discipline. He never should have healed the old man. It was a waste of power, one he'd be kicking himself for when he'd used up that which he'd taken from Hope.

Still, as stupid as it had been, he wasn't sure he would do differently now, given the opportunity.

Renewing Charlie's strength, driving away some of the pain of his years . . . It was rewarding in a way Logan had nearly forgotten. It had been centuries since there had been enough strongly blooded humans roaming Earth to fuel his kind properly. Long gone was the time when he could walk into a village and heal the sick and lame knowing there would be ample offers to feed him.

Back then, he could squander his power, letting it flow freely into the world. He could do good.

It had been . . . satisfying.

But now things were different. Bloodlines were too diluted. The power of the ancient Athanasians—a race of amazingly strong beings on a distant planet that was the source of all Sentinel magic—was nearly wiped from the world, traces of it so minute, he and his kind spent nearly all their time searching for them.

Until Hope. Her blood was powerful in a way he hadn't experienced for years. It was rivaled only by a few Theronai women, such as Helen, who'd been recently discovered—women whose blood was carefully guarded by their dangerous, sword-wielding husbands.

Once again he wondered if Hope might be one of them—a Theronai, the child of an Athanasian man and a human woman. It was possible. The women they'd found had no idea what they really were. Hope could be one more.

And if so, then the stirring in his groin when he looked upon her was more than inconvenient. It was forbidden. If she was a Theronai, touching her could start a war. If she was a Slayer, touching her could get him killed. If she was human, she belonged to Project Lullaby, and touching her would be akin to betraying his own kind.

Perhaps it was time to call in one of the Theronai. They were far better suited to protect her than Logan was—at least once the power Hope's blood had given him was gone and he was once again weak.

He found himself resisting the idea of handing her safekeeping to another. He'd found her. He'd fed from her. He'd bargained with her. They were tied together.

That was the thought that spurred Logan to action. He was already growing too attached to the woman, and whether she was human, Theronai, or Slayer, that simply could not stand.

Logan retrieved his phone and dialed Joseph, the Theronai leader. Let him send someone to see to her safety and test her identity. If she was a Theronai, one of her own kind would know. If she wasn't, she'd be in safe hands until such time as Logan or Tynan could find her a suitable mate. It was the safest course of action—one that would preserve the power flowing through her veins, and prevent Logan from doing something unforgivable.

Chapter 8

It was still early in the evening when Iain finished cleaning out the nest and went back to his Suburban.

Fucking demons hadn't even put up enough of a fight to make him breathe hard. And the paltry battle sure as hell hadn't done a thing to ease the pain swelling in his chest more with every day that passed.

He would have thought that after his soul died off some of that pain would have gone away. But no. No such luck.

His blood was running hot and he was way past the point where meditation would do him any good. The only thing that would help now was more fighting.

Iain pulled up an electronic map on his phone. Nicholas had rigged the thing to pinpoint the known locations of the child-face abominations. He selected the little pink dot that indicated his current location and deleted it. The next closest one was northern Kansas, which was a good two-hour drive on backcountry roads.

He hoped like hell that by the time he got there, the pain wouldn't be any worse. Too much more and he wouldn't be able to fight. And that he simply could not stand.

Iain put the vehicle in gear and headed for a road. He'd made a bit of a mess of some farmer's field getting out here, but there was no help for that. At least he'd taken care of their infestation.

He'd just eased back onto a pitted blacktop road

when he heard a noise rise up from behind him. It was low. Faint. More a brush of air than a sound.

A slow, satisfied smile stretched his mouth as he pulled to the side of the road.

Apparently, one of the demons had slipped past him and hitched a ride with the wrong man.

Ava's body clenched hard, driving the breath from her lungs. The baby was coming. Right now.

She huddled under the blanket she'd found, crouched in the far backseat of the big SUV, trying to be quiet. She curled around her child, hugging her knees as close as possible in an effort to ward off the pain. A coppery taste filled her mouth as she bit down on her lip, struggling to be silent in the face of so much pain.

The tires bounced, jostling her hard. A second later, the car tilted sideways as it was parked in a deep ditch.

A car door opened, but Ava didn't dare lift her head to peer out a window to see where they were. They hadn't been driving long enough yet for her to have made a clean escape. She was still too close to the caves.

The back door at her feet was ripped open. The man she'd seen in the cave was standing there, holding a gleaming sword, looking ready to kill her. His face was a snarl of rage and veins in his neck stood out.

Fear, her faithful companion these long months, was there at her side, holding her close, refusing to let go. She held her dirty hands up as if they could do anything to shield her from his blade.

Her voice came out raw and scratchy from the fight to keep from screaming. "Please don't hurt me."

The man's expression altered from rage to suspicion, but his blade stayed high and ready to strike. "Who are you? And how the hell did you get in my ride?"

"I was in those caves. I escaped. I didn't know where else to go."

She started to ask for his help, but her words were cut off as another wave of pain crushed her body. This time, there was nothing she could do to stop a low moan of agony.

"Are you hurt?" The man sheathed his sword, leaned inside, and grabbed her arms. He pulled on her, but her body was too tense to cooperate as he tried to pull her from the car.

She couldn't speak. Pressure grew inside her as her body contracted. There was a wrenching kind of pain. She felt her skin tear as the baby's head crowned.

Ava pushed the blanket away and reached between her legs, heedless of her lack of clothing. The jeans she'd been wearing when she was taken hadn't fit her for months. Even the stretchy T-shirt she wore couldn't cover her belly. Her immodesty had stopped having meaning a long time ago, and she only vaguely remembered now that there had been a time when she cared.

The man jerked the blanket away, finally seeing what was going on. "You're pregnant."

"Not for long," she grated out between clenched teeth.

"Hell. Hold on." He didn't look worried. Simply resigned.

"Have you done this before?" she asked him.

"What?"

"Delivered a baby."

"Yeah. Couple of times."

That made her feel better. Safer. And then another contraction hit and all she could feel was pain and pressure. Her body took over, forcing her to bare down. Another searing sting burned her as the baby's shoulders passed. Her child slid from her. The pressure faded, leaving her panting for breath. She caught her baby's slippery body and brought him up to her chest.

She had a baby boy. A wave of something nameless and profound washed over her, altering her forever. She was a mom. In this single, still moment, nothing else mattered.

Her boy let out his first choked cry. It grew louder as the seconds passed, reassuring her as nothing else could.

She'd done it. She'd delivered a healthy baby despite the torture she'd endured for almost a year.

The man was hunched over, his body filling the doorway. He was staring at her with an odd look on his face. A kind of resignation. "I'll find something to tie off the cord."

The wetness beneath her began to cool, making her shiver. She covered them both, reveling in the squawking cries of her boy.

The man came back a moment later with two strips of frayed cloth. She allowed him to tie off the cord and sever it with a sharp knife.

Something hot and wet slid from between her legs, followed by a gush of fluid.

The man glanced down and a grim look tightened his hard features. "You're bleeding. I need to get you to a doctor."

It was his speed that gave away the urgency of the situation. So far, his movements had been methodical and easy—fast but not rushed.

He was rushing now.

As the car jolted over the road, Ava held her baby, protecting him from the rough ride as well as she could. She could feel the slow trickle of blood flowing from her, but didn't know what to do to stop it. She wadded the blanket up between her thighs and clenched them together.

"Hold on," said the man. "Bump."

The car lurched, going airborne for a second before landing hard. Ava was getting nauseated from the ride, but she didn't dare sit up and look out a window. Moving might make the bleeding worse.

She heard him talk to someone on the phone, but couldn't hear the words over the roar of the engine. All she could hear was the pissed-off tone in his voice.

"How much farther?" she asked.

"Not much. You just hold on."

"I'm cold. Can you turn on the heat?"

He didn't say anything for a moment, then responded with, "Sure."

The next time they went over a big bump, Ava's arms didn't seem to work. Her baby shifted and she had to struggle to keep him safe against her chest. When her head began to spin, she realized that the weakness wasn't a simple mistake. The blanket between her legs was soaked.

She was bleeding out.

Her vision blurred, going dark around the edges. She focused on her baby and swallowed a lump of regret. She wanted to see him grow up. Wanted to play with him and teach him things. She wanted to protect him from the monsters that had taken her.

They'd put this baby inside her. She knew they were going to want him back.

Her strength was fading. She wasn't going to make it much longer. She forced her voice out so it was loud enough for the man to hear. "Promise me you'll take care of him."

"That's your job."

"It's yours now. Promise me." Her voice was getting weaker. She wasn't sure if he heard her. If so, he didn't answer.

Ava could no longer keep her eyes open. She was so cold. She kissed her baby's head and gathered her strength for one last plea for help. "Please," she said. "Protect my son."

Iain didn't dare give his promise. If that child was one of the abominations, it was his job to kill it. From what little he'd seen, he couldn't tell if there were signs of Synestryn blood flowing through the infant's veins, but with her in that cave, pregnant and alone, chances were good the father wasn't human.

Several silent minutes passed as Iain sped over the rutted road. She didn't speak again.

"Are you still with me?" he asked.

When she didn't answer, he knew she was either dead or unconscious. And that the child was back there, unrestrained.

If it was human, he could kill it if he hit a bump the wrong way.

Iain slowed the Suburban and pulled off the road. He got out and drew his sword before approaching the back door. If the child came springing toward him, fangs bared, he was going to be ready for it.

Logan found more blood on the second floor. He crouched next to the spot. It was fresh, only a few drops, but enough to know it was from a heavily blooded human male. And he'd shed it tonight.

Hope let out a breath laced with fear. "Is that ... ?"

"I think it's time to get you out of here," said Logan. "I'll continue my search and find you when I'm done."

"You don't even know where I live."

He stood and looked in her eyes. The need to reach out and stroke her cheek slammed into him, blindsiding him. He fisted his hands in the pockets of his coat to keep from touching her. "I have your blood inside me. I'll be able to find you."

"Do you have any idea how stalkerish that sounds?" she asked.

"Go home. Get warm. I'll come find you soon."

"At least take my cell phone number. In case you run into trouble."

"I will gladly take your number, but there are others I can call for help if necessary."

"Big, strong men with lots of guns?" she asked, forcing a smile.

Logan's hand was on her face before he'd realized how foolish his touch of reassurance was. Her skin was warm and soft under his fingers. The planes of her smooth cheek were basked in shadow, casting an air of mystery around her. She leaned into his touch just the slightest bit, but he sensed the subtle movement. Reveled in it.

He heard her pulse speed and felt her skin warm. She looked up at him, her amber eyes shining with trust and something else. Something hot and womanly.

There was desire in that look, and while Logan was used to such things, he wasn't used to feeling a physical response to them.

His own pulse sped and he felt a wave of heat sweep down his body, settling in his groin. The untimely swelling of his manhood made him wish for things he could not have—made him wish for the man he had been once upon a time, before the blood of the ancients had dwindled from this world.

No longer. Duty had to come before pleasure. If he failed in that, others would die. Perhaps even the woman standing before him.

She covered his hand with hers, holding it in place against her cheek. "I don't know what you're doing to me. But I'm starting to like it."

Logan refused to touch that comment. He couldn't think about giving her pleasure. If he did, his thoughts would stray beyond duty to a place much more enticing.

He pulled his hand away and took her elbow in a firm grip, guiding her to the stairwell exit. "You must go now. I have colleagues on the way. If you don't hear from me before sunrise, I'll seek you out tomorrow night."

"I'll wait up for you," she said. "No matter how late it gets."

Regret burned in his chest. "I cannot come to you in daylight. I'll send another to protect you."

"I don't want another."

"We rarely get what we want in this life. I suggest you become accustomed to it."

They exited the stairwell and walked toward the hole in the overhead door. "Believe me. I already am."

Rather than stop and interrogate her about her intriguing answer, Logan escorted her outside to his van. "I'll drive you home, then come back here and investigate the blood."

"How?"

He unlocked the doors and opened hers. "I'll follow the trail and see where it leads."

"What trail? I only saw a few drops."

"There is a scent trail."

"Again with your sense of smell. That's not normal, you know."

"No, it's not. But it is useful." He shut her door and went around to his side. The van's engine started smoothly. He turned to ask her how to get to her home and saw her staring in the back of his van.

There was a narrow mattress back there. All the windows were blacked out.

"Are you some kind of pervert?" she asked.

"Hardly. But sometimes I'm forced to sleep here."

She relaxed a little and toyed with the blackout curtain, which currently hung open. "Don't you have a home?"

"I do, but I travel frequently."

The night was running out and he still had a lot of work to do. "Which way?" he asked her.

"North two blocks. Take a right. The studio is three blocks down on the right."

"Studio?"

"A photography studio where I work. I live upstairs."

Logan drove her there and pulled up in front of the studio. "Stay inside around as many people as possible. I'll contact you as soon as I can."

Hope hopped out of the van. "Don't make me wait, Logan. I'm not a patient woman."

Logan nodded. "I'll be swift."

Hope hurried up the stairs and disappeared into the building. Logan sat there for a long moment, feeling the cold sink into him more with every step she took.

It was all in his head. It had to be. He was simply worried over losing sight of such a precious source of power. There was no other explanation—at least none he'd allow himself.

Before he could dwell on that too long, he put his van in gear and headed back for the building where the blood trail began.

It was time to go blood hunting.

Chapter 9

Jackie Patton refused to hide in her room. She'd spent the last two years as a prisoner in a cave. That was as much of her life as she was willing to allow the Synestryn to steal from her. It was time to move on. To what, she wasn't sure, but whatever it was, it wouldn't be in this room the Sentinels had provided for her.

She was still weak from her ordeal, but getting stronger every day. Food was settling better in her stomach, and now that she'd cut the matted tangles from her hair and put on real clothes rather than tattered rags, she felt almost human.

Funny how ironic that was, all things considered.

Jackie opened her door to find Helen standing there, her fist poised to knock. "I was just coming to see you."

Jackie looked at the other woman, studying her, looking for the family resemblance in the woman who was apparently her half sister.

Helen's brown hair was braided, with each of her twin braids falling forward over her shoulders. Her face was sweetly rounded, which seemed at odds with the power the woman wielded.

Jackie had seen firsthand what that woman could do with magical fire.

"I was just going down to the dining hall for some food," said Jackie.

"Mind if I join you?"

Jackie did, but manners won out. "Sure."

They walked down the winding halls. Jackie had already gotten lost a couple of times before she learned the numbering system that helped her navigate. The numbers got smaller the closer she was to the public areas.

"How are you feeling?" asked Helen.

"Better. Thank you."

"Is there anything you need?"

"No. You've all been very solicitous."

"I spoke with Tynan about you. He said he thought you were well enough to discuss your plans."

Jackie didn't much like the idea that the vampire-healer, or Sanguinar as they called him, had spoken about her condition with others. "I don't suppose HIPPA means anything to you people, does it?"

Helen had the decency to blush. "I promise I didn't ask for details. I just needed to know if you were well enough to start thinking about your future."

"You should ask me. Not some blood-drinking monster."

"Tynan isn't a monster."

Jackie held her tongue. Anyone who lived on the blood of another was a monster. Period. It didn't matter if he used that blood to save lives or not. "I'd prefer we don't discuss him over food. I'd rather be able to eat."

Helen's mouth flattened, but she nodded. "I understand."

Jackie truly doubted that. "What exactly is it you want from me?"

"You're a Theronai. You may be able to save the life of one of our men and yet you've avoided all of them."

"I'm not exactly good company right now."

Helen pulled Jackie to a halt. There was no one in the hallway, giving them privacy. It served only to make Jackie that much more nervous.

She wasn't ready for this kind of pressure. She was barely able to keep from screaming in anger and grief every time she opened her mouth.

Jackie knew Helen was trying to help, but it didn't change the fact that it made Jackie feel used and dirty. She'd had enough of that for one lifetime.

"I can only imagine what you're going through. You were held captive, starved, fed on."

Jackie cringed, pulling away from Helen and her words. As bad as those memories were, they paled in comparison to the suffering she'd been forced to witness. There had been children in those caves with her. The things they'd endured had been much worse than Jackie's torture. No matter how hard she'd tried, she hadn't been able to save them all. "I don't want to talk about it."

"I'm not asking you to. All I'm asking is that you stop hiding from the men. While you may be able to save one of their lives, what I really hope is that one of them might be able to save yours in return."

No. Jackie had seen the way Drake looked at Helen. The way Paul looked at Andra. And she couldn't even stand to see the way Madoc looked at Nika. It was too much. Too full of need. Jackie had been looked at like that for two years. She'd seen bloodlust glowing in the eyes of beasts too hideous to be considered men.

She never again wanted to be used. Ever. And any man who tried to do so was going to wish he hadn't.

Her hands balled into fists and she had to unclench her jaw so she could speak. "Don't ask me to do this. I simply can't."

"I think you can. I think you're stronger than that."

"Whatever strength I had I used up over the last two years, keeping those children alive. It's all gone now. Your leader promised me a safe place to rest and recover. If there are strings attached, I'll go someplace else." She wasn't sure where. Her house had likely been sold. Her job was certainly filled by now. The manufacturing facility couldn't have stayed open without a manager, and there was an endless list of people eager to take her place.

She had nowhere to go, but she'd leave all the same if these people wanted to use her.

"No strings," Helen hurried to say. "I swear. I only meant to let you know that joining with one of the men may be as much of a help to you as it is to them."

"It's not going to happen. Please don't ask me again."

Helen nodded, sadness plain on her pretty face. "I'm sorry if I upset you. We won't talk about it again. Let's just go share a meal and get to know one another."

Jackie couldn't do that. She couldn't face the dining hall knowing those men would be there, staring at her, wishing for something she could never give. "I've changed my mind. I'm going back to my room now."

"Okay. I'll go with you. We'll order some food to be brought up."

"No. I'd rather be alone."

At least that way no one would ask the impossible of her. It might make her a coward to hide in her room like that. It might even make her a virtual prisoner. It didn't matter. She could not be what these people wanted her to be. And if she didn't get out of here soon, what was left of her humanity might soon vanish.

Logan followed the scent trail into the basement of the run-down furniture factory. Water had seeped in down here, leaving behind the musty smell of mildew. Beneath that was the unmistakable smell of wet animal hide, cloying sweetness, and malevolence. Synestryn.

Logan cloaked himself with his power, hoping to avoid any unnecessary combat. He was strong enough now to fend for himself, but he didn't want to squander his power in that way. It was better to save battle for the Theronai, or even the Slayers. He was more valuable in other ways.

He checked his watch. There was still an hour before backup arrived. He worried that by then the trail would grow cold, or lead him to another location. He needed to gather intelligence so that when the Theronai did arrive, he could put them to good use.

Assuming the man he hunted was still alive.

The basement wasn't open like the floors above. It was sectioned off into what had once been storage rooms or offices. A long hallway led down the center of the level with a dozen doors on either side.

He followed the hall to where the scent of blood was strongest. There were a few more drops of blood on the floor here. From beneath the door, he scented much, much more.

A muffled cry of pain sounded on the far side of the wood. The man was still alive.

Logan twisted the knob, strengthening his shield to prevent anything from seeing his presence. A rush of power slid from him, and he mourned the loss of it. That was power he could have shared with his brothers.

But only if he made it out of this alive.

He stepped inside, forcing his eyes to adjust to the inky blackness of the room. The first thing he saw was the faint glow of the man's body heat. As he fueled his vision further, he saw half a dozen demons surrounding the man's body. They licked the blood seeping from his wounds.

The man remained still, as if immobilized. "Is someone there?" he asked, his voice faint and weak, almost garbled.

Logan stayed silent.

One of the Synestryn lifted its head, which swiveled back over its narrow body. It was the size of a large cat with a long snout. It had no ears, only gaping holes at the sides of its head. The front legs were shorter than the back ones, and all of them were tipped with gleaming, sharp claws. Bright green eyes peered out at Logan, but they did not flare with recognition of his presence.

Logan's mask had held.

A wide, flat tongue swept over its bloody muzzle before it returned to its meal.

The man moaned, the sound one of hopeless despair. He knew he was dying. So did Logan.

He couldn't let it happen. This man was blooded. He was too valuable to waste his blood on such creatures.

Warrior or not, Logan had to save this man's life. For all he knew, he might be Hope's perfect mate.

Logan slid his dagger from his coat. He approached silently, keeping his shields up until the last possible second. He slashed across the neck of one demon. Black blood spurted out of the wound. It hissed and flailed, raking blindly at him.

He fell back out of its reach. His shielding faltered and he didn't have time to get it back up.

He grabbed the demon's thin body and hurled it across the room. A few flecks of its blood landed across the back of his hand, burning his skin. He bit off a cry of pain and shoved a burst of power toward the wound to heal it.

The other demons sensed an easy meal and bounded after their wounded pack mate, leaving the man's side.

Logan had little time before the distraction no longer held their attention. He bent down, tossed the man over his shoulder, and headed for the door.

He hadn't quite reached the hallway when sharp, stabbing pain radiated across his back. It took him a moment to realize that at least one of the things had attacked him, slashing at him with claws.

He shifted the man's weight, pulling him forward to protect him from attack. Cradling the man in his arms made his weight more awkward, and Logan stumbled.

A wobbling weakness slid up his legs, and his body reacted before his mind could. Instantly, his blood went to work manufacturing an antidote for the paralytic. He felt a wave of power flow over him, weakening as it passed.

Hope's power.

He was using up the strength she'd given him much faster than he'd hoped. And now it seemed that he was going to have to use even more of it to get out of this alive.

The idea of never seeing her again tore at him, making an anger he'd rarely felt before rise up and bellow in outrage.

Logan stumbled out the door, turning his body to ward off any more attacks from behind. One of the beasts still clung to his back, so he slammed his weight into the wall, crushing it.

A hiss of pain rang in his ears as the demon fell and lay twitching on its side. He kicked it away and lifted his eyes in time to see another two charging.

Logan used a flash of power to slam the door shut. An instant later, the creatures thudded into it and began to claw at the wood.

He didn't wait to see if they made it out. Already his body was weakening, dragging down the hall as his blood struggled to cure the growing paralysis.

He'd made it to the stairway and looked up at what seemed like an insurmountable task. Each jagged step looked like a mountain he had to scale. With every beat of his heart, his strength faded. The weight of the man in his arms bore down on him, crushing the air from his lungs.

Logan shoved more of his dwindling power reserves into creating the antidote, hoping to speed the process. He could feel the cells within his body jumping to obey, squeezing out tiny droplets.

It wasn't enough.

The scratching at the end of the hall grew in intensity. Logan leaned against a wall to hold himself up.

It didn't work. His legs went rubbery beneath him and he slid to the floor, panting and sweating.

A moment later, one of the doors midway down the hall slid open. Out from it stepped a creature like those trying to claw their way through the door. Only this one was much larger, filling the hallway as it rose up on hind legs.

Apparently, the demons he'd fought had been off-spring. And this one was a fully grown adult.

Its elongated muzzle opened, letting out a feral hiss. Then it charged.

Chapter 10

Something was wrong. Hope could feel it in her blood. Her insides itched. She couldn't sit still. All of that she could have brushed off as her nerves—her worry for Logan—but there was one thing she couldn't ignore. That glowing-sunshine type of warmth she'd felt since meeting Logan was starting to fade. Without it, she felt cold and strangely lonely.

He was in trouble. She was certain of it.

She dialed his cell phone. He didn't answer. His cultured voice came over the line, asking her to leave a message.

"Call me if you get this. I'm worried."

Hope hung up, feeling no better. That pervasive itching deepened until she was curled around herself, panting and sweating.

Screw this. She wasn't going to sit here, waiting for a call, when he might be out there, dying. She didn't understand this connection they had, and she sure as heck didn't like it. But that didn't change the fact that she had to do something.

The only thing she could think to do was to go back and check on him.

Sister Olive didn't allow guns in the shelter where Hope had grown up. She had never even considered getting a gun, but was cursing that decision now. She didn't know who or what she was going to face once she found

Logan, but she doubted they would respond to reason and a nice, civil discussion.

She did, however, have a baseball bat tucked under her bed, just in case. She was definitely taking that with her.

Hope went out the back exit and cut through alleys, running as fast as she dared over the slippery pavement. Cold wind whipped her hair around her face, sucking the air from her lungs.

Even with the shortcut, it seemed to take forever for her to get to the defunct furniture factory. Every step she took seemed to ease some of that restless itching.

Without even pausing to get through the creeps this place gave her, she hurried through the busted door, following her instincts and the last bit of fading warmth she knew came from Logan. They led her to the basement entrance.

Hope had never been down there before. The door loomed over her, daring her to open it.

She clenched the bat in one hand and reached out for the handle with the other. Her hand shook, and oddly, she just now realized she'd forgotten her gloves.

A rough sound of pain echoed behind the door. There was a harsh breath of air and a low, snakelike hiss.

The pained sound came again, giving Hope the courage to do the right thing.

She turned the knob and pulled the door toward her. She braced it open with her foot and took a solid grip on the bat.

It was pitch-black inside. Not even the lights she'd flipped on as she came in reached this far into the corner. She leaned in and felt blindly for a light switch.

She heard a scuffling sound and a shocked breath. It came from below her—several feet below.

Her heart pounded fast, vibrating in her chest with fear. Her breathing was so rapid, a steady stream of silvery mist bloomed in front of her, blocking her vision even more.

She took a step inside, reaching, feeling for a switch with her hand and the top step with her foot.

The door shut behind her, shoving her forward as it latched. It banged against the bat, and the hollow racket echoed in the darkness stretching before her.

She thought she heard her name, but couldn't tell over the frantic pounding of her heart.

Finally, she found a switch and shoved it up with clumsy, cold fingers.

Light flared to life in the hallway below. An enraged bellow of pain blasted up the stairwell. Crumpled at the bottom of the cement stairs was Logan. Halfway up the flight was another man. Logan turned his head slowly, and looked up at her, fear shining in his eyes. His mouth moved, but no sound came out. His aura was dim, tinted red with pain.

A shadow fell over him. A heartbeat later, a paw came into view. It was black, tipped with shiny black claws. Its aura was the black nothingness that haunted her nightmares.

Hope didn't need to see the rest of it to know it was bad. Really bad.

"Run!" Logan shouted, but the word came out as more of a breath than a yell.

The other man with him—the one lying unmoving and bleeding—stared up at her with pleading eyes. The faint aura hovering around him was threaded with tentacles of that black nothingness, as if it had somehow infected him. He looked broken, paralyzed. She couldn't leave him lying there. She had to at least try to help them.

A vibrant humming exploded inside her skull. Pressure pulsed inside her as something tried to break its way free.

Memories. She was teetering on the edge of seeing something from her past, but didn't dare take the time to examine it. If she did, none of them would live long enough to celebrate.

She shoved the memory back, screaming inside to let out some of the frustrating disappointment she suffered. For all she knew, that memory would never again bubble to the surface, leaving it lost forever.

As soon as the pressure passed, her body disconnected from her mind, acting on its own. She moved down the stairs as if dreaming, gliding in a smooth, fluid way she'd never felt before.

An odd buzzing tingled through her limbs. Her muscles rippled, tightening as the shuddering feeling passed through her body. She had no idea what had caused it or what it had done to her, but right now, she simply didn't care. Her focus was on getting all three of them out of here alive.

She saw the creature hunched below, cringing from the light she'd turned on. She felt an inky fear hover around her, not quite penetrating. The demon was huge. Frightening. It could kill her with one well-placed swipe of its paw and still she wasn't afraid.

At least not yet.

She grabbed the back of the man's shirt and hauled him up the flight of stairs before she'd even thought about how it should have been impossible for her to move that much weight.

The adrenaline. That had to be what was making her stronger, helping her compartmentalize.

She didn't stop to think, simply dropped the man on the first floor and went back downstairs where Logan was. She had to go down farther, which allowed her to view more of the demon. She'd been gone only a few seconds, but in that time, the demon had knocked out the bulb over its head and was covering its eyes with one paw while blindly swinging for the next light—the one over Logan.

Hope grabbed Logan's leather coat and began hauling him up the stairs, too. He was heavier than the last man—much heavier than he should have been, given his lean build. He thudded along, his body jerking with ev-

ery stair, but she was able to keep only his head from
hitting. Nothing else. He'd have to deal with the bruises
left behind if they made it out of this alive.

"Leave me," he whispered. "I'm nearly recovered."

"Yeah," she snorted out. "You look like it. Shut up
and think light thoughts."

"It's coming," he warned her. "Drop me and run. Save
the human."

Hope spared a quick glance over her shoulder and
saw the demon had managed to knock out another light.
It oozed forward up the stairs, moving methodically,
catching up with them more by the second.

Hope pulled harder, dropping the bat for more leverage. It clattered as it fell, bouncing off the steps until it
hit the demon.

The monster swiped at the bat, slicing it in half with
its claws. Two large pieces as well as three smaller ones
flew out, slamming into the walls so hard they splintered.

Hope did not want to be on the receiving end of that
kind of power.

They had only a few steps to go. Then she'd find a way
to bar the door and keep that thing below.

Logan's hands began to move and he started pushing
himself up, helping her. They moved faster, but it wasn't
fast enough.

The demon slinked up the steps, catlike in its grace. It
opened its jaws wide, showing off tiny, serrated teeth.
Primal fear exploded inside her chest, shoving the breath
from her lungs.

She reached behind her, one hand feeling for the door
handle. She found it and pulled, wrenching her shoulder
in the process. Logan reached for the door, shoving it
open, trying to help her as much as he could.

Hope had just stepped across the threshold when the
monster sprang up at them. It leapt forward, closing the
distance. It dug its long claws deep into Logan's legs. He
bellowed in pain.

The demon pulled. Logan's coat ripped out of her

hands and he slid down the stairs, snatched away by the demon.

Hope lunged for him, but the thing was too fast. He was gone—dragged into the blackness the monster had created below.

Jackie knocked on Joseph Rayd's office door. He was the leader of these people, and if she wanted something, it was best to go straight to him and forgo all the middlemen.

He looked up from whatever he was working on, his hazel eyes meeting hers. His spine straightened, but his shoulders were still bowed as if he carried some great burden.

"Please come in," he said as he rose from his desk. He was a big man and with every step he took closer to her, she wanted to shrink away.

Jackie held up her hand to stop his advance. "No need to get up. I was hoping I could speak to you for a moment."

He stepped back, motioning to a chair across from his desk. "Sure. Have a seat."

It had been a long time since Jackie had been in such a civilized setting, though she was used to being on the other side of the desk. This side seemed odd and alien, putting her in a position of servitude somehow.

She didn't like it. She wanted her old life back—the one full of boardroom meetings and schedules and making things happen.

Sadly, that life was over. She knew better than to believe otherwise.

Jackie sat perched on the edge of the chair. If he made a sudden move to touch her as so many of the men here had, she could bolt and avoid him. "I want to leave."

Joseph frowned. "Leave?"

"This place. These people."

"Leave Dabyr? But you just got here."

"It's become apparent that my presence here is causing problems. These men of yours are looking to me as some kind of savior. I can't handle the pressure. Not so soon after . . ." She couldn't bring herself to verbalize even one of the things she'd endured.

He leaned forward, bracing his elbows on the desk. Silvery strands of hair gleamed at his temples. "I'll tell them to back off."

"It's not that simple and you know it." She squeezed her eyes shut. "Even you look at me with hope in your eyes."

"I would think that would be a good thing. Not everyone has the power to give people hope."

"What I offer is false. I've seen the unions between your people—what you think I'll be a part of one day. I'm telling you now that it can never happen."

"You don't know that."

"I do. I'm a grown woman. I know my own limits, and after . . . everything, I know that I'll never again be able to tolerate the touch of a man. Especially one who isn't human."

"What you've suffered is horrible. But you're strong. You may not be able to see how you can come through it, but I know you can." He stood and moved around the desk. Jackie gritted her teeth and held her ground. "I also know that if you trust us enough to stay and find a compatible Theronai, he could help you through this. Help you heal."

Joseph was too close. She slid in her chair, pressing up against the far edge so hard she knew it would leave a bruise. "I need to leave. I need to go somewhere where the expectations are not so high. And I need to work. Be useful. Find some reason to get up in the morning."

Joseph let out a sigh and nodded. "The Synestryn will want you back. I can't let them have you."

"They won't know where I am."

"They'll be drawn to you."

That thought made her blood thicken in her veins. She could feel their taint inside her, dirtying her soul.

"So you're saying I'm a prisoner here as I was in those caves?"

"No. I'm saying that if you leave, you can't do it alone. You'll have an armed escort."

"To a job? I don't see that working out."

"It would with the right job." He said it like he already had something in mind.

"And what job would that be?"

"We know why you were taken. The Synestryn are trying to breed more human-looking demons so they can more easily mingle among people. I'm certain there are other women like you out there—women who were taken and need to be saved."

"It's not the women you have to worry about," said Jackie before she thought better. "It's the children."

"What do you mean?"

"I was used for my blood. I was food. Fuel. The children were not so lucky. They were altered. Fed the blood of the monsters so they changed."

Joseph nodded. "Like Tori. They took her as a child so that she could grow up and give them children."

Jackie swallowed hard, struggling not to throw up on his carpet. She'd seen what happened to those kids. She'd heard their screams.

"You were a prisoner a long time," said Joseph. "You might have heard or seen things that can lead us to others. I was going to ask you to lead a team, but I didn't want to push you before you'd had time to recover."

"I'm recovered." At least as much as she was going to.

"Tynan will have to clear you for field work, but if he does, you can get out of here and have a job all at the same time."

Just the idea of it made her feel like she could breathe again. She knew she couldn't go into those caves again, but they'd moved her a couple of times. She might see something that would help find the location of the other caves. "Who would you send with me?"

"That would be your choice. At least in part. If

you're more comfortable with bonded Theronai, I understand, but you have to have some strong sword arms with you."

"Not Helen. Not Lexi."

"They're your sisters. I would have thought they'd be your first choice."

Jackie shook her head. "It's too much pressure. We may be related by blood, but I don't know those women. I don't want to pretend that I do. Or that I want to."

Joseph stared at her for a long time. Even though she guessed he was trying not to, he looked at her with hopeful expectation lighting his eyes. "How about Paul and Andra?"

"Fine."

"Go pack what you need," said Joseph. "You'll leave tonight."

Jackie stood up to leave but Joseph's voice stopped her. "I'd like to know if it's true," he said.

"If what's true?" she asked.

"I've heard rumors that every Theronai you've met has felt something. That their lucerias have reacted. They're saying you're compatible with anyone."

"I wouldn't know."

"If it's true, I need to be prepared for the fallout."

"What fallout?"

"Things could get ugly. My men could turn on one another, fighting over you."

"None of them can have me, so why should they bother?"

"Logic won't play much of a role if it's true," said Joseph. "I was hoping you'd indulge me so I'm at least armed with the truth." He held out his hand. It was wide and square with shiny callused patches.

Jackie looked at his hand, then back to his face. He wore no expression. No hope, no excitement. He didn't move toward her or show any signs of impatience.

It was his stoicism that gave her the courage to step forward. She closed her eyes and pretended she was in a boardroom, meeting customers. She grabbed his hand and gave it a quick shake.

Jackie felt nothing but heat, strength, and the fine trembling of her own hand. But when she opened her eyes and looked at him, he'd gone white with shock. His hazel eyes were wide and he stared at the ring on his left hand, watching colors swirl within the band.

She didn't wait for him to speak. She didn't want to hear what he had to say. She turned and ran down the hall, getting away as fast as she could.

The rumors were right. She was some kind of freak.

Logan was consumed by pain. His legs burned with it as the demon's claws sank deep into his bones. The antidote his blood had created to combat the paralytic was working, but not nearly fast enough to save his life.

At least Hope had gotten out safely. Logan took solace in that.

As the Synestryn dragged him down the hall to its den, Logan forced the antidote to his arms, giving him the strength to pull his dagger. It wasn't going to do much good, but he refused to let this creature kill him without a fight.

He sat up enough to reach down and slam the blade into one of the demon's paws. The tip went through the soft tissue and into Logan's leg.

He gritted his teeth against a scream of pain and lifted the blade to strike again.

The demon jerked back its paw, licking at the black blood dripping from the wound. A menacing growl rose from the beast, promising retribution.

Logan didn't wait to see what it had in mind. He lifted his blade and struck again, swiping at the closest paw, praying he'd hit a tendon.

The demon was too fast. It snatched back its paw and batted at Logan before he could strike. The dagger flew from his numbed hand, ringing against the concrete floor several feet away.

Logan's legs still hadn't started to work yet, so he called on some of his dwindling power to draw the weapon back to him.

It vibrated on the floor and slid only a few inches before it stopped.

Hunger roared inside Logan. The power in the blood he'd taken from Hope was gone. He was out of energy. And time.

Chapter 11

Hope scrambled to find her cell phone. Logan had said the police couldn't help, but at this point, she didn't think they could hurt, either.

Her cell phone was gone. It must have fallen out during her run or while she was dragging people around.

Frustrated panic gripped her as she looked around, making a futile search of the area.

The man she'd rescued still hadn't spoken or moved. He watched her with wide eyes the color of golf course grass. He had short, sandy blond hair and wore ripped-out jeans and a concert T-shirt.

He might have a cell phone.

Hope rushed to his side and started searching his pockets. Her voice was an octave higher than normal. "I'm going to call for help and get you out of here. Just hang on, okay?"

Her hands shook as she slid them over his body, searching for the hard edges of a cell phone. She found a small one lodged in his front pocket and dug in his jeans for it. "Sorry to be so forward. I don't normally fondle strange men."

He said nothing in return. Not that she'd expected him to.

She grabbed the small phone and pulled it out, only to discover that it wasn't a phone at all. It was a lighter inside a rumpled, mostly empty pack of cigarettes.

Shit.

"I can't leave him down there alone," she told the stranger. "I can't stand by and let him die. I have to do something."

But what? She was no superhero. She couldn't handle something like that monster, alone and unarmed.

She needed help and she needed it now. Sadly, there wasn't a pay phone for blocks and she didn't dare leave this paralyzed man alone, either.

Maybe her phone was on the stairs. If she could get it and call for help, then it might save both men's lives.

The creature had dragged Logan away. It was safe to go down there. She was sure it was.

Hope swallowed down an acidic bubble of fear and walked to the door. She heard nothing on the far side. Of course, her heart was hammering so hard it probably masked plenty of noise.

With a prayer for courage, she cracked the door open and peeked inside. Nothing sprang at her. No demons lurked within sight.

The stairs marched down into blackness, mocking her ability to do the same. The demon had destroyed the lightbulbs, making it impossible for her to see past the sixth step.

She'd rushed out without her satchel. Which meant she'd also left behind her flashlight. What she wouldn't have given to have that light now.

Or a torch.

Right. She had fire. She could make a torch. Couldn't she?

It was worth a shot.

Hope sprinted over the dusty floor to the toppled stack of pallets. She braced her foot against it and pulled on one of the boards. The nail screamed as it was wrenched out of place, but she was able to get it free.

She grabbed a wad of discarded newspaper she found on the floor and crumpled it into a tight ball. She stabbed the ball onto the bent nail and went back to the stranger's side where she'd left the lighter.

It took a moment for her to fumble it free of the cigarette package, and even longer for her to get her fingers to work the thing. The tiny flare of light made her rejoice.

The flame wobbled as she set the newspaper on fire. She angled it so the dry wood would catch fire, holding her breath the whole time.

A few seconds later, the pallet board caught flame and victory surged inside Hope.

She was going after her phone, and if she didn't find that, she was going after Logan.

Iain readied himself for the infant to attack. He flung the back door open, sword poised to strike.

Nothing happened. He saw no movement, heard no warning hiss coming from inside the vehicle.

The woman lay still. The blanket covering her was soaked with blood. Her face was lax, her eyes staring unfocused and fixed in death. She'd bled out. He'd failed to get her help in time to save her life.

There had been a time not so long ago that Iain's failure would have bothered him. But no longer. The life of one human woman apparently wasn't enough to stir his dead soul.

Not that he cared. He'd long since stopped caring. His entire focus now was on playing the part of a healthy Theronai long enough to give his brothers hope—to help them cling to life long enough to find their mates.

He could remember a time when his desire to help had burned fierce and bright inside his chest. It no longer did, and his actions were more from habit than anything else. Still, those habits ran deep, giving him a reason to pull in his next breath.

Atop the woman's chest, the blanket shifted as something beneath it stirred.

The child. It let out a faint cry of distress.

Iain used the tip of his sword to move the blanket, pulling it down, uncovering the child.

It didn't lunge for him. In fact, it flailed around, its

tiny arms and legs jerking in the air. It had four limbs. No tentacles. It didn't even have teeth, much less fangs.

It looked like a normal human baby.

A flicker of relief fluttered deep inside Iain, so faint it barely registered. He wasn't going to have to kill it.

Him. The baby was a boy, not an it.

Iain sheathed his sword and gathered the squalling infant. He was tiny. Iain's hands swallowed him up.

The child screamed louder, his cries vibrating with demand to fix what was wrong.

He was probably cold.

The blanket was too wet and bloody, so Iain tucked the naked baby inside his shirt, warming him against his chest. He zipped up his jacket to keep the wind out.

Something warm and wet slid down Iain's stomach.

The child had peed on him. Of course.

Iain covered the dead woman with the blanket and got behind the wheel. He needed to get the baby back to Dabyr where someone could care for it. Unfortunately, that trip was going to take several hours and he doubted the child would hold its bodily functions for that long.

Time to find some diapers.

He pulled back onto the road, holding the baby in place with one hand while he drove. After a few minutes, the child's cries quieted, then stopped completely. He could feel the warm brush of air against his skin as the baby breathed, telling him he was fine.

Not that Iain was worried. Death was probably the best thing that could happen to the boy. His mother was gone. His father was likely dead. The Synestryn would have had no reason to keep a man alive. They would have drained his blood and eaten him.

This child's life would no doubt be filled with pain and suffering. It would be a kindness to simply let him die. If it weren't for Iain's vow to protect humans, he probably would have.

The vow stayed his hand, removing the choice from his conscience. Whatever hardships the boy would face were his to bear. He'd have to suck it up and deal like the rest of the world.

Iain found an all-night convenience store and pulled into the parking lot. He parked away from the entrance, as far away from lights as he could. Anyone who glanced in his ride would see the bloody blanket covering the woman's body. He really didn't want any trouble with the police.

As soon as he shifted, the child let out a disgruntled breath at being disturbed. He patted the lump under his coat and hurried into the store.

He found diapers and bought the smallest ones they had. He also grabbed some wet wipes, a can of formula, a plastic bottle sporting yellow ducks, and some bottled water. The boy was going to have to eat sometime, though hopefully not before he got back home.

The clerk behind the counter was a man in his early twenties with as many piercings as pimples. He grinned at Iain's purchases. "Daddy duty, huh?"

Iain ignored the kid and pulled out his wallet.

The baby squirmed and let out a shrill scream.

The kid's grin faded. "You got a baby under there?"

Iain laid more than enough money on the counter, grabbed his sack, and left. As he got back in his car, he could see the clerk on the phone, talking fast.

Shit. He was probably calling the police, telling them all about the big, scary man with the stolen baby under his coat.

A venomous anger streaked through Iain's blood. The baby screamed and he realized he'd tightened his hold and had to ease up.

If he hit the highway now, every cop in the area would find him, the baby, and the dead woman. He needed to stick to the back roads and hide for a while—maybe switch vehicles.

He couldn't drive, dial his phone, and hold the baby all at the same time, so he sped out of the parking lot and headed for the closest Gerai house. They were scattered all over this part of the country, and there were two less than an hour away. He picked the one closest to Dabyr and raced for it as fast as he dared.

The demon crouched over Logan's legs, feeding from the blood that seeped from his wounds. His body was fighting the paralysis, but not fast enough. He couldn't feel his legs anymore, though perhaps the demon's saliva contained yet another toxin he couldn't combat.

Logan scoured his mind for options, but the churning hunger inside him was distracting.

Being a meal for a Synestryn was even more distracting.

He closed his eyes, gathering up what little bit of power remained. He wasn't yet sure what to do with it— there wasn't enough for a powerful assault—but he'd think of something.

Light seeped through his closed eyelids. The beast at his legs hissed in annoyance.

Logan looked up to see what it was. Standing a few feet down the hall was Hope, holding a burning board aloft. Her hair seemed to glow in response to the fire-light, and her eyes burned a bright, determined gold. Fear tightened her mouth and widened her eyes. Her chest rose and fell with her rapid breathing.

He'd never seen anything more beautiful in his long, long life.

"Get out of here!" he ordered, using a bit of his remaining power to spike the command with a compulsion for her to obey.

He must have been weaker than he thought, because she didn't even pause long enough to blink before striding forward, flame first.

"How do I kill it?" she asked.

"You don't. You run. Now." A little more power left him as he struggled to force her obedience.

"And leave you here for it to snack on. I don't think so." She stabbed the torch forward and the demon flinched back. "It doesn't like light. I know that much."

She stepped forward. The demon batted at the torch, missing. Its eyes streamed with tears.

"Give me the torch," he said. "I'll kill it while you run."

"You can't even stand."

"I'll manage."

Hope took another step forward, jabbing the fire near the demon. It inched back, hissing in frustration and rage.

"Can you hold the torch?" she asked.

"Yes."

She handed it to him. The wood was rough in his palm. He kept his grip tight, not wanting to lose their only real weapon.

"Keep it back. I'm dragging you out of here."

Before he could argue, she grabbed the collar of his coat and began pulling him back faster than he would have thought possible for a woman her size.

She was strong. Inhumanly so.

The importance of that would have to be examined later. For now, he had to pour all his concentration into holding the demon back with nothing more than a chunk of burning wood and steadily weakening arms.

As they moved down the hall, the Synestryn followed them, keeping out of reach of the firelight. Occasionally, it would bend its head and lap up a spot of blood on the floor left behind from Logan's wounds.

Its eyes burned a bright, eerie green, telling Logan that it hadn't given up on a meal yet.

They hit the first step. Hope grunted with effort. Through the leather, he felt her arm quivering with the strain of dragging his weight. Logan lifted himself, helping her as much as he could with one arm.

The demon kept up its pace, searching for an opening. Fire had eaten its way down the wood and was now only a few inches from his hand. Once he had to drop it, the demon would pounce.

They had to be out of here before that eventuality.

"You need to go faster," he told her.

Her voice was breathless. "I'll try."

Even without looking at her, he could almost feel her gather her will, as if the air around her had shifted at her command. The torchlight wavered, the flame eating its way toward Logan's hand.

The demon made a grab for Logan's leg. Its claws raked across his skin, but sliced cleanly through his flesh, leaving nothing for them to catch on.

Pain burned his limb and he felt more poison enter his bloodstream.

The torch became heavier. So did his eyelids. His arm drooped and the demon lurched forward.

Logan raised it up at the last second, singeing away a spot of fur on its paw. It howled in pain and its eyes glowed brighter.

The last few steps bumped beneath him, rattling his spine. He heard the squeak of door hinges and felt a cool rush of air pass his cheek.

The demon flinched away from the relatively bright light of the first floor. Crackling power gathered around them, like static electricity. A moment later, Logan's body nearly flew across the concrete, landing a few feet away. Hope slammed the door shut, picked up a discarded length of pipe, and slammed it down on the handle.

The metal doorknob bent slightly, jamming it shut.

The demon pounded against the door, rattling it on its hinges. That bent knob wasn't going to hold it off for long.

Hope came over, grabbed the torch from his hands, and shoved it in the crack under the door, swinging it from side to side.

The demon screamed, but the pounding stopped. For now.

She came over and crumpled beside Logan, panting. "Please tell me you have a cell phone on you. Mine's gone and we need to call for help."

"We need to get out of here. That demon will be back."

She let out a heavy sigh and her head hung limp from her neck in exhaustion. "I don't know if I can drag you both out of here. I barely made it up those last few steps."

Not to mention the fact that he was bleeding and the scent would eventually draw other Synestryn to him to feed.

He was too weak to heal himself. Too weak to even stand. He needed blood. If she wasn't going to leave his side, he had to be strong enough to defend her.

"Feed me," he whispered, feeling ashamed that he had to ask. "Give me some of your blood and I'll get us all out of this mess."

Hope's hand covered the spot where he'd fed from her last night. Uncertainty drew her pale brows together before she gave him a resigned nod. "No more hospitals," she warned him. "Deal?"

Logan couldn't speak. His mouth had already begun to water in anticipation. His body clenched at the thought of holding her close again, of feeling her power sliding into him to become a part of him.

He returned her nod, sealing the deal. Even unspoken, the promise he'd given her had power. It fell across him, warm and sweet like a lover's kiss.

Hope brushed her hair away from her neck and bent down. "Don't you dare make a habit of this," she said.

Logan feared he already had.

Krag stilled as that flash of power slammed into him again, coming out of nowhere. This time he was ready for it.

He closed his eyes and concentrated on the path, letting his mind slide out and through the ribbon that led to the source of that power.

The frozen landscape flew past him, giving way to homes and then to the run-down buildings at the edge of the city. The speed at which they passed was dizzying, but he held tight, needing to know who the source of such a vast amount of power was.

Krag caught only a glimpse of honey blond hair and a slender neck for an instant. A Sanguinar was feeding from the source. A woman.

How dare that leech touch what belonged to Krag? All blooded humans in this region belonged to him. Their blood was *his*.

Rage broke Krag's concentration and he was flung away from the scene, dragged back into his body against his will. He fought it, struggling to go back to the woman and see her face, but it was useless. The connection was already gone.

At least he'd seen her location. It was an old, run-down building some of his minions used for shelter. The Tyler building.

Krag sent his mind back out, racing across space until he touched the thoughts of the demon lurking in the basement of the Tyler building. He shoved his orders into the demon's mind, forcing it to obey. It shuddered in defiance, but in the end, Krag's will won out.

Now all he had to do was send one of his Dorjan—his human servants—to fetch her and bring her back here. With any luck at all, he'd have her at his feet before sunrise.

Chapter 12

The flash of pain was gone, leaving Hope floating in blissful warmth. It was better than she remembered. Pleasure became a palpable thing, winding around her cells and soaking into them. The gentle tugging at her throat, the feel of Logan's lips moving against her skin, made her head spin, and not with loss of blood, either. As the seconds passed, he became stronger, gathering her up in his arms and holding her tight.

He sat up and swung her around until she was cradled in his lap. She felt his muscles swell and harden against her body. His erection throbbed against her hip, sending zingers of need arcing through her.

She heard a strangled sound of shock coming from somewhere nearby, but it didn't matter to her. Nothing mattered but the scent of Logan in her lungs and his strength surrounding her, keeping her safe. Here, there were no worries. No fears. No monsters could touch her here, in this place of blissful peace.

Weakness slid into her, but even that was welcome. Her eyes drifted shut and sleep beckoned.

Hope fought it off only because she didn't want to miss even a moment of what Logan was doing to her. It was too good to miss.

His tongue slid across her skin, sending a parade of shivers marching down her spine. A moment later, his mouth pulled away and she lay in his arms, looking up at him.

He was so beautiful. His jaw was tight and that lovely silvery light in his eyes was back, glowing with need—a kind of need she'd never seen on a man's face before. It made her feel special. Cherished.

"If there were more time . . ." he whispered, his voice stroking over her like a caress. He didn't finish what he was saying, but she enjoyed filling in the blanks for herself.

If there were more time, he'd kiss her. Touch her.

And then he laid her down on the cold floor, leaving her feeling weak and alone.

Hope struggled to sit up.

"Not yet," he said from somewhere behind her. "Give yourself a moment."

She didn't want to, but her body had other ideas. That unexplained strength she'd experienced before was gone now, leaving the opposite in its wake. She could barely hold up her own head. She had to settle for rolling onto her side to see what he was doing.

He was at the stranger's side, bent over his neck. Feeding from him.

Feral jealousy rose up inside Hope. She didn't want Logan doing that to anyone else. Ever. Only her.

The reaction was so strange and unwanted, it shocked her. Of course she didn't want Logan to drink her blood all the time. What kind of an idiot wished for a thing like that?

Logan leaned back and pressed an elegant hand to the man's head. The stranger closed his eyes as if falling asleep.

"What did you do to him?"

"He was poisoned. I had to administer an antidote."

"How did you get it?"

He ignored her question. "I'll take him to a human hospital."

"But not me. You said so."

"No, not you. You I get to keep an eye on myself." He said it in a way that made her wonder if he saw the task as a chore or a pleasure. "Can you walk?"

Hope was wobbly, but she could walk as long as it was out of here. "Yeah."

"I'll carry him. Follow me."

They hurried outside to Logan's van. He loaded the unconscious man in the back and drove to the hospital. He parked at the emergency entrance and got out. "I'll just be a few minutes," he told her. "Will you please await me here?"

Hope nodded and leaned her head back against the seat to rest. She was still feeling woozy, but she'd take that over dead any day of the week.

Logan came back out wearing scrubs. He had a trash sack full of something clenched in his fist.

"Where are your clothes?" she asked as he got back in the van.

"Bloodied. I have to dispose of them properly."

"You make it sound like you have some kind of disease. I really hope that's not the case with all the neck-sucking you've done."

A faint smile lifted one side of his mouth. "I can assure you there's nothing for you to worry about. You're perfectly healthy."

Except for a slight case of brain damage that made me enjoy getting fed on by a vampire. Not that she was going to bring that up.

He drove onto the highway and headed east. "Where are we going?"

"There are too many people here for me to simply toss my clothing out the window. I have to go to a safe place where I can burn them. You're coming with me until I'm certain there will be no lasting damage."

Worry crept into her. "Damage?"

"I tried not to take too much from you—just enough for us to escape—but after what I took from you last night . . . I just want to be careful."

"So you're not trying to scare me?"

"No, Hope. That's the last thing I want to do."

He opened a compartment between them and pulled out a bottle of water. "Here. You need the fluids."

Hope popped it open and drank, struggling to make sense of everything. She'd let a vampire suck her blood. Twice. Sure, he didn't call himself that, but that's what he was.

And she'd almost died tonight. So had Logan and that other man. If she hadn't shown up, they probably would have died.

If she hadn't had that odd burst of strength, all three of them would have bought the farm right then and there in that creepy old building.

She opened her mouth to ask Logan if he knew anything about what might have caused her to get so strong so fast, but closed it again before she could speak. She didn't know this man. She didn't know anything about him other than he could drink her blood and feel better.

That was not something that recommended him for a confidant.

She leaned her head back on the seat, wondering why she trusted him enough not to jump out at the first stop. Maybe it was what he'd done for Charlie. He'd done something to help the old man, to ease his pain. And he hadn't even wanted credit for it.

That went a long way in her book. Not many people would bother to help, and those who did wanted recognition. But not Logan. He'd hidden what he'd done, though she didn't understand why.

"How are you feeling?" he asked.

"Fine."

"Dizzy?"

"A little."

He reached over and wrapped his long fingers around her wrist, checking her pulse. His touch was warm, gentle. Warmth radiated out from him, streaking through her blood.

Hope shivered in response.

"Cold?" he asked.

"Yes," she said, more because she didn't want to admit his effect on her than anything.

Logan cranked up the heat until it was pouring out of the vents by her feet. "If that doesn't help, tell me so I can care for you properly."

"Properly?"

He glanced at her quickly before returning his attention to the road. "I might need to restore some of the strength I took from you."

"You mean you want me to drink *your* blood?" The idea should have grossed her out. Yesterday morning, it would have. But a lot had happened since then, and she found the idea of giving him the kind of pleasure he'd given her more compelling than she would have ever imagined.

She wanted to make him feel good. The fact that she'd get her mouth on his neck was simply an added bonus.

"No," he hurried to say, as if the idea was somehow forbidden. "Of course not. It would merely be a transference of energy."

"I don't understand."

"You don't need to. All you need to know is that I'll take care of you."

While Hope wouldn't mind a little of that, she didn't like being treated like a child. "I want to understand. You don't get to turn my life upside down and not tell me the whole story."

"There's a good chance I'm going to have to remove your memories of tonight's events. The less you know, the more comfortable that process will be for you."

Remove her . . . ? "Excuse me?"

Logan sighed. "It won't hurt. And it's for your own good. Synestryn can sense those memories. They're like a beacon that calls them to you. If I can't scrub them away, you'll be in danger."

Anger burned hot and bright in her belly. She had to

force words out between clenched teeth. "You touch my memories and you're a dead man."

He let out a musical laugh. "You are such a fetching creature. As if you could actually stop me."

"No one is taking any more memories from me. Ever."

His laughter died off suddenly. "Hope, I'm sorry. I forgot you already face a substantial loss. Forgive me."

"Only if you promise not to touch a single memory I still have left."

He was silent for a long moment with only the sound of the tires on pavement filling the space. His jaw was tight with righteous determination. "I'm sorry. I cannot do that."

A void opened up inside her and was instantly filled with a sense of betrayal. "Stop the car. Let me out here."

They were through the suburbs and towns were getting smaller as each one passed. If she didn't want to be stuck out in the middle of nowhere, now was the time.

"No. If I leave you alone in the dark, chances are you won't survive until sunrise."

"You don't know that."

A silvery light flared, splashing across the steering wheel. "I do. I've seen it happen often enough to know. Now, you can be as angry with me as you like, but you're going to do it here, next to me, where I can protect you."

"I saved your life," she reminded him. Sure, it made her a smaller person to bring it up, but the way she saw it, he owed her at least a little respect for what she'd done.

"You did. And I'm repaying the favor by keeping you from needlessly going to your slaughter."

"Fine, then drop me off somewhere public. A police station. I'll be safe there."

"I'm sorry," he said, remorse softening his tone. "You're too precious to entrust your safety to humans. I have to insist that you come with me."

"And do what? Where are we going? What, exactly, do you want from me?"

"We're meeting friends. They will see to your safety."

"And what about our deal? What about those missing people?"

"My friends are far better equipped to handle that task than I."

"So, you're handing me off. I'm too much of a bother?"

"Hardly. I find your company . . . stimulating."

Hope couldn't stop herself from looking at his crotch. It was a knee-jerk reaction. Uncontrollable.

He was hard. His erection tented against the loose fabric of his borrowed scrubs.

The idea that she could do that to him was more than a little exciting. A thrill winged through her belly, exploding into a thousand tiny, shimmering streamers.

She'd never been very physical. She'd dated a few men. Had sex with a couple of them. But not even all-out sex with all the bells and whistles made her feel half as good as she did now, thinking about how Logan would feel sliding inside her.

Hope squirmed in her seat.

Logan's nostrils flared as he pulled in a deep breath. His eyes fluttered shut for a brief second and a shudder shook his big body. "We cannot."

She didn't ask him what they couldn't do. She knew what he meant. No sense in playing coy. "You're married," she stated, knowing a man like him had to be taken.

"I'm not married. I'm also not human."

"Point taken. Not that I would have slept with you anyway."

He sent her a brief, pointed stare so full of arrogance she had to marvel at the trick. A small smile played at his mouth. "You think not?"

"You're awfully full of yourself."

"Indeed."

"Someone should cure you of that conceit."

"Feel free to try. But do so in a hurry. Our time together is nearly at an end."

Instantly, Hope began to grieve. Sure, he was arrogant and strange, but there was something compelling about him—something that called to a part of her soul that hovered on the dark side of her memories. She didn't know what it was or what it meant, but what she did know was that she didn't want Logan to leave her life. At least not yet.

If Logan didn't hand Hope's care to another soon, he was going to do something unforgivable. Already he could see her slim body writhing beneath his as he drove his cock deep into her, over and over.

She was warm and soft, and the way she went pliant as he fed from her, letting out those quiet little noises of pleasure, nearly drove him mad.

He could smell her arousal as they drove. Combined with the sharp scent of her anger, breathing her in was intoxicating. It made him forget his purpose and think only of how she would smell and sound if he stripped her bare and tasted every inch of her skin.

Down that road lay the destruction of his race, so Logan shoved aside his inconvenient desire for the woman and focused solely on doing what must be done.

As soon as he had her settled safely inside the closest Gerai house, his bloodied clothing burning in the fireplace, he excused himself and snuck outside.

"I need you to come and handle this woman," he told Tynan as soon as he answered the call. He knew he sounded desperate, but he couldn't help it. He *was* desperate.

"What happened?"

Logan considered veiling the truth, but that would get him nowhere. Tynan needed to know the risk in order to respond appropriately. "I want her."

"So have her."

"It's not that simple. The longer I'm with her, the more convinced I am she might be a Theronai."

"Are you sure?"

"No, but her blood is pure enough that there is a chance. You know what happened the last time someone stole away one of the Theronai's mates."

"I remember. And with a truce between the Slayers and Theronai closer than it's ever been, I don't want anything reminding either side of why the war began in the first place."

"Neither do I, which is why you must come. Now."

"I cannot get away. I've tried. Between Grace and Tori, my hands are full. Why not escort her back to Dabyr and wash your hands of her?"

"I promised to help her find the cause of some locals gone missing in exchange for her cooperation."

"Foolish," chided Tynan.

"I realize that now. Too late."

"I'll contact Joseph. He'll send one of his unbonded men to deal with her problem."

"I already spoke to him. I'm expecting his men to show up at any time." Logan didn't like the idea. He didn't like the thought of some giant pawing at Hope, desperate for her to save his life.

She would if she was able. The fact that she'd gone back for Logan in that basement proved she was selfless and courageous. If she thought she could save a man's life, she'd tie herself to him. Logan was sure of it.

And the thought made a dangerous anger swell deep inside him. He didn't want her tied to a Theronai. He didn't want her tied to anyone except him.

"You need to come," he told Tynan, desperation lifting his voice. "You need to take over her placement— wherever that might be."

"You're far better at finding good matches than I am. And I'm a stronger healer than you. My place is here, doing what I can to help Grace and Tori."

"Then send someone else in your stead. Please."

Tynan's sigh filled the phone line. "I need to know you can handle this. And so do you. There aren't enough of us left to be handing duties off to another."

A cold wind whipped around Logan. He stared up at the sky, watching stars twinkle. "You're right. I know this. But the things I'm feeling—"

"Will need to be controlled. Remember the goal. Think of a life without hunger. A life with children."

Tynan wanted a child of his own and had for as long as Logan could remember. He deprived himself of the joy, knowing that any child born to them would be doomed to a life of starvation and pain. None of the Sanguinar could do that to a child. Especially Tynan.

If Logan could change the lives of his people for the better, there was no other choice for him to make. He'd keep his urges in check, stay as far away from Hope as his job would allow, and do what needed to be done.

"I'll remember," he told Tynan. "Joseph's warriors will show up soon. We'll find Hope's mate and be one step closer to the life we want."

Chapter 13

Iain hid his car behind the Gerai house so it wasn't easily visible from the street. Not that it was much of a street or that anyone would pass by.

He let himself into the safe house and dumped all of his supplies on the living room floor.

The baby had been crying for the last half hour, and if that smell was any indication, he was tired of lying in his own shit.

Iain wasn't a fan, either.

He stripped out of his coat and eased the child out from under his reeking T-shirt. The mess was impressive, covering both of them equally.

Iain toed out of his boots, unfastened his sword belt, and stripped naked. He made a quick call for backup, started up the shower, and carried the child inside. He'd never before held something quite as slippery as a naked, soapy baby, so he took great care not to drop him on his head.

By the time they were both clean, the boy was screaming his head off and Iain's was beginning to pound.

He dried the baby off, diapered him, and wrapped him up in a clean, dry towel. Then he set him in the center of a bed while he dressed in fresh clothes. His boots and sword went back on.

The child was still crying.

Iain read the instructions on the can of powdered formula and followed them to the letter. It took a while for the infant to get the hang of drinking from a bottle, and he made a soggy mess, but after a few tries, they both figured out the best way to make it work.

The child fell asleep. Iain tried to remove the bottle only to have him start sucking again.

Fine. If that was the way he was going to be, then Iain might as well get comfortable.

He sat down in a recliner and eased it back. Some Gerai would be here soon to take the child off his hands. Then he'd take care of arrangements for the mother's body and be back out there fighting right around sunrise.

Iain looked down at the tiny life in his arms. Every detail was perfect. Once upon a time he'd wanted children of his own. He remembered the fact, though he couldn't quite remember why he'd felt that way. Babies were too much work. Their lives too easy to end.

Still, there was something soothing about the boy. Holding him settled some of the seething rage that was always bubbling below the surface. It was probably some kind of survival instinct Iain had never experienced before—something that prevented adults from simply killing a messy, loud, stinky inconvenience.

Whatever it was, it was nice. Peaceful.

Iain closed his eyes. He didn't think about what he'd done or what he had to do. He didn't worry about his brothers—those who looked to him for guidance when their lifemarks became barren. He simply existed.

If his eyes hadn't been closed, his heartbeat slow, he might not have heard the faint howl coming from the north.

Synestryn.

He'd been so concerned about caring for the child he had forgotten to consider the mother's blood. If she was blooded, every nasty within scent of her would be on its way here.

He couldn't take the car and run. Her blood was all over it. Gerai hadn't brought him a new ride yet.

There was no help for it. Iain was going to have to

fight off an attack and hope the kid didn't start crying
and draw attention to himself.

When Logan came back inside, he was a different man.
Colder. More distant. Hope tried to find out what had
happened, but he avoided her and went to shower.

She sat on the couch, flipping through TV stations in
an effort not to think about Logan's naked body streaming with hot water. The door of the little house opened,
interrupting her inappropriate thoughts.

Hope's heart jumped and she sprang from the couch,
holding the remote control out like a weapon.

The man who'd come in was big. Tall. Broad. He had
dark blond hair and laser blue eyes. A fine network of
scars crossed his face, puckering the skin. His aura
throbbed with red-hot pain, consuming the other colors.
She could see faint streaks of pale silvery honor and no-
bility peeking out through the red.

Seeing so much pain, having it blasted into her retinas
made her reel back in horror. She held up her hands to
ward it off, shaking and speechless.

Sadness bowed the man's shoulders for a second. A
flash of gray-blue disappointment spread out over his
aura before it was eaten up by cool green resignation. "I
won't hurt you. My name is Nicholas. Logan sent for
me."

His voice was quiet and reassuring. The fact that he
stayed on his side of the room was even more reassuring.

"I'm Hope Serrien. Logan's in the shower."

He glanced at the hearth, where the clothing had
been burned and a fire still crackled away. "You were in
a battle?"

She nodded.

He started forward, only to stop himself after a couple of steps. "Were you hurt?"

Hope shook her head. "Logan was. He's better now."

Nicholas's jaw tightened with a pulse of anger. "Did
he . . . hurt you?"

"No. Why would you ask that?"

"I thought he might have ... Never mind. I'll speak to him about it." He motioned to the couch. "Please, sit down. I didn't mean to disturb you."

Logan stepped out into the living room, his hair black with dampness. A pristine towel hung around his neck and he wore fresh jeans and a T-shirt that clung to his chest. "Nicholas. I'm glad you could come. Where are the others?"

"There's only me. We're stretched too thin."

Logan nodded, his face grim. "I understand. Have you touched her yet?"

The odd question rocked Hope back on her heels. "What?"

Nicholas eyed Logan in irritation. "We've only just met."

"Touch me?" asked Hope again, looking from one man to the other.

"Touch her," ordered Logan.

Hope crossed her arms over her chest, pinning her fingers under her arms. "What the hell are you two talking about?"

"You haven't talked to her about this?" Nicholas asked Logan.

Her voice got louder until she was almost yelling. "About what?"

Nicholas looked at her with an apology shining in his blue eyes. "I'm sorry, ma'am. You'll have to forgive us. I know this must all seem strange to you."

"You have no idea."

"Just touch her and be done with it," said Logan.

"Back off," warned Nicholas. "Way off."

Logan stared at Hope for a moment, then nodded his head once. "Fine. I'll be in the kitchen."

"Please sit down," said Nicholas. "I'll explain everything."

Hope sat, perched on the edge of the seat. "Make it quick. I'm tired of all the mystery already."

"That is a problem with Sanguinar. I'll try to clear things up the best I can." Nicholas lowered his body into a chair across the room from her, clearly trying to come off as nonthreatening. "I assume you know Logan's not human, right?"

"Right."

"I'm not either. Our question is whether you're one of us—like me."

"Are you a vampire, too?"

Amusement pulled at Nicholas's scars. "No. I'm a Theronai. My people work in pairs. One man, one woman. Only there aren't many women of our kind left. Logan thinks you might be one of them."

"Why does he want you to touch me?" Even asking the question hurt. She didn't want Logan to hand her off to someone else as if she weren't good enough for him.

"Because there's a chance that if I touch you, my luceria will react." He held up a wide hand. On it was a simple band that swirled with flecks of color—so many she had trouble focusing on it.

She blinked rapidly, concentrating on the lines crossing his face. Whatever had left those scars had been one hell of an opponent. A man built like Nicholas would not have been easy to hurt.

"So, can we just shake hands or something?"

"Sure. If you're okay with that. I've waited a long, long time to find my partner. A few more minutes won't kill me."

Hope didn't want to spend a few more minutes with him. She wanted to be back with Logan. Best to just get this over with and figure out if she was who he thought.

She might not be human. The idea was so bizarre, and yet it explained a lot. Maybe that's why she saw auras. "If I am like you, would that explain why I can't remember anything before about ten years ago?"

Nicholas shrugged. "I don't know. It's possible. What I do know is that if you are meant to be my partner, I'll do anything in my power to make you happy. Including getting your memory back."

His earnestness touched her. She sensed he was a sweet man. A good man.

Hope held out her hand. She couldn't stop it from shaking. She closed her eyes, cringing at her own cowardice.

Warm, callused fingers closed around her hand. His touch was gentle, careful.

She looked up at him. He stared in rapt attention at his ring as if it held the secret to life. She didn't know what he was looking for, but she saw nothing.

After a long moment, he bowed his head in defeat. He blew out a long, weary breath and a wave of deep blue sadness smothered the vibrant red pain for a moment before it, too, got swallowed up.

"I'm sorry to have bothered you," he whispered, grief plain in his voice. Then he turned and left out the front door.

Nicholas had known better than to get his hopes up. She wasn't the one. She couldn't save him.

Pain bore down on him, crushing him under the weight of disappointment. He didn't know how much longer he could keep going. And even if he did, even if he kept fighting the good fight and miraculously managed to find a woman who was compatible with his power, what then?

He saw the way Hope had looked at him, flinching back in revulsion. He knew his scars had either frightened or disgusted her. Not that he blamed her for the honest reaction. His appearance was shocking. There was no help for it.

He heard the front door open behind him. The heavy fall of footsteps told him it was Logan and not Hope.

"I presume things did not go well," said Logan.

"No."

"I'm sorry for your disappointment."

"Forget it. Time to move on. Demons to slay."

"Will you stay?"

The last thing Nicholas wanted to do was hang around, wishing for something that wasn't going to happen. He respected himself too much to beat himself up like that. "Why?"

"To protect her. She's blooded. She risked her life to save mine tonight. I fear she would do the same thing again if necessary."

Nicholas's opinion of Hope rose a notch. "No kidding?"

Logan nodded. "I don't know how she managed it. There were two of us, both paralyzed. She dragged us up a flight of stairs."

Nicholas let out a low whistle. "Strong woman."

"Foolish woman. Her blood is too valuable to spill. I need someone who can take care of her."

"I'll take her back to Dabyr."

"She won't go," said Logan. "At least not until she finds the answer to her mystery."

"And what mystery is that?"

"Apparently, people she knows are going missing. She's certain of foul play."

"Is she right?" asked Nicholas.

"I've seen eight Synestryn in two nights near her home. Inside the city limits."

Normally, Synestryn stayed out of sight. They avoided public areas, like cities, preferring suburbs and rural locations. The hunting might be sparser, but the risk of being caught was much lower.

Nicholas had to get rid of the infestation. It was too dangerous to allow demons to live among so many people. "Give me the details. I'll take care of it."

"And the woman?"

"I can't take her into combat with me," said Nicholas. "She needs to go to Dabyr."

"We're bound by a promise. I can make her go, but only after the cause of the missing people is determined."

Nicholas stared at Logan. He didn't trust the Sanguinar. Logan was way too pretty to be trusted. He was used to getting his way. The fact that this woman had managed to wring a bargain out of him was one more sign that she was one of their own.

Which meant she might be able to save one of his brothers.

"I'll have Joseph send more men. If she won't go willingly to Dabyr now, then we'll keep her safe until she will."

"And in the meantime, the other unbounded warriors can test her for compatibility."

"Exactly," said Nicholas.

Logan nodded. "It will be as you say."

"Do you want to tell her, or do you want me to?"

"Tell her what?"

"What our plans are."

Logan frowned in confusion. "Why would we tell her?"

For a smart guy, Logan was a complete idiot. "Because it's *her* life. Because she's a grown-up and gets to make her own decisions. Because you don't muck around in someone else's life without at least telling them you're doing it."

Logan smiled in amusement. "You truly are naïve if you believe that. The *best* way to muck around in someone else's life is by keeping it a secret from them."

Nicholas stared at Logan for a long time, unsure whether he wanted to punch the man or weep for him. "People are not here for your amusement. We're responsible for the things we do to them. I truly hope you understand that."

"You don't have to lecture me about responsibility. I know that lesson all too well."

"Then you won't mind telling Hope what we plan to do so she won't be frightened."

Logan's phone rang. He answered it, listened briefly. "I'll come immediately. Before dawn." He hung up and said to Nicholas, "I have to go. Urgent matters. You understand."

What Nicholas understood was he was being handed responsibility for Hope's safety and comfort. And while he was equipped to manage both, he couldn't help but feel like Logan was using him to avoid something. Or someone.

Logan got in his van and drove away.

Nicholas sighed and turned back to the house, trying to figure out how he was going to explain everything to Hope in a way that wouldn't frighten her or piss her off.

He told himself it was good practice for the day he found his other half. If he was lucky enough to live that long.

Krag's Dorjan came back empty-handed.

"Where is the woman?" he asked the human he'd sent to find her.

"She wasn't there. We searched the whole building. There were signs of a fight. Blood. But nothing else."

If that Sanguinar had bled her dry, Krag was going to stake him out in the sun for the Solarc's Wardens. "Where did she go?"

"I don't know."

The Dorjan's failure grated against Krag's patience. He needed that woman. If her blood was as pure as Krag hoped, she could be enough of a prize to appease his father's anger. Krag could return home and take his rightful place as his father's heir.

The domain he'd scratched out for himself here was nothing compared to his father's realm. The sources of food there were rich and plentiful, as if someone had been raising blooded human children as one would cattle. Krag wanted that power. He was the firstborn. He deserved it.

But when his father had beheld his second son—the one who could walk among humans, unnoticed—Krag had been shunned and banished.

He had to prove to his father he was worthy of his inheritance, that he could rule over his domain, destroying any rebellion or attack.

The woman he'd sensed would go a long way toward proving he was worthy. Especially if he could breed her and give his father a grandchild more perfect than Krag's brother could ever be.

The thought warmed his blood, making him merciful. Rather than torturing the man kneeling before him for his failure, Krag drew his dagger and rammed it into the man's heart. He fell over, a look of shock frozen on his face.

Demons snarled nearby, but did not dare to come feed without Krag's approval.

He nodded to them, stepping back as they flooded around his feet to clean up the mess.

Krag turned to his right-hand man, a Dorjan who went by the improbable name Hacksaw. "Can you find her?" he asked his servant.

The Dorjan lifted his dark eyes from the floor. A scar bisected his lip where a piercing had been ripped out. His wide shoulders straightened with purpose and his meaty fists clenched. "I can, Master."

Krag went to the man and pressed a finger to his forehead. He shoved the knowledge he had of the woman into Hacksaw's head. The skin under his finger sizzled and blistered as the memories were implanted.

Hacksaw shuddered in pleasure or pain. Krag couldn't tell which and didn't care.

Once the information was in place, Krag dismissed him and turned away. "Don't take long," he warned the Dorjan. "Don't make me wait."

Chapter 14

Hope listened quietly to everything Nicholas had to say.

There were more men like him. She might be able to save one of them, and if she did, she'd have access to magic.

As she listened, she kept waiting for a spark of recognition—something that told her she was on the right path, that she was what he thought she was. Unfortunately, as his story went on, she began to realize that nothing he said resonated with her. It simply didn't *feel* right.

With Logan, she felt like the veil between her and her memories became thinner, like she was getting closer to the truth. And while Nicholas was gentle with her feelings and careful not to shock her, she felt . . . nothing.

Finally, she had to stop him before he got his hopes up too high. "I'm sorry, Nicholas, but I'm not a Theronai."

"You don't know that. None of the others knew, either."

"You said I'd have a ring-shaped birthmark. I don't."

"It could be in a place you can't see, under your hair."

Hope didn't know how to explain to him that it didn't feel right. That while she was beginning to believe that she wasn't human, what he told her left her feeling unconnected.

She offered him a wistful smile. "I can't be someone just because you want me to."

"I know that," he said. "I also know that no matter who or what you are, we'll protect you."

"I'd rather you protect the people on the streets—the ones who keep disappearing."

"We'll do that, too. Logan told me it was important to you."

"It is. While I'm not close with everyone who's gone missing, I still feel a responsibility toward them, as if it's my job to ensure their safety."

Nicholas smiled, making his scars pucker. "See? That's the kind of thing that proves my point. You feel your sense of duty even without your memories. That has to count for something."

"I know you want it to. Believe me, the idea of being some magical woman who can save people's lives is compelling, but I have to be honest with myself. And so do you."

He shook his head, his blue eyes sad. An answering plume of blue swirled in his aura of pain. "No, what I have to do is keep hope alive. For us, it's more important than food or water. Without hope, we're already defeated."

She understood that. She'd lived in hope of learning her past for a long time. "I'm not going to lie to you. I don't think I am who you want me to be. But I'll do what you ask. As soon as we find what happened to all these missing people, I'll meet your friends. Let them touch me. And if I can save one of them, I will."

Nicholas swallowed hard, then nodded. When he spoke, his voice was tight with emotion. "Thank you. That means more than you can ever know."

He got up and walked out of the house. Hope got the sense he needed to be alone. So did she. There were so many things to work out in her head, all of them crammed together one on top of another.

She'd just committed to lining up for savior auditions for a group of men she'd never met. On top of that, chances were she was going to let them all down the way she had Nicholas.

She was no savior. She didn't look forward to the moment that these Theronai came to realize that.

A feeling of inadequacy hung over her, making her feel heavy. She leaned back on the couch and covered her eyes with her arm.

She was tired. Lonely. Logan had left without even saying good-bye, and his brush-off stung.

She'd thought they had a connection. He'd drunk her blood. Twice. She'd saved his life. And yet, apparently, that wasn't enough to even warrant a quick word of farewell.

He'd abandoned her. And whether he felt connected to her or not, she felt him. Even now, lying here with her eyes closed, she knew which way he'd gone. She could feel him glowing against her left side like the sunshine she craved so much.

She glanced at her watch. It would be dawn in a few hours. She'd have Nicholas take her home, bundle up against the cold, and enjoy the sunrise. It would calm her, center her, give her strength.

She could hardly wait for summer to get here so she could strip down and bask in the sun. Winter had been long and was hanging on for dear life. Maybe once all of this bizarre stuff was behind her, she'd take some time off and drive down to Florida. She could lie on the beach and listen to the ocean. Maybe if she relaxed enough, her memories would loosen up and simply come to her.

That would be nice.

At least she thought so. There was still a part of her that wondered if that mental wall was there for a reason. Maybe what was on the other side was too dark and scary to stand. Maybe her mind had blocked it out as a way of protecting her.

If so, did she really want to see what was on the other side?

The question rolled around in her head, rattling in annoyance. She'd had this debate with herself a hundred times. In the end, there was only one answer. Those memories were *hers*. Ugly or beautiful, she wanted them back.

Jackie sat in the back of the SUV trying not to pay attention to all the lovey-dovey stuff going on up front. Paul and Andra were the perfect couple: beautiful, tall, strong, working together as one unit in complete accord.

It was more than a little nauseating.

Jackie stared out the window, watching the dark landscape slide by. After living so long in darkness, her eyes had no trouble seeing into the inky blackness of the countryside. And while she saw no demons, she knew they were out there. One wrong move and she could be right back where she was only a couple of weeks ago.

She patted her purse, feeling the hard lump of the handgun she'd insisted on having before leaving the safety of Dabyr. No matter what happened, those demons were not taking her again. At least not alive.

Andra's phone rang. She said something quiet Jackie couldn't hear, and then hung up. "Change of plans," she announced. "Iain is in trouble. We're going to go help him since we're close."

Iain. The man who'd pulled her out of her cage and then looked at her with a dark hunger she'd never seen before.

Jackie fought against the memories, but in the end, she relived every moment of her rescue again. The fear of that night flooded her, making her body tremble. She could almost smell the blood and filth of unwashed bodies as she and the others ran from the cave. Big men were on all sides, hurrying them forward.

Iain had gone back for the others. For the children. He'd saved them all that night—all those who were left to save.

Jackie didn't want to think about the ones who hadn't made it out. She didn't want to see the faces of those who were born and died in captivity, never to know the warmth of the sun.

The car lurched around a corner, hitting a rut in the gravel road. Jackie's head bumped into the glass, breaking the hold those bleak memories had on her.

"I don't know what we'll find," said Paul as he sped down the lane. "Stay close to me and Andra, okay?"

Jackie nodded, her throat too clogged with emotion to find any room for words to escape.

Andra turned her long, lean body in her seat and looked at Jackie. Her short, dark hair framed her face, making her blue eyes stand out in contrast. "If things get ugly, I'll put a shield around you. You don't have to be afraid."

Jackie didn't bother to tell her she was constantly afraid these days, and there wasn't a shield in the world that could change that.

They came to a rocking stop in front of an aging farmhouse. Paul didn't even turn off the engine before he slammed out of the SUV, drawing his sword. Andra was only half a second behind him.

Now that they were gone, Jackie had a clear view out the front windshield. The SUV's headlights flowed over the icy landscape, glinting off trees and tall, dead grass. Everything was coated in a thin layer of ice, giving the area an almost fairy-tale type of feel. Only this wasn't a friendly tale; it was one of the dark, twisted, cautionary tales from long ago, filled with monsters and death.

Half a dozen demons littered the area, their eyes glowing with a hungry light. They were furry, with thick, heavy limbs like a bear, but they had almost human features. Their mouths were too big to be human, their teeth too long. And the pale green light spilling from their eyes was definitely not human.

Jackie had seen these things before. She'd seen them feed on the bodies of the dead. She'd seen them fight and kill one another for a scrap of food, then consume their own when one fell.

Her body froze in the vehicle, unable to move. She sat

there, staring, shaking. A cold sweat seeped from her pores.

Paul's sword gleamed as he fought the demons. Andra was by his side, her attention split between the monsters and Jackie.

Andra shouted something Jackie couldn't understand. Her heart was pounding too loud for her to hear anything else. She closed her eyes to block out the sight of the things that had stolen her life and instead concentrated on breathing.

The SUV rocked as if something had jumped on top of it. Jackie's eyes shot open, but she saw nothing. Her breath fogged up the window on her left. Andra lifted a hand and a faint blue light spilled out over the hood, sweeping back to engulf the left side of the vehicle.

"Get out!" shouted Andra, and this time Jackie understood her words.

Panic forced her into motion. She fumbled for the latch on the seat belt, but her sweaty fingers slipped from the plastic. The sound of metal scraping over glass squealed out from behind her.

Jackie spun her head around to see what was behind her only to discover that it wasn't metal on glass she'd heard; it was one of the demons clawing at the back window. Pale blue sparks spewed up from the claws, keeping the thing from doing any damage to the glass. But for how long?

With that thing only inches away, Jackie's world began to cave in. She remembered all the cold, dark nights she spent in terror for her life. She remembered the faces of every one of the women and children who were slain and eaten by those monsters. She'd known from the moment of her escape that they would want her back. And here they were, clawing at her, trying to reach her so they could take her back to that nightmare.

Jackie wasn't going to let that happen.

A calmness settled over her as she made her decision.

She reached for her purse and the revolver inside. Her hand settled around the textured grip, keeping it from slipping out of her sweaty palm. It was already loaded. All she had to do was disengage the safety and it was ready to fire.

Five bullets for the demon. One for her.

Iain didn't know how long Andra's shield was going to hold, but he knew that he had to get the woman out of the SUV before it failed. There were three Synestryn back there, and every one of them was going to want a bite.

He finished off the demon in front of him, then shifted to his left, forcing the rest of the beasties to hit Andra's shield. She'd created a tunnellike barrier, forcing the demons to come at them only one or two at a time. Paul could handle that for as long as it took Iain to get to the woman.

He'd seen panic enough times to know its face, and the woman he'd found in those caves—Jackie—was wearing it now.

Iain opened the car door nearest the house and leaned inside, trying to ignore the slavering demons only inches away from Jackie's head.

They were so going to die when he got a minute.

As soon as his head and shoulders were inside the vehicle, he saw the muzzle of a .45 aimed at his face.

Iain was impressed. Apparently she hadn't completely panicked.

"Save it for the Synestryn. We need to get you out of here," he told her as he reached in and pressed the release button on her seat belt. The canvas strap slithered away from her body, catching on her arm.

She wasn't moving. She was staring at him, holding that gun so tight her knuckles were white from the strain.

"Move your arm," he told her.

She didn't.

Iain held back a sigh as he pushed the gun down and

pried her fingers from the grip. "The seat belt is stuck on your arm."

Jackie looked down where he indicated and recognition flared in her wild gray eyes. Her slim arm moved, freeing the seat belt.

As soon as he touched her, Iain's heartbeat slowed. His luceria leapt away from his neck as if reaching for her. The ring vibrated, humming close to his skin. A sense of calm descended over him, contrasting sharply against the chaos of combat and the rage of his dead soul. He knew he didn't have time to study the odd reaction, but he couldn't bring himself to care.

He'd felt like this only once before—the night he took Jackie from her cage. It had passed so quickly, he hadn't even allowed himself to believe it had ever happened.

It meant she could save his life. Too bad she was too late to do anything for his soul.

Iain shoved away all thoughts of salvation and forced himself to focus on keeping the woman alive. The Band of the Barren was full of men that needed a woman like her, and he was going to see to it that she lived long enough to meet them.

Blue sparks jumped from the Synestryn's claws for a second; then they stopped as the thing made its way through to the glass.

"Time to go." Iain grabbed her arm and pulled her across the seats, practically dragging her from the SUV.

Her feet hit the ground, slipping on the ice. Iain kept a tight hold to keep her from falling and ushered her inside the house, where she'd at least have the protective wards of the Gerai house to keep her safe. They might not hold for long, but they were better than the SUV.

He pushed her through the door, grabbed the handle to shut it behind him, and said, "There's a baby in the bathtub. Don't let the Synestryn get him."

*   *   *

Logan had to hurry if he was going to meet Alexander and check in on Hope before sunrise.

He sped down the highway, finally pulling into a secluded Gerai house tucked at the end of a long driveway. Trees surrounded the old farmhouse, sheltering it from prying eyes.

Logan jumped out of his van and hurried to the front door. By the time he got there, Alexander Siah had opened it, beckoning him inside.

Alexander had been instrumental in the success of Project Lullaby. The man had an ability to cure cancer that was unparalleled. Even Tynan couldn't match his skill when it came to the disease.

For years, Alexander had been gaining the cooperation of heavily blooded humans in exchange for cures for themselves or loved ones. He saved lives, and the humans paired up and created new ones.

Their breeding program was of questionable morals, but necessary. Without Alexander's aid, they would be years behind where they were now, so when he'd told Logan they needed to meet, Logan had not questioned him.

Alexander was several inches taller than Logan. He wasn't as thin as the last time Logan had seen him, proof that he'd fed well recently. His icy green eyes flashed with impatience beneath his steeply arched eyebrows.

"Come inside. We must hurry," said Alexander.

Logan stepped inside and came to an abrupt stop. A man stood there, imposing in his size. An air of power and menace wafted from him, forcing Logan to dial down his senses so he wouldn't be overpowered by his presence.

The man had medium brown hair and golden brown eyes. He stood a bit over six feet and his limbs were thick with muscle. His stance was belligerent, his booted feet braced apart and his hands fisted on his hips. The tops of his ears were slightly pointed, displayed openly, rather than hidden as many Slayers did.

Logan looked at Alexander in disbelief. "You brought a Slayer to a Gerai house? Are you mad?"

While the war between the Theronai and Slayers had stagnated over the decades, bringing a Slayer onto Theronai soil was a surefire way to reignite violence.

Alexander shook his head. "Tynan sent the word out. You wanted the most powerfully blooded males we could find. Eric Phelan is the man you're looking for."

Logan absorbed that shocking news for a moment. As far as he knew, the Slayers had bred with humans to the point where their bloodlines were too diluted to be of much use. But if Alexander said differently, Logan believed him.

Eric's jaw clenched in anger. "You said you'd make this quick. I have places to be."

"We have a bargain," said Alexander.

"And I'll abide by it, but you two better hurry the hell up. If my brother finds out I'm here, taking a chance of messing up his precious plans for peace, you'll be sucking blood from my corpse."

"Your brother?" asked Logan.

"Andreas Phelan."

That name rang a loud bell. "The new leader of the Slayers."

"Yeah. And he earned his title through beating the hell out of everyone else who wanted it, so I suggest you don't cross him."

"No, of course not," said Logan. His mind was reeling, trying to sort out this new twist of events. "Why am I here, Alexander?"

"Eric's blood is strong. He's the man you're looking for to breed with Hope."

A slight snarl lifted Eric's lip. "I'll fuck whoever you want, but we have laws about breeding. You know that."

"I do," said Alexander. "Your brother has been clear about that. I assure you that if he doesn't find Hope a suitable mate—if he doesn't accept her bloodline—our bargain will be fulfilled."

"Fair enough," said Eric. "Where's the woman?"

Logan looked at Alexander. "You want me to have Hope breed with a Slayer?"

"His blood is stronger than any human. Why not?"

"Because she's with a Theronai right now. He's convinced she is one, too. He'll take her back to Dabyr for all the other Theronai there to test her."

"Whoa," said Eric. "I'm not fucking some Theronai's woman. My brother would kill me, and he'd take years doing it, too."

"We don't know if she's a Theronai or not," said Alexander. He looked at Logan. "Test his blood. You've had hers, right? You'll know if they blend."

He would. All he needed was a few drops of Eric's blood. It would react strongly to Hope's if they were a good match. "Fine. We'll try that, but if he's not a match, then this meeting never happened."

Logan didn't dare step closer to Eric without permission. Slayers were violent. And quick. Logan had already been injured enough for one night. "May I?" he asked Eric.

Eric held out a beefy arm. "Knock yourself out. Just don't make me do the same. Mind your manners. Understand?"

Logan did. He would take only a little—just enough to answer his question.

He took Eric's wrist and brought it to his mouth. The man's skin was hot, but that was natural. Slayers' body temperature was above that of humans or Theronai. Their metabolisms burned hot and fast.

As soon as Logan's fangs broke the skin, it began to heal. He hurried to finish the job, to prevent him from having to bite Eric a second time.

As his blood pooled in Logan's stomach and spread through his system, it combined with Hope's blood. Logan let go of Eric and closed his eyes, focusing on what was going on inside him.

Eric's blood cells sought out Hope's, merging with

them. The two combined, much stronger than the sum of their separate parts. Logan's body warmed and sparks of power filled his limbs.

The effect didn't last long, but it was unmistakable. Hope and Eric would make a powerful couple. Their children would be strong, their blood possibly as strong as a Theronai's.

As good as that news was, it rang hollow inside Logan's chest.

He looked at Eric, imagining him with Hope, their bodies entwined, creating life.

Jealousy rose up in Logan so swiftly he didn't have time to stop it from taking root. It wove its way through his bones, making him writhe with possessive rage. Hope was his. He did not want to share her. Not with Eric. Not with anyone.

Not that he had a choice. He'd never had a choice.

Logan swallowed down that jealousy and looked at Alexander. He knew if he so much as glimpsed at Eric, those violent urges would return. "It is as you say. They are a good match."

"Excellent," said Alexander.

"You'll have to gain permission from Andreas," said Eric. "I can't have a kid with her unless he approves."

Logan barely kept the sneer from his voice. "You've never even met her, yet you're willing to create a life with her? What if she doesn't want it?"

Eric crossed his thick arms over his chest. "I thought it was your job to see that she did. Isn't that what you do?"

"Why are you so willing to help?" asked Logan.

Eric gave a careless shrug. "I'll be saddled with a wife as soon as my brother finds one for me. What's the difference if you do it first?"

"What about love?"

"What about it?" asked Eric. "Do I look like a child who believes in such things? I've always known I'd marry out of duty to the race. It's no big surprise, unless you count the fact that I've avoided it this long."

"And what about Hope? Doesn't she deserve love?"

"She'll be safe. She'll have family. Children. She'll have a home and a place she belongs and people who would give their lives for her. If that's not enough for her, she doesn't deserve more."

Yes, she did. She deserved to be loved for the exquisite creature she was. If Eric couldn't see that, he didn't deserve *her*.

Alexander put a staying hand on Logan's arm. "I'm sure Eric will come to care for her in time. Let them meet. We'll see what comes of that and then go from there."

He was right. Logan knew this was the best course of action—or at least the most logical. "There's only one problem."

"What's that?" asked Eric.

"Hope is with Nicholas, and there's no way he'd ever allow a Slayer anywhere near her."

"Then get rid of him," said Alexander. "Send him away and bring her to us."

"It's not that easy," he told the men. "Nicholas thinks she might be a Theronai. He's going to take her back to Dabyr."

"I could get rid of him," said Eric. "Make it look like an accident."

"Absolutely not," said Logan. "We're too close to a truce to do anything to upset it."

"So I'll put on a hat. Cover my ears. Go to meet her. He'll never know what I am."

"No. We need Nicholas. I'll take care of him. I'll find some way to separate them. And then I'll bring her here."

"Not here," said Alexander.

"You're right. The risk of a Theronai showing up here is too great. We'll find another place."

"Agreed."

Eric grabbed his jacket from the couch. "You boys

figure it out and let me know. I'll show up and marry the girl so we can get on with our lives."

"A true romantic," said Logan.

Eric looked him in the eye. "Romance is for children and women. I'm not either of those. And neither are you. Do your job and you'll get what you want. So will I."

"What is it you want, Eric? Exactly?"

"Same as you. To be left the hell alone so I can do my job."

Eric walked out. His motorcycle started up, making Logan wonder how he could stand riding it in this weather.

"You're having second thoughts, aren't you?" asked Alexander.

"About what?"

"Mating Hope to him. You know they're a match. I could see it on your face when you fed from him."

"They are," admitted Logan. "At least their blood is."

"You say that as if it's not enough."

"It's not. I want her to be happy."

"She will be. So will Eric. He blusters, but we both know what happens to a man when he falls in love. He grows softer, more pliable."

"I'm not sure that man is capable of love."

"He will be. For her. For their children."

Logan could easily see an infant with Eric's eyes and Hope's smile. Their children would be beautiful. Strong.

The image should have comforted him and given him hope for the future of his race, but all it did was leave a hollow ache in his chest, as if something vital had been removed.

His feelings for the woman were getting in the way and they were growing stronger by the hour.

He opened his mouth to demand that Alexander take over her care, but the words would not come out. He couldn't stand the thought of not seeing her again.

It was a warning—a screaming siren of doom—but

Logan couldn't bring himself to back away. She'd saved his life. She'd fed him. He was tied to her in a way no other man was. If Alexander took over, he'd feed from her and that bond that Logan shared with her would be diluted. It would no longer be something only he and Hope shared.

Besides, he needed to prove to himself he was strong enough to do this. She wouldn't be the only woman he felt a connection to as the years passed. If he walked away before he could overcome his attraction to her enough to do his job, he'd forever wonder if he could. The worry would plague him. He'd question his confidence at a time when there could be no question.

"I'll do what must be done," he told Alexander.

His friend nodded. "I know you will. You always have."

Chapter 15

A baby in the bathtub?

Jackie gathered herself and searched the small house until she found the infant. He was wrapped up tight, screaming his little head off. His face was red and his squawking cry was hoarse, as if he'd been screaming for a long time.

She picked him up and cuddled him to her body. He quieted after a few seconds, sucking in gulping breaths of air.

She'd seen what the Synestryn did to babies born in those caves. She wasn't about to let it happen to this one.

Jackie retrieved her gun from where Iain had set it next to the front door. She checked to make sure the safety was off, then stood with her back to the wall.

If the people outside didn't finish off the demons, she was going to have to do it herself.

Rory crouched on top of a rusting file cabinet to get out of the water. She was so cold her bones ached. She hugged herself, shivering, trying to stay awake. She hadn't slept in days. Maybe longer. Time meant nothing down here. Every hour was an endless progression of hunger, thirst, and fear.

In the murky water below, something slithered just below the surface. Ripples spread out in three places, and she couldn't tell if there were three different creatures down there, or one really big one. Either way, it wasn't good.

She stood, reaching overhead to the tiled ceiling. A lifetime ago, Rory had hung paper snowflakes from fishing line at school to decorate. She remembered the teacher showing her how to lift the ceiling tiles so she could wrap the line around the metal bars that held them up.

Maybe she could pull one of those metal bars free and use it as a weapon. It was worth a shot.

Rory slid two dingy tiles aside and wiggled the bars. Dust and insect carcasses rained down on her, but it was better than whatever was in the water below. After what she'd waded through, she wasn't sure she'd ever be clean again.

It took some work, but she managed to free a short piece. The end was blunt and the metal was light, but it was better than no weapon at all.

Rory went back to her crouch, clutching her prize in her hands. If that thing came for her, she was going to kill it.

Fatigue made Hope's body sluggish as she climbed the stairs to her room. It was five in the morning, and she had only a couple of hours to sleep before she had to be up for work.

She flopped back onto her bed, feeling something hard under her. She pulled it out. It was her cell phone, which seemed almost comical.

Hope entered the phone number Nicholas had given her, which was scrawled in ink on the back of her hand. He'd said he'd stay nearby until dawn, that she'd be safe during the day without him, but insisted she take his number, just in case. Which worked for her. She didn't like the idea of having a babysitter sleeping on her couch, which was what he said he'd do if she didn't cooperate.

She wasn't used to being bossed around, and she

didn't much care for it, even if she knew Nicholas was right about the danger.

Hope fell into a fast, hard sleep and when she woke, it was growing light outside. It wasn't time for her alarm, but something had woken her.

She blinked her blurry eyes and tried to get her sleep-deprived brain to function. The lights were off. Only a faint slice of streetlights gleamed from the edge of her blinds. The smell of cold, fresh air filled her room, along with a darker, more intoxicating scent.

Logan.

Hope reached for her lamp, fumbling to turn it on. The lightweight base rocked as her knuckles slammed into it. Finally, she found the knob and light flared through the room, blinding her for a moment.

When the stinging eased, she saw Logan. He sat on the foot of her bed, watching her.

Hope should have been scared. She should have been outraged that he'd slip uninvited into her room. But all she could feel was curiosity and a slow, budding warmth.

"What are you doing here?" she asked. "It's not even six in the morning."

"I came to see you."

"Practicing your stalker technique?"

He frowned for a second, the action creasing his beautiful face. His hair was damp as if he'd just showered, falling perfectly over his pale brow. There was a healthy glow brightening his cheeks, which made her wonder if he'd taken blood from someone tonight.

The spike of jealousy that rammed through her was as unexpected as it was unwanted. She didn't care whose blood he drank so long as it wasn't hers. It was none of her business.

Mocking laughter flooded her mind as she tried to get herself to believe the ridiculous lie. She wanted him to need her again—to make her feel that exquisite pleasure only he could give her.

"I had to come before dawn," he said. "We need to talk."

Not until she'd cleared her head. He was too potent to face so soon after waking up.

"Give me a minute." Hope pushed herself out of bed and went into the bathroom and shut the door. She took her time washing up, content to make him wait.

Assuming he was there at all. For all she knew this could be some kind of vivid dream.

As soon as the thought entered her mind, she dismissed it. If this had been a dream, Logan would have already had her naked and been making love to her while he fed from her neck. And while she'd never admit that to another soul, she had to be honest with herself. Logan excited her, even the scary parts. Perhaps *especially* the scary parts. She felt drawn to him, connected to him. When he'd left her with Nicholas, she'd felt abandoned—like some vital part of herself had been ripped away and held hostage.

She'd never had fantasies about vampires before. All these wayward thoughts were his fault—no doubt the result of some kind of vampire cooties. Having her blood taken had changed her somehow, and part of her wondered if it wasn't an improvement.

While she'd been with other men before, not one of them had made her feel even half of what Logan had. And he hadn't even taken off her clothes. She could only imagine the kind of pleasure being naked with him could bring, feeling his skin against hers. No clothing to mute the sensation. And now that the thought was in her head, it was going to occupy all free space.

Hope dried her face and straightened her shoulders to face him. When she opened the bathroom door, he was sitting exactly where she'd left him, so beautiful she forgot to breathe.

He'd replaced the long leather coat that he'd burned with an identical one. The sweater beneath it was the same pale silvery gray as his eyes, and it clung to muscles she swore hadn't been there when she'd first seen him. His gaze roamed over her long sleep shirt to the bare legs beneath. Her toes curled under his scrutiny, and she wondered if he liked what he saw.

A faint shimmer of light glowed in his pale eyes for just a split second before he squeezed them shut. "What I have to say can wait until you're dressed."

"But not until I'm awake?"

"My apologies for that. I had to come before dawn."

"You could have knocked."

"No. I didn't want Nicholas to see me."

"Why?" she asked as she gathered up a fresh set of clothing.

"His kind tend to be a bit . . . possessive."

"His kind? You mean men?"

"I mean Theronai."

"How did you get in here?"

"The window."

"It was locked."

He shrugged. "That posed no problem."

"Did you turn into mist and come in through tiny cracks?"

"You've watched too much TV." A smile lifted one side of his mouth. Instantly, the need to feel her lips against his exploded inside her. She needed to see if he tasted as good as he smelled, and if that wicked smile was teasing or a promise of more to come.

"TV?" she asked, all her thoughts dribbling from her ears.

Logan rose and glided toward her, holding her gaze. Her head tilted up as he came closer so she wouldn't have to look away. She really didn't want to look away.

"I'm not here to discuss myths and fiction. I'm here for more important matters. I want you to come with me."

Hope had to blink several times to get the gears in her head to spin again. "I already told you I would, once we find those missing people."

"Let the police handle that. You and I can leave now. Together."

That sounded nice. "Where will we go?"

"I know a special place. Secluded. Romantic. Eric is there, waiting for you."

Hope jerked, reeling back at the mention of another man's name. He might as well have thrown ice water down her shirt.

She turned away, grabbed up her clean clothes, and went into the bathroom.

It was clear Logan didn't want her. He kept shoving other men at her, and like a fool, she kept letting him. Not this time. She wasn't going anywhere with him. And it didn't matter how many men he brought around. She was staying put in her life, where she belonged.

When she came out of the bathroom armored in comfortable clothing, she faced him down. "Tell Eric to find someone else. I'm not interested. I'm done letting you play matchmaker. I don't care if I never get my memories back. I don't care if I have to find Rory on my own. You're using me and I don't like it. I'm not playing anymore."

One second he was a few feet away, and the next he was right in front of her, his strong hands wrapped around her upper arms. "You made me a promise. You can't escape that, so don't even try."

"I'll do what I want, and if you try to stop me, I'll call the police."

"Human police. There's nothing they can do to me."

"I'm willing to test that theory," she shot back.

"Don't, Hope. Don't do this."

"I'm not doing anything. You're the one who keeps trying to foist me off on other people. I don't understand why. What is it you want with me?"

His grip loosened as his gaze slid over her face. There was longing in that look. Needful desire that went beyond sex.

He was into her. He couldn't hide that. A man didn't

look at her the way he did if he wasn't at least thinking about getting her naked. And Hope wanted that. Bad. A man like Logan didn't come by more than once in a lifetime, and she wanted to at least give them a chance. She wasn't a fool. She knew things would probably end in disaster, like they always did. But for Logan, the risk of heartbreak was worth whatever time they might have together, no matter how fleeting.

His eyelids lowered, masking his emotions. "The things I want don't matter. Only the things my people need."

"I don't understand."

"I know. Trust me when I tell you that I would never allow anything bad to happen to you. I want you to be happy. Safe. Loved."

"Why? You don't even know me."

"I know enough to realize you're deserving of only the best." Pain creased his brow, shimmering in his eyes. "And that's something I simply cannot give you."

"You're not even willing to try?"

"I'm not willing to risk disaster."

Maybe he wasn't, but she was. He deserved to be happy, too, and from the way he looked at her, he wanted her as much as she did him. If there was a chance for them to find some joy in each other, she owed it to both of them to make it happen. Even if it was only a little fling.

Hope broke his grip on her arms and slid her fingers through his hair. As soon as she had two fists full of his silky locks, she held him still while she went up on tiptoe. She pressed her lips to his, testing the theory that they'd be good together.

At first he was stiff and resistant, but it didn't take long for that to change. He yielded with a rough groan of defeat. His mouth opened and melded to hers. She licked over the inside of his bottom lip, tasting him as she'd been dying to do. He growled in excitement and she felt a shudder race through him. His hands slid around her, gripping her hips, pulling her body against his. Heat bloomed between them and she swore she could feel his heart pounding through their clothes.

Her feet left the floor as he lifted her and pressed her against the wall. His body held her pinned, freeing his hands. Those long, elegant fingers caressed her face and neck while their kiss deepened. Her tongue traced over his teeth until she found the sharp tip of one fang. A thrill raced through her as her body remembered how good his bite had made her feel.

Sweet tremors fluttered in her belly where his erection pressed against her. His scent grew stronger and darker as the fever between them increased.

There was no more question in her mind. Despite the fact that he kept trying to set her up with other men, he wanted her. She could feel it in every rapid breath and every heated touch. Only a man who wanted her would kiss her like he was, demanding and thorough.

She wasn't going to let him deny it again.

Hope's fingers trailed down his back, enjoying the hard planes and contours beneath his leather coat. And while she totally dug the whole black-leather, bad-boy look, what she really wanted was to feel his naked skin.

She slid her fingers beneath his sweater, shoving it up so he'd know she wanted it off. Instead of giving her the space to strip him bare, he held her pinned by her shoulders to the wall and took a long step back.

A stain of lust darkened his cheeks and his lips were shiny from hers. His nostrils flared wide and his face twisted in a grimace of pain. "We cannot do this."

Her throat was tight as she fought the need to shut him up and get his mouth on hers where it belonged. "Why?"

"Because it's wrong."

"It felt right."

He squeezed his eyes shut as if trying to gather his control. "You're meant for another."

"*Meant?* The only person I'm meant for is the one I pick. And right now, I pick you."

He shook his head and stepped back out of her reach. "No. I can't allow myself to do this."

"Do what?"

"To... feel strongly for you. My job is to see you safely in the arms of another. That is all."

She ignored the fact that he didn't get to decide she was meant for anyone and focused on the more important issue. "You want me. You can't deny that," she said, her voice rough with budding anger.

"I must deny it. Please. Don't test me again."

His rejection hurt, which pissed her off. She didn't know him well enough to allow him to hurt her. Why should she care so much if he didn't want to be with her? She hardly knew him. Just because he made her feel good didn't mean he'd done it on purpose. For all she knew that was an involuntary action on his part—a package deal with all the bloodsucking.

Sadly, whether he should be able to hurt her didn't matter. He had.

Her tone came out flippant and snippy. "Fine. But you stay the hell away from me, understand?"

"I wish I could. It would be easier for both of us. But I made you a promise, and I intend to see it fulfilled."

"I don't need your help, Logan. Just go on with your life and let me do the same."

He reached out as if to touch her, but pulled his hand back before he could. "I'm going to help you. And you will help me. We struck a bargain, and we will both fulfill our ends."

He walked out of her room, but she didn't follow him. If he didn't want her, fine. She had enough self-respect not to chase after him.

Chapter 16

Synestryn kept attacking until sunrise, drawn by the dead woman's blood. Iain finished off the last of them and wiped his sword on the fur of the closest one. Exhaustion hung heavy on his frame, but at least some of the pain had eased. He felt like he could think straight for the first time in days.

Paul held Andra close, supporting her weight over the icy ground. Blood, severed limbs, and twisted bodies were everywhere. Little droplets of black blood froze along blades of grass, clinging like chunks of malignant coal. It was going to take at least an hour for the sun to burn away so much filth.

"You okay?" asked Paul. He was breathing hard and each breath froze as it hit the air.

"Fine," said Iain.

Paul nodded. "I need to refuel. We'll be inside in a few minutes."

The couple shuffled off to find a clean patch of ground that wasn't covered in blood. Paul could draw strength from the earth and feed it to Andra, who looked like she could use about a week's vacation.

Iain left them to it and went inside to check on the kid. As soon as he opened the door, he was met with the muzzle of a .45. Again.

Jackie had a baby in one hand and a revolver in the other. A fierce expression twisted her mouth and made her gray eyes stand out.

Iain waited there, giving her time to realize who he was. Slowly, recognition registered and she lowered the weapon.

Her whole body seemed to sag as if the life had drained out of her. Her face was pale and she was shaking like crazy. She weaved on her feet and Iain was sure she was going to drop the baby on his head.

He reached for the child and that gun came right back up.

"Whoa." He held his hands up. "Just trying to help."

"Your clothes. You stink of them. Go wash."

Iain looked down and sure enough, there were a few places on the front of his shirt where their blood had burned holes through the fabric. His coat had hung open, and the magic shielding on his leather coat hadn't been able to protect the fabric.

"Be right back. The fight's over. Sun's up. Relax."

He cleaned up, changed shirts, and came back out. The woman hadn't relaxed. Not even close. She was still armed, watching out the windows, moving from one to the next as if something was going to jump out at them.

"They won't come for us in the daylight," he assured her.

"I'm not taking any chances."

"Except you're holding a gun and a baby and shaking so hard I'm surprised you haven't shot your own foot off."

She ignored him.

"How about you set the gun down."

She turned then, and something in her face pulled at him, making him take a step closer. There was a vulnerability there—one that didn't belong. From all accounts, this woman had spent years in a Synestryn nest, and not only had she survived, but several of the others they'd rescued that night had reported that Jackie was the reason they were still alive. She'd protected them as much as she was able, finding them food and warmth when there was none to be had.

She swallowed, her eyes pleading. "I can't set it down. My hand won't let go."

He looked at her hand. Her knuckles were white. Tendons stood out, stretched to the limit. She'd been gripping it so hard for so long her hand had probably gone numb.

Iain moved toward her slowly. He really didn't want his head blown off because he made a sudden move around an armed, skittish woman.

"I'm going to help, okay?"

"I don't want you to touch me."

"Why not?" he asked.

"Something happens when your kind touches me. I don't like it."

"Fine. Then give me the baby."

"No. I don't trust you. I'll keep him safe."

He crossed his arms over his chest and stepped close enough he could loom over her. "The gun or the baby. I'm taking one of them. Your choice."

A helpless kind of vulnerability settled over her expression for an instant before she banished it. She squared her shoulders and slowly lifted her arm toward him. It was the one holding the gun.

Iain nodded, accepting her choice, engaged the safety, and started prying her fingers away from the grip. The instant he touched her skin his luceria began to hum. The gaping hole in his chest where his soul had been before it died seemed to shrink. His monster—the dark, dangerous creature that had started growing inside him the day his soul had died—was lulled to sleep, and until now he hadn't realized just how much control the beast had stolen from him. For the briefest second, he remembered what it was like to feel things deeply. Good things, not just anger and fear.

The baby grunted, and rather than coldly calculating the odds of his survival, Iain *felt* something. Some connection. He . . . cared.

The feeling rattled him so much his heart started pounding hard and he broke out in a sweat.

"See?" she said, her voice tight and strained.

"Oh yeah."

"Please hurry."

Iain did as she asked and made quick work of loosening her grip enough to ease the weapon away. Her hand was curved into the shape of a claw, and without thinking, he massaged it, rubbing all the delicate muscles so they'd start working again.

Jackie stared at him, but she didn't pull her hand away. She let him ease her, which somehow served to ease him as well.

His luceria trembled at his throat and finger, but he could detect no colors swirling in its pale depths. All the color had been leeched away by time and the decay of his soul. His lifemark was bare. His soul was dead. And no matter how excited the luceria got, there was nothing Jackie could do to save him.

He was already dead. His body just hadn't caught up with his soul yet, because he wouldn't let it. There was too much work left to do. He couldn't leave yet. His brothers needed him.

Jackie tugged her hand away and shook it. "Thank you."

With her touch gone, the ragged emptiness in his chest opened up again. The monster roared back to life, thrashing around within Iain's head. He had to grit his teeth and lock his knees to keep from staggering back in pain.

"Are you okay?" she asked.

"Yeah," he lied. He was good at lying. It was the only thing keeping him and the Band of the Barren alive. "We should go as soon as Paul and Andra get back. We need to get the kid to Dabyr where he'll be safe. And I need to bury his mother."

"His mother?"

"She died in childbirth."

Sadness painted Jackie's face. "That happens a lot with their babies."

"Whose babies?"

"The Synestryn."

A quiet rage seeped in, filling him from his feet up. "That's not a Synestryn baby."

"Yes, it is."

He shook his head in denial. "No. It's not. It can't be."

"Look at his eyes."

Iain leaned over. The baby was awake, staring up at him. His eyes were blue. "What about them?"

"Give it a second."

He kept staring, his hand on his sword. He did not want to kill this child.

Then he saw it. A black plume of movement swirled in the boy's eyes, tainting the iris.

Iain stumbled back. "No."

Jackie frowned in confusion. "I thought you knew. I thought you'd found him in one of the caves."

He shook his head, his belly filling with acid. The baby had seemed so human. So perfect. He'd cared for it, cuddled it. And now he had to kill it. "Give it to me."

Jackie turned away, shielding the child with her body. "No."

"It has to die."

"You asshole! You'd kill him because of who his father was?"

"It. I'd kill *it*. That's my job."

She picked up the gun again, and stared at him with a look so feral he was certain she'd use it on him. "It's a job you don't have to do. None of their babies survive. None of them. He'll last a day. Maybe two. That's all he gets and there's no way in hell I'm letting you take even one second of that away from him."

"You don't know that."

"I do. I've seen it over and over. I wish I didn't, but I do." Pain radiated out from her, so strong Iain could feel it bombarding his skin. Whatever she'd been through, it had been bad. She'd witnessed horrible things. They all had. But that didn't change his duty.

"I can't let it live."

"I will kill you if I have to," she warned him, leveling the weapon. "He's innocent. You're clearly not. There's no question for me about who should live and who should die here."

Iain didn't dare test her. He knew she wasn't bluffing. He could see her firm resolve in her stance, in her face. She would pull that trigger.

If it weren't for his carefully developed sense of duty, Iain would have let her. But he had to survive. The lives of too many of his brothers depended on it.

"You really want to watch it die?" he asked her.

"No. I really don't. It breaks my heart and tears me up inside. I still see the faces of each one of the babies we lost in those caves. When he's gone, I'll see his, too."

"And you're certain he'll die?"

"As certain as I am that I'll shoot you in the head if you take another step closer."

He nodded. Fine. Let her have her way. If she wanted to watch the thing die a slow death, that was her business. But it wasn't something Iain could tolerate.

He walked out, got behind the wheel of Paul's ride, and took off without them. Let them find their own way. He had things to do.

Jackie stepped outside, making sure Iain was gone. As fast as he was driving, she didn't think he was coming back.

Good. She didn't like the way he made her feel, all soft and weak.

She cuddled the baby close, seeking the comfort of its tiny presence. As short as his life would be, there was still magic in it. She'd seen it over and over. Women found love they never would have known without those few hours with their children. Their heartbreak was soul-crushing, but for those few hours, they were happy and knew a special kind of peace only a baby could bring.

Jackie stared down at him, uncovering his face just enough so that he could see the sun. None of the others had ever had that joy and she wanted to share it with him.

"See," she said, holding his little body upright. "That's the sun. Isn't it pretty?"

The baby blinked and started crying like the light hurt his eyes. She hadn't thought about that, though she probably should have. His father would have hated sunlight.

She tugged the towel up to shield his eyes and noticed that as soon as she did, the black plumes rioted in his eyes as if the sun had held them back.

A spark of hope lit inside her. She tugged the towel down again, letting sunlight spill onto his soft head without shining directly into his eyes.

The plumes shrank and disappeared.

Holding her breath, she covered and uncovered him several times. The black in his eyes responded as if hiding from the light.

Maybe the sun was the key. Maybe all those babies in the caves died because they had no sun.

She didn't dare get her hopes up too high, but she allowed herself enough to fight back the desolate surety of death. This child could survive. The odds weren't good, but it was possible.

If he was to survive, he needed two special things: She needed to get him somewhere safe—back to Dabyr, where the Synestryn couldn't reach him and there were Sanguinar around to help keep him alive. And he needed a name.

Hacksaw's mind burned with the information the master had put into it. Even the pain of such a gift was its own kind of pleasure. He'd gained the notice of the master, which was something he'd only dreamed about.

A thread of power connected the two of them, allowing Hacksaw to feel closer to the master than he ever had before. And while that leash hurt, he reveled in the agony that would allow him to please the master.

Hacksaw went where he was led, driving into the city as fast as he dared. By the time he found the building where the master had seen the woman, the sun was already bright in the sky.

Sunlight streamed through his car windows, blocking some of the pain screaming in his mind. For a split second, Hacksaw remembered a time before the master. He'd been happy then. He hadn't hurt. He hadn't been afraid.

And then, as quick as the feeling came, it was gone again, leaving Hacksaw disoriented.

Had there been a time before the master? If so he didn't want to know about it. That time wasn't important. The only thing that mattered was obedience.

A search of the run-down building showed no signs of the woman. There was only one young man there, huddled in a corner against the cold.

Hacksaw grabbed him by the front of his shirt and hauled him to his feet.

The man cried out in fear and batted at Hacksaw's hands. "Please don't hurt me."

"I'm looking for a woman. Pretty. Blond. She was here last night."

"I don't know about any woman. I only found this place today. I wasn't here last night. I swear."

"You're lying."

"No. I'm—"

Hacksaw pulled out a switchblade and shoved it against the man's throat. "Tell me where she is or I trigger the blade."

The man started to blubber. "I swear I don't know."

Hacksaw's thumb moved to the switch.

The man's words tumbled from his mouth, almost too fast to hear. "It could be Hope. She's blond. I've seen her on the streets trying to get people to come to a homeless shelter where she works."

"Where?"

"A few blocks north. I could show you."

Hacksaw moved the knife and let go of the man. He shoved him toward the door. "Show me."

The man led him through back alleys until they reached the shelter. It was an aging building that someone had tried to keep from decaying. The sign out front was plain, its paint fading, welcoming all who came.

Hacksaw spun the young man so he was in front of him, facing away. Then he slit his throat. Blood arced onto the pavement, but it didn't touch Hacksaw's clothes. He didn't want anything rousing the suspicion of those inside, including this kid.

A few seconds later, the guy had bled out and wasn't nearly so messy. Hacksaw dumped him in a trash bin, covering him with garbage. Someone would find him soon, so he didn't have much time to get the job done.

He walked around to the front entrance and went inside to find the master's woman.

Sibyl stumbled over her feet as she crossed her bedroom floor. She fell into the small table where she used to take tea, bumping her arm hard enough that it went numb for a moment.

She didn't fit in the little wooden chairs anymore. She was sure she'd grown more overnight, despite the fact that her mother's clothes still fit the same. The gray silk gown clung to her new curves, and no matter how long she looked at herself in the mirror, this body still seemed alien to her.

For centuries she'd wanted to grow up and be normal. She'd never thought that doing so would cause her to pay such a high price.

Sibyl hugged the porcelain doll to her chest and sat on the edge of her bed. She'd always been able to reach her sister, Maura, before. Even when she wasn't invited.

But now, even with the doll that looked like her sister to help strengthen the link, she couldn't get through. It was as if there was no one on the other end of the line—all she heard was silence.

She refused to believe that Maura had died. Sibyl would have known if she had.

Wouldn't she?

Cain knocked on her door. "I brought you food."

She opened her mouth to tell him to leave it outside as he'd been doing, but instead, she heard a tool rattle in the lock on her door.

Sibyl raced across the room to prevent him from opening it, but her clumsy body thwarted her. She didn't pick up her too-long feet far enough and ended up stubbing her toe. She tried to catch her balance, but that only made things worse.

She toppled forward, barely missing the edge of her dresser as she fell.

Her bedroom door opened and Cain stood there with a tray in his hands, staring for a long moment.

Then he dropped the tray and drew his sword. It became visible as he pointed it down at her, thrusting the tip toward her face. "Who are you and where the hell is Sibyl?"

She stayed there, frozen for a moment, trying to ignore the pain in her stubbed toes and wrists. They'd been taking a beating over the last few days as she struggled to adjust to her new size.

Slowly, so she wouldn't set him off, Sibyl pushed herself up. She kept her giant hands in sight and lifted her chin to look into his eyes. She was as tall as his shoulder now, when she'd always come only to his waist, and seeing him from this height was odd.

"I am Sibyl."

The tip of his sword dipped, then fell to his side. The look of shock on his face was almost comical. His dark green eyes widened and he leaned forward as if the distance was causing him to hallucinate.

"Sibyl?"

She nodded, feeling her hair sway around her thighs. It had grown as well, and she hadn't dared ask for scissors to cut it, fearing he'd get worried and barge in here.

Like he had just now. "I didn't want you to see me like this."

"You're a grown woman. How did this happen?"

A flutter of grief passed through her. She'd thought she'd grieved for her parents when she'd seen the vision of their deaths years ago, but the past few days had proven her wrong. Now, facing the man who'd seen to her protection for longer than her own father, she felt unwanted tears burning in her eyes.

She willed them away and straightened her spine. "I believe Gilda's death freed me from the prison of that child's body."

"How?"

"I can only guess, but I believe that whatever magic she wrought to keep Maura and me small was destroyed the night of her death."

"Your mother freed you?" said Cain, staring openly at her.

Sibyl had long since stopped referring to Gilda as her mother. Cain knew that and yet he persisted in constantly reminding her of their relationship. "Or simply confined me to a new prison. This body is defective."

"Defective? How?"

"I'm hungry all the time. I fall constantly. Look," she said, shoving up the too-short sleeves of the inherited gown. Dozens of bruises marred her arms. She raised the hem of her skirt, showing even more bruises on her shins. "This isn't normal."

"In days you've gone from a small child to an adult. There's bound to be adjustment issues."

"Perhaps," she allowed.

Cain recovered an apple from the discarded tray and wiped it on his sleeve. "Here. Eat this. I'll get you something else in a minute. But first you've got to tell me why you were hiding. I can understand how you wouldn't feel like celebrating, considering how this happened, but why would you hide it from me?"

Sibyl bit into the apple, unable to resist the offer of food. "I didn't feel like myself. I didn't want to worry you."

"Well, I was worried as hell, wondering if you were in here crying all day and night. At least this is something I can deal with."

He kept staring, his eyes going from the top of her head to her bare feet. She felt like some kind of zoo animal put on display. And that was with Cain—the man she trusted more than any other in the world. Once the others saw her, she was going to feel even worse.

"We need to get you some different clothes. Something that fits. And I need to tell Joseph. Your change has a lot of implications."

"Like what?"

"Like the fact that now that your body has caught up with your mind, you may be compatible with one of the men."

No. Sibyl wasn't ready for that. She'd lived as a child for hundreds of years. She wasn't willing to step from that directly into the role of wife. She needed some time. Some freedom.

"I don't want the men to know."

Cain frowned at her. "Of course they're going to know. Knowing will give them hope."

"No. I can't even walk across a room without tripping. Any man who sees me like this will coddle me. I can't stand the thought of being treated like a child. Ever again."

He nodded slowly, his lips flat in unhappy acceptance. "You can take the time you need to adjust, but this isn't something we can hide. You've had the mind of an adult for a long time. You know what we're up against."

"And I will take my place in the war. I will bind myself to a man and fight by his side. But not now. Not yet."

"Then when? And what will you do in the meantime?"

"I'm going to live. Finally. I've been alive for centuries, but I've never really lived my life on my terms. I've always been under the control of someone else. My parents. You."

He jerked back as if she'd struck him. "I didn't control you. I protected you as I would my own daughter."

"You watched over me day and night. You knew where I was all the time. You kept tabs on my life and the company I kept. I understand why you did it. I even accept that there was no other way, but that was when I was small. Weak."

"You're still weak," he pointed out.

"For now. But I'll get stronger every day. And I'm going to do it on my own."

"What do you mean?"

"I'm leaving Dabyr."

"Leaving . . . ? Are you crazy? Do you have any idea how dangerous that is?"

"I don't care. I've been a prisoner my whole life. I've thought about this for days, and I realize that as long as I stay here, I'll be treated like a child."

"Do you hear yourself? You've only thought about this for days. What's the rush? Your parents died. You haven't even processed that yet, haven't grieved. You need to stay where I can take care of you."

"No. I can't. If I do, my life will stay as it has been. I can't stand that, Cain. I need some space. Some freedom."

He turned away from her, peering through the lacy curtains. "Where will you go?"

"I don't know. Away from here."

"You won't be safe. What if your sister finds you?"

Sibyl didn't dare tell him that her powers were gone. He'd see that only as a further weakness and reason why she should stay caged. "I won't let her. I'll go somewhere safe. Perhaps one of the other strongholds."

When he turned back to her, his eyes were suspiciously shiny. "If anything happened to you, it would end me. I get that that's a terrible burden to lay at anyone's feet, but I have to be honest. I love you. I'll always love you. You've been my little girl for hundreds of years, and that's not something that goes away no matter how big you grow. You're always going to be a part of me."

Because Sibyl loved him, she refused to lie. "I love you, too. I promise I'll be careful."

Cain nodded. Sadness bowed his body as he turned toward the door. "I'll talk to Joseph. I'll make sure you get what you need."

Just like he always had.

Cain didn't know how he was going to stand losing Sibyl. Caring for her had been his greatest joy in life. And now she was leaving.

He couldn't blame her for wanting to go, but that didn't stop the mountain of grief he felt from crushing him.

His baby girl was leaving him. It didn't matter that she wasn't his biological child, or that she hadn't even really been a child for a long time. The only thing that mattered was that he'd felt like a father. And now she was taking that away.

He knew she'd always love him. He also knew that it was healthy for her to move out on her own, but after so many years, he wasn't sure if his heart could handle the shock.

He arranged for more food to be taken to their suite as he headed for Joseph's office. He wasn't sure how he was going to convince their leader to let an unbound female Theronai out on her own, but he had to find a way. Sibyl deserved to be happy. He wanted that for her more than he wanted anything. And if he had to fight Joseph to make it happen, then that's what he'd do.

A searing pain hit his chest, nearly knocking him over. It felt like something had stabbed him, and he jerked his shirt up to see what it was.

A trio of leaves fell from his lifemark, fluttering down over his skin as they fell.

Cain braced himself against the wall. He'd always had a healthy batch of leaves. His pain had always been manageable.

That had been Sibyl's doing. She'd needed him, and because of that, he'd stayed strong and solid.

She didn't need him anymore, and based on the proof gathering at the base of his lifemark, his soul knew it.

Chapter 17

"I saw two new faces today," said Sister Olive that night as she loaded blankets into the washing machine. "A man and a young woman. The man was asking some of the others about you. Do you know him?"

Hope stifled a yawn as she folded laundry. The easy, mundane chore helped soothe her nerves, giving her time to think. Fatigue grated against her eyes and ached in her joints.

She'd finished her last appointment and closed up shop early, leaving Jodi to her work. The whole day had oozed by in a fog of fatigue and frustration and she needed to get out and clear her head.

She wasn't sure if she was going to see Logan again or not. She tried to convince herself that having him out of her life was for the best, but she couldn't quite choke down that lie.

"I didn't see a man. I only saw the young woman," she told Sister Olive. "The pretty one with the dark, frightened eyes. The one in the too-small clothes." Not only had they been too small, they'd also been slutty, like something a streetwalker would wear. That coupled with the fear screaming through her aura made Hope wonder what had happened to the poor girl.

"I found her something that fits in the donation box. And I called Dr. Oakes to see if she could stop by for a visit."

"You think she was abused," said Hope. She'd thought

the same thing when she'd seen the small, black-eyed woman stumble in here as if dazed.

"Dr. Oakes will be the judge of that. We'll get her any help she might need."

Hope stacked a folded towel onto the pile. "Do you think she'll stay that long?"

Sister Olive shrugged. "I don't know. We can only pray she does."

"Do you want me to talk to her?"

"No. I think she's too skittish for that. Give her some space and we'll let Dr. Oakes approach her."

Hope nodded. "I'm sorry I haven't been here as much lately."

"Child, I'm surprised you stuck around this long. Your business is growing. You need to nurture it like a plant or it'll die on the vine."

"My business is fine. And I like being here. You're my family. Besides, I seem to be the only one around here that's convinced people are going missing."

Sister Olive smoothed stray strands of iron gray hair behind her ear and gave Hope a hard stare. "People come and go. You know that as well as I do. If you go out there trying to keep tabs on everyone, you're going to scare them away."

"What if you're wrong? What if this feeling I have is right and they're out there, hoping someone will save them?"

"You plan to save them?"

"Why not?"

"Don't you think that's a bit dangerous? You need to leave that kind of work to the police."

"They're doing what they can," said Hope, repeating what the cops had told her over and over.

Sister Olive abandoned the laundry and gave Hope a tight hug. "Don't you dare get yourself hurt. I don't know what I'd do without you."

"I'll be fine."

"You're going out again tonight, aren't you?"

Hope nodded. "I have to. I can't sit around and do nothing."

Sister Olive gave her a maternal smile. "I understand. You have a calling you need to answer. I won't stop you."

That was good, because while Hope desperately wanted Sister Olive's blessing, she knew she'd continue on her chosen path even without it. She didn't need anyone's approval to do what she thought was right. Not Sister Olive's and certainly not Logan's.

Tynan had done what he could for Grace and was on his way out to finally meet Logan when Nika stopped him in his path. Her white hair and pale skin made her blue eyes stand out in stark contrast. She was dressed from head to toe in black leather, and Tynan would have bet his fangs that Madoc had made sure it was imbued with the strongest protective wards the Sentinels had to offer.

"You have to do something," she said, hands on her hips, her booted feet braced apart.

"I am doing something. You're getting in my way."

"You have to do something about Tori," she clarified. "She's slipping away."

"I saw her last night. She's suffering, but she's not getting any worse. I've done all I can."

"She is getting worse." Nika frowned in confusion, shaking her head. "I can't touch her mind much anymore. She keeps me out. But sometimes, I get a glimpse of her thoughts and they're not healthy. She's consumed with thoughts of revenge."

"I'd say that's good. She needs something to work toward, and while I'd rather she be pushing herself to become well enough to take her place among the Theronai, I won't complain about her choice of motivation. So long as she stays motivated."

"Your efforts to clean her blood have failed."

"I can only do so much for her at a time. You have no idea how exhausting—how painful—it is to fight back the taint that's in her."

Nika stripped off her leather jacket and tossed it on the floor. She shoved up her sleeve and offered him her delicate, pale arm. "Go ahead. Chow down."

Tynan shook his head and backed up a step. Not only would Madoc kill him—again—if he touched her, he didn't want her blood inside him. It would give her too much power, allowing her to see into his thoughts.

Tynan had far too many secrets to keep to let that happen. His as well as those of others he'd fed from. "No, thanks. I'm on my way to meet Logan. He'll give me what I need."

"You're not leaving. Not with Tori like this."

Frustration grated along his nerves. He knew better than to let it out on Nika, but the urge to vent at someone was nearly overwhelming. "I've been stuck here for days, taking care of both your sister as well as Grace, who is, by the way, much worse off than Tori. I have done everything within my power to see to it that they both recover. Logan has found a new source of power, and if you value your sister's life, you will step out of my way and let me pass."

"Not until you promise me you'll fix her."

Tynan had no idea what kind of control a promise like that would hold over him, so he refused. "You're only standing in the way of what you want most. Please, step aside."

"Is there a problem?" boomed a deep voice from behind Tynan.

Madoc.

Tynan's neck tensed involuntarily. Madoc had broken it only days earlier, and it was going to take a lot longer than that for Tynan to forget.

He spun around to face the warrior. "Nika has decided I should take her blood rather than go out hunting for it. I was explaining to her that you would not approve."

"The leech is right," said Madoc. "He's not getting another fucking drop of your blood, Nika."

Nika glared at Tynan. "He's leaving. Tori is still sick and he's going to walk away. We can't let him do that."

Madoc picked up her jacket and draped it over her slender shoulders. With a touch so gentle that Tynan wasn't even sure Madoc was capable of it, he lifted Nika's chin. "He's been busting his ass, love. I know you're worried. We all are, but what's wrong with Tori is going to take time to fix."

Nika's eyes flooded with tears. "She's in pain. I have to find a way to make it stop."

Madoc pulled her against his body, wrapping his thick arms around her. He held her head against his shoulder, smoothing her hair with comforting strokes.

He looked at Tynan over Nika's head. "Is there anything else you can do?"

"The only thing left is to put her to sleep while we work on driving the Synestryn blood from her system. I offered her the option and she refused."

"We'll talk to her about it. If she agrees, will you do it?"

"As soon as I return," said Tynan. "But I need to go now."

"Go," said Madoc. "We'll talk to Tori."

"If anything happens while I'm away, Alexander is here at Dabyr tonight. I'll try to be back before sunrise."

"We're not going to let anything happen," said Madoc, more to Nika than to Tynan. "We'll take good care of Tori while you're gone."

After dinner, Hacksaw saw the blond woman dart through the swinging door that led to the kitchen. She had her coat on like she was leaving.

He couldn't let her get away. The master would not be pleased if he failed to bring the woman back. Alive. He had to remind himself of that part so he didn't accidentally mess up and kill her, no matter how much easier it would be.

He didn't dare follow her out the back way for fear of being noticed. Instead he hurried through the growing crowd of stinking men, out the front, and ran around the side of the building to intercept her.

She moved between buildings fast, huddled against the cold. She had a bag slung over her shoulder, which meant he had to be cautious of weapons. She didn't look to be the sort to shoot him, but anything was possible.

The switchblade in his pocket grew cold, reminding him that it was there, waiting to be used. It had been a long time since he'd killed a woman, but he could still remember how easily the knife slid into her soft skin. And that look of fear on her face had been better than any drug he'd ever used.

It wasn't as good as a word of praise from the master, but it was close.

The woman turned a corner, disappearing from sight. Hacksaw hurried to catch up to her, unwilling to lose sight of her for even a minute.

She was behind buildings now—out of sight of the street and passing cars. It wasn't dark yet, but that was too bad. He'd have to risk attacking her in what was left of the daylight. No one was out in this cold, anyway. All he had to do was knock her out, tie her up, and drive his car back here and dump her in it. He'd be back to the master in time for him to wake and see the gift Hacksaw had brought him.

The rest of the night he'd spend basking in the master's praise.

A shiver of anticipation raced down his spine. He couldn't make that happen fast enough. He had to act. Now. Get the woman and get his reward.

He was only a few yards behind her now. As quietly as he could, he broke into a run.

She glanced over her shoulder. Saw him. Her eyes widened with fear and she froze for a second before she sprinted away.

Hacksaw followed at a dead run.

Cold air sawed in and out of his lungs, but did nothing

to cool his blood. He loved the chase. He was going to love catching her even more.

She was fast, but he was gaining on her. He'd have her before she cleared the next corner.

Panic pounded through Hope's blood. The man chasing her was a killer. She could see it in the bleak, empty spots in his aura. Black surrounded them, like the rotting edge of a wound. He looked human, and maybe he was, but not completely. He'd been touched by something dark and malevolent. Infected.

She sprinted, sucking in huge gulps of frigid air. Her feet slipped on the ice. She cursed herself for not calling Nicholas to come with her. It was an hour until dark. She thought she'd be safe until the sun went down.

The man chasing her proved her wrong.

Hope fumbled for her cell phone. Nicholas's number was programmed on speed dial as he'd insisted. Her gloves made the phone slippery, but she didn't dare take the time to strip them off.

She tried to punch Nicholas's number, but her gloves got in the way and she pressed too many buttons.

The phone bobbed in her vision and she couldn't focus on it, so she went by the feel of the buttons, hoping she remembered right.

Before she could hit send, something hard slammed into her from behind. The phone spun out of her grasp. She landed hard on the icy pavement, hitting her chin. Her teeth snapped together. Her head spun and confusion swamped her.

She couldn't figure out what she was doing on the ground, especially in this cold.

Hope was flipped over. A man hovered over her. His teeth were locked together in a snarl. His bottom lip was scarred, as if someone had sliced it open and it had healed crookedly. A scraggly beard hid his jaw and a feral light burned in his gaze.

"Got you," he growled at her. "The master will be pleased."

Hope didn't know who or what he was talking about. She'd never seen this man before. She would have remembered his rotting aura if she had.

Blood seeped from her chin, cooling as it ran along her neck. She tried to say something that would stop him, but her mouth seemed to be frozen shut. Whether from the fall or from fear she wasn't sure, but nothing was working right. She couldn't figure out how to fix it.

The man balled up his fist. Hope realized he was going to hit her and she tried to fight him. She shoved with her arms and legs, but not fast enough. That beefy fist flew toward her. The impact registered for a split second and then everything went away.

Logan was jarred from a deep sleep. Something was wrong.

His hand jerked to the dagger sitting next to him as he prepared to defend himself. He surveyed the back of his van, looking for signs of an intruder, but there were none. He was parked inside a locked, rented storage unit, and there were no signs that sunlight had breached his hiding place.

He felt a flash of fear, followed by a sharp pain. Instantly, he knew the sensations weren't his, but belonged to someone close to him. Someone with whom he'd shared blood.

Tynan? Alexander?

Logan closed his eyes and concentrated. He sought out the source of that fear, hoping to feel it again now that he was alert enough to study it.

He felt nothing.

Perhaps it was a dream? That seemed unlikely. He rarely dreamed, though he had yesterday. He'd dreamed of Hope, of feeling her body tensing beneath his as she climaxed. He'd dreamed of her pleasure, of the soft sounds she made and the way she'd dug her fingernails into his back. He'd dreamed of her taking his blood, of accepting him and claiming him for her own.

Just the memory of that dream was enough to make him painfully hard. He didn't have time to be distracted by lust. He had to determine what had woken him.

He closed his eyes, pulling his power around him. He let some of it fly out in a wave, like a ripple on a pond.

The magical disturbance bounced some of that energy back, and with it came the scent of Hope's fear.

She was being attacked.

Rage detonated deep inside him, giving his weak body strength. The sun was still up, but he refused to let that stop him. Hope needed him. He had to go to her.

He shoved his dagger into his coat pocket and briefly considered the folly of his actions. If even a single ray of sunlight touched his skin, he'd summon one of the Solarc's Wardens—the powerful, deadly warriors that enforced the Solarc's curse upon the Sanguinar. Not only would the Warden cut Logan down for allowing the sun to touch his skin, but it would take with it anyone else in sight. The Wardens had no emotion. They felt nothing. They were programmed to kill, and would continue to do so until they were destroyed.

He had to be careful. He had to be sure that did not happen.

Logan found his protective clothing. He covered every inch of his skin, donning a mask and gloves, then sped out of the storage facility where he'd parked his van to sleep away the daylight.

The sun glared at him, as if detesting his presence. It was low on the horizon, but even so, Logan felt it draining his strength.

He concentrated on the part of Hope that was inside him, allowing it to lead him toward her. He couldn't tell how far away she was, but what he did know was she was alive and he was going to do everything in his power to make sure she stayed that way.

The van's engine screamed as he sped through the

streets. He'd stayed near Hope's home, unable to make himself go too far away from her. It was a silly notion to want to sleep near her, but one he'd been unwilling to resist.

Her pull on him intensified, telling him he was getting close. He took a turn too fast, his van lurching over the curb as it hit. A horn behind him blared at his mistake. Not that he cared.

He sped down the side street only blocks from the shelter. This part of town was run-down, having been mostly abandoned for the brighter, cleaner parts of town.

Another hard turn brought him to a private drive that had once been delivery access for several of the surrounding buildings. Now it was a dumping ground for old couches and rusted appliances. A toppled water heater barred his path, forcing him to skid to a stop.

He rushed out of the van, following the delicate connection he had to Hope through her blood.

When he rounded the corner and saw a man loading her limp body into the trunk of a car, he realized he hadn't considered what he'd do once he found her.

Rage gathered like a storm inside him. He felt it crackle along his skin. Even with the sun weakening him, feral power roared through him.

How dare someone hurt Hope? How dare they touch her, dumping her body in a trunk like so much dirty laundry?

He was silent as he approached. The car was running. The man had accessed this area via another street, giving him the ability to escape by car if Logan didn't stop him.

Logan was definitely going to stop him.

He gathered up some of his power, waiting for that bastard's hands to be off of Logan's woman. As soon as he laid her body down and stood straight, Logan struck.

He hurled that power out, slamming the man into the back wall of a brick building. His head hit with an audible thunk; then he crumpled to the dirty ground.

Logan hurried to the back of the car. Hope was curled up so she fit. Blood smeared over her face and neck.

Some of his rage burst free in the form of a bellow. The man who'd done this to his Hope was going to die. If he hadn't already. But first he had to get her to safety.

Logan gathered her in his arms and lifted her from the trunk. He couldn't heal her easily here. He needed to touch her skin, and if he bared his, he risked summoning one of the Solarc's Wardens. If that happened, both he and Hope were dead.

He had to get her into his van where he could tend her.

Hope's head was limp against his shoulder. He could hear her breathing and heartbeat, but he wasn't going to be satisfied until she was whole and awake, looking at him with those beautiful golden eyes.

As soon as he knew she was going to be okay, he'd go back for the unconscious man lying in the trash. And drain him dry.

Logan laid Hope in the back of his van, pulled the curtain and door shut, and then removed his gloves and mask. The smell of Hope's blood caused an odd combination of anger and hunger to roil in his stomach. For now, he couldn't act on either.

He smoothed her hair away from her face and soaked up the warmth of her skin. While he would have enjoyed stroking her until she woke, he resisted the urge and focused on his task.

He let his power slide inside her, seeking out her injuries and knitting them shut. He closed her skin, being careful not to leave behind a scar. It took more energy to work slowly, but he couldn't stand the thought of marring her perfect skin.

The small fracture in her jaw was harder to heal. But even that was nothing compared to the bruising inside her skull. He did what he could to heal her, but there was too much damage for him to finish the task as weak as he was. He made sure she was stabilized and retreated from her body.

He was shaking with effort. The sun was setting, but not down all the way. It bore down on him, sucking his strength, making every task ten times as hard.

He covered his skin again and moved to the front of the van. Nearby buildings shaded them from the last rays of sunlight, making it safe for him to open the door.

Logan went back to the human garbage lying on the ground and stared long and hard at the man who dared hurt his woman.

No. Not Logan's woman. He couldn't think of her like that. Just because he was drawn to her did not mean he could stake a claim. He had to stay objective. Distance himself.

With her lying in the back of his van, that was an impossible task. The need to tear her attacker apart and drain him dry of blood pounded on Logan, demanding he take repayment for the injustice done to her.

Logan dragged the man deeper into the shadows and lifted his mask over his mouth. He craned the man's head back at a brutal angle and bit deep.

The taste of rotting filth filled his mouth. Logan jerked back, vomiting the tainted blood onto the ground.

Dorjan. This man was filled with Synestryn blood, protecting him from Logan's hunger.

Logan's body fought to purge him of every last bit of that vile blood. He struggled against the nausea that roiled in his stomach and the dizziness that spun his head.

The blood that flowed through that man's veins was strong. The Synestryn that had infected him was powerful. Even now, Logan could feel the demon stirring, waking. If he didn't rid himself of every last drop, the demon might be able to sense his presence, or even possibly read his thoughts.

Logan thrust up a mental wall to surround his mind. He kept his thoughts light, inconsequential. He didn't look at his surroundings or allow any other image that might identify his location to pass by his eyes.

He gathered up the tainted blood that had escaped and forced it up his throat and into his mouth. He spat the rest onto the ground. It oozed toward him, and he scrambled back, avoiding its touch.

The man who'd stolen Hope moved behind Logan, rising to his feet. Dark red blood seeped down his neck where Logan had bitten him. The man's eyes were wild, but filled with an uncanny intelligence.

"I see you," said the man, though his voice echoed with an eerie hollowness.

That wasn't the human who spoke. It was the voice of the Synestryn who controlled him.

Logan wasn't strong enough for a battle of wills. Not while the sun was still up. Not when Hope needed every bit of his strength to heal her.

The human lurched forward, his legs moving awkwardly as if controlled by a puppeteer.

Logan scrambled to his feet and backed away. He needed to get back to Hope and get both of them out of here.

The human moved faster than should have been possible. He dropped to a crouch and sprang at Logan, teeth bared.

Logan tried to dodge, but his body was heavy with fatigue. Both the poisoned blood and the last bit of daylight served to weaken him until he was barely able to stand upright, much less combat an attack.

The man's weight plowed into him, knocking him to the ground. Logan's head hit the pavement, and he was stunned for a second. Something cold and hard slid over his back, and it took him a moment to realize that he was being dragged across the ground.

Toward the last, dying rays of sunlight streaming between the buildings.

Logan tried to clear his head enough to figure out a way to stop his slow, deadly progress toward the light. His hands were clumsy. His mind was clouded and slow.

He remembered his spare dagger, which he'd slid into

his coat pocket earlier. He pulled it out and swiped at the man's arm, slicing him deep. Dark blood poured from the wound, but the man didn't slow or even show signs that he'd been hit.

The human was no longer controlling his body. His master was behind the wheel.

Dirty concrete slid under Logan as he was dragged closer to the sunlight.

He stabbed again. This time his blade hit bone and stuck.

The man lifted him up with his other hand and shoved him the last few inches into the light. Sunlight hit his chin, which was bare from his earlier attempt to feed.

The air around them shuddered and groaned as a portal was ripped open. Searing light burned Logan's eyes. The ground shook and a horrible tearing sound deafened him.

The human turned and fled. Logan's dagger clattered to the ground. He scooped it up, even though he knew it would likely do no good against a Warden.

The light died down just as Logan regained his footing. He didn't dare waste even a second looking to see if one of the Solarc's enforcers had appeared. He knew one had.

And if he didn't get back to his van and drive her away, Hope would be slain.

Chapter 18

Joseph rubbed his eyes. The headache that had become his nearly constant companion was back with a vengeance. Ever since that meeting with Andreas, it had been getting worse.

The stress of leadership was getting to him. He wasn't cut out for this job. He'd never asked for it. It was just pure, dumb luck that had his people thinking he was the right choice to lead them.

It hadn't exactly worked out well.

Gilda and Angus were dead. Jackie refused to choose one of his men despite the fact that she seemed to be compatible with all of them. Whatever had happened to her in those caves had left deep scars, and Joseph had no idea if or when they would heal enough for her to take her rightful place in the war against the Synestryn.

Joseph couldn't even bring himself to ask Tori to search for her partner among the Theronai. She was still a kid, and the things she'd suffered were not the kinds of things that led a woman to trust a man. Ever. She needed time to heal—years of time they didn't have.

Torr's paralysis was gone, but the man refused to go out and fight. He was glued to Grace's side, watching her die slowly. There was nothing any of the Sanguinar could do to save her, and they'd wasted precious resources trying.

The human women and children they'd rescued from a Synestryn nest a couple of weeks ago were not adjusting well to their freedom. The kids had nightmares. One of the women had killed herself three days ago, and Tynan had suggested that more may follow in her footsteps. He'd put all of them on suicide watch.

Demons were closing in around them. Some of them had human faces—something Joseph knew would cause even the coldest Theronai to hesitate in battle. Their vows to protect humans ran deep and the Synestryn were using it against them.

Things were falling apart. Even with the discovery of Theronai women in the world, they'd only found a few—not enough to turn the tide of war. His men lost more leaves every day, putting each of them closer to death. He'd had to sentence Chris to death only days ago, and he spent too much time wondering who would be next.

He had to do something—anything—to give his people hope.

Perhaps Andreas's offer was the key to that hope.

Joseph had talked to several of his most trusted men, along with Tynan, who spoke for all the Sanguinar. They all agreed that ending the stagnant war with the Slayers—believing it wasn't a trick—was a risk they had to take.

If it was a trick, at least Joseph wouldn't have to worry about his headaches anymore.

He left his office and went to the dining hall where Andreas had been spending his time, out in the open, very publicly. It was like the man was trying to make a point that he had nothing to hide, which made Joseph nervous.

Still, reports indicated that the human children were drawn to him. Madoc had even gone so far as to tell them to stay away, but as soon as his back was turned, the kids came back, begging Andreas to play a game with them.

Kids were good judges of character. They had no idea what was at stake or what Andreas was trying to do. They just knew that a new guy had come to play with them and break up some of the monotony of life at Dabyr. They weren't afraid of him.

That went a long way in Joseph's book.

He found Andreas sitting on the floor in front of a TV, playing some kind of racing video game. One of the little girls they'd found in the caves with Jackie was racing him and he was doing a good job of not being obvious about letting her win.

"We need to talk," said Joseph.

Andreas handed his controller to another child and stood up. The children grabbed onto his legs, begging him to stay. "I'll be back in a few minutes. We just have a little boring grown-up stuff to do."

He extracted himself from the children and gave Joseph a level stare. "I hope you have good news for me."

Joseph led him to a table at the far side of the dining area. He'd spotted at least four of his men nearby, keeping watch on Andreas, and there were several more out in the courtyard, working out. If things turned ugly, help would be here in seconds.

Carmen sat only two tables away, typing on her laptop. He knew she was taking online classes, but had no idea which ones. She'd hardly spoken to him since he'd claimed her as his daughter, thinking he was doing so out of pity rather than honoring the memory of their fallen brother-in-arms, Thomas.

Thomas's dying wish was that Joseph claim her as kin, and Joseph was honor bound to uphold that wish. But Carmen was human. She didn't understand their ways, and had yet to come around and forgive him for doing what was right.

Maybe she never would.

"Where is your sister?" he asked. Joseph hadn't seen a single glimpse of Lyka since their arrival.

"She's in our suite, pouting."

Joseph couldn't imagine her doing anything quite so petulant, though he could easily see her lower lip all full and begging for a kiss.

The wayward thought shocked him and he shoved the image away, putting his head firmly in the game.

"Have you decided?" asked Andreas, his body tense with anticipation.

"I have. I agree to a truce with your people."

Andreas blew out a long, relieved breath. "Thank you, Joseph. You won't regret your decision."

"Not so fast. You need to understand that our truce is in your hands. We will not attack you first. If provoked, we will defend ourselves."

Andreas thrust out his hand. "Good," he said as Joseph and he shook. "That is all I ask."

"If any of your people break this truce, there will not be another."

"I understand. They won't. We want peace as much as you do."

"I hope you're right," said Joseph. "Your people are prone to violence. It's in their blood."

"So is obedience. They will do as I say, or they will challenge me for the right to lead our people in a different direction."

Joseph had heard about their customs, how their leader was chosen through combat. Andreas would have had to beat dozens of challengers for the right to lead his people. Which meant he was one tough son of a bitch.

Andreas rubbed his hands together in eagerness. "Excellent. Now all we need to do is settle the formalities of our bargain."

"Formalities?"

The Slayer frowned like he didn't understand why Joseph was confused. "Of course. I'm leaving Lyka here to guarantee my trust; now I need the same from you. Who have you chosen to come with me?"

Outrage flooded Joseph's blood. His voice rose, drawing the attention of people nearby. "You want me to give you a hostage?"

Carmen turned and looked at them. From behind him, Joseph heard the rasp of steel on steel as one of his men freed his sword. Apparently, his voice had carried farther than he'd intended.

He held up his hand, signaling his men to stop.

"That is the way these things are done," said Andreas, as if his request was perfectly reasonable.

"That's not the way *we* do things."

"I already told you that we're following the old ways. You keep my sister and I keep yours. It's a civilized tradition, and tradition is the only thing keeping peace among my people now. I would have hoped you'd see that."

"You can rule however you choose. But once your traditions start involving my people, they've gone too far. Even if I had a sister, which I don't, I wouldn't send her with you."

Andreas's jaw tightened. "I can see my work here is not yet done. Perhaps you'd allow us to stay for a while and give you time to get used to the idea."

"You can stay here for a century and I'm still not going to give you one of my people. It's just not going to happen."

"You don't know me. I get that. But I can't go back to my people empty-handed and expect them to go along with this. I can show no sign of weakness."

"Are you revoking your offer of peace?"

"No, I'm asking you for a show of good faith. If you can't do that . . ."

Carmen shoved her chair back and came to their table. She glared at Joseph, and then said to Andreas, "I'm his daughter. Take me."

An awful, ear-grating, tearing sound woke Hope. It sounded like a giant had ripped a Mack truck in two with its bare hands. Searing light burned her eyes, even through her closed lids. As soon as the flash faded, she forced her eyes open so she could look out of the open van doors.

The first thing she saw was Logan sprinting toward

her. His gaunt face twisted in fear and his lips parted around a shouted order she couldn't understand. He was several yards away. His leather coat was flapping behind him like a cape. He held a big, bloody knife in one hand, and for a split second, she was afraid of what he'd done.

And then her focus shifted to the thing behind him—the thing he was running from.

It was beautiful. It gleamed with an internal light that surrounded it almost like an aura, but not quite. Shaped like a heavily muscled man, it was easily eight feet tall, made from what looked like shards of ice or crystal. It held a transparent sword in each fist, and the blades were so thin they seemed to disappear when the angle was right.

If it had been still, she would have sworn it was a work of art, perfectly sculpted into the shape of an ideal male. But it wasn't still. It moved like water, gliding over the pavement on bare feet. She could see the grime of the street through it, and was suddenly embarrassed that it was seeing her world so dirty.

There was no question that this thing was from another world. It was far too beautiful to be earthly—so beautiful it made even Logan seem plain in comparison.

Hope blinked and felt tears spill onto her cheeks and cool in the frigid air.

"Go!" shouted Logan, pulling her from her trance.

She didn't understand why he'd want to leave such a thing of beauty behind. It belonged in a museum or in an art gallery, on display for all to see.

And then it struck. One of its paper thin swords sliced through the air and the trailing length of Logan's leather coat was sheared off.

It was trying to kill him.

Shock trilled through her, spiking her adrenaline. Her heart kicked against her ribs, and her body broke into clumsy movement. She didn't know what she was going to do, but she had to move.

"Drive!" screamed Logan, his voice fading. He was

only a few yards away, but she couldn't leave without him.

Hope scrambled into the driver's seat and started the engine. She felt the van bounce as Logan's weight landed in back. She put it in gear and hit the accelerator.

The tires squealed as they slipped on the icy street. The back doors of the van were still open, and in the rearview mirror she could see the crystalline man lift both of its blades to strike.

Smoke poured out of the back as the tires spun; then, finally, the van jumped forward as it gained some traction.

It was then that Hope realized that there was nowhere to go. Ahead of her stood a brick building. The alley running along it, both to her right and left, was barred with junk. The only way out was through that junk, or backward. Where the giant, armed, ice man lurked.

"Hold on," she yelled as the front bumper rammed into an old water heater.

She heard Logan grunt in pain. The water heater spun sideways. The right tire went over something it shouldn't have and exploded.

Hope lost her grip on the wheel for a second, but the loss of control was long enough that they came precariously close to ramming into the brick building.

Which gave her an idea. Whatever that thing was made of—glass, crystal, ice—it was bound not to like being smooshed into a hard wall.

Hope spun the wheel hard, making the van screech about in a half circle. Something hit the inside wall of the van and she wondered if it was Logan's head. She winced at the thought, but held the wheel firm.

Looming in front of her, as tall as the van, was the crystalline man. His swords were raised to strike.

Time slowed. Hope gunned the engine. The thing sliced downward. Its swords ripped through the van's hood like it was tin foil. The engine died, but the van's momentum carried it into the creature, pinning it against a wall.

One of its swords snapped off, giving her hope that she might have actually defeated it. Then it held the broken stub of its sword aloft and the sounds of wind chimes and cracking ice filled the air. New crystals grew, forming a fresh blade in a matter of seconds.

A strong hand grabbed her arm. "We must go," said Logan.

He pulled her from the seat toward the back of the van. The ground beneath her shifted and she lost her balance. Logan held her up as the crystalline man kicked the van away from the wall to free itself.

Logan's grip was tight, keeping her on her feet. They jumped out and he pulled her toward the closest building.

With one hard hit from his shoulder, the locked door caved in. He pushed her inside. "It will follow. We need to find a defensible position."

"Does it have a weakness?"

"Blunt force. Lots of it."

"I rammed it into a wall with a van. If that doesn't kill it, what will?"

"A wrecking ball would be nice." Logan urged her forward into the vacant building. It smelled of sawdust and fresh paint. Shiny new cubicle walls showed that this place was being remodeled. Blue wires dangled from the ceiling and stacks of carpet tiles sat neatly in one corner. Toward the front of the building, near the lobby, the ceiling opened up to create an airy foyer. Several large windows let in what was left of the daylight.

Despite their dire situation, Hope was still impressed by the remodeling job. Sadly, it was devoid of any wrecking balls. "I don't see anything like that here. Do you?"

"Hide," he ordered. "I'll hold it off while you get away."

"I'm not leaving you."

They wove through the cubicles until they found the

front exit of the building. A hard vibration shook the walls.

"The Warden is here," said Logan. "Go."

"Not until you tell me how you're going to kill it."

"I'll think of something." He looked up at the impressive two-story entrance. "Perhaps drop something heavy on its head as it passes."

He shoved the front door open, cracking the glass with the force of breaking the lock. Then he pushed her through the opening. "Run. Hide."

Logan turned his back on her, crouched, and jumped up. She saw him cling to the railing of the walkway above, and then he disappeared from sight.

Through the cracked glass, she saw a cleanly severed cubicle wall fly across the room.

As strong as Logan was, he was no match for that thing. And neither was she.

Logan waited until the last second. The Warden lumbered into view in the foyer below, its wicked blades slicing the air as it searched for prey.

A harmonic hum filled the air, the sound beautiful and deadly.

As soon as he had a clear view, Logan hefted the tile saw over the edge of the railing and tossed it at the Warden's head.

It spun around, striking out at the projectile. The saw was halved by the Warden's blade, but one of those halves struck home, taking a chunk of its shoulder with it.

The musical sound of growing crystal rose up as the Warden began to heal itself.

It looked up. Its transparent eyes fixed on Logan. A white light of recognition flared. Shards sprouted from its toes and forearms. It went to the nearest wall and began crawling up it, using those shards to dig deep and propel itself upward.

Logan backed away from the railing and darted along the catwalk.

Below, he saw a flash of movement and honey blond hair.

Hope. She'd come back in to help him.

Fear and rage pooled in his stomach. With every second that passed, the sun sank farther below the horizon, giving him strength. He was a long way from his best, but he'd find a way to kill that Warden and save Hope. There was no other option. He couldn't let this creature loose on a city full of unsuspecting humans.

Especially Hope. She was precious.

Logan heard footsteps behind the stairwell door. On his right, the Warden vaulted over the railing and headed for Logan at a dead run.

The stairwell door opened. "Here!" shouted Hope, holding the door open for his escape.

There was no time to argue. He darted through the door and grabbed her arm as he passed. He started to drag her down, but she resisted.

"Up. I have an idea."

Logan went with it, simply because fighting her would waste seconds they didn't have. He'd stash her on one of the upper floors and continue on without her.

Even if he had to knock her out.

"We'll push it off the roof," she panted as they ran up the stairs.

That might work. He wasn't sure how many stories tall this building was, but it was possible the impact would kill it.

The scream of bending metal and wind chimes rose up from below, getting closer. If they kept up this pace, the Warden would catch up with them before they reached the top of the next floor.

Logan slammed his shoulder into the door leading to the sixth floor. More signs of construction showed up here, though it hadn't progressed as far as on the first floor. The elevator shaft was easy to spot.

He ran for it and jabbed the up button, hoping it was

functional. Surely, they hadn't been carrying all these construction supplies up the stairs.

Lights over the door moved as the elevator car slid toward them.

Through the window in the stairwell door one transparent eye gleamed. It saw them.

Hope stabbed the up button. He could smell her fear, and the need to protect her from it rose up in him, roaring with the need for violence.

The stairwell door exploded inward. It flew across the room, gouging a deep scratch in the concrete floor.

Hope let out a frightened breath. "Oh God."

The elevator doors opened with a cheerful chime. Logan backed her inside with his body. He hit the button for the top floor, then the close-doors button. He waited until the doors began closing, and then darted out through the opening, knowing the Warden would come after the closest target.

The sun was down, but the last lingering glow on the horizon made everything he did harder. With his strength hampered, he was going to have only one chance to trick the Warden and shove him out through a window.

The Warden charged. Logan waited until the last second to duck behind the brick-and-steel-encased elevator shaft.

Crystal blades swung at him, lodging deep in the wall, their tips only inches from Logan's face. While the Warden struggled to pull them free, Logan sprinted to one of the large floor-to-ceiling windows. The wet street six stories down gleamed under streetlights that had just begun to flicker to life.

He picked up a drill lying nearby and swung it by the cord, smashing out the window.

The Warden freed itself and turned. It saw Logan and let out a howl that sounded like shattering glass. Its feet slipped on the floor as it gathered speed.

Logan stood in front of the open window, his feet

braced. He focused inward, collecting sparks of power as he wrung them from his blood cells.

The glow of sunset behind him seemed to burn his back, but he ignored it. There was no time for pain now.

The Warden's crystalline muscles bunched and it lunged for Logan. Logan dodged. The Warden flew out the window. Logan turned to watch it fall, to be sure it shattered on impact.

The Warden was right there, clinging to the window frame.

Logan heard its swords shatter as they hit the pavement below. Too late, he realized his mistake.

The Warden grabbed Logan's arm and hurled him out of the window.

The feeling of free fall registered as his arms and legs flailed to find purchase. There was nothing to catch himself on. He was between buildings, dropping like a stone.

Above him, he saw Hope's head peek out over the edge of the rooftop. Her eyes widened and her mouth opened around a scream of horror and loss.

"No!" she shouted.

The Warden's head craned around, looking up at Hope, and through its transparent skull, Logan could see its eyes glow with the sight of its next victim.

Chapter 19

Hope stared in shock as Logan's body fell. An unnatural wind whipped around her head, sending her hair into a frenzy. She swiped it out of her face in time to see Logan hit.

She flinched and a cry of denial was ripped from her mouth by the wind. Tears stung her eyes as she stared down, hoping for a miracle.

For a second, she thought she saw him move, but that was just wishful thinking. He couldn't have survived a fall like that.

The crystalline monster that Logan had called a Warden stuck to the side of the building like a spider. It looked up at her. Light poured from its eyes as it began climbing the wall, right for her.

Rage and grief flooded her system, making her fingers curl into fists. That thing had killed Logan. She was going to kill it.

She scanned the rooftop, searching for some kind of weapon. A pipe. A two-by-four. Something.

There was nothing up here but an air handling unit.

The Warden crawled over the edge. It had lost its swords somewhere along the way, but she could see a new growth of crystals beginning in its fists. It was growing new ones.

Hope couldn't let that happen. She had to strike now, while she could. Once it had its weapons back, it would slice her in two before she could even get close enough to kick it in the shin.

She didn't want to die, but she didn't see any other choice. She had to knock it off the roof and send it careening to the pavement below.

She'd catch herself at the last second if she could, but she didn't think that would be possible.

The brief ten years of her life—those she could remember—flashed through her mind. Of them, the brightest memories were those she'd shared with Logan. She wondered if she'd see him again in whatever afterlife awaited her, or if the only thing waiting was the deep black void that mirrored her forgotten past.

Either way, her decision was made. There was no time for regrets or second thoughts. The Warden had to die before it could kill anyone else.

Hope let loose all of her rage and fear, channeling it into her legs. They propelled her forward over the tarry roof. Strength poured through her limbs like it had when she'd carried those men up the steps.

She screamed and jumped up, hitting the Warden in its chest.

It swiped at her, but its blades had not yet finished growing back. It missed and jerked back.

The Warden teetered. Hope threw her weight up and back, grabbing its head to throw it off balance. The slight shift worked. The Warden fell backward, the back of its knees catching on the ledge.

Its arms spun in the air as it tried to regain its balance. There was nothing to hold on to and it fell, going headfirst over the edge.

Hope scrambled to grab the ledge, but it was too late. It was too far away and getting farther with every microsecond.

Ten stories down, the ground waited for her.

"Like hell!" Joseph shouted at Carmen. "You're not going anywhere with a Slayer."

"Why not?" she asked, her hands on her hips, her stance belligerent. "It makes perfect sense. Unless of course I don't mean enough to you to serve as a hostage."

"Of course you do. And you really shouldn't be offering to do something you know nothing about."

"People talk. It's all over Dabyr about how the Slayer brought his sister here so you knew you could trust him. It makes sense he'd want the same insurance policy in return."

"Go to your suite. Stay out of this. No one is going with him and that's final."

A small muscle under her eye twitched, making Joseph realize his mistake too late.

"Final?" she asked, her tone frighteningly calm.

Andreas stood up. "I think I'll leave you two to chat."

Carmen grabbed his arm. "Stay. This won't take long."

The Slayer looked down at her fingers, which were curled around his biceps. His nostrils flared and Joseph felt more than he saw a shift in Andreas's posture. His muscles tensed, as if readying for a fight. He pulled in a deep breath and shifted slightly, partially blocking her from Joseph's sight.

The Slayer was giving off huge protective vibes. As if Joseph would ever do anything to hurt Carmen.

She looked up at Joseph, seemingly unaware of the response Andreas was having to her. "I can't stay here. I'm suffocating with all these rules and restrictions."

"They're for your safety."

"My safety is my responsibility, not yours."

"Not true," said Joseph. "Thomas put your care into my hands."

"I'm a grown woman. You can't see that." She turned to Andreas. "Can you?"

"Depends. You act like an adult, you get treated like one."

"That's better than I have here."

"Their society isn't like ours," warned Joseph. "You may not like it."

"Then I'll leave."

"Not if you're a hostage."

"Hostage is such a loaded term," said Andreas. "You'll be our guest."

This wasn't good. Joseph had done nothing but screw things up with Carmen since she'd shown up. She'd had a rough life. She felt like no one had wanted her—not her father, not her uncle, and now Joseph was inadvertently following in those assholes' footsteps. "Please don't go. We need you here."

"No, you don't. You've already got more screwed-up humans to take care of than you know what to do with. Let me go. I need to do this."

"Who will teach you to fight if you leave?"

"I will," said Andreas. "She'll learn alongside all the other women."

"See?" said Carmen. "I already fit in better there."

Joseph hated letting her go. He was responsible for her. But he'd made mistakes in dealing with her, and now he was reaping the results of those mistakes.

If he didn't let her go with Andreas, where she'd at least have the Slayers to protect her, chances were she'd leave anyway. Without any safety at all.

Joseph looked Andreas in the eye. "Promise me you'll protect her with your life."

Carmen sighed. "I don't need—"

"I promise," vowed Andreas.

Joseph felt the weight of his vow settle over him, giving him some comfort. It seemed only fair to offer that same comfort in return. "I promise to keep your sister safe as well. She may hate living here, but she'll be safe."

Andreas nodded and offered Joseph his hand. They shook, sealing their bargain.

There would be peace among the Sentinels. At least for now.

*   *   *

Logan was still panting with the effort of using the wind to slow his own fall when he saw Hope and the Warden topple from the rooftop.

He didn't know how he was going to find the power to save her, but he knew that he would do it or die trying.

Pain seared along his veins as he wrung every last speck of power from his blood. He felt his body shrivel and his skin sag on his frame. His bones felt brittle and he stooped under the strain.

He took one weak step toward the falling pair and reached out a hand. Wind answered his call and he sent a wedge of it toward them, shoving it between the two.

The Warden's fall sped as Hope's slowed. He gritted his teeth and pushed harder, commanding the wind to obey.

A few feet away, the Warden smashed into the concrete, shattering into countless pieces. Its dying scream was deafening, smashing several windows nearby.

Hope flailed high above. Logan shoved the last dregs of his power at the wind. It pushed her up and over the ledge of the building. His vision failed and he fell to his knees. He didn't know if his aim was good, or if he'd merely sent her flying over the far side of the building.

All he knew was that what he'd done would cost him his life.

His heart stuttered, then stopped. His body toppled and cold consumed him.

Hope landed hard on the rooftop. The wind was knocked from her lungs. Her head spun. She had no idea how she was alive, but she'd seen Logan standing below, reaching for her.

He'd saved her.

She pushed herself to her feet and stumbled to the edge of the building. Below she saw the remains of the Warden sparkling on the pavement. Next to it was Logan, lying too still.

Panic gripped her hard and she scrambled for the door. She went back the way she'd come, but the elevator ride seemed to take half a year. By the time she shoved through the doors and out to Logan's side, she'd had time to build up hope that he was alive.

As soon as she saw him, shriveled and still, that hope died.

He was only a shell of the man he'd been before. He looked old and dried up, as if the life had literally been wrung from him.

She fell to her knees at his side. He wasn't breathing. She felt no pulse.

Tears blurred her vision as the weight of grief tumbled down on her.

She couldn't let him die. Not like this.

Hope grabbed up a shard of crystal and sliced her wrist open. Blood splashed across his cheek before she managed to press the wound to his mouth.

"Don't you dare die," she warned him.

Blood leaked from the side of his mouth. He wasn't swallowing it.

Hope stroked his throat, trying to make it work, trying to get her blood into him.

He jerked as if a current had been sent through his body. He pulled in a deep breath. His eyes opened and he grabbed her arm, holding it to his mouth.

He drank down her blood, gulping audibly. Hope rejoiced in the sound, knowing her blood had saved him.

Weakness descended on her, but she didn't care. She wasn't going to fight him. He could take whatever he needed so long as he lived.

Her body melted, but Logan caught her before she could fall. He gathered her against his hard body and kept her warm.

Hope let go and drifted down into sleep. She didn't know if she'd wake again, but she hardly cared. If she died like this, she'd do so feeling good.

*   *   *

Krag felt the presence of the blooded woman flare into existence again. She was near Hacksaw and the Warden Krag had instructed him how to summon. Any Sanguinar foolish enough to risk daylight deserved to die.

Krag, however, was glad to know that the woman had survived. At least for now. There was no way to know if the Warden would find her and slay her, which made him impatient.

"You failed," Krag shouted into the mind of his servant, who had run in fear at the sight of the Warden.

Hope was protected. He came for her.

The Sanguinar. Of course he did. The leech would want her blood for himself.

That simply could not stand. She and her powerful blood were Krag's.

"Find a way to draw her out. Find a lever that will force her to leave the side of her protector."

A lever?

The idiot human had done too many drugs and mangled his brain. "Family. Friends. Some mangy beast she lets pee on her rug. Someone or something you can use against her."

Right. A lever. I know just the one to use.

It took every scrap of willpower built over the centuries for Logan to release Hope. Her blood spread through him, renewing his strength and waking his senses. He held her close, curling his body around hers while he waited for his light-headedness to ease.

He'd been only moments from death. Hope had saved him. Again.

Shards of the Warden glistened against the dirty pavement. None of them moved, proving the Solarc's servant was truly dead.

Logan lifted Hope in his arms. Her limp body felt almost insubstantial. How could something so delicate carry such strength and selflessness?

His van was destroyed, but her home was not far. He

took her there, shielding her from sight of the passersby
on the street. He carried her upstairs to her room,
stripped her dirty clothing from her limbs, wiped away
all traces of her blood, and tucked her into her bed. The
sight of her in only her bra and panties sent waves of
need crashing through him. He should have been too
weak to even consider the carnal delights she could offer, but when it came to Hope, Logan seemed to have the
boundless ability to torture himself.

There was no fireplace, so he set the bloodied cloth in
a metal trash can, put it on the fire escape, and lit a fire.
Sure that there were no traces of blood around to draw
any Synestryn to her, he fetched a cup of water and compelled her to drink.

Perhaps he should have taken her to a human hospital, but he couldn't bring himself to do that, knowing
how much she detested the idea. Besides, there was no
way he would allow himself to be parted from her. Not
now, so soon after nearly losing her.

Logan pulled the covers up to her chin to hide her
lush body from sight. With that barrier in place, he allowed himself the pleasure of holding her, of knowing
she was alive.

He held one hand over her heart, trying to ignore the
swell of her breast so he could keep track of her pulse
and breathing. Both seemed normal, which was impossible. He'd taken too much blood from her, and on the
heels of the other times he'd fed from her, there was no
way that what he'd done tonight shouldn't have caused
some damage.

He could find none.

Logan slid into her mind to make sure he hadn't
missed some sign of distress.

She was sleeping. Dreaming.

Her consciousness reached for him as if detecting his
presence. It wrapped around him, pulling him into her.
He didn't fight it. If she wanted his company, it was the
least he could do.

The idea that she did want his company—that he could somehow ease her—was a powerful feeling. It filled him with purpose and gave him hope that her sacrifice would not be a lasting one.

She let out a soft sigh of contentment, her body melting into his. Her mind shifted to a dream state, taking him along for the ride.

The chaotic swell of images made little sense, but then dreams rarely did. He glided along, skimming the surface but not allowing himself to be tugged in. As much as he'd enjoy sharing dreams with her, he had work to do tonight. Hope's safety was foremost on that list, but there were other things that needed his attention. His devotion to Project Lullaby had to be absolute.

Hope's mental images morphed until she was on a beach at high noon. Logan could feel the warmth of the sun and a cool breeze on their skin. The sound of waves blocked out all others. She lounged there on the sand in her cheery yellow bathing suit, the picture of contentment and womanly perfection.

She lifted a hand to block out the light and turned to look at him. "Join me?"

He wasn't supposed to be participating, but he'd gone too far and allowed himself to slip deep inside her where her dreams resided.

He opened his mouth to refuse her invitation, but in the next moment, he was stripped of his clothing, lying next to her on a towel. He could almost feel what it would be like to soak up sunlight through her. It gave her strength, made her cells swell with power as if she was somehow feeding on the sun's energy.

It was such an odd feeling, Logan's mind nearly retreated from hers to figure out the puzzle. But he didn't want to leave yet. He wanted to be right here with her, where things were not real and his actions had fewer consequences.

She turned to her side and her slim fingers settled against his bare chest. The heat of them made him suck in a shocked breath. He longed to feel more of her skin on his—to feel her run her hands over him as a lover might.

"You're afraid of me," she said.

"I'm afraid of what you make me feel. My duty—"

She covered his mouth with her hand. "Shh. We're on vacation. There's no duty here."

Against his will, he kissed her fingers, his tongue flicking out to taste her skin. It was warmer here than he remembered, scented with coconut, and completely intoxicating.

She shuddered and a wicked smile curved her mouth. "You're not running from me now."

He should. He knew he should, but what harm could come of indulging within her dreams? None of this was real. It was simply a complex string of chemical and electrical signals in her mind she was allowing him to witness— a sort of shared hallucination. One he knew could never become reality.

Hope leaned over him, blocking out the sun. Her eyes seemed to glow with a golden light amidst the shadows of her face. He could stare into them for hours and never become bored.

But she had other ideas. She leaned down and kissed him. It was a soft kiss. Tentative. Chaste.

Logan's body did not translate it properly, and the animalistic side of him took it as a challenge. His blood heated and pounded through his veins. His heart sped and sweat broke out along his back.

He wanted more, and she was going to give it to him. Here, now, where no one would ever know.

Logan flipped her over, tucking her slim body beneath his. He liked her here, safe from harm and unable to escape. It appeased his predatory nature even as it fed it, making him want more.

Hope's fingers slid into his hair and she tugged him to her. He let her have her way, kissing her open mouth to claim the space for his own.

Ravenous need that had nothing to do with blood swelled inside him. His cock throbbed against her belly, demanding entrance into the slick heat of her body. The rub of her swimsuit angered him, so he took control of the dream long enough to rid them both of their clothing.

Her hot, naked skin against his felt better than any he'd ever touched. Her nipples rubbed over his chest until she was arching into him for more. The smooth skin of her stomach, made slick by his need, stroked his erection, teasing it with a promise of more. She set his nerve endings alight, sending shivers of desire coursing through him.

"I want you," she whispered, breaking their kiss. Her thighs opened, giving him room to settle between.

A deep groan rumbled in his chest as he tried to resist her invitation. It was too soon. He hadn't loved her enough yet for her to be ready.

Her hips thrust up, trying to mate them together. She grabbed his hair and forced his mouth to her throat. "Here," she said.

She was asking for his bite? The idea made his entire body clench in need. He'd never fed on a woman while he took her. The risk of losing control was too great.

But not here. Not in this dream where nothing was real.

Her fervent request couldn't be right, and his immediate reaction was to seek out the truth. He dove deeper into her mind, searching for some sign that he'd misinterpreted.

All he found was an image of him through her eyes—one too beautiful to be real—and her writhing desire to be with him and feel him take her body and her blood.

There was no question in Logan's mind. She wanted it.

And he was going to give it to her.

He thrust any hesitance from his thoughts and let the predator in him loose. It howled in victory, and an unusual strength flooded his body. He felt muscles grow and bones harden as he pinned her hands above her head. Her amber eyes widened, and he couldn't tell if it was from fear or surprise.

Part of him didn't even care. She was his now and he was going to make the most of it.

Need prowled through his blood, pounding in impatience. It would have been easy to shift his hips and push inside her, but more than wanting the pleasure of doing that, he wanted the pleasure of seeing her lose control. He wanted her to fall apart in his arms and scream in climax as he took her.

Logan pinned her writhing hips in place with one thigh while he brought his lips to her throat. His fangs scraped across her skin, making her suck in a breath. He teased her, kissing and nibbling his way down her throat. Her delicate collarbone intrigued him, and he licked his way across it to the hollow of her throat. Her pulse pounded hard and fast, in time with her rapid breathing.

"Please," she begged him, and the sound of pleading in her tone filled him with a deep satisfaction. There was no question whether she wanted him.

Logan kept her wrists pinned in one hand while he let his fingers slide down her arm. The heated silk of her skin made something dark and primitive rise up in celebration. Laid out like this for him, she was a feast. Her scent went to his head and the sound of her pounding heart and sighs of need made him feel invincible.

His pale hand cupped her breast. She arched as if trying to force him to brush over her nipple, but he resisted the urge, knowing how much better for her it would be if he made her wait for it.

She fit into his wide palm perfectly. The pounding of her heart beneath her flesh called to him, as did her struggles to get him to comply with her wishes.

A deep yearning hunger spread through Logan, making his mouth water. He needed to know how she tasted, how her nipple felt as it beaded against his tongue. He needed to hear her sounds of pleasure as he suckled her.

Waiting became impossible. Her strength grew with each languid twist of her body.

What if she woke up before they were done?

A searing sense of desperation gripped him at the thought. This was his one and only time to be with her. Never again would he allow himself to indulge in the feel of her skin or the gasping sighs of her pleasure.

A fever overtook him, stripping him of control. He covered the tip of her breast with his mouth, soaking in her satisfied cry. He licked and suckled her while his hand stole down between their bodies.

Her sex was slick and hot. It clenched around his finger, making Logan shake with the need to feel her around his cock.

He tried to be gentle, but his movements were rough and demanding as he pushed her thighs wide and lined up their bodies. She bathed the tip of his cock in silken heat, tempting him. He held himself back, barely resisting the urge to shove inside her until she could take no more.

Hope's lips lifted, meeting him with an urgency that neared desperation. Their bodies melded together per fectly as if they'd each been made for the other.

Once again, she guided his mouth to her neck. "Now, Logan. I can't wait."

Which suited him just fine. Held in the snug perfection of her body, stroking every slick inch, he wasn't go ing to last long.

"Are you sure?" he asked her because he couldn't stand not to, because he couldn't stand her looking at him in revulsion, even if what he'd done was only a dream.

"Yes."

He surged forward, sliding deep as his fangs pierced her skin. Hot blood filled his mouth, tasting of desire and pleasure. Hope moaned and clutched at his back, scoring his skin.

Physical sensations ricocheted through his body. He was overcome by the taste of her, the scent of her. The feel of her sex gripping him as he thrust savagely into her body stole his mind. Sweet cries of building pleasure vibrated under his lips as he consumed her blood, her power.

It wasn't like a normal feeding. It was more. Deeper. The two of them were connected in a way he'd never allowed himself before—in a way none of his kind allowed.

The thrill of the forbidden rose up inside him. He let it take over and send him crashing over the edge. He sucked hard on her throat, demanding she give up her blood. Her body clenched, every muscle locking down as a high-pitched scream of completion shattered the air. He'd made her feel good. Made her come. A sense of victory rang through him. His orgasm ripped from him, forcing his hips forward, shoving his cock deep into her soft body as he let go of all control.

Hope shuddered around him, shaking as the last waves of her orgasm held her in its grip. Complete and utter satisfaction made Logan's head spin.

He closed the wound on her neck and slumped to the ground, rolling her on top of him.

The sun shone down on them, reminding him that none of this was real. That should have made him feel better, but instead, it left him feeling hollow. Empty.

All this dream had done was to make him wish for things he could never have. It gave him a taste of what he was missing with Hope—of the pleasure and connection they could never share.

Logan stroked her back, lulling her dream self into a deeper sleep while he slipped from her mind and back into his own.

She was lying on top of him, draped over him as she'd been in her dream. The covers were bunched around her waist, leaving the soft skin of her back naked to his touch.

His cock was aching and hard, twitching in irritation beneath his jeans. He didn't know if Hope had come during her dream, but he hadn't. Not that he deserved the release. What he'd done was borderline unforgivable. If Hope's true mate ever found out about this, he could only imagine the consequences.

Logan allowed himself one single stroke of his hand on her skin before he pulled the blanket back up and slid away from her alluring body. She was even softer in real life than in the dream. Even more beautiful. He didn't know how he was going to resist her now that he'd had a taste, but he had to find a way.

He only hoped that for her the dream was lost in the fog of sleep and that she didn't remember a thing

Chapter 20

Hope woke in her own bed, unsure of reality. First, the horrible thing with the Warden had happened, but had been too horrible to be real. And then Logan had been with her, naked and drawing exquisite pleasure from her body, too wonderful to be real.

Maybe it all had been a dream brought about by too much stress and worry over her missing friends. She needed to get up and clear her head so she could sort out reality from dreams.

She shifted slightly and felt a strong, warm arm tighten around her waist.

"Rest, love." Logan's deep voice was out of place in the quiet of her room.

She'd never had a man in her bed before, but couldn't imagine wanting anything more than she wanted him at her side, knowing he was safe.

She turned around to face him. No lights were on, but his pale skin and eyes were easy to see in the deep shadows. She traced one finger over the dark arch of his brows and the fullness of his lips.

"Was it real?" she asked.

He stilled. "Was what real?"

With the heat of her dream shimmering through her, not even the fear of what had happened tonight could touch her. "The Warden. The attack."

"Too real. How do you feel?"

She was a little groggy, but it was passing more by the

second. She remembered the man chasing her down, catching her. Then Logan was there. "Fine. How did you find me?"

"Your blood. I'll always be able to find you."

Coming from someone else, that would have sounded creepy. Instead, she let his words comfort her, knowing he'd already used his ability to save her once.

"Who was he?" she asked.

"A Dorjan—a human who subjugates himself to the Synestryn in exchange for money, power, or some other coin."

"Why did he attack me?"

"For your blood."

It was one thing when Logan took her blood, but the idea of letting another do it was repulsive to her. The mere thought of it made her shiver in revulsion.

Logan reached out. His long fingers slid over her hair, tucking some of it behind her ear.

She could only imagine what a mess it was. In fact, she probably had a giant purple bruise forming on the side of her face where that man—that Dorjan—had punched her.

Her fingers gently pressed along her cheekbone, testing for damage. She found none.

"Do you hurt?" he asked.

"No, though I should. You healed me, didn't you?"

He bowed his head in acknowledgment. "Though perhaps I didn't go far enough."

"What do you mean?"

"Your movements are stiff. Not at all like your usual grace."

The compliment made her smile. "Very smooth, Logan."

"I do try to please."

"You do please me. Even in my dreams."

A flush of embarrassment crept over his cheeks. Until now, she had no idea that vampires could blush.

"It's the least I could do, considering you saved my

life. Without your help tonight, that Warden would likely have killed me along with many others."

"I couldn't let you die. I—" She cut herself off before she could admit her feelings for him. She wasn't entirely sure what those feelings were, but they ran through her, so deep she felt they'd always be a part of her. She settled with, "You kept me from falling."

His eyes roamed over her face as if memorizing it. "I'll always be there to catch you when you fall."

They were just words. She knew he didn't mean them, but hearing them was nice. Comforting. Hope had been on her own for as long as she could remember, and despite the fact that Sister Olive had taken her in, Hope had been considered an adult, responsible for herself and her actions.

"Thank you."

He nodded. "I'm sorry you went through that. It was never my intention to see you come to harm."

"I know."

"And that's why I must insist that you allow me to see to your safety. There's a man. A powerful man—"

"No," she said, covering his mouth, stopping what he was going to say. "Just don't. Not tonight. We both nearly died." And the dream she'd had of him on the beach was not the kind of thing a woman forgot. It may not have happened, but she felt changed by it all the same.

"Which is why we must speak of this. Your safety is of vital importance."

"So is right now, this very moment. I don't want to plan for the future or discuss the possibility of more violence. I just want to celebrate our survival." And get back to that shimmering moment when he was filling her, driving her toward a pleasure too intense to be real.

"Celebrate? There isn't time for such frivolity. Your safety—"

"I'm safe with you." She shed the blankets and pushed him down on the bed, straddling his hips. Until now, she hadn't realized he'd taken her clothes off, leaving her in only her underwear. Not that she minded that he'd undressed her. It was going to make this so much easier.

Logan's eyes slid down her body. By the time they'd started the journey back to her face, a silvery light was glowing inside those icy depths. "What are you doing?"

"Proving to you how healthy I am so you'll relax."

"You're not healthy. I took so much blood."

She wasn't going to let him go down the guilt road. She had other plans. "Do you have any idea how good it feels when you do that?"

His eyes closed tight as if blocking out the sight of her. Fine. She knew how to combat that move. She lifted up the hem of his shirt and slid her hands inside, stroking his bare chest. She leaned down close to his ear and whispered, "It's like being dipped in sunshine, only better. Has anyone ever done that to you? Have you ever had a woman bite you?"

His body clenched, but she was set in her path. She was tired of Logan trying to hand her off to someone else. She didn't want someone else. She wanted him.

He didn't respond, but that was okay. She could tell that regardless of whether he'd allowed someone to take his blood, the idea did not repulse him. In fact, if the thick bulge of his erection was any proof, he liked the idea.

Hope shifted, sliding herself so she stroked him as she inched up his body. She kissed his jaw, his earlobe, just beneath. And then she kissed his neck, parting her lips and sucking his skin against her teeth.

Logan's arms wrapped around her, holding her tight. A low rumble of warning vibrated in his chest, but she couldn't tell if he was warning her to stop or warning her not to.

The idea of pushing him far enough to find out the answer was too alluring to resist.

Hope nipped his hot skin. Logan let out a sound of torment that gave her pause.

"You mustn't." His voice was rough as if he'd spent a week screaming.

"Why? I only want to make you feel the way you make me feel."

"It's wrong."

"I used to think so, but not anymore. The longer I'm with you, the more my preconceived notions fly out the window. The idea of tasting your blood doesn't even bother me. Not anymore."

"It's not safe."

She scraped her teeth along his neck. "Why?"

"You belong to another."

That pissed her off. "I belong to myself. If I choose to give myself to someone else, that's my business. You don't get to decide who that person is. Or isn't."

"I can't want you, Hope."

She ground her crotch against his erection, eliciting a groan from both of them. "Clearly you can. And do."

"It's forbidden."

"Sex or me biting you?"

"Both."

"Why?"

"You don't want me to tell you the truth. It only makes you angry."

"What makes me angry is that you actually think the truth is I *belong* to someone else. I don't."

"You will. You'll give yourself to another man and be glad we resisted."

"Now you can see the future?"

"No, history. I've seen this course of events before. You'll meet Eric. You'll fall in love with him. His rough edges will fade away and the two of you will be happy together."

"You can't know that."

"I've seen it happen over and over. I cannot take that happiness away from you. Not for one night of pleasure."

"Assuming I believe you, which I don't, why can't I have both?"

"Our world is not like the humans' world. There are laws. Traditions."

"No one has to know but us."

"I'll know. I've worked for centuries to see the continuation of my race. I would give my life for you, but I can't offer theirs. I can't risk the life of a child we might conceive."

"I'm protected. I won't get pregnant."

"If you take my blood you might. I wouldn't have the control to fight you. I'd take you. I'd spill my seed inside you. You could conceive."

"I'm on the pill. We can go buy condoms."

"I cannot risk it. And any child we would have would be doomed to a life of humiliation and starvation. I will not allow it."

The thought of making a child suffer doused her lust. She scrambled away, pulling the blanket tightly around herself.

"That doesn't make any sense. You don't know any of that. You're just trying to frighten me."

Logan pulled his shirt down and sat up. He looked weary. Defeated. "I wish I were. I wish we could have our liaison and no one would come to harm, but that's not the way our world works. That dream we shared was all we'll ever have."

"You were there? In my dreams?"

He nodded. "Though I wish I hadn't been. It was wrong."

"I'm glad you were there," said Hope. "If that's all we can ever have, then it'll have to be better than nothing."

"I'm sorry. We must finish our bargain and go our separate ways."

Wanting Logan was hard, but loving him and knowing there would never be anything between them was torture. She needed to have him out of her life before she was so deeply in love with him she'd never find a way out.

She lowered her voice, unable to put any enthusiasm in the words. "The sooner, the better."

*   *   *

Hacksaw found the address of Hope's photography studio. The master's presence inside his mind propelled him forward, burning inside him as a punishment for his failure.

He'd lost the master's woman. The bloodsucker who guarded her still lived.

But the night was young and the master's hold on Hacksaw was strong. His guidance would lead him to victory, so Hacksaw didn't even try to fight it. Not that it would do any good if he had.

A bell tinkled as he walked into the posh studio. Ornately framed portraits lined the walls. Beyond a doorway curtained in heavy, fringed fabric, he heard the sound of a woman singing.

Hacksaw parted the curtain with a dirty hand and slipped silently inside.

The woman wasn't Hope. Disappointment filled him for a moment as he watched her. She was wearing headphones, singing along with a tune that made her bounce in time with the music. She was pretty. Clean. He'd seen women like this come into the master's domain and fall at his feet.

None of them were clean when they died, but the master didn't seem to mind. So long as they were obedient.

The woman hadn't noticed his presence. She was busy doing something with her hands—something that involved a razor blade.

Bring her to me.

The master's voice echoed in Hacksaw's head, blocking out all other thoughts. He didn't know what he'd want with her, but it didn't matter. What the master wanted, he got.

Hacksaw slipped around behind her. She didn't see him coming. He clamped a dirty hand over her nose and mouth, blocking off her air.

She yelped in shock and kicked back at him while her

fingers pried at his. But Hacksaw was strong. He didn't let go. Not even when she slashed at him with that razor blade, drawing blood—both his and hers.

Dark red and bright red drops splattered out across the picture of a chubby toddler.

His blood was so much darker than hers. He didn't know why that was.

The master's presence in his mind reassured him there was nothing to worry about. All was as it was supposed to be.

Hacksaw took comfort in that as he suffocated the small woman.

Her struggle slowed and finally stopped as she lost consciousness. Hacksaw didn't know how long he'd have before she woke, but his car was parked right outside and his trunk was ready for her body.

The master was going to be so pleased.

Logan smelled blood. Familiar blood.

He bolted from Hope's room and sprinted down the stairs to the studio below. She was right on his heels

"What's going on?" she demanded, her voice raised an octave in fear.

"Get dressed. Fast."

He didn't wait to see if she complied. He stepped into the hallway and pulled in a deep breath through his nose, smelling human blood. Tainted blood. The blood of the man who'd tried to steal Hope.

Beneath that scent was a cleaner one. The blood of a human with no taint. She was blooded, but not heavily. The sour stench of her fear still lingered in the air.

Logan followed his nose to the studio's workshop. Hope was only seconds behind him.

On a large, sturdy workbench was a child's portrait spattered with blood—both light and dark.

"Jodi," said Hope, the name filled with devastation. "Where's Jodi?"

Logan followed the drops of blood out the front door

and onto the sidewalk. Several congregated in a cluster at the end of an empty parking slot. He'd put her in the trunk. Just like he had done to Hope.

Her hand clenched his arm. She was weaving on her feet, and despite the emergency that faced them, Hope was his primary concern.

The Dorjan knew where she lived. He'd taken her roommate as leverage. Logan had to get Hope out of here. Now.

He reached around her waist and steadied her. "I'm going to find her."

"She's gone. Jodi's gone. It's my fault, isn't it?"

"No. You are not responsible for the choices of others."

Logan retrieved his cell phone and dialed Nicholas. "I need your assistance."

"Where?" asked Nicholas.

It wasn't safe to stay here, but he had no vehicle. It had been ruined by the Warden. "The coffee shop down the street from Hope's studio. As soon as you can."

"I'm nearby. It won't be long."

"And can you request a team of Gerai to tow my van? We ran into some difficulties and I don't want my license plate drawing any unwanted police attention." It was something he should have thought to do before, but he'd been too swept up in Hope and the shared pleasure of her dream.

"No problem," said Nicholas. "The tracker in it will give them the location."

"Thank you."

Logan hung up and swept Hope back inside. He kept a hold on her, making sure she didn't topple over. She was swaying on her feet, moving along wherever he led without question.

She was in shock. A lot had happened tonight, and she was likely weak from the remnants of her injuries as well as feeding him. It was no wonder that she needed some time to process the situation.

He found a coat in her closet and eased it over her arms. A knit scarf went around her neck and he pulled her hood up to ward off the cold.

Her eyes were wide and shining with tears. Her mouth was tight with worry. "Is he going to hurt her?"

"No," he lied.

Logan's heart ached for her and for her friend, who was no doubt terrified. If she was still alive.

He had to believe she was. Not much blood had been spilled, and what good was Jodi if she couldn't be used as a lever to pry Hope out into the open? She'd be of no use to them dead.

He kept his tone gentle as he pulled her to her feet. "We're going to go meet Nicholas now. We'll figure out where Jodi went and we'll find her."

"It was the same man who tried to take me, wasn't it?"

"That is my belief." He pushed through the front doors of her studio, not bothering to lock them.

"He's going to use her as bait, isn't he?" asked Hope.

She was smart, and now that the shock was wearing off, her mind was working and she had arrived at the same conclusion he had. He only wished it had taken her a bit longer—that they would have been closer to rescuing Jodi before her head had cleared. The fog of shock was much easier to tolerate than stark reality.

"That's good news," he assured her. "If they intend to use her in that manner, they'll keep her alive."

Hope's knees buckled and he tightened his hold, pressing her against his body to steady her. The slight tremors shaking her frame were easy to feel, even through their winter clothing. "They can't kill her."

"We'll find her, Hope. You hold on to that and all will be well. I promise."

As the weight of his vow fell on him, he realized his mistake. He should never have promised her such a thing. It was not in his power to give. But it was too late now.

He hurried her down the sidewalk, ignoring the curious stares of the few people they passed. He opened the door of the coffee shop and was immediately blasted by the smells of ground beans, cinnamon, and cocoa. His eyes watered from the intensity, but he managed to ignore it.

Logan settled Hope at the table nearest the counter and ordered her hot chocolate. It was done by the time he'd paid. He added extra sugar and used ice to cool it down. When the temperature no longer burned his mouth, he wrapped Hope's fingers around the paper cup and said, "Drink."

The wisp of compulsion he used was slight, but he wanted no argument. She needed sustenance and fluids.

She also needed to be behind the locked gates at Dabyr. That was clear now. The Synestryn who'd infected the Dorjan wanted her for some reason. It hardly mattered why. What did matter was that the demon was not likely to stop until he got what he wanted.

Logan would die before he let that happen.

Nicholas strode into the coffee shop, his scarred face grim. His black leather jacket clung to his wide shoulders. His hair was mussed from the wind and his cheeks were red from cold. The woman behind the counter gave him an uneasy look before she moved to the phone on the wall. If Nicholas noticed her mistrust, he gave no outward sign.

"What's up?" he asked, his voice quiet.

"Not here. Where are you parked?"

"Double-parked. I didn't want to wait for a spot."

Logan reached to help Hope from her chair, but stopped at the last moment, pulling himself back. Touching her was not his right, and the more he did so, the harder it became to remember that.

He looked at Nicholas. "She's weak. Shaken."

Nicholas nodded and wrapped his big hand around her arm to lift her from her chair. His thick arm came around her waist, making Logan grit his teeth against a jealous cry of outrage.

He averted his eyes and Nicholas helped her into the backseat of his SUV and buckled her in. "Don't you worry, Hope. We're going to take good care of you."

She looked up at Nicholas, her eyes bright with unshed tears. "They took Jodi. They couldn't get me so they took Jodi."

Nicholas stroked her hair to soothe her. "Everything's going to be okay."

Logan had to unclench his fists before he could open the car door. Possessiveness was going to get him nowhere. Worse, it could exacerbate their troubles immensely. He had to stay logical and focused.

They drove away and Logan wasted no time filling Nicholas in on what had passed. The Theronai assessed the situation quickly. "We need to find Jodi before it's too late. We'll take her back by force and kill the demons who took her. But first we need to get Hope to Dabyr."

"I'm not going anywhere," said Hope, her voice resonant with determination. "Jodi's my friend. She's in this mess because of me. I'm going with you."

"You'll only slow us down," said Nicholas.

"The longer we wait, the farther away they'll get. Logan can track them now, like he did the man in the warehouse."

Nicholas shot him a sideways glance. "That true?"

"Yes. But I'd feel better if Hope were at Dabyr."

"Every second counts." Hope put her hand on his shoulder. Her finger inadvertently stroked his neck, making his body clench in desire. "Please don't let her die. Find her. You promised."

He had. It had been stupid, but he'd made the mistake and now he had to live with it.

Logan eased the window down an inch. He hated letting the cold in to chill Hope, but there was no help for it.

He gathered some power and breathed in through his nose, seeking the scent of blood.

"What are you doing?" asked Nicholas.

"Blood hunting." His eyes cast a pale glow on the window as he eased himself into a trancelike state.

Minute particles of power wove through the air, creating faint, visible streams. Those particles seemed to be drawn to Nicholas. They bombarded him, adding to his already vast stores of energy—energy that was slowly killing him.

Logan sifted through the streams, searching for the ones that matched the scent of Jodi's blood or the Dorjan who'd taken her. He caught a slight glimpse and forced his mouth to move. "Turn right."

Their direction shifted and two delicate strands of power came into view. He breathed in deeply, testing them to see if they were the ones he sought.

The match was true. Both Jodi and the Dorjan had gone this way. He had their trail now and it was only a matter of time before he caught them.

You're being followed by a Sanguinar.

Hacksaw heard the master's voice in his head, booming like a loudspeaker. He swerved off the side of the road, nearly hitting a mile marker.

"What do I do?"

You cannot lead them here. Kill him.

Hacksaw didn't dare question the master. He didn't understand why the master wouldn't want the glory of slaying a Sanguinar himself, but it was not his place to talk back. Instead, he exited the highway and went down a quiet country road.

A few miles down was a turnoff on a hill that would give him an excellent view of the top. He got his machine gun from the backseat.

As soon as he saw the vampire, he'd blow him away and take his corpse back to the master as a treat for his pets.

Chapter 21

Krag split his attention between what Hacksaw was doing as well as the scene playing out before him. Two of his women had disagreed, and they were now rolling around on the floor, trying to kill each other.

He didn't know who'd win. He didn't even care. The sport was enough of an amusement that he'd see what he could do to enhance the experience in the future.

The brunette grabbed a chair and smashed it into the blonde's head. She stumbled back, arms flailing. When she fell, she landed wrong and something in her neck snapped.

She wasn't dead yet, but she soon would be.

He briefly considered draining her blood himself, but he preferred his meals to have a little more life in them. The blonde was of no use to him now.

He turned to the woman who'd bested her. "We eat what we kill around here."

The brunette's face paled as she realized what he was demanding of her. "I will feed her to your loyal servants."

"No. You will drink her blood and then I will feed you to them." He sent a compulsion to her, forcing her obedience. "Now."

The woman sobbed as she bent over the blonde. Krag watched her struggle with her human nature for a moment before it became boring.

He closed his eyes and reached out to Hacksaw. The man was good with a gun, but there was no guarantee it would be enough. He wanted the blooded woman. He was tired of waiting.

Krag sent a mental missive to a pack of Handlers he controlled. Touching their minds made him break out into a sweat, but he'd managed to give them his orders. Their excitement to be of service was unsettling in its enthusiasm. At least he knew they'd be thorough and his orders had been clear: Find anyone associated with the blooded woman and burn them alive. Once she had no place to go, flushing her out of hiding would be much easier.

Hope was freezing from the inside out. Jodi was gone and it was her fault. She wasn't sure what she'd done to cause it, but she knew that it had something to do with the black void of her forgotten past.

The auras of the men in front of her and those in the surrounding cars were too bright. They stung her eyes, nauseating her with their chaotic swirls of color. She closed her eyes and focused on the feeling of air sliding in and out of her lungs.

Too much had happened in the past few days, and she feared she wasn't strong enough to handle it. Not that she had any choice. This was her mess. Her responsibility. She had to find a way to fix things before it was too late.

Jodi.

She willed her friend to hang on and prayed that the merciful God Sister Olive had told her so much about would keep Jodi safe.

The reason for all of this was inside her somewhere, in her past. She'd done something bad or angered someone along the way, and now they were taking their revenge. She had to break through that mental wall and figure out what had caused this before anyone else was hurt.

Logan was speaking quiet directions to Nicholas in the front seat. Hope kept her eyes closed and let the low sound of his voice calm her nerves. There was something about him that called to her, pushing her to try to get closer no matter how much he shoved her away.

She knew her actions were destined to cause her heartbreak, but she felt out of control and unable to stop herself from careening toward the inevitable.

For the moment, she needed to do whatever was within her control, and that meant finding a way to uncover the source of this pain she was causing others. If she knew what she'd done to make this happen, maybe she could find a way to make up for it.

She moved back through her memories to the night they stopped. The first conscious thought she had was of being cold. Confusion set in swiftly and she wondered why she was there, in the dark, alone and naked.

Fear swiftly overcame the cold and confusion and she huddled, hugging herself in a futile effort to offer herself comfort. The lump in her palm drew her attention and she looked down and read the name on the wooden amulet.

She could read, which meant she'd been educated. She spoke English, though Sister Olive had commented on her strange accent early on.

Hope had rid herself of it, not wanting anything to draw attention to how different she was from others. It had been almost a year before she'd realized that other people didn't see auras the way she did. She'd mistakenly referred to the strange color surrounding a small child once and his mother had looked at her like she was insane.

Her research had revealed that others saw auras, but she'd never once had the courage to share that she did as well. Not even with one of them.

Hope pressed up against the spot where her past disappeared. She prodded at it, forcing herself to envision different scenarios, hoping one of them would feel right and click into place.

This was something she'd done a thousand times before, using characters from books and movies to give her ideas for who she was or from where she'd come.

Nothing fit. Even now, she forced herself to think of all the bad things she could have done to cause someone to hate her enough to hurt Jodi. Had she been involved in drugs? Gangs? Was she connected to organized crime?

Had she killed?

A heavy sigh of regret filled the air around her. She hoped she hadn't done any of those things, but proof was stacking up against her. There had to be someone out there who knew who she was and what she'd done. Maybe it had taken them this long to find her.

At least now she had an idea of why she wouldn't have wanted to be found. Maybe she'd erased her own memories, on purpose.

A resonant hum filled her head as that idea struck a chord. She held her breath, tentatively poking at the idea.

The blank wall that had always stood there seemed to bulge inward, like someone pressing on a balloon. It was no longer rock hard and unyielding. She'd found a soft spot—one that said that whatever had caused her amnesia had been self-inflicted.

No. That couldn't be right. She'd never do this to herself. She'd never take away something so precious as her memories. Those were the things that made a person who they were. Past actions defined people. How could she have willingly given up her identity without a fight?

She couldn't. She wouldn't. And yet it seemed to fit.

A pounding headache broke out behind her eyes as she began to question the kind of person she'd come to think of herself as. She wasn't the kind to give up, even when things were hard. She fought.

She'd fought for years to make a place for herself. A name for herself. She'd struggled for everything she had and would do so until the day she died. She created. She didn't destroy.

And yet, given the chance, she'd rip apart the man

who'd taken her friend. She wasn't afraid of violence. She'd been taught how to deal with it.

Hope stilled as that single thought broke free. She didn't remember a single lesson in fighting and yet the knowledge was there, as sure and solid as if it were part of her bones.

Someone had taught her the ways of violence, but she couldn't remember who, which led her to believe that it had happened in her past.

She pressed on that thought, being careful not to push too hard. She didn't want it to slip away. Not now. Not when she might well be given a reason to draw on those lessons in violence.

Nothing came to her. No new thoughts. No images. No ideas. Her mind kept whirling around the question of what kind of life would she have led that would have trained her to fight and then allowed her to wipe the slate clean?

She couldn't think of a single thing that made sense, and with every second that passed by, that soft spot seemed to harden again, thwarting her.

"Jodi's ahead," said Logan, breaking her concentration. "So is the Dorjan."

The front windshield shattered as bullets hit it, and they went sliding off the road in a violent spin.

Logan leaned to the left, ensuring that any bullet that hit Hope would at least be slowed down by going through his body first.

Nicholas made quick work of correcting their spin, then gunned the engine, charging the car from which the shot had been fired.

"Don't hit him," warned Logan. "Jodi is probably in the trunk, unprotected."

"Shit," spat Nicholas; then he unbuckled his seat belt. The SUV skidded to a halt, and as soon as it was in park, Nicholas jumped out and drew his sword.

"Stay here," said Logan. "Keep low."

He slid from his seat, using the front of the SUV as cover. Another gunshot rang out and Nicholas jerked back.

He'd been shot.

A scream of rage bellowed out of Nicholas as he lifted his sword and closed the distance.

Logan feared for Nicholas's life, but even more he worried about what would happen to Hope if she no longer had his sword to fight off this Dorjan and any other Synestryn who would be drawn to the scent of Nicholas's blood.

Logan darted across the frozen ground, using a burst of power to speed him. He arrived at the car only a split second before Nicholas.

Blood seeped from the Theronai's arm where the bullet had penetrated. The metallic scent of it filled his nose, making his mouth water. As rich as Nicholas's blood was, it wouldn't take long for nearby Synestryn to sense it and come running.

The Dorjan fired again, right into Nicholas's chest. The Theronai jerked back from the blow, snarling in pain. He brought his sword down, aiming for the man's hands poking out of the open window. The man jerked back at the last moment, but the blade knocked the gun from his hands.

Nicholas grabbed the man by his shirt and ripped him out through the window. His blade was in his fist, which he pulled back and struck the Dorjan with the butt of his sword. The blow landed, rattling the Dorjan's teeth. Nicholas's eyes opened wide in shock. He dropped the man and stumbled back to reveal the hilt of a knife protruding from his chest.

Logan closed the last few feet of distance as the Dorjan crumpled unconscious to the ground.

Nicholas slid down, barely catching himself on all fours. He reached for the knife.

"No!" shouted Logan, shoving a strong compulsion into his words. "Don't pull it out."

The Theronai could bleed to death before he could

prevent it if that blade was removed. He knelt beside Nicholas and helped ease him to the ground.

The warrior's breathing was shallow and uneven. The sound of his heart was all wrong, telling Logan that there was a good chance the knife had hit it.

Logan was vaguely aware of a car door slamming shut. He heard footfalls quickly approaching. Hope.

He didn't dare look up at her. The horror that would surely show on her face would be too much of a distraction and right now he needed to keep his wits about him.

"Jodi's in the trunk. Free her. There should be duct tape in our vehicle. Restrain the Dorjan." He didn't check to see if she complied. He trusted she'd do what was necessary.

Logan gathered his power and sought out the worst of Nicholas's injuries. The knife had indeed nicked his heart, but it wasn't as bad as it could have been. He grabbed the knife and slowly retracted it as he healed the wound shut from the inside out.

He blocked out the raw sounds of pain coming from Nicholas, shoving his consciousness into the other man's mind enough to hold him still while he worked. One inadvertent twitch and the damage could be fatal.

Strength fled his body as he worked. The knife was now out and the bleeding stopped, but he had two bullet wounds left to mend before he could rest.

"Take what you need," said Nicholas through gritted teeth. "We have to get the women out of here. My blood . . ."

Logan didn't ask if he was sure. He simply pulled Nicholas's head to the side and bit deep, drawing strength from the other man to heal his wounds.

The rush of power filled his head for a moment before he could control it and focus. He shoved the bullets out and used the quickest, most effective method of healing he could. It was also the most painful, making Nicholas's body bow off the ground in an arc of agony.

Logan hated the other man's suffering. He would

have preferred more time to ease the healing process along, but they had none. His only remaining choice was to will Nicholas to sleep, which he did with a harsh, unyielding command.

He finished the healing process, then stripped all the bloody clothing from Nicholas's body, leaving him bare from the waist up. He eased Nicholas's heavy body to the passenger's seat of the SUV. With the power the Theronai's blood had given him, it was no effort.

Jodi was lying in back, unconscious. Logan laid his hand on her head and closed the wound on her hand. Her blood wasn't powerful enough to draw demons unless they were close, but he used a paper napkin to wipe away what he could.

Hope was back near the Dorjan. His car door hung open and she'd taped his hands to the interior handle. Logan grabbed Nicholas's sword from the ground and handed it to her. "Please take this back to the others and wait for me in the car."

"What are you going to do?"

"I'm going to stop this man from hurting you again."

"You're going to kill him?"

Logan was riding along a thin edge, barely staying in control of the rage he wanted to let loose. He kept his voice even through a sheer act of will. "This man tried to hurt you. He abducted Jodi. He shot and stabbed Nicholas. Death is too good for him. Now go! We don't have much time before demons find us."

Hope nodded and stepped back.

Now there was no one standing between him and the man who'd attacked Hope.

He pressed his hand to the man's head and then touched his thoughts.

The taint of Synestryn hit his senses, making him gag. He stomped on that reflex, forcing himself to ignore the vile touch of evil. Without any grace, he shoved his way into the other man's mind, searching it for the motivation for his attack.

His name was Leonard, but he'd taken on the nick-name Hacksaw as a teen. His past had been plagued by drugs and violence. He had no education to speak of, but what he lacked in schooling he made up for in dedica-tion.

Leonard would do anything for the Synestryn named Krag, the one he referred to as the master.

The face of a Synestryn lord hovered over Leonard's thoughts, motivating every facet of his life. Krag's skin was hairless and scaly in places. His lips were so thin they were almost nonexistent, unable to hide his pointed teeth.

And despite all of that, Krag's resemblance to a hu-man was unsettling. Like the Synestryn lord, Zillah, Krag would have been able to walk among humans in the dark and likely go unnoticed.

The fact that another creature like Zillah existed was proof of just how far Synestryn kind had gone to blend in with their prey.

Logan let the import of that news pass him by. He'd consider it later, but for now he needed to finish this job and be out of this puppet's mind as fast as possible.

He passed images of other people who were in Krag's thrall. The stream of faces was impressive. The latest was a young woman with hot pink–tipped hair and matching high-tops.

Rory. Hope's missing friend.

That was not a coincidence. Logan was certain of that. Krag was somehow tied to the missing people. Maybe all of them. He couldn't be sure without descriptions, so he filed away those memories of Leonard's to ask Hope about later.

The man's vile thoughts twisted in Logan's mind, urg-ing him to hurry.

He homed in on Leonard's thoughts of Hope. He'd been sent to fetch her. He'd known what she looked like, where she lived.

Which meant only one thing: So did Krag.

If Hope was being hunted, she was in deep danger.
She couldn't stay here in the city. He had to get her to
safety. Now, while he still could.

He shoved deep into Leonard's mind, erasing from it
Nicholas's blow to his head. In its place he planted a
false memory of another battle, one in which Leonard
shot them all down. Hope died trying to free Jodi from
the trunk, and their bodies were left alongside the road.

Creating the vivid details of the scene made Logan's
stomach turn and his head pound. He could barely think
of Hope in those terms—dead and rotting in a ditch—
but he did what was necessary to protect her, no matter
how disturbing he found it.

Chapter 22

Hacksaw's head pounded. He was barely able to stay on the road long enough to drive home. His eyes kept losing focus. His arms felt weak and heavy.

He walked into the master's home, ashamed that he'd failed.

Hacksaw fell to his knees before the master's throne. He bowed his head in shame. He didn't dare look up. "The woman and her friend are dead."

"You failed."

"I'm sorry, Master."

"How did they die?"

"I . . . shot them. They tried to escape. I had no choice."

"Where are their bodies?"

Hacksaw looked up, startled that he hadn't considered to at least bring that much of an offering. "I . . ." He couldn't think of a single excuse for why he'd forgotten such an obvious thing.

The master's tongue flicked out over his teeth. "You didn't bring them?"

His head pounded. He was weaving on his knees, barely able to stay upright. His failure was making him sick, but he deserved every bit of suffering. "No, Master. But I'll go back and get them now."

"Come here," ordered the master.

Hacksaw pushed himself to his feet. He shuffled forward, his legs too heavy to lift.

"You smell of deception. Why is that?"

"I'd never lie to you, Master."

The master grabbed him by the throat and dragged him forward, forcing him to look into his eyes. Hacksaw couldn't breathe, but he accepted his punishment, refusing to struggle. His life belonged to the master and he could do with it as he willed.

The master's hand pressed to the side of Hacksaw's head. He had only three fingers, but each one burned like fire. It felt like they were gouging into Hacksaw's skull, drilling into his brain.

What little light there was in the throne room began to fade. A sense of failure weighed down on Hacksaw, driving tears from his eyes.

He'd displeased the master. He'd been chosen and he'd failed.

His legs went numb. Blood dripped down the side of his head. Images exploded in his mind only to be pulled from him.

The master shoved him away. Blood coated his fingers as if they'd been dipped in it.

Hacksaw lay crumpled on his side, unable to move.

The edges of his vision were fading, but he saw the master give a wave of permission to the demons beside him. "Eat him."

The demons approached, their yellow saliva glowing as it dripped from their jaws.

Hacksaw craned his neck to see past them. He wanted the master's face to be the last thing he saw before he died.

The mess Krag's minions had made of Hacksaw was impressive in its enthusiasm. Not that he minded. They'd clean it up before they were finished feeding on his remains, licking every last drop of blood from the concrete floor.

Maybe he needed a rug to cover the stain. Of course that would last only until the next human failed him.

Though Hacksaw's failure hadn't been complete. The

memory of the girl's death had been planted by a fucking Sanguinar, but after rummaging through Hacksaw's mind, the means to find her was also now clear.

The Sentinels would have no doubt hidden her already. Krag would have done the same thing. The trick was going to be drawing her out of hiding so he could find out what made her special—why she appeared, glowing in his mind as if calling to him. Thanks to Hacksaw, he knew just how to do it.

Hope held on to Jodi's hand while Logan drove like a bat out of hell. Both Nicholas and Jodi were still unconscious, though Jodi had been making some noises that indicated she might start coming around. Nicholas wasn't so lucky. He was pale and way too still.

Hope tried to keep Jodi's head from sloshing around as Logan took the next hard turn. "Where are we going?"

"A Gerai house. We'll be safe here for now. We need a place to rest. And we need a place to talk."

"About what?"

His pale eyes met hers in the rearview mirror. "Not now."

Because he was focusing on not sending them flying off the road, Hope let it go. A few minutes later, they pulled up in front of a pristine home well off the main road. It was surrounded by trees, with so much land between it and every other home she couldn't even see any neighbors.

"I'll unlock the house and carry them inside. If you could see to lighting a fire, that would be nice."

"Are you cold?"

"I used quite a bit of power tonight." He said it as if that answered her question.

"Sure. I'll make some coffee, too."

"Thank you."

Logan slipped out of the car and had the front door open in a few seconds. Hope waited until he came back for Jodi before she slipped inside and lit the fire. Everything was already laid out, ready to go. All she had to do was light the newspapers crumpled under some kindling.

By the time she had coffee brewing, Logan had settled Nicholas and Jodi in separate beds and was warming his hands by the fire.

Hope found the thermostat and kicked it up a couple of degrees, then went and sat on the couch. "You said we needed to talk."

He didn't turn around when he spoke, but she could see by the rigid set of his shoulders that he wasn't pleased. "I touched that man's mind. I saw what he's seen. I think I know where your friend Rory is. It's not good news."

Hope held back her worry, refusing to let it loose until she heard him out. "Where?"

"That man, Leonard, is controlled by a Synestryn. I don't know where his nest is, but what I do know is that Leonard had recently seen a woman with dyed pink hair and bright pink high-tops. It could be someone else, but that seems a bit of a stretch."

Shock shielded Hope from that news, insulating her from the fear she knew would settle in at any moment. "You think he saw Rory?"

"It's likely."

"Do you think he was taking Jodi to wherever she is?"

"Also likely."

For a second, she wished Logan hadn't interfered. If he hadn't, maybe they would have found Rory. Maybe. Then again, they could all have died, too.

Logan frowned as if reading her thoughts. "We'll find her. Nicholas and I will go after her as soon as possible."

"I want to help."

"That's out of the question. Your safety is too important to risk."

"And yours isn't?"

He lifted a black brow. "I have superpowers, and

apart from your sudden bursts of strength, I'm not aware of you having the same. Do you?"

Hope almost mentioned her ability to see auras, but she wondered if Logan and his kind would want to study her or something. She couldn't afford to be locked away, kept from stopping whomever was stealing souls from the street. No one else seemed worried enough to look for them. She had to do it herself. She didn't have time for all the questions her ability would raise.

"Of course not," she said, hoping she sounded convincing. "Don't be silly."

Logan pulled in a deep breath through his nose and eyed her skeptically. "You're hiding something from me."

"No, I'm not."

He tilted his head, scrutinizing her. "You are. Which makes me intensely curious."

"Stop worrying about me and tell me what we're going to do to get Rory and the others back."

A knowing smiled played about his lips, and the sudden desire to kiss him again had her breaking out in a sweat. Her dream of the two of them together came back hard and fast, making her thighs clench together in lust. She sat on her hands to keep them to herself and looked at a boring landscape painting on the far wall of the little house.

"There were other humans there, too. There's only one way for me to know if they are among the missing as well."

"And what way is that?"

"You'd have to let me see your thoughts, share your memories of them so I can compare those images to the ones I pulled from Leonard."

His eagerness was almost palpable, which made warning bells ring loud and clear. "Assuming I let you do something like that, what's to stop you from poking around where you're not wanted to satisfy your intense curiosity?"

His smile widened to victorious proportions. "Nothing."

"I don't suppose you'd give me your word not to poke your brain into my business?"

"My dear, I find you far too compelling to resist. I'd never paint myself into such a corner. You're the one who raised my suspicions. You're going to have to live with the consequences of rousing my natural curiosity."

While Hope loved the idea of having him inside her again, sharing her thoughts as they had in her dream, she also wasn't sure just how much she wanted to reveal to him. She didn't want him seeing her as more of a freak than he already did. She didn't want anyone seeing that side of her.

"Fine," she said. "We'll stick with the assumption that wherever Rory is, so are the others."

"Assumptions can be dangerous. Are you sure you don't want to reconsider?"

She scooted past him and stood, putting a little distance between them in an effort to help her think clearly. "While I appreciate you saving me, even your charm isn't enough to get me to tell you my secrets."

He rose, standing in front of her so she was right on eye level with his throat. "Ah. Then you do admit you have them."

For a single, crazy moment, she wanted to kiss him there, right over the steady beat pounding in his veins. "I'm a woman. Of course I do. That's my job."

"And it's mine to uncover those secrets."

Nicholas staggered into the living room, filling the wide doorway.

Logan took a long step back, looking like a kid caught stealing a cookie.

Nicholas's laser blue eyes glared in suspicion at Logan. "What's going on?"

Hope suffered through a moment of confusion while she translated the macho-speak. Clearly, Nicholas didn't like the idea of her being close to Logan, and it appeared as though Logan agreed it was wrong as well.

The idea that two men would decide what was right or wrong regarding her made her furious. This was her life. She may not have known exactly how old she was, but she knew she was a grown woman, completely capable of making her own decisions.

She decided to let them know loud and clear she was in control of her own life.

Hope stepped closer to Logan. He backed away. She followed him until he was close to the fire with nowhere else to run.

"Problem?" she asked sweetly.

Logan lifted his hands to his sides so they were in plain view. "What are you doing?" he asked her.

"I'd like to know that, too," said Nicholas.

Hope looked at Logan's eyes, then back to his mouth. His lips were a dark red, full, beautiful. She wanted to kiss him again so much it made her shake.

"You mustn't," whispered Logan. "Please."

"Why not?" she asked.

"Mustn't what?" asked Nicholas.

Logan swallowed. "There are things you don't understand."

"Explain them to me."

"I will."

"No," said Nicholas. "I'll be the one to do the explaining. She's getting all sucked in by your pretty face and I can't let that happen."

"It's not your decision," said Hope.

"It's not yours, either," said Logan. "Any more than it is mine. Things are as they are and neither of us can alter that truth."

"That's it," said Nicholas. "She's going to Dabyr. Tonight."

Hope whirled around and glared at him. "I'm not going anywhere but to a hospital with my friend."

Logan slipped out from behind her, putting the couch between them. She didn't understand his actions, but she didn't like the way he went cold whenever others were around.

He wanted her. She knew he did. She'd seen proof of it more than once. She didn't understand why he kept avoiding her.

Unless he was ashamed to be attracted to her. Maybe vampires were too good for humans. Or whatever she was—even they didn't seem to know for sure. What she did know was his rejection stung.

Good thing she had more important worries to distract her.

"I need to leave," said Logan.

"The hell you do," said Nicholas.

Logan's lips thinned in anger. "Would you prefer I stay with her? My attraction isn't exactly convenient for me, either. I'd think you'd be willing to keep me busy elsewhere."

The thrill that he admitted an attraction to her was steamrollered by his desire to avoid it. And her.

"Okay. Whatever," said Hope. "I'm done dealing with you all. I'm taking Jodi to a hospital. Will one of you take us? Or are you going to make me call a cab?"

Nicholas was scowling at Logan, puckering his scars. Logan's face was smooth and stoic, but he was avoiding her gaze.

She reached for her cell phone only to find it missing, lost back in that alley where she'd been attacked. "Is there a phone in this house?"

"I'll take you somewhere safe," said Nicholas.

"What about Jodi?"

"Jodi, too. She'll need to have her memories altered."

"Not only no, but *hell* no. No one is touching my friend's memories."

"We must," said Logan. "Any Synestryn taint must be removed or demons could be drawn to her."

"To kill her and eat her," added Nicholas, scowling. A

bright plume of fiery anger exploded in his aura, drowning out the pain and flashes of silvery honor she'd come to associate with him. "This is nonnegotiable. Logan cleans your friend's memories or she dies. Period."

Hope didn't know what to think. If Nicholas had been lying, she would have seen a hint of deception surrounding him. There had been none, which meant he was telling the truth, at least as he believed it.

"I don't want her to live like I have," she whispered, her eyes pleading with Logan.

His voice was gentle. "It won't be like that. I'll be careful. I'll make her think she went out drinking with friends and had a little too much. She'll wake up tomorrow and go on with her life. Safe."

"I don't like it."

"I know. I'm afraid we can't let that matter. I'll be as gentle as I can."

She needed a few minutes alone. These two men sucked all the oxygen out of a room. And she couldn't stand to watch the man she'd grown to care about do something as despicable as erasing her friend's memories.

Hope pushed past Nicholas and went outside.

Logan had to lock his knees to keep from going after her. "Go," he told Nicholas.

"Do you want to explain what's going on between you two?"

"I wish I knew."

Nicholas ran a hand through his hair in frustration. "I'm used to women tripping over their tongues when you're around, but I've never once seen you do the same."

"Just go. She's not even wearing a coat."

The Theronai stared at Logan for a long second. "She's not a Theronai, is she?"

"I don't believe so, but that could simply be a case of wishful thinking."

Nicholas closed his eyes and let out a long breath, as if he'd come to a hard decision. "You go and I'll watch Jodi. Hope trusts you, as foolish as that may be."

"Around her, I don't trust myself."

"Do you think you'd hurt her?"

"Never."

"Then go. Calm her down so we can gain her cooperation. It's the only way to ensure her safety in the long run."

Logan knew it was a mistake, that he was tempting himself with something he could never have. Still, his feet moved toward the door and carried him out into the night.

Finding Hope was easy. Even blinded, even without her blood flowing through him, he'd be able to find her by scent alone. No other woman called to him like she did. It may have been a cruel twist of fate, but that didn't change how he felt.

She was sitting on the porch steps, hugging her knees, shivering.

Logan stripped out of his coat and draped it over her shoulders before moving away. He didn't dare stay within reach of her. Not because of what she might do, but because of what he *wanted* to do.

Cold air slid around him, but he barely felt it. Not with her this close. She seemed to drive the chill away by her mere presence.

"Will you come back inside?" he asked.

She looked up at him. "I didn't want to distract the two of you from your plans to control our lives."

"It's not like that, Hope. We only want you to be safe."

She shook her head. Moonlight gleamed off her pale hair. "That man came after me for some reason. Maybe he knows who I am. *What* I am."

"Does it matter?"

"Apparently it does to you. And Nicholas."

"His kind are desperate. It's his pain that makes him possessive. You can understand that, can't you?"

"Now you're just trying to manipulate me. Again."

She was right. He spent so much time manipulating others he barely even realized he was doing it. "I apologize."

"Don't. You don't really mean it."

"Tell me what you want, Hope. Tell me how I can help."

"I want Rory and the others found. I want the monsters who took them stopped. I want Jodi safe and happy. And I want my memories back."

"We're already working on the first two. The last will take more time, but it is possible."

"You can't know that. You're just telling me what I want to hear so I'll play along."

Was she right? Was he fooling himself into thinking he could help her so he'd feel less guilty over forever altering the course of her life?

"We could try now," he offered.

"Try what?"

"Accessing your memories again."

"How?"

He wanted this for her, but she was so skeptical right now. He needed her to let down her guard, and the only time she did that was when he got close enough to distract her and slip past her defenses.

"Come, we'll get out of the wind and find some quiet."

"I don't want to go inside. It's too . . . crowded."

"As you wish." He reached out his hands to her.

Hope looked at his hands, then back to his face. Her shoulders slumped on a sigh of defeat and she put her fingers in his.

They were cold, and the need to see her warm and safe brought out a dangerous, feral side of him.

He'd kill to see to this woman's comfort. Or worse.

If the man she ended up with did not treat her right, Logan wouldn't hesitate to tear his mind to shreds until even her slightest whim was a compulsion he couldn't resist.

It was the ultimate form of evil to take away someone's free will, to strip them of what made them human and destroy it. It was what the Synestryn did to their Dorjan. And yet if the options were to go against everything he held sacred or watch Hope suffer, he knew which he'd choose. Without hesitation.

Logan shoved those bleak thoughts from his mind and led her to a nearby barn. The structure was showing its age. Some of the boards had rotted out near the ground, and the dingy white paint was peeling. The doors were unlocked. He turned on the lights so she could see, but only one was working. The bare bulb hung from a wire near the back, barely bright enough to illuminate all four corners.

The interior was empty but for a few sacks of grass seed, a lawn mower, and lawn furniture that had been stored for the winter. It smelled of gasoline and the hay that had once been stored here, but without the wind, it was definitely warmer than outside.

He unfolded a lounge chair, retrieved the thick cushions from their plastic storage bin, and made her a comfortable place to lie. "Have a seat."

"Why do I feel like this is a couch at a psychiatrist's office?"

"How does that make you feel?" he joked.

A smile pulled at her soft lips, and a glow of satisfaction radiated from his core, warming him. He'd made her smile. Surely that was as close as he'd ever get to having the sun warm his skin, and if so, he'd count himself lucky to have come this close.

Hope took his coat from her shoulders and handed it to him. He was sure she'd meant to give it back, but as soon as she was settled, he draped the leather over her like a blanket.

He did not miss the shiver that coursed through her, though he couldn't tell whether it was from the cold, regaining the warmth of his coat, or from fear.

"We don't have to do this," he told her.

"I want to. Something changed tonight as we were searching for Jodi."

"Changed?"

She frowned and shook her head. "I felt a kind of soft spot in the barrier to my memories when something struck a chord."

"What was it?"

Her lips pressed together as if she wasn't going to tell him.

Logan sat down beside her and took her hand. There wasn't much space on the lounge chair, but that only gave him a reason to touch her, to press his thigh to hers. He knew their time together was drawing to a close, and he wanted to take from it what he could for as long as he could.

"Tell me," he urged her. "It could help."

She pulled in a deep breath, but when she spoke, she did not meet his gaze. Her amber eyes were fixed firmly on the opposite wall. "I thought that if I remembered, we might know why Jodi was taken or where she'd gone."

"How would that have helped?"

"These things that have been happening—the people that are going missing are all connected to me. None of the other shelters are suffering the same problem. Just ours. That could have connected to anyone at the shelter, but then Jodi was taken. She doesn't go there, which means that the common connection was me."

He cupped her chin and turned her head until she was looking at him. He needed her to see the truth in his eyes. "This is not your fault."

"It is. I can feel it."

"No. The choices these monsters make are theirs alone."

"How do you know? For all we know, I worked with them. Hell, maybe I even ran the whole damn group."

"It's simply not possible. I would have felt their taint upon you, tasted it in your blood. All I taste in you is purity and light. You're a good person, Hope. Don't allow yourself to think otherwise."

"You're sweet to say it. I really do want to believe you."

"Then do. I swear I'm being honest."

She gave a small nod, though he wasn't sure if she was relenting or simply moving on. "I may not have worked for them, but I'm still the cause of all of this. Somehow. And there's something else."

"What?"

"I think I might have allowed someone to take my memories. I might have even done it to myself."

Logan tried not to let any of his shock show through. He slid his hand down her arm until he was holding her chilly fingers within his own to warm them. "What makes you think that?"

"I don't know. It just feels . . . right. I don't think my memory loss was due to trauma. I think it was done on purpose."

That changed everything. If someone had done this to her, there had to be a reason. And the list of reasons why someone would steal another's memory wasn't very long. Either they were protecting her or they were protecting themselves.

Logan was going to find out which one, because if it was the latter, things were much more desperate than even he had thought.

He leaned forward and his fingers settled lightly at her temple. Her skin was so soft and warm, he forgot why he was touching her for a brief moment. He could spend all night touching her, learning the different textures of her skin and the sounds she made as he stroked each one.

No. That was not for him—not outside of dreams. He couldn't allow himself to think like that. Down that path lay starvation.

"Close your eyes, Hope. I want you to relax and let me inside."

Chapter 23

Tori tensed as the footsteps grew louder. She dragged herself out from under the bed and scurried under the covers to pretend she'd been there all along.

People looked at her funny when she was under the bed, like she didn't belong there. It made them come back with more people to help her—something she wanted to avoid. She didn't need people. All she needed was a plan. A good plan. One that would earn her the sight of Zillah's blood draining from his body.

Nika walked in with her grumpy boyfriend only a few steps behind her. Tori didn't like having them visit. She owed them her life for rescuing her, but she wished they'd just leave her alone.

"We need to talk," said Nika as she sat on the edge of the bed.

Tori had grown to hate that word. Every time someone said they wanted to talk, it meant they wanted her to do something she didn't want.

"What?" she asked, hoping to get this over with.

"Tynan thought of something we can do to help you." She pulled in a deep breath. Madoc laid his giant hand on her shoulder, making Tori flinch. Even the thought of a man touching her like that made her want to puke.

Tori shifted away from the pair, moving to the edge of the bed.

"He says that he can put you to sleep while he heals

you. That way, you won't have to hurt. You can go to sleep and when you wake up, you'll be all better."

Liar! screamed a voice in her head. She had to fight back the urge to scream it at her sister.

"No. I don't want to sleep." Zillah crawled into her dreams when she slept. She could feel his slimy touch on her thoughts, forcing her to remember the things he'd done to her. She didn't want to remember, and if she was forced to sleep, she'd be trapped there with him with no way to escape.

She'd spent years as his prisoner. He wasn't stealing another second of her life.

"But you're hurting so much," said Nika.

Anger swirled deep inside her, making her muscles clench against the need for violence. Her heart was pounding hard, driving infected blood through her body, readying it for action. She knotted her fingers together to keep from lashing out at her sister. "I don't need anyone telling me how much I hurt. I know."

"And so do I. We're linked, no matter how much you fight to keep me out."

Tori wrapped her arms around her knees. "You don't belong in my head. I wish you'd quit trying to put your nose in my business."

"I can't help it. You're my sister. I have to find a way to help you."

"Then leave me alone. Quit coming here. Quit shoving your thoughts in mine. Just go away."

Nika rocked back as if Tori had hit her. It made Tori feel bad, but only for a second. Then all she felt was anger. The constant, pulsing anger she'd grown so used to. It was always with her, growing every day. One day, she'd kill Zillah and it would all go away, but until then, she needed that anger to keep her going—to help her fight the pain of the poisonous blood flowing through her veins.

"I won't leave you," said Nika. "I promised you that years ago, the night you were stolen. I meant it then and I still mean it now. You can't make me go away."

She could. She'd learned lots of ways to kill in the years she'd spent with the Synestryn. And when the rage inside her got bad enough, all she wanted was to lash out at whoever was nearby. She didn't care who it was or what happened to them. Andra knew it. So did Madoc. That was why they never let Nika come in here alone.

Tori looked at Madoc, fighting down that rage. She remembered the gift he'd given her while she was still imprisoned—the gift of sunshine. Because of that gift, she offered him one now. "I don't want to see her again. If you love her, don't let her come back here."

Hope was as beautiful inside as she was out. Being inside her mind was like Logan imagined bathing in sunshine would be. Warm. Soft. Gentle. He could live here forever and never grow bored.

He slid along her thoughts with ease, but it was different from being inside a human. The connection he felt to her was stronger and took less effort to sustain. There were no convoluted paths of logic he had to overcome, or flittering distractions that led him in the wrong direction. With Hope, sharing the same mental space was easy.

Perhaps this was what it felt like when mated Theronai connected.

Before that thought could bloom into something dangerous, Logan pushed forward, heading right to where her amnesia began.

"Show me this soft spot," he whispered to her, though whether his mouth moved, he wasn't sure.

Hope wrapped around his consciousness to guide him, and the instant she did, everything else ceased to exist. He was surrounded by light and joy, bathed in it. Time no longer mattered. His body could have shriveled and died and he would not have mourned the loss. This place or feeling—whatever it was—was magic, pure, perfect magic.

"Did you feel that?" she asked him. Her voice swept

through him, shimmering along his nerve endings as it passed.

"Yes," was all he could manage.

"What is it?"

"I don't know. I've never felt it before with anyone."

"Stay close. It could be some kind of trick, like a booby trap."

Confusion flittered across him for a brief second. "What makes you say that?"

"Because nothing that feels that good can be real. It must be some kind of trick."

Logan questioned her logic, but kept it to himself. "I'll be careful. Show me."

Hope guided him along her thoughts, taking him with her on the chain of logic that had led her to the soft spot.

There. He sensed what she'd felt earlier—a kind of dent in an otherwise pristine plane of do-not-pass.

"This wasn't there before," he said.

"It happened when I thought about how I might have allowed someone to take my memories. I can't imagine ever letting that happen, but this seems to be proof that I might have."

Logan prodded the spot and instantly felt a stab of pain vibrate through Hope. He pulled back, fighting against an instant flare of anger at himself. "Are you hurt?"

He was still connected to her mind, but his eyes opened so he could scan her body as well. She'd pulled her knees up as if someone had punched her in the stomach.

"That's just a tender spot, I guess."

"I won't touch it again."

"No. I want you to. I want you to see if this is a way into my memories."

The idea of causing her more pain repulsed him. She must have felt it, because in the next instant, she was stroking over his consciousness as if to comfort him.

"Please, Logan. I don't care if it hurts. I need to know what I did to cause these people harm."

"You did nothing."

"You don't know that. Maybe I didn't do it on purpose. Maybe this is all about someone I know who's holding a grudge—someone I can't remember."

She could be right. If she recognized Krag, it could create another soft spot, or perhaps break through the one she'd found.

He took the image from Leonard's mind—the one of the Synestryn lord with scaly, hairless skin and lips that did not cover his pointed teeth—and showed it to Hope.

She recoiled in revulsion, but there was no flash of recognition he could sense. "Have you seen him before?"

"No. What is he?"

"Synestryn. He's the beast who ordered Leonard to hurt you, to abduct Jodi."

He felt her take the image deeper, dragging it inside her mind where she turned it over and ran it along the barrier to her past. There was no reaction, no dent formed.

Her sense of defeat hit him hard. His immediate reaction was to wipe it away—to blunt the emotion artificially, but he doubted she'd appreciate his help. Instead, he wrapped himself around her and offered her what reassurance he could.

"We'll find a way to get back what you've lost. I promise." The weight that settled over him as he gave his vow wasn't heavy. It was comforting. Given freely, without any thought of repayment, it reminded him of the man he used to be—the one he wished he could be again.

That man would have been good enough for a woman like Hope.

"I like the man you are now," she told him, her words fervent and heartfelt. "The fact that you wish you could do more counts for a lot."

"Not nearly enough. My weakness is shameful."

He felt her hand on his skin and pulled back into his body enough to revel in her touch. Until now, he hadn't realized he'd draped his body over hers at some point in his effort to comfort her. His arms were wrapped around her tightly, and her legs were hanging from the sides of the lounge chair to allow room for his body between her thighs.

Instantly, his cock swelled and hardened, painful in its haste to be ready for her. Pressed against her belly like this, there was no way to mask her effect on him—no way to hide his desire for her.

Her golden eyes glowed with womanly need. "You aren't weak. It's not your fault that you don't have the strength to do what you want. Except when you take my blood."

The mere mention made his mouth water and his hips kick forward against his will. The smell of her skin was intoxicating, but it was the scent of her growing arousal that pushed him to the limit of control.

She tilted her head aside, stretching her elegant neck, tempting him. "You can do it again if you want. I like it. A lot."

Logan's body clenched, his muscles knotted against the need for him to hold perfectly still. If he so much as breathed, he knew his self-control would give in and he'd take what she offered. "I cannot."

"I feel fine. You're not as hard on me as you think." She reached between their bodies and rubbed her palm over his erection. "Except here."

He pulled in a deep breath, hoping it would cool down the inferno raging inside him. She was so beautiful laid out like this, open and trusting. Her skin glowed in the dim light and the gold of her eyes seemed to brighten as they moved to his mouth.

She was going to kiss him. He could feel her muscles tensing to move, to lift her head forward toward his. Her lips parted and she pulled in the air that he breathed out.

Heat swirled between them. He could feel it fighting back the chill surrounding them. Her pupils dilated and her tongue swept out to wet her bottom lip.

He needed to get up—to push himself away from her. He gathered his power to shove himself back, not caring if he slammed into the rotting barn wall. He'd take an injury over betraying her.

And if he took her, it would be a betrayal. She didn't realize that now, but once she was settled with the man meant for her, she'd see that he'd used her for his pleasure, that he knew there could never be anything more between them than a few shared moments of physical bliss.

But after so many years of famine, he wanted the feast. He wanted to feel the slide of skin on skin, the damp heat of shivering lust as it overtook a woman. He wanted to hear her soft moans of pleasure and strive to make them louder. But most of all, he wanted to find a way to be closer to her, to make her feel good. Safe. Loved.

He could love a woman like Hope. Part of him already did, which was all the more reason to hold himself back.

She wrapped her hand around his nape and pulled him down, meeting him halfway. The touch of her lips to his was electric. Every rational thought in his head shorted out and in that space was the ravenous need to possess something he so desperately wanted.

Her tongue swept inside his mouth, playing along his teeth until she found one of his fangs. Her sigh of need filled his lungs, and he drank it in, greedy for more. His stomach tightened and his cock jerked against her belly, desperate to be closer.

He was lost, and while part of him screamed in defiance at his weakness, the rest of him was cheering in a roaring scream of encouragement.

Logan ripped the leather coat from between their bodies and kissed Hope back like she deserved. He shoved her shirt up and caressed the smooth skin over her stomach and ribs. She pushed him up, using more strength than he would have thought possible.

Not that he'd let her shove him away now. Not anymore.

He pulled his mouth from hers to tell her it was too late to change her mind, but from the flush of desire painting her cheeks, that wasn't what she had in mind. Instead, she stripped her shirt over her head and shed her bra, baring herself to him. Her eyes dared him to stop her from getting what she wanted.

Logan stared down at her, reveling in her beauty. She was exquisitely formed, perfectly curved. Her dream self did not do her justice. Her nipples were hard and cherry red. A pink flush spread down her neck over her chest. As he watched, she reached for the button on her jeans.

"We're doing this," she warned him, her tone fierce and demanding.

He wasn't sure if he found her assumption more amusing or alluring. Either way, he was along for the ride. He could barely speak, but he managed to push out a rough, "As you wish."

Her smile of approval drove the breath from his body with the sheer power of her beauty. To possess something as perfect and potent as she was seemed too good to be true. His actions didn't merit such a reward and yet he was going to take it, nonetheless.

Her hands slid up his ribs, shoving his shirt up as they went. He stripped the fabric from his body, not wanting anything to get in the way of her touch.

Her nails dug into his skin, scraping just hard enough to send a shiver up his spine.

"The jeans," she ordered.

He obliged, stripping hers off before seeing to his own.

She lounged, one leg dangling over the side of the chair. The slim lines of her body had a perfectness of symmetry he'd never seen before in a human. Her hips flared just enough to fit his hands, before tapering to long, smooth legs. Faint tan lines marked her skin, and he stroked a finger over them, intrigued by the marks the sun had left upon her.

What he wouldn't give to lie in the sun with her and make love, drinking in its warmth.

It was a fantasy that could never be, but he found himself hoping despite all logic. After all, if Hope was here, sharing her body with him, then anything seemed possible.

He tossed another cushion onto the floor and draped his coat across it to form their bed. "If I take you on that flimsy thing, we're both going to end up on the ground, anyway."

She lifted a brow in challenge. "Take me? That sounds awfully barbaric."

"It fits my mood, then."

She rose from the chair, naked and glorious. She didn't try to hide from his sight, or strike any artificial poses. She needed no such artifice. Hope was perfect as she was.

He took her hand and eased her to the cushion, ensuring her comfort before he perched along the edge. A chill roughened her arms, and before he considered the consequences, he rolled atop her to cover her body with his.

The skin on skin contact was too much sensation. It stole his breath and made his heart pound in his chest. His head spun at the feel of her hard little nipples and the slide of her legs along his own.

She speared her fingers through his hair and brought his head down for a kiss.

He'd meant to be gentle. Slow and careful. But as soon as her lips touched his, thoughts vanished. The man in him gave way to the more feral part of him—the baser part of him. A sweet wooing was no longer an option. He needed her. He needed to be inside her and drive as much pleasure from her body as she could stand. He needed to fill her up and claim her for his own so no other man would ever dare to touch her. Only him.

The thought gave him pause, but he brushed it aside, refusing to let anything come in the way of what she offered.

Logan pulled his mouth from hers. She tried to follow him up, but he had other ideas, other needs. He laid his hand across the center of her collarbone to hold her still while he kissed his way from her shoulder down to her breast. He took her nipple into his mouth, dragging his fangs across it in a way that made her gasp and lift toward him.

"Yes," she hissed out, grabbing and holding his head in place. "Just like that."

Logan suckled her hard, then eased up, swirling his tongue over her to ease away the sting. Every time his teeth grazed her, her body tightened in anticipation.

He knew what she wanted. He could feel her need shimmering between them. She wanted his bite and the pleasure it could bring.

He refused. He'd already lost enough of himself coming this far. If he went any farther, he might never be able to return. And she would be the one who suffered—something he simply could not allow.

Her fingernails bit into his scalp. She slid her ankle up his flank, wrapping her leg around the small of his back. The move opened her so that his manhood nudged the wet heat of her core. And then she started pulling, using her leg to urge him closer.

Against his will, his hips shifted, gliding the slippery tip of his cock along her folds. There was still time to turn back. Somewhere deep in his mind, part of him was screaming for him to stop this before it was too late.

She reached between them and wrapped her fingers around him, giving him a long, hard stroke. Her fingers slid over him, lining up their bodies. One hard tug from her leg and he slid a couple of inches inside her core.

There was no place he wanted to be more than right here, right now. Despite his reservations, the perfection of the two of them like this, joining together, was simply too much to deny.

Hope held her breath and became still. He reached out for her, searching for signs of pain. He brushed against her mind, intending only to seek out what was causing her distress, and too late realized the folly of that plan.

She was writhing with need. Her body ached to be filled. Lust was a tangible thing inside her, demanding and insistent. It gripped her belly and twisted, making her desperate. Her skin sizzled with sensation, each nerve ending pushed to its limits. And the emptiness churning within her reminded him all too keenly of what it was like to need blood. It was more than merely a want, and he could not stand her suffering.

Her body was tight, but he pushed forward, needing to fill the ache and ease her suffering. She was slick and hot, accepting each small thrust as he worked his way inside her sweet body.

She twisted beneath him, trying to help ease his way and join them more quickly. He held himself back only enough to prevent her any discomfort and refused to let her hurry him.

Finally, only when he was seated inside her, the tip of his erection nudging her womb, did she subside. The need was still there, but it had shifted, morphing into something else. Something darker and more taboo.

Taking her body was not nearly enough. She wanted him to take her blood as well.

The image of it burned bright in her thoughts as if she'd spent hours fantasizing about it. Every detail was laid out before him, from the way his muscles clenched as he moved within her to her firm hold on his head as he fed from her throat.

Logan tried to pull back to rid himself of the tempting image, but it was with him now, part of him as much as her blood flowing through his veins was a part of him. Forever.

Her sheath clenched and he sucked in a breath. Stillness was no longer an option.

He pulled from her, feeling her slickness easing the way. Her body had accepted his invasion, making room for him to push deep without causing her pain.

Part of him still hovered inside her thoughts, gauging her reaction. It didn't take long for him to perfect his angle and technique to bring her the most pleasure with every stroke.

His nerve endings felt like they were glowing. Sweat formed on his back only to evaporate in the cool, dry air. Her nipples grazed his chest, sending zingers of sensation to the base of his shaft. Small muscles inside her quivered around his erection, making it hard for him to concentrate. He tried to keep his wits so he could bring her the most pleasure, but his own was too great to ignore.

With each thrust, he lost a little more sanity, a little more reason. All that mattered was the sound of her increasingly loud sighs and the hard, steady pace of their mating bodies.

Hope kissed him, taking his breath away with her enthusiasm. Her lips were swollen and wet from his mouth. The growing scent of her arousal made his head spin. She was close. He could feel it in the way her body was winding up, tightening with the impending explosion.

Logan wanted nothing more than to give her the pleasure of climax and to feel that climax flutter along his cock as he filled her with his seed. Nothing else was important now. Only Hope.

He would give her anything she needed to see her fulfilled.

Anything? he heard her voice whisper within his mind. And the image of his mouth working at her throat while his hips worked to drive her higher flashed in his mind's eye, brilliant and clear and forbidden.

He opened his mouth to tell her that he couldn't, but her lips covered his, and her tongue thrust inside to flick across his fangs.

She wanted it. The idea compelled her, consumed her.

Hope guided his head to her neck. The slender length arched, giving him unhindered access. Beneath her delicate skin, her pulse pounded hard and fast. Steady and strong.

She wasn't too weak. He would have sensed it if she had been. He didn't understand how that was possible considering how much he'd fed from her, but it was true all the same.

"Do it," she whispered, breathless with anticipation. "Bite me. Just a little."

There was no little about this. If he bit her, he'd lose control. He knew he would. He was nearly already at his limit just thinking about it.

Her grip was strong. It forced his mouth against her skin. He couldn't help but kiss her. She was so smooth and soft. She tasted so good.

His fangs ached. His tongue felt swollen. There wasn't enough oxygen to fill his lungs as his body thrust, keeping up the pace she liked best—one that had him fighting to stave off his own release for as long as possible. With each deep plunge, she quivered around him as if her body were trying to hold him inside.

"Please," she said. "I want to feel it all. Just once."

He could deny her nothing. Even if it was forbidden. Even if he knew he might never recover from the stain on his conscience.

His fangs grazed her skin. She let out a soft gasp and shivered.

He promised himself he'd be careful. He wouldn't bite deep. Just enough to fulfill her fantasy.

Logan took charge of her body, holding her tight so she couldn't thwart his plans to stay in control. Her sudden bursts of strength were unpredictable, and one of those could put all of them in danger.

It took only one spilled drop of blood to bring an entire nest of Synestryn down on them.

But he wouldn't spill any. He'd swallow it all down, staying sealed to her throat until every trace of scent was licked clean.

Her hips bucked as she struggled to make him hurry. Her impatience shimmered in the air, but he wasn't going to let it alter his course.

Logan thrust deep, pinning her in place with his weight and his cock. He felt an answering quiver inside her and a hot rush of wetness as she neared climax.

She was close. One little nip would send her over the edge.

He stroked his fangs across her neck, sealed his lips against her skin, and bit down gently.

The taste of her blood hit his tongue and filled his senses. His mind was connected to hers, and because of that, he felt her searing spike of pleasure caused by his bite.

Logan had been foolish to think he could control himself in this. It was too much sensation to control. Too much desire. Too much pleasure.

He bit deeper, needing to increase the flow of blood. A trickle would never do. He needed more. As much as he could get.

Her body shuddered as an orgasm swept through her. It shook her to her core and milked his erection as if trying to hurry his release. A feminine cry of completion echoed inside the barn's high walls. Heat poured from her until he was sure he'd see steam rise from her body if he opened his eyes.

He didn't. He was too busy drinking her in, letting the strength of her climax fill him as it raced through her blood. There was power in this moment, more than he'd ever thought possible. It was like drinking from one of the Athanasians, pure and perfect and laced with a reverent sort of magic.

His cock throbbed inside her, demanding to be heard.

Until now, he'd stayed still, pinning her in place. But that was no longer possible. He needed to move.

Logan stroked in and out, using some of his newfound power to speed his movements. Hope's climax had just eased, but he felt another building, her need swelling as the tempo of his thrusts and feeding sped.

Her hands had held his head in place, but they now slipped away as her arms went limp. Weakness filled her, but he wasn't done with her yet. He was going to wring one more searing burst of pleasure from her. Now.

He drank deep, tugging on her throat as he fed. Each tug coincided with the movement of his hips until she was careening over the edge again, screaming out her orgasm

Logan lost control and let the climax have him. It crashed against him, choking the air from his body. His seed spurted deep, wringing another soft cry from Hope.

Her pulse slowed, became weaker.

As the last shivering wave of his orgasm passed, he realized just what he'd done. He'd nearly drained her dry.

Panic ricocheted in his chest. He healed the puncture wounds closed and cleaned away every drop of blood before he dared lift his mouth. He felt her mind touch his, offering him reassurance, but guilt weighed down on him.

"I'm so sorry," he said as he lifted his head to look into her pale face.

She gave him a sleepy smile. "Don't be. It was . . . perfect."

She didn't realize what he'd done. She was probably delirious.

Logan briefly considered feeding her some of his blood to strengthen her, but the risk of doing so was too great. His seed was inside her. If she drank his blood, she could conceive.

The idea of a child—his child—growing inside her was bittersweet. He would have loved the idea if he

hadn't known how it would end for the child. All Sanguinar children, even half-breeds, had been cursed with the
thirst for blood. Creating more mouths to feed was not
just irresponsible, it was unforgivable.

So he did the only thing he could. He gathered up a
burst of power and transferred it back into her, directing
it to make new blood. Some fluids and some rest and
she'd recover.

"Mmm," she sighed. "I like that. Not nearly as much
as the other way, but that's nice, too."

He was still joined to her. Still inside her, which made
his betrayal seem even worse. "We need to get you inside
where it's warm."

"I'm warm here. With you."

Logan slid from her body and gathered up her clothes.
He didn't bother with her undergarments, simply pulled
her jeans and shirt on to keep her warm while he dressed
himself. He loathed every second it took, but if Nicholas
knew what he'd just done, the consequences could be
unpleasant.

He eased her limp body up enough to slip the sleeves
of the coat over her arms.

"Will you stop? You're harshing my buzz."

Logan blinked in incomprehension. "You're delirious."

She smiled at him. "You're just that good, baby."

He lifted her into his arms. She snuggled against his
shoulder. "The real thing was so much better than my
dreams."

"You mustn't speak of it," he warned her. "No one
can know what we've done."

He could hear the frown in her voice. "Why not?"

"Promise me, Hope. Promise me you will not tell anyone what I did to you."

"I believe I did some of that to you, too."

"Please. Promise me."

"Fine," she said, exasperation filling her tone. "I
promise."

He staggered under the weight of that promise for a step, knowing that not only had he violated her, he'd also forced her to help him cover it up.

"Put me down," she said.

"That is not going to happen."

"I can walk."

"Tomorrow. Perhaps."

"You're treating me like I'm dying. Will you just stop?"

Logan did. They were halfway across the icy lawn between the barn and the house.

"Put. Me. Down."

He did that, too, though he kept a careful hold on her arm in case she fainted.

Hope got right into his face, her eyes blazing. "Look. We just had the most fantastic sex in history and you're acting like we murdered a litter of kittens. We did nothing wrong."

"Yes, we did. You're meant for another man."

"No, I'm not. I get that you have some really antiquated ideas, but that doesn't mean I'm playing along with them. I'm not going to hook up with some guy—not until you and I have had time to see if what we have together works."

Logan closed his eyes to block out the sight of her beautiful face. She was confused. Weak. He'd caused those things by taking too much blood. No matter how much pleasure it had given her, he knew better. That was why his kind never mixed sex and blood. It was too easy to lose control.

Another minute or two and he could have killed her.

"What we have is duty. That is all I can allow myself."

"Fuck duty. You've been toting that burden around for too long. Let someone else have a turn."

"That's not the way it works. All must help if we are to survive."

"Then let me help you."

He looked down at her, unable to keep his eyes

averted any longer. The sight of her was precious, a treasure to be cherished for as long as it lasted. "I hope you will help us. But not like this. Not with me."

"Then how?"

He owed her the truth. "Eric is like you. His blood is rich and powerful. My hope is that the two of you will be happy together and have many children."

"Children?"

He nodded, his mouth suddenly dry. "We need the blood."

She stepped away from him. "You're telling me that you want me to sleep with this Eric guy and let him knock me up? You're telling me this while your semen is still inside me? That you *want* me to sleep with another man?"

"Yes." He took a step toward her.

She held up her hands to ward him off. "You are out of your fucking mind. I'm not going to be some baby factory so that you and your buddies have a nice, hot meal whenever you want one."

"It's not like that. We're very careful in our efforts."

"Careful? Is that what you tell the women you've done this to? Sorry, Mom, we're going to snack on your babies, but we'll be careful."

"It's not like that and you know it."

"What I know is that I offered you my blood. Repeatedly. That's not enough for you?"

"I wish it were."

She shook her head in disbelief. "This is too messed up. I can't believe anyone could be so cold as to manipulate the lives of innocents for their blood."

"We have no choice. We're starving."

"Ever thought about asking people first, rather than trying to trick them into it the way you did with me?"

"We only mate those people who will be happy together."

"Yeah, do you go into their minds and brainwash them to make it happen? Are they just drooling fuck-puppets meant to squeeze out kids once a year?"

"Stop it, Hope. You're twisting it into something it's not. We go to great pains to make sure our subjects are happy."

"Subjects? Is that what I am to you? Some kind of lab rat?"

Anger was gathering inside him, threatening a storm. "I wish you were. I never would have been drawn to you, never would have lain with you."

She let out a scoffing bite of laughter. "You're even colder than I thought. Here I was, all moon-eyed, thinking I was falling in love with you. I had no idea of the man you really were."

"That's because I'm not a man. You'd do well to remember that."

"That's it. I'm out of here." She stormed off, but her anger supported her only so far. Her knees gave out and she started to crumple to the ground.

Logan caught her and pulled her against his body, hating the immediate reaction she caused. He'd had her only moments ago and yet he was already aching to slide inside her again. He could smell the scent of their bodies mingling, becoming something darker and more intoxicating. The muskiness of his seed was deep within her, and any Sanguinar or Slayer who met her would know in an instant that she was his.

Not that she wanted to have anything to do with him. The way she was twisting the truth about made it seem ugly and sinister. Project Lullaby was nothing like that. It was necessary.

He needed her to see that. To know it. She didn't understand the kind of suffering they endured, because if she had, she wouldn't have been so quick to judge him. They didn't kill people. They worked themselves sick ensuring that their subjects were happy and healthy.

The scales were even. And soon, she would know it, too.

Chapter 24

Logan's hold on Hope tightened and he pressed his hand to her temple. She could feel his anger vibrating through his body, but that was just too bad. She didn't have time for him or any of his tricks.

She tried to pull away but his grip was too tight. She willed one of those surges of adrenaline-induced strength to fill her, but nothing came. A second later, all thoughts of struggling evaporated.

A strong, solid presence filled her, and she recognized it easily. Logan.

Normally, she felt a gentleness surround him, but not now. His presence was draped with purpose, like a man on a mission.

"Feel," he ordered.

And she did. She was swept up in a wave of memories and sensations unlike anything she'd ever felt before. There was hunger. Mountains of it. So much that it ate away at her sanity, making her cry out in agony. Her belly churned and nothing could fill it but ancient, powerful blood.

But there was none to be had. A hopeless desperation descended on her, driving strength from her limbs and the will to live from her soul. She was so hungry and yet there was no more food. There would never again be more food. She was going to die here, now, and it couldn't come soon enough.

Hope pleaded for death to take her, to end the relentless gnawing in her guts and the weakness that robbed her of the ability to do more than sit and stare, helpless and useless, while people around her died.

She couldn't go on like this. What was the point of living if all that life had to offer was hunger and weakness and death?

And then she felt it, a faint stirring of hope, a dim light gleaming on the horizon of her suffering.

Blood. Rich, powerful blood. She could make it, grow it. It would take time. Centuries, perhaps, but for the first time in memory, there was a chance.

Hope reached for that chance, grabbing onto it with both hands. It slipped through her fingers, intangible and insubstantial. It flitted in her vision, teasing her as it darted around, never fully in sight.

But she could have it. She could have that blood. All she had to do was one little thing: Create families.

It didn't sound so bad. Surely, she could find people who would love each other, people who belonged together, who would be happy together. The search would be hard, but the reward would be survival. She would hold each new life in her arms and cherish it for the blessing it was. It would never go hungry. It would never die of disease or sickness. She would be there, right by its side, seeing to its needs.

She had plenty of money, so that was no issue. None of her children would live in poverty or squalor. She'd see to it that they got a good education and made a place for themselves in the world so that when the time came, they, too, could help create a new and precious life.

And while she knew she'd have to take their blood to survive, she'd be careful about it. She'd screen them for disease and heal any injuries she found. She'd imbue them with long lives so their cells would not age and die as a normal human's would. She'd do everything in her power to see them happy.

All she needed in return was the power to help them—the power only their blood could give her. It didn't seem too high a price to ask. After all, if she didn't do this, the dark things in the night would find them and eat them. If she wasn't strong, she couldn't keep them safe, and she desperately wanted to keep them safe.

As the idea sank in, she turned it around, looking at it from all sides. It didn't seem nearly so terrible as it had before. The faces of dozens of people filled her head—all of them had been touched by the Sanguinar. They'd been paired up; they'd been fed on. None of them seemed to show any signs of abuse or neglect. They were . . . happy with the arrangement.

Who was she to say they weren't?

Hope felt Logan's presence release her, and with a little pang of regret, she let him go. The images he'd shown her were still a part of her, as was the memory of that hunger. If he'd endured that kind of torture, it was no wonder he'd been desperate to find any means necessary to escape it.

But what if all that mental hocus pocus was just a lie? What if he'd planted it to sway her opinion? "I want to talk to them," she said.

"Talk to whom?"

"The people you've manipulated."

He flinched at her wording, but she didn't back down. She couldn't. If she let up even a little, she knew he'd find a way to break through her defenses.

"The couple who was attacked the night we met. They were paired by me. Will that suffice?"

She nodded, remembering how concerned the man had been for his wife. She'd had no idea they were some of Logan's "subjects."

He pulled out his phone and dialed. "Steve, are you all well?" He listened for a moment. "Good, that's good." His eyes met Hope's. "I was wondering if you had a moment to speak to someone for me. Just answer her questions with the truth, please." He paused. "No, your vow of secrecy does not apply to Hope. You may speak freely."

Logan handed her the phone. She put it to her ear, half expecting a trick. "Steve?"

"What can I do for you?"

She didn't dare blurt out her real question, which was whether he knew he'd been manipulated. "How did you and your wife meet?"

"Uh. Logan set us up."

"Can you be more specific?"

He hesitated. "My sister was dying. Car accident. Her brain was swelling and she was in a coma. Logan came into her room and said he'd help in exchange for a favor."

"What kind of favor?"

"He wanted me to meet Pam, though I didn't know her name at the time."

"Did you find that odd?" she asked.

"Yeah, but I was kinda out of my head with worry. Nothing made any sense at the time. She was my kid sister. My responsibility. Mom and Dad were gone and I was the only one left to take care of her, but there was nothing I could do."

"So you agreed?"

"Yeah. I was desperate. I thought it was worth a shot—a hell of a lot better than watching my sister die." He pulled in a deep breath. "So I agreed. It was the first night Logan took my . . you know."

"Blood?"

"Yeah. He took my sister's, too. Whatever he did after that must have worked. The swelling went away. She woke up. She's a medical student now."

"And Pam? What happened when you met her?"

She could hear a smile creep into his voice and a distant quality filled it, like her presence on the line was suddenly unimportant. "She was my other half. A part of my soul I hadn't realized I lost."

A sense of jealousy filled Hope, but she ignored it. No sense in being jealous over something artificial. "How long have you been together?"

"Five years. Married three."

"And you have a baby on the way?"

"Yeah. A son."

"Did Logan order you to have children?"

"What?" The way he squawked the word made it sound like her question was ridiculous. "Of course not. What the hell is that supposed to mean?"

"Didn't he tell you that's why he put you together? So you could have babies and he could drink their blood, too."

"Listen, lady. I don't know who the hell you think you are, but Logan's not like that. He's a good man. He's nearly killed himself helping me twice now. I owe him everything, and I know without a doubt that when my son is here, Logan would do the same for him."

"But what about the blood?"

"What about it? It's no big deal. Doesn't even hurt."

"Are you going to let him have your son's blood?"

"The minute he's old enough to handle it, you bet your ass I will. None of us have been sick a single day since we met Logan, and the one time I fell and broke my leg, he came right over and patched me up so I wouldn't miss any work. Sure, the whole magical thing is a little far-fetched, but as far as I'm concerned, I don't know how a CAT scan works, either. It's all a mystery to me. Logan just happens to be better, faster, and a hell of a lot cheaper. I don't care what anyone says. He's a fucking superhero."

What could she say to that? Either Steve was being completely honest with her and he truly didn't mind the arrangement, or he was so brainwashed he didn't even know the truth.

Hope knew which one she thought was more likely. The man had been way too smooth to be reciting things he'd been force fed.

Which meant she had a lot to think about. She didn't like Logan's tactics, but that didn't mean everyone hated them. Steve certainly had benefitted from Logan's interference in his life.

And she remembered how bright Steve's love for his wife had shone in his aura. That was not something that could be faked. His love was real. He was connected to his wife in a way Hope could only dream about.

But she didn't dream about it with this Eric guy. She'd lied about falling in love with Logan. She wasn't falling. She'd fallen. Past tense. She'd thought that his manipulative ways would have kept it from happening, but they hadn't. If anything, the things he'd done to others had only cemented her feelings.

Not only did Logan have to fight for every drop of blood, he also had to take care of every life he touched. On top of that, there were people like her whose mistrust probably didn't make his efforts any easier.

She opened her mouth to apologize when Nicholas burst out the front door, his face grim. "You need to come inside. We have a situation."

Logan tensed beside her and took a protective step closer, scanning their surroundings.

"What?" she asked.

"I'm so sorry, Hope," said Nicholas. "The shelter and your studio. They're both on fire."

Hope stared in horror at the TV screen. One side showed an image of her studio. Firefighters blasted it with thick jets of water, but it seemed to be doing little good. On the other side of the screen was the homeless shelter where a reporter stood out front.

The reporter's words slid past her, not sinking in. All she saw were the flames rising up in the background as the fire crews worked to control the blaze. Huge plumes of black smoke billowed from the barred windows.

She scanned the surrounding crowd as the camera panned across the scene. She searched for a glimpse of Sister Olive or any of the regulars who visited. There was a growing group of people outside gawking, but she recognized none of them.

Fear weighed down on her, making it hard to breathe.

Logan's arm slid around her shoulders. She huddled against his side, waiting for someone to tell her this was all a mistake. "Where are the people who were inside?"

Nicholas sent Logan a meaningful look—one she didn't understand.

"What?" she asked.

Sympathy filled Nicholas's gaze. "They don't know about your studio, but the reporter said the fire at the shelter was obviously arson. The doors were barricaded from the outside."

The significance of what he said sank in, freezing Hope from the inside out.

It was cold tonight. The shelter would have been full. All those people had been trapped inside. Along with Sister Olive.

Grief choked her. Her knees gave out. Logan's strong arm held her up, supporting her.

She struggled to regain her balance. She needed to be strong right now and figure out what had happened. She needed to go back and find out how many people had escaped—broken the bars on the windows. Surely some of them had found a way out.

Maybe even Sister Olive.

"I need to leave," she announced, her voice sounding weak and hollow.

"You can't," said Logan. "That fire was set purposefully. We know a powerful Synestryn wants you. And while I tried to plant false memories in that Dorjan's head, it may have failed. They attacked your home as well as the shelter. I think it's more than possible that fire was meant to either kill you or force you to come out of hiding."

His words took longer than normal to sink in. "You're saying you won't take me back?"

"No. I won't."

"Neither will I," said Nicholas. "I'm sorry for your loss, but our priority now has to be your safety."

Hope pulled away from Logan's hold and sank to the couch. Her knees were still weak. Her body was shaking. Ice coated her insides, numbing her from the pain she knew would hit at any moment.

She had to hold it together long enough to find out if Sister Olive was still alive. The woman had been like a mother to her. Hope couldn't simply sit around and wait to find out if she was still alive.

What if she was injured? What if she needed Hope at her side, praying for her recovery?

Hope reached for her cell phone, before she remembered it was gone. She needed to call for a cab, but she didn't even know where she was.

Flashing lights, smoke, and flames filled the TV screen. A bright red banner scrolled across the bottom, mocking her inability to move forward as it did. She didn't know what to do next.

Sister Olive may be dead.

Grief crashed into her, making her sway. A low sound of mourning filled her ears. Hot tears slid down her cold cheeks, stinging as they passed.

Nothing was ever going to be the same again. Her whole world had gone up in flames and now she had nothing. No family. No home. No job. Everything had been stripped from her, laying her bare.

The air was too thin. She couldn't seem to get enough of it to fill her lungs. Her chest burned and she held herself as she rocked. The ice inside her had melted, and now she felt everything. All the fear and pain and grief. It slammed down on top of her, over and over, beating the life from her body.

Her mind struggled to make sense of things, to find some course of action that would help. But nothing came to her. There was nothing she could do to fix this. Her life was gone.

Again.

For the second time in less than thirty years, every-thing had been taken from her. She couldn't go through it again. She couldn't start from scratch and rebuild her life. She wasn't that strong.

If that Synestryn had meant to kill her in that fire, he'd succeeded, because Hope was certain she wasn't go-ing to survive. She wasn't even sure she wanted to try.

Hope's anguish assaulted Logan's senses. He could hear her heart race and her breath wheezing in and out of her lungs. The heavy scent of mourning flooded his nose, and the sight of her tears made something dark and violent writhe in his chest.

He had to do something.

Logan turned to Nicholas. "Do not try to stop me," he told the Theronai.

"What are you going to do?"

"Ease her pain."

"Why would I stop that?"

Logan didn't answer. Instead he gathered her trem-bling body in his arms and carried her back to one of the bedrooms. She didn't fight him. She didn't even seem to acknowledge his existence.

Nicholas was right on his heels. "Whatever you're go-ing to do, I'm going to watch."

"No, you're not."

"The hell I'm not. She's my responsibility."

Logan whirled around, snarling at Nicholas. He tried to keep his voice quiet, but he managed only to sound more feral. "Hope is *mine*."

Nicholas stopped in his tracks, looking stunned. "I've never seen you act like this before. What's gotten into you?"

"A woman I care for is in pain."

A silent sob shook Hope's body, making Logan wish she'd turn to him for comfort.

"You care for her? Since when do you care about anyone but yourself?"

Logan restrained his anger long enough to lay Hope down on the bed. She curled into a ball, hugging herself. Every moment Nicholas delayed him was another moment of suffering for Hope.

That was simply unacceptable.

He gathered his power and grabbed Nicholas by the throat. He slammed the beefy man into the door frame. "I care not what your opinion of me is. Hope is the one who matters here. She's in pain. I intend to ease her suffering. Back. The. Hell. Off."

Logan let go of Nicholas. The man's neck was red, but he didn't even rub away the sting. Instead, he filled the doorway, crossing his thick arms over his chest. "I'm not leaving you alone with her when you're like this. Not unless you kill me."

Which he knew Logan would not do. His blood was far too valuable, as was his sword arm.

Logan was going to have to ease Hope with an audience, which was awkward, but necessary. He didn't want to waste even one more second on Nicholas.

Hope was facing away from them. Quiet sobs of pain shook her shoulders.

Logan sat next to her, shoving all emotion from his mind in preparation for what he was going to do. After several deep breaths, he laid his hand on her forehead and forced his blood to give up its stores of power.

He sought out her grief and gathered it up. It swarmed about him, stinging like a hundred wasps. The pain grew the longer he controlled the emotion, but he needed to accumulate all he could. He wouldn't have the will to do this twice.

Once he controlled her pain, he shoved it into himself, holding his breath as her emotions became his own.

A sense of loss so deep it would never heal split him open. His soul wept boiling tears of mourning that burned until he was sure the pain would kill him. Every empty part of him was filled with grief and loneliness.

Intellectually, he knew that these emotions were not

his, but that made them no less real. Hope felt things deeply. More so than any other human he'd ever known. Her sorrow invaded every part of her until her very cells were drowning in it.

Logan didn't know how she'd survived feeling like this, even for a moment. He carried only a portion of her anguish and it was enough to drive him mad.

Normally, he would have adapted to the feelings, absorbed them, and transformed them into chemical and electrical signals that would fade in moments. But this was too much. He couldn't process it all. He didn't know how she could stand it.

He heard Nicholas's concerned voice, but couldn't make out the words. Not that they'd matter. Nothing seemed to matter now except Hope.

Logan gathered her into his arms and held on tight. Her warmth sank into him, anchoring him in place.

He needed just a little more time to fight off these feelings. To let them dissipate. And then, when they had, he'd go back to gather up more, despite the pain it caused him.

He couldn't stand the thought of leaving her to suffer alone.

Chapter 25

Nicholas didn't like this situation. He didn't know what Logan was doing to the woman, but whatever it was, it was costing him dearly. The Sanguinar's skin had gone so pale it was nearly translucent. His body shook, and Nicholas could see Logan's flesh wasting away before his eyes. Muscles that had been there only moments ago were shrinking and fading, leaving the other man's clothing hanging on his frame.

He went to Logan's side and put his hand on his bony shoulder. "You need to stop."

Logan didn't seem to hear him. His grip on Hope was tight, his body curled around her almost possessively.

Or maybe not almost. The Sanguinar *had* claimed her. Backing up that claim was a different story entirely, and modern women tended to be a bit prickly about such things. Their independent streaks were wide and tender. Treading on one was risky.

Not that Nicholas wouldn't have done the same thing if he'd thought Hope could save him. He would have. He would have done anything in his power to hold on to her. Just the way Logan was doing.

He heard the door to the Gerai house open. He put his hand on his sword and went to see who was there.

Tynan shut the front door behind him, gathering his coat about his lean body to ward off the chill. The Sanguinar was strikingly perfect in his appearance, with the kind of good looks that made women stare in lust-filled awe. Like all the Sanguinar, he had pale skin and eyes that had the ability to shed light when their emotions ran hot or they were using their magical mojo.

A Sanguinar with glowing eyes was a dangerous beast. Of course, even without the glowing eyes, Logan and Tynan's kind were not to be trusted. Unless it was to trust that they would do whatever benefitted them.

Which made Nicholas wonder what Logan stood to gain by easing Hope's pain. Perhaps her cooperation?

"What are you doing here?" asked Nicholas.

"I'm looking for Logan. Where is he?"

"In the bedroom. With a woman."

Only a faint flicker of surprise lifted Tynan's brow before he controlled his reaction and his face once again became impassive. "I see. Perhaps I shouldn't disturb them then."

"Actually, you probably should. I don't know what he's doing, but it doesn't seem to be too healthy for him."

Tynan hurried past Nicholas and down the hall until he found Logan. He watched for a moment before he went to the bed.

"Stop," said Tynan in such a forceful tone that Nicholas found himself freezing in place, not even daring to breathe for a second.

Logan growled. The quiet warning was unmistakable.

"You must stop," repeated Tynan, this time with more force.

Logan ignored him.

Tynan turned to Nicholas. "Strike him."

"What?"

"Hit him. Hard. Disrupt his concentration."

"Do it yourself."

"As you wish. I would have thought you'd enjoy the task."

There had been times when Nicholas would have bled for the chance to slap one of the Sanguinar, but not like this.

Tynan drew back his fist and slammed it into the side of Logan's face.

Logan was lying still one moment, and the next, he was flying at Tynan, claws and teeth bared, eyes glowing. The snarl on his face was a deadly warning, as was the hiss pouring from his mouth.

Nicholas yanked Tynan out of the way and took the brunt of Logan's attack. The Sanguinar's claws raked across his face, drawing blood, but Logan was no match for Nicholas's strength. He spun Logan around and tossed him to the floor. His head bounced off the wall and he stayed down.

Logan shook his head as if to clear it. Tynan knelt down by his side. "Are you well?"

Logan nodded. The light had gone out of his eyes, leaving them the normal, pale silver color. He looked up at Nicholas. "I apologize. I will repair the damage."

"No, I will," said Tynan.

"It's just a scratch."

"One that is bleeding and will draw unwanted company."

The leech was right.

Nicholas stood still while Tynan worked his mojo, closing up the small wounds. As soon as the searing heat faded from his cheek, Nicholas went to wash away the blood. When he got back, they were all going to have a serious talk about what the hell had just happened.

Rory had managed to fight off the smaller monsters that had come for her, but she was no match for this one. It was huge—easily three times her size. Its skin was covered in a slimy layer of filth, pulsing as if something was crawling beneath it. It stood upright; the lower half of its body was submerged. Above the waterline, it widened as it went up, getting bigger and thicker as it neared the ceiling. Its nostrils were above its eyes, leaving an odd, empty spot in the middle of its face. Fleshy lips protruded from its jaws, the bottom one sagging under its own weight.

Beyond the mottled gray lips, she could see the glint of teeth. Not that it needed those. The wicked claws extending from its flipperlike hands were more than enough to kill her.

It regarded her with a kind of curiosity, blinking and sniffing as it neared.

Rory didn't think she could be any more afraid than she had been since she'd been dumped down here, but this thing was proving her wrong. Her body found the strength to send a spurt of fear rocketing through her system.

She gripped her makeshift weapon harder, until the edges of it dug into her palm. She'd sharpened the tip by rubbing it on the concrete walls, and now that tip was caked with the black blood of the things she'd used it to kill.

As she looked at the two-foot length of metal, a bubble of nervous laughter rose up inside her. There was no way she could even get close enough to this thing to hit it without it being able to strike her first.

But as the thing glided closer to her, parting the dirty water, she realized it was going to make her test that theory.

A shrill whistle sounded from somewhere outside this room. The monster spun around and sank below the water, swimming out the door. Four thick tentacles broke the surface as it fled. It didn't have legs at all.

Rory had no idea what had happened, but she didn't question her good fortune. She was too busy trying to think of a way out. She couldn't be here when that thing came back. Her last attempt to crawl over the ceiling tiles had ended in disaster. The stairway was blocked by more monsters than she could possibly kill, and so far, she'd found no other means of escape. No windows, no tunnels, just an endless stretch of concrete walls and cold, disgusting water.

She heard the slosh of that water as something came her way. She crouched into the corner and lifted her weapon.

One of the guards who'd thrown her down here came into view. "You're still alive. Good. Come with me."

She tried to tell him to go to hell, but her mouth was too dry to speak. She hadn't been able to get back to the leaking water pipe at the far end of the building today, and she sure as hell wasn't going to drink the muck these things lived in.

He motioned for her to come. "Hurry. The food I gave them will hold their interest for only so long."

What choice did she have? There was no way out down here. At least if she went with him, she'd have a fighting chance to escape. Or at least a chance to die warm and dry. Even that would be an improvement.

Rory hopped down from her perch. The cold water sucked the life from her and stole her breath. The guard grabbed her arm and practically hauled her through the sludge.

As they neared the stairway door, she saw a throbbing mass of twisted bodies fighting a few yards away. She didn't want to see what they were fighting over. All she cared about was getting out of here.

Her legs barely worked to push her up the steps. She was weak from dehydration, hunger, and exhaustion. There was no way she could run in her condition—at least not without falling on her face.

Even her curse—or her *gift*, as her grandma called it—had quit working, which she counted in the pro column of situational accounting. At least without it, she didn't have to see the horrible things that were going on around her.

Funny. She'd prayed to be released from her curse for years. She'd spent the last two shadowing the only person in the world who had made her feel normal—the only person who seemed to be able to block her visions. So either that person was here—which seemed unlikely—or the whole time, all she'd had to do to get rid of the visions was to get captured, tossed into a den of monsters, starved, and to live in constant fear.

It was such an easy fix. She should have done it years ago. Or not.

Rory would have giggled at her situation had she had the energy. As it was, she was swaying on her feet, not even bothering to look for an opening to escape.

Stupid.

She gathered what little strength she had left and lifted her head. Standing in front of her was the asshole who'd taken her hostage, the one who ran this place like some kind of freakish cult. He was surrounded by adoring humans, most of whom were covered in ragged bite marks that burned red with infection. The women were mostly naked, staring in rapt attention at the ugly guy on the throne.

"Kneel," he ordered her.

"I'd rather go back downstairs, fuckhead." Her voice was rough and dry, but she stayed on her feet and that was what mattered.

He waved a scaly, three-fingered hand and two guards dragged a woman forward. Her head was covered with a dirty pillowcase, which shifted with her rapid, frightened breathing.

They ripped the pillowcase off, revealing Sister Olive, the nun who ran the homeless shelter where Rory sometimes ate.

Shock shot through Rory like a stroke of lightning. It jolted her, stealing her breath and melting her in place.

The guards forced Sister Olive forward until she was standing at the foot of the asshole's throne. Her eyes were wide, but the set of her mouth was hard. She hadn't given up hope and she hadn't been broken like the other women here. Yet.

He reached out and wrapped his scaly fingers around Sister Olive's throat. There was a malicious gleam in his eyes, one that told how much he enjoyed Rory's shock. "Kneel, or I'll kill her."

Sister Olive closed her eyes and started praying. Quiet, fervent words spilled from her mouth as she called upon the God she believed in so deeply.

Rory had seen the woman's faith run through her actions. She'd seen how kind and selfless Sister Olive had been. She'd devoted her life to others, and now that life was in Rory's feeble hands.

She couldn't fight. She couldn't run. She couldn't even call upon her rebellious streak and lip off in the hopes that he'd kill her. If she died, Sister Olive would suffer, and that was something Rory couldn't stand. She had to swallow her pride and do the right thing. Chances were it would be the last thing she ever did—at least of her own free will.

Rory knelt.

"You know better," chided Tynan.

Logan was not in the mood for a lecture. "She was in pain."

"It was foolish. A waste of power."

Logan didn't care. He couldn't stand to see Hope hurt like that, not if it was in his power to fix it. "Why are you here?"

"You said you had blood to share. Grace's condition is getting worse and I need more power."

Logan looked away, focusing on the slim lines of Hope's back. She was resting peacefully now. He could hear the steady beat of her heart and her even breathing. "I'm sorry. I used much of it."

Tynan's mouth flattened in disapproval. "You squandered it."

"No. She was grieving. Too much. It wasn't normal."

"It would have passed."

"Not soon enough."

Tynan looked at her, and it was all Logan could do not to block sight of her with his body. "Is she well now?"

"Yes."

"Fine. Then I will feed from her myself."

Rage coated Logan's vision. It took over his body, compelling him to act. Hope's heavy grief still hung over him, but it faded in comparison to the ferocious need to kill.

The sound that came from Logan's throat was not normal. It was feral, vicious. "I will kill you if you touch her."

Tynan tilted his head, unfazed by Logan's threat. "Is that so? You seem too weak to do anything of the sort."

"So are you. Don't test me."

Nicholas came back in, his face clean of blood. "What the hell is going on here? I've never seen you two act like this."

Tynan kept his eyes on Logan as he spoke. "Logan has absorbed the human woman's emotions. It's making him cranky."

"Absorbed her emotions?"

"Her grief," said Logan, hoping Nicholas would understand and take his side if they came to blows. Which was a definite possibility.

"Ah," said Nicholas. "So that's what you were doing."

"It's incredibly dangerous," explained Tynan. "And foolish. The woman would have healed on her own. Eventually."

"I don't know," said Nicholas. "She was pretty upset. If Logan here helped her out, then good for him. Way to take one for the team."

"What team?" asked Tynan.

Nicholas rolled his eyes. "It's a figure of speech. We're all on the same side here, right?"

Tynan gave Logan a steady gaze. "Perhaps."

"Whatever. It's over now. It's done. Time to move on already."

"He does have a point," said Tynan. "The power cannot be recovered now. I'll have to find a new source."

"Not Hope. She's off-limits."

Tynan smiled as if Logan had told a joke. "Off-limits?"

Logan heard Hope's heartbeat speed up a second before her eyes opened. "What's going on?" she asked, her voice groggy.

Nicholas lounged against the door frame, smirking. "These two were just having a pissing contest over you."

She pushed herself upright. "Really?" she asked looking at each of them. "Who won?"

"How are you feeling?" asked Logan, stepping over anything else Nicholas might say.

Hope rubbed her temples. "I had the worst dream. There was a fire at my studio and the shelter. Everyone was locked inside." She swallowed twice before continuing. "The woman who took me in years ago died."

Logan sat down, needing to touch her. He used the gentlest voice he could. "I'm sorry, but it wasn't a dream."

Her forehead wrinkled in confusion, and a moment later, sorrow overtook her expression as his words sank in. "It was real? Sister Olive is dead?"

"We don't know that," he offered. "But the fire was real."

Hope slid past him to stand. "I need to get back and find her. See if she's . . ."

"You can't," said Nicholas. "The fire was set on purpose."

"Then whoever set it will think I'm dead."

"Or maybe they did it to flush you out of hiding," said Logan.

She looked at the trio of men gathered. "The closest thing I have to a mother may be dead and you're telling me I can't even go and find out?"

"I'll make a few calls," said Tynan. "Perhaps we can learn of her fate without risking your safety."

"I don't know you," she shot at Tynan. "Why would you help me?"

"Because your safety is of great importance to me. As is your well-being."

Logan cupped his hands over her shoulders. The slender lines of her body called to him, even through his hunger and fatigue. He wished everyone else would simply go away, evaporate into space so he could be alone with her.

His thumbs smoothed over her shirt. "I trust him. Please, let him do this. If we can't find out about Sister Olive, then one of us will go investigate. But this will be quicker."

Hope nodded. Sadness radiated out from her, but it was no longer the gushing, unnatural grief that had been there before.

"You stay here and rest," said Tynan. "I'll go make my calls."

"I want to help." She began to move forward, but Logan stopped her with his body.

"He doesn't need any help." Tynan would use his powers of persuasion over the phone to get the answers he needed. Hope would only get in the way.

Before she could argue further, Tynan left.

Nicholas shot Logan a meaningful look. "Are you going to make it? You're looking a little pale. Even for you."

Logan was weak from his efforts, but that weakness was nothing new. "Give Tynan your blood if you're willing to share. Grace won't survive without him."

Nicholas nodded and left the room, shutting the door behind him. Whether he'd meant to offer them privacy or he'd done it in an effort to protect Hope from hearing any bad news, Logan wasn't sure. But he was glad of it all the same.

"Who is Grace?" asked Hope.

"A human woman who sacrificed herself for the sake of another. She's not likely to survive."

"I'm so sorry."

"I refuse to dwell on it. We've had enough sadness for one night."

"Nicholas seemed worried about you."

"Would you believe me if I said he's just a mother hen type?"

"Hardly." A faint smile curved her lips, making him ache to kiss her again. He knew it was wrong, but that didn't stop him from wanting it anyway.

Logan smoothed her hair away from her face. The honey blond strands were tangled and damp from her tears. "You should rest. It's been a rough night for you."

"For you, too. You need more blood. I can tell just by looking at you."

"Not yours. It's too soon."

"You did something for me, didn't you?"

"What do you mean?"

"If that wasn't a dream, then neither were the feelings I had. I felt you inside me. I felt you hold me."

He wished he could hold her still, but every second he spent touching her was another betrayal. "I'm going to go check in with Tynan."

She pushed to her feet. "I'm going to do the same with Jodi. Is she awake yet?"

"No, but she's fine. We want her to sleep as much as possible to prevent her from forming more memories we might have to remove."

"I told you I'm not going to let you—"

He pressed a finger to her lips to keep her from saying something she'd have to take back later. "We're going to do whatever is best for her. You're her friend. I know you want that for her."

"She has a right to her memories."

"She also has a right to stay alive and not be haunted by the things that have happened to her. So far, I believe she's only seen a human, but if I'm wrong, or if that was to change, I'd have no choice."

"And I'd have no choice but to stop you. Don't push me on this."

This argument was getting them nowhere. He'd do what he must to save Jodi's life, and if that drove a wedge between him and Hope, then so be it. Anything that pushed her away from him was for the best, anyway, because he wasn't sure if he'd ever be able to walk away from her.

"Go to her," he said. "It's a waste of time to argue with you over possibilities."

Hope left, her spine rigid. Logan found Tynan at the kitchen table, speaking on the phone. He waited until Tynan hung up.

"So?" asked Logan.

"The human authorities know nothing yet. The fire burned hot and they haven't yet been able to get in to investigate for bodies."

"Are you sure they're not simply hiding the truth from you?"

"I'm certain. The police chief was easy enough to compel to give me the truth."

"So we don't know if Hope's Sister Olive survived."

"No." Tynan gave him a level look. "Does Nicholas know you've slept with her?"

"How did you know?"

"Your scents cling to each other. Along with the scent of sex."

"I was weak."

"Based on your reaction in there, you have not yet worked her out of your system."

He said it like she was some kind of toxin—a malady to be remedied. That was not the case at all. Hope was no disease. She was a balm to his soul, comforting and infuriating in a way no other woman had ever been.

Logan loved her. There was no more denying it, and no matter who she ended up mated to, he believed he would continue to love her. "I will do what is right for our people."

Tynan laid a hand on his shoulder. His fingers were cold, the chill sinking all the way through to Logan's skin. "I know you will. I trust you."

"You're cold."

"Keeping Grace alive has been taxing, but it's Tori who's taking up most of my strength. I have yet to find a way to filter her blood and I fear that if I don't find an answer soon, her sanity will be the first casualty."

"She's lasted so many years. Certainly a few more weeks is not too much for her to stand."

Tynan shook his head. His mouth flattened to a grim line. "She has dark, violent urges and they're not getting better with time. I think being inside Dabyr with its protective wards is somehow irritating the Synestryn infection, bringing it to the surface."

"You can't take her outside the walls. Zillah would find her within hours."

"I know. I also know that nothing I've tried has worked. I'm going to have to put her to sleep in the way of our people. Maybe if we find and kill Zillah, whatever influence he has over her will die with him."

"Are you strong enough for that?"

Tynan sighed. "Not while Grace still lives. But I can't let her die, either. Without her, I have no clue what Torr might do. And as violent as Tori's urges are, I promise you that Torr would be much more destructive. He's losing leaves every day now."

"Grace can't save him. She's human, not Theronai."

"No, but if she dies, I fear that Torr's hope will die with her. I truly do not know what to do."

"You need to save them both. And for that you need strength. Take some of mine. I don't have as much to offer as I should, but what I have is yours." Logan held out his arm.

Tynan didn't hesitate, which told Logan just how close to the end of his strength he was. His fangs sliced through Logan's skin, opening his vein. Tynan held his wrist tightly, making the transfer as fast as possible.

None of their kind enjoyed giving up power. The sooner it was over, the better it was for everyone.

A few seconds later, Logan felt his skin knit shut and Tynan pulled away. He frowned at Logan. "You said she was strongly blooded."

"She is."

"I sensed her cells within you, but they were as empty of power as a non-blooded human."

"What are you talking about? Of course they're not. Without her blood I'd be dead."

Tynan's eyes lit, flaring for a brief moment. "You're right. They're not empty. They're . . . sleeping. I cannot wake them."

"You're saying that you can't access the power in her blood but I can?"

"It seems so."

"Have you ever run into this before?"

"No."

The memory of Hope's bursts of strength and the odd glow of colors she saw came rushing back to Logan. "Could it be some kind of Theronai power? You know how Helen has a gift for fire and Andra is adept at shields. Could her sleeping blood be some kind of gift meant to protect her from Synestryn?"

"It's possible. Does she bear the mark?"

"No." He'd seen her body, and unless the ring-shaped birthmark of the Theronai was hidden, she did not bear it.

Tynan glanced over his shoulder, checked the doorway, and lowered his voice. "We must be very careful here. Very certain. Has she shown any signs of magical power?"

Logan nodded. "Physical strength. And something else I can't name. It's like she has another sense; she can see things others cannot."

"I truly don't know what to think. It's like she's a mix we've never seen before—some kind of genetic anomaly or a mix of races."

"She could be part Slayer."

"That would certainly please Eric."

Logan bit back a bitter laugh. Eric didn't seem the type to be pleased about anything. "If we can prove it, Andreas will approve the match."

"And you're content with that?"

"No. I am not. Even thinking about Hope with another man puts me in a killing mood. But I know what's at stake. I will do what's right."

"We'll make sure she's happily settled," Tynan assured him.

It wasn't enough. Logan wanted her to be happy with him. It was selfish and juvenile, but it was his wish nonetheless. "She's not even going to meet a man of our choosing unless we find out what's going on. I promised her I'd help her find where her missing friends had gone. Until I do that, her side of the bargain will not go into effect. We find these people or she'll never meet Eric."

"Do you think the fires are connected?"

"Yes. Don't you?"

"There's something about them that bothers me."

"What?" asked Logan.

"The police chief said the fire department had never seen a fire burn this hot this fast."

"You think it was of magical origin?"

"You tell me."

Logan wasn't naturally one to share more details than necessary, but he guessed this situation qualified. "There's a Synestryn lord after Hope. His name is Krag and he's got several humans under his thrall. He sent one after Hope. It wouldn't surprise me at all if he has control of one of the demons who use fire."

"What if it's a Handler?" asked Tynan.

Denial rose up hard and fast, blocking out even the thought. Those demons were as rare as they were deadly. They were smarter than most, armed with whips that could set fire to nearly anything. With their ability to control weaker demons, Handlers could raze entire towns in a single night, if left unchecked. He still remembered what they'd done to Helen's home the night they'd found her. "It's not."

"With fire like that, it could be a Handler, and if this Krag has sent one after her, its hounds will have her scent. They've been to her home. She won't be safe anywhere."

Slick, oily fear rose up in Logan's throat, nearly choking him. He sprang from the table as he spoke. "We need to get both her and Jodi to Dabyr. Tonight."

"Is Krag after Jodi as well?"

"I don't know, but she lives and works with Hope. If the Handler has Hope's scent, he also has Jodi's."

"We'll go to Dabyr immediately."

"No. You take them both to Dabyr. I'm covered in her scent. Nicholas and I can go in the opposite direction and try to throw them off the trail."

The front door burst open. "Incoming!" shouted Nicholas as he sprinted into the living room, sword drawn. "There's too many for me to fight. We need to run."

Chapter 26

Hope heard the commotion and shook Jodi's shoulder. Something was coming and they needed to run.

Jodi's body was limp and unresponsive. Whatever Logan had done to her to make her sleep had worked too well.

The drop-dead beautiful man who'd been here earlier walked in and picked up Jodi. "Come with me. Now."

Hope didn't argue. She went where Jodi went.

They passed through the living room. Nicholas had his sword out. Logan was putting on the leather coat he'd made love to her on only a little while ago. His jaw was tight and his eyes glowed with a feral light.

Hope reached for him as she passed. He stepped aside, refusing to look at her. "Go," he said. "We'll catch up."

"Catch up? We have to run."

"There's no time to argue." Logan grabbed her arm and marched her toward the door, down the steps, and over the icy ground. In the distance, she saw shapes moving and flickering wisps of flames. They were surrounded by auras of black nothingness.

Fear slowed her feet, but Logan practically lifted her, hurrying her to the van. Despite the cold, her palms broke out in a nervous sweat and her heart raced.

"You'll be fine," he assured her. "We won't let them reach you."

Hope had seen him like this before—all business, focused and calm. It wasn't a good sign of things to come.

Tynan set Jodi in the backseat of his van, leaving the
door open for Hope. He went around and got in behind
the wheel. Logan all but shoved Hope up into the van.
"Stay with Tynan."

"What about you?" she called after him as he jogged
away.

"I'll be fine."

Tynan started the engine. Nicholas positioned himself
between the barn and a sturdy oak tree. His sword
gleamed under the moonlight.

Something small shot through the dark. Hope got
only a tiny glimpse of it, but she swore it was surrounded
by that same black aura as the monsters. It struck Logan,
sending him falling back.

He'd been hit by a projectile.

Synestryn closed in on Nicholas.

Logan let out a roar and grabbed at whatever had
struck him. Something long and skinny, like the tail of a
snake, wriggled in his grasp.

Whatever had hit him was . . . alive.

She had to help him. She couldn't leave him alone
and prone while monsters closed in.

Hope yelled at Tynan, "Go!" and slammed the van
door shut.

She sprinted over the ground to Logan's side. He'd
managed to dislodge the snake from his shoulder. He
tossed it to the ground and Hope stomped on it.

Tynan's tires spit gravel as he shot down the long
driveway.

Blood gleamed wetly on Logan's leather coat. It
didn't have the metallic smell she was used to. It was
sweeter than that, like honeysuckle. The urge to see if it
tasted as sweet as it smelled swept through her and she
had to grit her teeth to stop herself.

She pressed her hand to the wound to slow the bleeding. Logan's face was grim. "You should have left."

"I couldn't leave you behind."

He rose to his feet in one smooth, powerful motion. His injury had to hurt, but he showed no sign of pain.

Movement caught her eye. A pair of furry, rust-colored monsters were slinking toward them. While they vaguely resembled wolves, their jaws were too wide, showing off hundreds of triangular teeth, like a shark. There were burned-out holes where their eyes should have been, but their lack of sight didn't seem to impede them. Their nostrils flared as they sniffed the air, heading right toward her and Logan.

He grabbed her wrist, ripping her hand away from his wound, and pulled her toward Nicholas. Another two of those furry things were lunging at him, jaws snapping. Three more lay dead at his feet.

"Stay here," ordered Logan as he positioned her between himself and Nicholas.

Blue-white light spilled from his eyes. He lifted his hand and more light erupted from his fingertips. It splashed out, flattening into a flat disc between them and the two approaching Synestryn.

The air shivered with electricity. It crackled through her hair and slid along her skin like a caress. She didn't know what he was doing, but it was beautiful and felt good. She could hear Nicholas fighting, sense his sudden movements in the shifting air, but she was too busy watching the light to care what he did.

Beyond that disc, she saw the flicker of flames. Something came out of the shadows, striding toward them. It was taller than a human with hairless, snow-white skin. It had no nose or lips, just openings in its skull. Wicked teeth dripped with saliva that ran down its chin to wet the rust-colored fur cloak it wore. Its legs were oddly jointed, bending the wrong way, making its movements jarring to watch. In one hand it held a whip made from something silver and in the other hand was a red-hot poker.

"Handler," whispered Logan, his jaw clenched in concentration. "Stay still."

Hope did. Only her chest moved, sucking in huge gulping breaths of air that smelled of honeysuckle.

Her hand was wet with his blood—blood she needed. She didn't understand why she needed it, but the urge to taste it was growing uncontrollably.

Her black, hidden past swelled inside her head, taunting her with its presence. She couldn't see it, but she could feel it, looming right there, so close she could almost touch it. If it got only a little closer, if she reached out just a fraction, it would be right there, in her grasp.

The blood. It was the scent of his blood that was tugging at her memories, making them roil to the surface.

Hope lifted her hand and covered her nose and mouth with it, sucking in the scent. Her head spun. She heard a roaring in her ears, like waves breaking against a cliff.

Her mouth was dry. She licked her lips and tasted something sweet. Logan's blood.

She waited for a feeling of revulsion to sweep over her, but it never came. His blood wasn't repulsive. It was powerful. She could feel it sweeping through her system, spreading out to become a part of her. She licked her lips again, her body wanting more of that power.

A faint flicker of a face appeared for a split second. It was a woman. She was stunningly beautiful, with silver hair falling down to her hips. She didn't have a single wrinkle, but Hope knew instantly that she was old. Ancient. Powerful.

Hope felt a sense of warmth at the memory. She'd loved this woman. Trusted her. The feelings ran so deep and wide, Hope had no idea how she'd ever managed to forget someone who was so obviously a huge part of her life.

But as soon as the flash was gone and the image faded, the feelings began to fade as well, melting like snowflakes over a flame.

Hope trembled with excitement. There was something there, and for the first time she'd been able to touch it.

Light flared nearby, breaking her out of her stunned shock. That light was spewing from Logan's hand. She blinked, realizing that whatever Logan had done to shield them had failed.

He'd told her not to move and she'd moved.

The Handler looked right at her and lifted his whip to strike. It was made from fine links of chain and each one glowed white hot. Wisps of smoke rose up from the sinuous length, melting snow and ice wherever it touched.

The Handler's arm swept in a deadly arc, dragging the chain through the air. Hope froze in place, unable to move.

A pencil-thin beam of light slashed through the air, landing on the Handler's snow-white skin. It screamed in pain and reared back. The two furry demons snarled in rage, bared their sharklike teeth, reared back onto their hind legs, and lunged at Hope.

Krag felt the woman's presence explode in his mind. He saw her standing in the moonlight, her blond hair whipping around her face. Her mouth was open around a scream and her golden eyes glowed with fear.

She was beautiful. And she was his.

He sent out a silent command to the Handler nearest her, commanding him to take her hostage. The Handler tried to resist the compulsion, but his feeble mind was no match for Krag's powers. He'd learned at the feet of his father. There wasn't a lesser Synestryn alive who could defy him.

Krag's vision of the woman faded, but he could still feel her this time, as if a light inside her had been switched on and he could see it glowing across the miles.

Wherever she went, he would now be able to find her. Forever.

Logan shoved Hope out of the way of the charging demons. They rammed into the barn wall, yelping as they struck.

The move threw him out of position, earning him a searing lash from the Handler's whip. It burned right through his coat and jeans and blistered his skin. The pain crushed the breath from his body and made his vision waver.

Logan pushed Hope behind him, putting her back to the barn. Nicholas was on their right, fighting off another pair of demons. Logan could smell the Theronai's blood, proving that at least one of them had landed a strike.

The Handler lifted his whip again. It burned through a thin branch overhead. The branch fell at Logan's feet, the severed end still smoldering. He grabbed it up and swung at the Handler. His injured shoulder and thigh burned. He'd stopped the bleeding, but the pain was sucking up his strength, making him weak.

His blow missed and the Handler's whip wrapped around the branch, slicing through it in three places. The burning chunks of wood fell, useless.

"Nicholas," he called. He used one hand to maneuver Hope so she was between him and Nicholas.

"Almost there."

A ragged yelp of pain rose up and Logan hoped it was the sound of a dying Synestryn.

Logan gathered his power and sent another burst of light streaking toward the Handler. The beam landed on his face. He shrieked and jerked back, growling through his bare teeth.

Nicholas's sword appeared, gleaming in the moonlight. With one strike, he severed a paw from one of the demons. The one next to it turned its burned-out eyes onto its brother and attacked.

The two rolled away in a snarling ball of rust-colored fur.

The Handler backed up, out of melee range—out of reach of Nicholas's blade. The demon lifted his whip. Nicholas charged. Only one of the two furry demons lived, and it pounced over the ground, lunging for Nicholas's throat.

The chain slashed out, striking a thick limb overhead. It wrapped around the tree, sizzling and popping as it burned through the heavy wood.

The limb started to fall. Logan pushed Hope back out of the way. He reached for Nicholas, but there was no more time. The branch fell, slamming both men to the ground.

Logan heard the unmistakable sound of bone breaking. He was too stunned to figure out whose it was. He was hurting all over, from whatever had tried to burrow into his shoulder, and the deep burn on his thigh. Add to that the crushing weight of the branch and his whole world was pain.

"Run!" he screamed at Hope.

He couldn't see her. His body was pinned in place so that he couldn't lift his head. He didn't think she'd been under the branch when it fell. Maybe she could get away.

A feral cry of rage filled the icy air. That was Hope's voice, roughened with a battle cry. She was still alive.

One of the rust-colored beasts flew across the sky, landing out of his line of sight. Nicholas shoved at the branch. Pain exploded in Logan's hip, but he ignored it and helped Nicholas push.

The branch rocked but did not move.

The Handler stepped up onto the branch. Nicholas cried out in pain and swiped at the Handler's legs with his sword. The angle was awkward and he missed. The Handler snapped his chain whip, wrapping it around Nicholas's blade.

Nicholas jerked his arm back, trying to pull the Handler off balance. Logan smelled burning flesh and saw smoke rising from the sword's hilt.

Nicholas refused to let go. To give up his sword to a Synestryn could cause his entire life's work to be undone. A Theronai would die before he let that happen, and from the looks of it, that was exactly where this situation was heading.

The Handler stepped over them toward where Logan

thought Hope was. His whip slithered away from Nicholas's blade, but the damage was done. The back of his hand was blistered, some of the flesh charred black. Logan could only imagine what the man's palm looked like.

Hope's terrified scream filled Logan's ears. Then suddenly, it was cut off.

The Handler came back into view. Hope was draped over his shoulder. She was struggling weakly, her head hanging down over his back.

He stepped back onto the log, crushing them beneath it. Bone grated against bone, sending his nerve endings into a frenzy of agony. Logan strangled on a cry of pain.

Hope met his gaze. Her focus seemed off, but she was looking at his face. "Logan," she whispered, reaching for him.

He couldn't reach her hand. He couldn't touch her. The Synestryn was dragging her away and there was nothing he could do to stop it.

The Handler let out a shrill whistle, and the remaining demon came to heel.

His whip stuck out from his belt, looped in a neat bundle. As he stepped over the branch, Hope grabbed it and tossed it back over the branch. The wood started to smoke as the chain sank through it, burning its way down.

It was going to take only a few seconds to burn through. Then Logan could push the branch away and take Hope back.

And then the Handler broke into a run, sprinting away on its oddly jointed legs. It ran faster than Logan could have thought possible, disappearing into a stand of evergreens a few yards away.

"Help me," ordered Logan.

Nicholas didn't respond.

Panic spread through Logan's blood, thickening it until his heart had to struggle for each beat. The chain burned so slowly it was maddening. Logan shoved with all his strength, needing to go after Hope.

Finally, the chain burned through and the section of branch holding Logan down became moveable. He pushed it up and slid out from under it. As soon as the weight was gone, the extent of his injuries became clear.

His pelvis was broken. So was one of his legs.

There was no time to do this gently, so he jerked the bones into place and knitted them together as fast as possible. It felt like someone had taken a blowtorch to his bones, but they fused together, leaving him panting and sweating.

He levered himself up and leaned over to check on Nicholas. He was unconscious. Now that Logan was closer, he could smell the man's blood being driven away by the wind.

If he didn't get them out of here, more demons would descend upon them and Logan was too weak to fight them off.

He stood, holding himself still while the dizziness passed, then reached down and lifted the burned end of the branch. He pivoted it off Nicholas.

The smell of blood grew. Logan wasted no time debating what he had to do. He knelt down beside Nicholas and lifted his arm to feed.

Blood flowed weakly into his mouth. He sent his senses out, sliding through Nicholas's veins until he found the openings. He closed them systematically, healing the worst ones first. It took only a few seconds to finish, but every one took Hope farther away from him.

He could still find her. Her blood was within him. He'd always be able to find her. He simply wasn't sure if he'd find her in time.

The need to run after her pounded at him, but he couldn't leave Nicholas here to die. There was no time to clean him up, so he dumped him onto the backseat of his SUV and got behind the wheel.

Logan dialed Dabyr. One of the Gerai answered.

"I need help. Locate Nicholas's vehicle and send every Theronai in the area."

The woman on the other end of the line sounded young, but she responded to the emergency with a calm, even voice. "Yes, sir. I'm tracking you now. Morgan is in your area. I'll guide him to you."

Logan hung up and focused on his driving—on taking the roads that most closely corresponded to the path the Handler was taking overland.

The sun would be up soon and he'd have to go into hiding. He had to find her before then. He'd seen the things Synestryn had done to young women. That couldn't happen to Hope. He had to find a way to stop it. Before the sun rose and Hope was lost.

Chapter 27

Paul and Andra left for some emergency. Jackie had gone back to Dabyr with a pair of heavily armed Gerai. Baby Samson slept the whole way, waking only when she pulled him from his car seat.

His eyes opened, showing signs of the demon who'd fathered him, but it was the only hint she could find that he wasn't fully human.

Jackie carried him inside, heading straight for her suite. She'd already talked to Joseph, who had grudgingly allowed her to bring him here. She wasn't sure what these men thought an infant would do, but they all seemed to think he was like the others—the children that had been born more Synestryn than human.

She'd seen those things, and knew firsthand that Samson was different. He had no teeth or claws. He had no scales, no tentacles, no extra limbs. He was no threat and she was going to prove it.

Both Gerai followed behind her, lugging in the purchases she'd asked them to make along the way. They needed a car seat for the ride, and while they were at it, she had them buy a few clothes and other essentials.

They laid everything inside her suite and left just as Joseph arrived at her door. He looked at the infant sitting quietly in the carrier, then back to her. "Are you okay?"

"Why wouldn't I be? A baby can't hurt me."

"Iain said you were attacked."

Embarrassment rose in her cheeks. "Oh. Sorry."

He nodded. "Can I see it?"

"Him. You can see him so long as you don't call him an it."

Joseph crossed to the carrier and crouched beside it, moving as if he were nearing a box of live snakes.

"Samson's not going to hurt you," she said.

Joseph lifted a brow and looked up at her. "Samson?"

"His mother is dead. He needed a name."

"Okay. Samson." Joseph unfastened the clips and eased the baby from the carrier. His big hands wrapped around him, making Samson look tiny and fragile. "What do you propose we do with him?"

"Take care of him. He's innocent. He deserves a chance."

"So, you think it's a good idea to have a part-demon child running around, playing with all the humans?"

Sadness made her limbs feel heavy. She slumped onto the couch. "Chances are he won't live that long. The human-looking babies never do."

"You mean there are more like him?"

"Were. Three that I know of. All of them died within a day or two of birth."

"And you saw this? With your own eyes?"

She nodded, unable to speak past the lump of regret and pain in her throat.

Joseph carefully set the baby down and buckled the straps to hold him in place. He sat on the chair across from her, leaving plenty of distance between them. She was sure it wasn't an accident.

His voice was low and gentle. "Jackie, are you sure you want to put yourself through that again? Watching another baby die?"

"Of course I don't want to!" she shouted, unable to contain the sudden roar of anger that erupted inside her.

Samson jumped and let out a squeal of fear.

Jackie gathered her emotions and got them back under control as she gathered up Samson in her arms. She jiggled him until he calmed down.

"We'll take care of him," said Joseph. "I don't know if it will help, but we'll get Tynan to look him over and see if there's anything that can be done."

"The sun," she said. "He needs to spend time in the sun."

"Why?"

"I think it combats whatever part of him is Synestryn. He doesn't seem to like it, but I think it might help him survive."

"Okay. I'll make sure to mention that to Tynan."

"I'll do it."

"I have to insist that you let me place him with a family —people who can watch out for him."

"I can watch out for him."

"You can barely watch out for yourself. I hate to spell it out for you, but you're a mess. You've been through hell and you need to give yourself more than a few days to recover."

"I'm fine."

"No. You're not. You nearly shot Iain."

"He was going to *kill a baby*."

"A Synestryn."

Jackie held Samson out, forcing Joseph to look at him. "Does he look like a demon to you?"

"No, he doesn't."

"His mother was human. Doesn't that count for something?"

"It does, but I can't have him here. It's too great a risk. If he changes suddenly, he could attack someone. We have no way of knowing what might happen."

"He's a baby!"

Joseph grabbed her shoulders. She held Samson close to her chest, shielding him.

Joseph's grip lightened, and she could feel his ring humming through her shirt. His mouth was tight and he split his attention between her, the ring, and Samson.

"Listen to me. The people here are my responsibility. I will not risk them. Samson is a risk—an unknown quantity. We need to put him somewhere where we can care for him and make sure that what we hope is true is true."

"And if it's not?"

"I'm not going to discuss that with you now. We'll deal with the situation as it changes, but my decision is final. I'll place Samson in the home of a Gerai couple and we'll see what happens."

"You can't take him away from me."

"He's not yours. But you are one of our own—a Theronai—and like it or not, you have to abide by the rules like everyone else. It's the only way to keep everyone safe."

"If he goes, so do I."

"I won't force you to stay. But you can't stay with Samson, either. You're already too attached."

"He needs me."

"No, he needs someone, but it doesn't have to be you. It's not going to be you. Do you understand?"

She didn't. She didn't understand any of this. She didn't understand why she'd been taken captive two years ago. She didn't understand why they hurt all those young girls. She didn't understand why Samson's mother had to die, but most of all she didn't understand why she hadn't. Why had she survived when so many others had died?

She couldn't let Samson be one more wasted life.

"Promise me you won't kill him," she demanded.

"I can't. But I will promise you that we will do everything in our power to see that he grows up safe, happy, and healthy. So long as he doesn't try to hurt anyone."

She felt the weight of his vow settle over her, calming her nerves. "He won't. He's innocent. You'll see."

"I hope so. I truly do."

He held out his hands for the baby. Jackie didn't want to let go, but every second she spent with him made it harder for her to give him up. If she didn't let him take Samson now, she might never be able to let go.

Jackie kissed his head and looked him in the eye. "I

know you're a good boy. You show everyone the truth, okay?"

Samson blinked his pale blue eyes. There was no sign that he was anything but a normal, human boy and she prayed it would stay that way.

Joseph took the baby and buckled him into the carrier. He picked it up. "You're doing the right thing. I know it's hard, but the right thing usually is."

Jackie hoped like hell he was right, because if he wasn't and Samson suffered, Joseph would as well. She'd make sure of it.

Hope woke up. She was lying on a cold cement floor, shivering. She lifted her head, but her eyes had trouble focusing more than a foot or two away. Dizziness slammed into her, so she focused on taking slow, deep breaths. When she opened her eyes again, she saw a dark stain on the floor beneath her. Blood. Lots of it. There were layers, some older than others.

She struggled through her confusion, trying to figure out where she was.

Her situation came rushing back to her. The fight. Logan and Nicholas pinned under the tree branch. The pale, disgusting demon had grabbed her. The moment of strength she'd felt when she'd flung that furry wolf monster had disappeared, leaving her weak and shaking. She'd barely been able to dislodge the fiery whip, leaving Logan at least a hope of escaping.

The ringing in her ears started to fade and she began to hear more than her own rapid heartbeat. There were voices nearby, but her eyes couldn't see more than blurry shapes surrounded by strange auras. The colors swirling around these people were dull, muted. Thick black tendrils wound through them, cutting off even the faintest flicker of hope before it could grow.

Slowly, her vision cleared, allowing her to see a group of mostly naked women sitting around a large black hole of nothingness. The aura of a powerful Synestryn.

That nothingness rose and came toward her, parting the group of women as he passed.

Hope shoved herself upright, but she was too weak to stand. She craned her neck up, staring at one of the most disgusting things she'd ever seen. He had patchy skin that was part human, part reptile. His teeth looked like they'd been filed to points. He had only three fingers on each hand, and they were tipped with thick, yellow claws. Maliciousness hung in his aura like a trophy, adding festering spots to the evil blackness that surrounded him.

He stared down at her, his posture screaming victorious arrogance. "You're awake. Just in time."

"Who the hell are you?" she asked, her voice weaker than she would have liked.

"My name is Krag, but you will call me Master."

She forced out a harsh laugh. "Wow. Been watching a lot of B movies lately?"

He jerked her to her feet, bringing her up to his face, so close she could smell rotting meat on his breath. "You will kneel before me. You will worship me. I am the master of all that you see, and you are in my sight."

"Not for long."

"We shall see."

His touch made her stomach roil in protest. His claws dug into the tender skin under her arm.

The desire to fight him off raged through her, but she was so weak, she could barely keep her knees from buckling. She wasn't sure what was wrong with her, but whatever it was, she had to get over it. Now.

Her head became too heavy to hold up and it slumped limply toward her chest.

"None of that now," said Krag. "I want you awake and alert for what's next."

Whatever it was, Hope was certain she wanted no part in it. This monster was rotten from the core out, infecting everyone near him with the same malignance.

She was not going to let him do to her whatever it was he'd done to these women. She was going to escape and take as many of these people with her as she could. Right after she was able to stand up under her own power.

His scaly, reptilian fingers cupped her chin, shoving her head up. Her eyes struggled to focus across the dimly lit space. The building was huge—larger than she could see. Steel I beams supported the ceiling, which was easily twenty feet up. Large, industrial lights hung down, but they were off. The only light in the space came from dozens of candles scattered throughout. They sat on defunct workbenches and conveyor belts. Several giant wooden spools had been set up to act as tables. They were covered in pounds of melted wax and hundreds of spent candles.

Based on the dusty machinery and air-powered tools hanging above rows of benches, Hope guessed that this place had once been a factory of some kind.

Sitting in the middle of all of it was an ornate throne that looked like a movie prop. It was painted a gaudy gold and set up on a raised platform. Flanking it were wrought iron candelabras that were as tall as she was. Blood red candles burned bright, casting a wavering glow over the dozen or so women lounging on the chilly concrete floor.

Her first thought was that he could have at least given his harem a few pillows or something.

Beyond the throne she was able to make out vague shapes slinking around in the shadows. Some of them appeared human, but her eyes were too fuzzy to tell for sure. What she did know was that some of them were definitely *not* human. Their eerie green eyes, black auras, and glow-in-the-dark yellow saliva gave them away.

Part of her was scared out of her mind, but the rest of her was taking everything in, searching for a way out of this mess.

"Nice place," she quipped. "Could use a woman's touch though."

Krag smiled, baring his fetid teeth. "Save your touch for my cock."

That got through her sense of detachment. Just the thought of him looking at her in a sexual way made her stomach churn. "Pardon me while I throw up on your cloven hooves."

He shook her hard, jarring her teeth. "You will learn obedience. So will our children."

Children?

Hope shrank away from that thought, unable to process it. There was no way she'd let him touch her like that. She'd die first, even if she had to take her own life.

"Ah. Now I know how to reach you," he said. "Good." He looked toward the shadows and ordered, "Bring them out."

A moment later, a man who appeared human walked away and came back with two more people. Their hands were bound behind their backs and their clothes were dirty and torn. There was something familiar about them, but in the darkness, with them a hundred feet away, she couldn't tell who they were.

Hope squinted, trying to make them out. Finally, her eyes cleared up enough that she could see them. Rory's pink hair was brown with filth, but her pretty face was unmistakable. As was Sister Olive's.

The floor seemed to evaporate. Hope's legs gave way in shock. Her head pounded. Sweat broke out over her skin.

This monster had her friends, her sweet, innocent friends. There would be no limits to what a monster like Krag would do to them. A sense of bleak, hopeless despair washed over her. There was nothing she wouldn't do to save them, which meant only one thing.

Krag had won.

Chapter 28

Logan pushed the vehicle to travel as fast as he dared over the backcountry roads.

Nicholas let out a stifled noise of pain, but Logan heard it anyway. He couldn't imagine how much the Theronai had to be suffering right now with his horrible burns.

"I wish I could aid you," said Logan.

"I'll be fine," he hissed. "Just find Hope."

If Nicholas was in any shape to drive, Logan may have been able to help him, but his sword was still seared inside his grip, and based on the rate at which his heart was beating, his ability to focus on the road would have been dangerously limited.

"I will help you as soon as I can."

"I know, man. Just drive. I'll call for backup."

"Will they reach us in time?" asked Logan, knowing Nicholas had access to the location of all Sentinel vehicles on his phone.

"We're spread pretty thin. I'm calling Joseph now to get him and any other men there to hop on the chopper."

The invisible pull Hope had on him seemed to be getting stronger, which meant they were getting closer. He guessed she'd stopped moving.

Logan could feel sunrise creeping up on him. Already there was a faint gray glow in the sky warning him of the approaching danger. He couldn't drive any faster or they'd slide off the road. At least there was no traffic to impede their progress.

He took the next exit, hoping it would bring him closer to Hope's location. He had no idea which way the roads would go once he left the highway. He'd have to slow down, but he hoped that what he lost in speed he'd make up in distance by taking a more direct route.

They sped through a small town that was still sleeping. Past that was where he felt Hope the strongest, north of them. He barely noticed the buildings, nor did he care. His whole focus was on that faint connection he had to the woman he loved.

Just the thought of seeing her again, of smelling her skin and feeling her warmth, was enough to calm his nerves. He would find her. And once he did, he'd find a way to save her, help or not.

Nicholas groaned quietly, followed by a speeding of his pulse. He was used to pain, but this was different. The physical damage done to his body tonight was great. Logan hadn't healed any of it but the bleeding.

"I don't know how much good I'm going to be in a fight," said Nicholas.

"I'll heal you as soon as we find her."

"As much as I like that idea, I think you might be better off just taking my blood and going after her solo."

"Don't be ridiculous."

"I'm covered in blood. They'll smell me as soon as we get close."

"You carry spare clothes, do you not?"

"Sure, but—"

"But nothing. We'll toss your bloody clothes out as a distraction. It will draw them away from Hope's location, giving us time to free her and get out."

"I'm digging the positive thinking thing you've got going here. Most of your kind would have jumped on my offer of blood."

"Most of my kind don't need your sword to free the woman they—" He stopped himself before he said something he'd regret.

"The woman they what?"

"You misheard me."

"Bullshit I did. You love her. No shame in that."

No shame in love, perhaps, but certainly there was shame in choosing a woman over his duty to his people. Hope didn't need his love. There were others who could love her better than he. Thinking otherwise would simply make him a selfish, reckless fool. "You wouldn't say that if you thought she was one of your own."

"No, but she's not. She's yours. Anyone with eyes could see it in the way she looks at you."

Logan wanted that to be true. Part of him wanted to believe that there was something real between them, but the rest of him knew it didn't matter how she felt. They couldn't be together. He couldn't put his own selfish needs above the survival of his people. No matter how much he loved her.

Regret burned hot in his gut, making his words come out clipped and angry. "We will not speak of this again. We need to concentrate on getting her back."

"Fine. Have it your way. If you've got a plan, I'm all ears."

They were getting closer. The SUV sailed over some railroad tracks and suddenly, he could feel Hope on his left. He'd just passed her.

Logan kept going another mile before he pulled over. He turned around in his seat and looked at Nicholas. The man was pale and sweating. His right hand was blackened around the hilt of his weapon, red and blistered everywhere else. Repairing that damage wasn't going to be easy.

"Give me your left arm," he told the Theronai.

Nicholas offered up his wrist. Logan shoved his coat up, baring his vein.

"Take a deep breath," said Logan as he brought the other man's wrist to his mouth. "This is going to hurt."

Logan was getting closer. Hope could feel that familiar sunlight warmth he caused glowing along her skin.

She silently screamed for him to stay away, pleading with him not to come here. There were too many monsters here, too many humans under Krag's control. They would hurt him, use him against her, and then they'd kill him.

She couldn't stand the thought of being the cause of his pain and death. She wanted him alive and happy, healing people and sticking his nose into their business.

What about all the happy couples he had yet to help create? If he came here, those people may never meet each other, may never fall in love.

Krag dragged her across the concrete floor, mostly carrying her. Hope's legs still weren't working right, and she was starting to wonder if the pounding in her skull was due to an injury she'd sustained while being brought here.

She couldn't remember much about the trip—just the cold and being jostled so hard she thought her teeth would fall out. The creature who'd carried her had no regard for her comfort. He ran inhumanly fast, sloshing her about as he leapt over any obstacle in his path.

Maybe she had a concussion from all the jarring her brain had suffered. That would explain a lot.

For some reason, believing that made her feel better. A concussion was normal. Human. There was nothing magical about it. She just had to grit her teeth and get through this. So what if her movements were clumsy and her vision sucked? She'd get better. She just had to hold herself together long enough to regain her strength and get out of this mess.

Krag had no idea that she got those odd bursts of power. She'd bide her time and use it against him when he thought her weak.

Maybe if she killed him, all of these poor people under his control would snap out of it.

He let go of her arm and she slumped to the floor, unable to hold herself up. He grabbed a fistful of her hair and craned her neck back.

Sister Olive stood there, tears running down her sooty cheeks. Fuzzy strands of hair had worked their way free of her bun, and her clothing was singed in spots. Her mouth was moving in quiet prayer.

Rory stood next to her, the set of her jaw defiant. She glared at Krag. Her dark eyes glittered with the promise of vengeance. The muscles in her arms shifted as she tested the strength of her bonds.

Krag let go of Hope, and reached out to stroke Rory's face. She bit him. He jerked his scaly hand back, and she spit onto the floor.

Black blood leaked from the bite wound. Krag held his three-fingered hand close to his body and struck her across the face with the other hand. Her head whipped around so hard Hope cried out for her friend, worried he'd broken Rory's neck.

That noise was a mistake.

Krag turned around slowly, a grin showing off sharp, pointed teeth. "You do care for the humans. Excellent. That will make this so much more enjoyable."

Anger and fear collided inside her, mashing together in an ugly, rancid pile in her stomach. "Don't you dare touch them again."

"You warning me? You seem to lack an understanding of who, exactly, is in control. I shall educate you."

Hope could feel the malevolence surrounding him. She could see it swirling within the bleak nothingness of his aura, like rotten spots of decay. Before he even moved, she realized that the lesson he was about to teach her would be horrible. Irrevocable.

She tried to grab his leg to stop him, but he was already gone, too far away for her to reach.

Krag snatched Sister Olive from the hand of the human who held her, grabbed her bun, jerked her head back, and bit her neck, tearing into delicate flesh.

Sister Olive let out a strangled yell before falling deathly silent. The only sounds Hope could hear were the frenetic pounding of her heart and the sickening gulping sounds of that monster stealing Sister Olive's life.

Hope shoved herself to her feet and lurched for him. She was weak and her knees buckled as soon as she gained her feet. She slammed down into the concrete, hitting so hard her skin split against her kneecaps.

She didn't feel the blow. She was a hollow shell, with room for nothing but fear and rage.

Hope crawled over the floor, scurrying to do something—anything—to stop him. She grabbed his ankle, digging her fingernails into his skin.

He kicked her away, sending her skidding a few feet. She hit her head on a steel I beam. Her vision faltered for a moment and when it cleared, she saw Krag release Sister Olive's lifeless body.

The nun's face was fixed in horror. The skin of her throat was ravaged and bloody, and the rest of her was pale.

He'd drained all of Sister Olive's blood. It had taken only a few seconds. A moment ago, she'd been alive, with a fighting chance at survival, and now she was . . . gone.

Hope stared in shock, waiting to wake up and have this nightmare end. This wasn't the way things were supposed to be. She was supposed to fight back, defeat the villain, save the day. That was the way it went in movies.

This was definitely no movie. The woman Hope loved like a mother was dead. Forever. And this time there was no question whether she'd survived. The proof of her death was staring Hope in the face, slicing at her, trying to penetrate the thick fog of shock that surrounded her.

Hope was lifted up by strong hands. Not Krag's, but someone else's. She didn't care whose.

Krag stood in front of her, only inches from Rory. Sister Olive's blood coated his chin and ran down his neck to wet his shirt. His teeth were stained by it.

He grabbed Rory's hair and jerked her head back, displaying her neck at an obscene angle. Rory grunted in pain and struggled to get away, but her efforts were futile. She was bound, and even if she hadn't been, she was no match for Krag's strength.

"Would you like to issue another warning?" he asked with an eerie calm, as if he already knew the answer. "Shall I kill her as well?"

He would. There was no question in Hope's mind as to his earnestness. He wasn't a man. He had no soul. He was a demon.

And for some reason, he wanted Hope.

Rory was young. She had her whole life ahead of her and, perhaps even more important, she had a past. Hope didn't. Jodi and Sister Olive were the only two people who might miss her, and now Sister Olive was dead. Even Logan wouldn't really notice she was gone after a while. He'd made it clear that he'd planned to fix her up with some other man. That wasn't the action of someone who loved her.

If Hope didn't cooperate, Jodi could die, too. Krag had already managed to find her once. He could do it again. And even if he couldn't, Rory was here now. She would suffer. Maybe even die as Sister Olive had.

"No," said Hope. "Don't kill her. Please."

Krag eased up and set his black, soulless gaze on Hope. "Promise to obey me."

There was power in a bargain. She'd felt it when she'd promised Logan to meet Eric if he helped her find her missing friends. Now that their path had led her here, she could feel that bargain pushing her, making her worry more and more about whether she was going to be able to uphold her end. She didn't know if it worked both ways, but as weak as she was, it was worth a shot.

Hope chose her words carefully. "If you let Rory go and never harm her again, I'll cooperate so long as no one else gets hurt."

"She goes nowhere."

"Then it's clear you intend to kill her, in which case you'll have no one left for leverage."

His nostrils flared in anger. "I'll kill her slowly. I'll make you watch her suffer."

"I'll be dead either way," said Rory.

Krag jerked her head, making her gasp in pain. "Shut up! You are an animal. Meat."

False bravado was hard in the face of evil like him, but Hope didn't know what else to do. Logan was getting closer, and unless he had an army with him—one he wouldn't have had time to gather—once he was here, he was going to be another pawn for Krag to use against her.

Hope squared her shoulders, carefully keeping her gaze away from Sister Olive's body. She shoved as much strength as she could into her words. "Let Rory go or you'll never get what you want."

Krag released her and stalked over to loom over Hope. "Are you saying you'll give me what I want? Unquestioning obedience?"

"I won't hurt anyone. You can never make me do that."

"We'll see," he said, confidence dripping from his words like the bloody saliva from his teeth. "But I accept your bargain. The meat will go free and you will be mine."

A crushing weight slammed down onto her, driving the breath from her lungs. She didn't know what he'd done to her, but she wasn't going to live through it for long. She sucked in a wheezing breath. Dark spots formed in her vision. Krag jerked her to her feet.

He bent over her. His stench made her gag. She couldn't breathe. She felt his hot breath hit her neck and a moment later, all she felt was pain as his teeth ripped into her skin.

Searing cold slid through her veins, burning them as some kind of toxin sped through her. Her heart slowed. Sweat broke out over her limbs and she started to shake.

Krag shoved her head back until her spine felt like it would snap. With a deep growl of anger, he pulled back, his teeth coated in her blood.

Revulsion shook her to her soul and her stomach heaved. Hunger twisted his face, and she knew that while he may have been able to stop himself this time, the next time he might not.

Hope couldn't face the thought of dying by his hands like that. Her blood was Logan's. Letting this monster have even a drop felt like a deep betrayal. Not that she could stop him from doing it again.

Rory was led away by a human. She was screaming something Hope couldn't hear over the roar of her own heartbeat.

Dizziness weighed her down. Krag's horrible face filled her field of vision. He was smiling, pleased with himself.

He lifted his hand and placed his reptilian fingers on her temple. A cold, searing pain whipped through her head, like being stabbed with knives made of ice.

Dark, twisted images flickered through her thoughts. Sinister, alien impulses invaded her. The urge to hunt and kill surged inside her, making her legs twitch with the need to run. Her senses sharpened until she could hear the heartbeats of every creature nearby. The pumping rush of blood through their veins made her mouth water and her hands flex in preparation for digging her nails into their flesh. Hunger bore down on her, hollowing out her insides until the need for blood writhed inside her, demanding to be appeased.

"That's it," she heard Krag whisper over her thoughts. "My vicious, hungry bride."

Chapter 29

Logan was close. He could feel Hope, smell a faint hint of her skin on the breeze.

She was inside the run-down factory across the street. He'd circled it, making sure he'd pinpointed her location before wasting time breaking in.

Nicholas was in bad shape. Logan had managed to patch the worst of his injuries, but the blood he'd needed to take had left Nicholas drained and weak— too weak to stand, much less fight. The warrior was sweating and shaking, but Logan thought he'd at least saved the man's hand from amputation. It was a long way from usable, but was the best he could do under the circumstances.

"You can't go in there alone," said Nicholas, his voice trembling with fatigue.

"I don't have a choice. Sunrise is coming soon. I can't wait for reinforcements."

"Paul and Andra are on their way. So are others."

"They won't be here soon enough. There's no end to the damage Krag could cause in the time it would take them to get here."

"So you're going to go in alone and die?"

"No. I'm going to scout out the situation. If there's an opportunity for me to grab her and run, I will."

"You're not a fighter," said Nicholas.

"For her I am. I'd do anything for her. *Be* anything for her."

Nicholas nodded. "Keep your phone with you. I'll be able to track your movements."

Logan made sure it was silenced, then shoved it into his jeans pocket. He found a spare sword stashed in back with the rest of Nicholas's supplies. It wasn't a Theronai blade. It wasn't imbued with any magic he could sense. It was common and simple, but it was better than nothing—certainly better than relying on what little power he had left in his blood.

"I plan to go in from the west. This close to sunrise I'll probably only have human guards to contend with."

"You can't kill them."

He could. His vow to protect humans ended where the threat to Hope began. "Killing them would draw too much attention. I have better ways to dispatch them."

Logan made sure the engine was running and Nicholas had some bottled water nearby. If Hope made it out without him, at least she'd have a way of getting free.

Once the sun was up, Logan was trapped indoors with the Synestryn until sunset. Assuming he lived that long.

Logan slipped around the building to the back. He smelled dozens of Synestryn nearby, within the building. There had to be a way in and out for them —one that probably involved a simple hole through the steel siding.

Instead of a hole, he found a dock door partially open, the entrance covered with heavy rubber flaps. The stink of demons clung to the area and there were trails of mud, blood, and filth staining the concrete below.

He held his breath and listened. The sky had lightened to a pale gray, signaling dawn. His instincts screamed at him to rush inside and escape the sun, but haste now could get him killed.

Logan parted the rubber flaps with the tip of his sword. A few feet away from the opening was a tall stack of wooden crates—likely a screen against any possible rays of sunlight that might filter in. He saw no signs of demons or humans. He could smell them, he could even hear the heartbeat of at least two humans nearby, but that was all.

He eased himself up and through the opening. He crouched behind the crates, listening for signs of guards. After a few seconds, he was able to locate those heartbeats. They were on the other side of the crates. Definitely human.

Logan shielded himself from sight and scratched on the wood.

"Did you hear that?" asked one of them.

"What?"

A man came around the wall of crates, squinting into the darkness. Silently, he urged the man forward.

He was young, maybe twenty-five. His clothes were dirty and his hair hadn't been cut in months. He was too thin, as if he'd simply forgotten to eat. Ragged bite marks marred his throat where he'd been fed on by demons.

The question was, did he contain any of their blood? If so, feeding from him would only weaken Logan further. But if the man was blooded and his blood was clean, he could give Logan the strength he needed to help rescue Hope.

Logan scratched again, luring the man forward. Two steps later, he was in reach.

Logan dropped the shield and caught the man's gaze. Pale light spilled out over the young man's face, accentuating the gaunt hollows under his cheeks.

The other guard's heartbeat picked up. "Jeff?"

Logan held the man still and silent while he willed him into a deep sleep.

The second guard came around the crates. This one was bigger, healthier. He had only one bite mark on his neck and it was recent. He hadn't been here long. Perhaps not long enough to become infected.

Logan was visible, and as soon as the man saw Jeff lying at his feet, he pulled in a breath to raise the alarm.

Logan was at his side in an instant, cutting off that

scream with a tight grip on his throat. Panic hammered inside the man's chest, giving him added strength.

Before it was too late, Logan took hold of the human's mind and control over his body. Inside the man was screaming, but outside he was still and compliant.

Logan scored a small cut on his neck and breathed deeply.

He was blooded. Clean of Synestryn infection. He would do nicely.

Logan bit deep and sucked the man's blood into himself. There wasn't much power here to be had, but every little bit would help.

He took enough to render the guard unconscious, then eased him to the ground next to Jeff. The two of them would remain here for hours.

Logan shielded himself from sight again and eased around the wall of crates. There was a brief maze of twists and turns, but with every step he drew closer to Hope.

Someone approached from around the next turn. Logan stood still and held his breath.

A woman rounded the corner and came to an abrupt stop. She was wearing a strip of dirty lace wrapped around her hips and nothing else. Her skin was pale, streaked with red from infection. Puffy bite marks covered her neck, arms, and breasts. The smell of rotting skin nearly gagged him.

"I know you're here," she said. "The master knows you came for the woman."

Logan said nothing, refusing to reveal his presence.

She jerked, then stiffened, and her eyes turned black and her lips curled back from her teeth. "Show yourself, leech," she hissed in a voice not her own. "We shall bargain for your woman."

Someone else was controlling her. Krag.

Logan hesitated. The woman's eyes cleared and she shook herself. Tears slid down her dirty cheeks. "Please. Don't defy him. He'll kill her."

Logan couldn't let that happen. He released the shield. "What do you want in return for her freedom?"

The woman's mouth stretched obscenely around a grin. Her eyes blackened and that hissing voice vibrated out of her mouth. "Your blood. All of it."

Logan had expected no less. He was more than willing to trade his life for Hope's, but he had to be careful that his sacrifice wasn't in vain. All he really needed to do was buy enough time for the Theronai to arrive, kill Krag, and release himself from any bargain he made. Of course, staying alive that long was going to be difficult.

The woman doubled over, coughing, and spat blood onto the floor. It was too dark to be fully human blood. She'd been tainted, the same way Hacksaw had.

When she spoke, her words were slow and halting, her breath wheezing out of her lungs. Black swirled in her eyes, and Logan could sense some kind of internal struggle going on within the woman. Krag was controlling her—using her to communicate—and she didn't like it.

Her mouth opened as if someone had pried it. "Surrender yourself and I will free the woman."

"Unharmed," demanded Logan. "She goes free before you take so much as a drop of my blood."

The woman shuddered and clenched her head between her hands. "Agreed."

"Vow it. Make it binding."

"I . . . promise," she whispered, and crumpled to the ground.

Logan nodded, bracing himself for the weight of their bargain. It slammed down into him, rocking him back on his feet. He stumbled for a moment before finally regaining his balance.

The woman stood up, turned, and walked away, her movements rigid and artificial, like a puppet.

Logan followed her, keeping his sword at the ready. Krag would look for a way out of their bargain. He could have one of his minions attack and kill Logan, freeing him from his promise to release Hope. Logan could not trust this demon beyond the letter of their vow.

The woman led him to an open area full of Dorjan and demons. Candles lit the space, circling a gaudy throne on a raised platform. Krag sat atop that throne. Kneeling at his feet was Hope.

Her head was in his lap, and he stroked her hair, petting her like a dog. A dazed look filled her golden eyes as she stared off into space. There was a raw, angry bite wound on her neck, and two burn marks the size of Krag's fingerprints on her temple.

Krag had already damaged her, taken her blood, altered her mind.

Rage boiled from a deep, hidden recess in Logan's soul. He hadn't promised not to kill Krag, only that the demon could have his blood in exchange for Hope's release. The first chance he got, he was going to rip that monster's head from his neck, even if he had to do it with his bare hands.

"Let her go," Logan ordered.

Krag snapped his fingers, and the woman who'd escorted Logan hurried over to Hope's side. She pulled Hope to her feet, helping her stand. Hope trembled, her whole body shaking as she gained her balance.

Whatever Krag had done to her had damaged her enough she hadn't even noticed Logan's presence.

Krag stood from his throne and walked over to the pair of women. He grabbed the head of the woman who had served as his messenger and twisted it until her neck broke.

The woman fell to the ground.

"I guess her bargain with you no longer applies," he said, smiling.

"She spoke on your behalf."

"No, you only assumed she did. You know what they say about assumptions." Krag's hand twitched in a small motion.

Synestryn slid out from the shadows, closing in on Logan. They were all shapes and sizes, from ones he could stomp under his boot, to powerfully built, canine-shaped creatures, to a couple who walked upright and looked startlingly human.

Logan lifted his sword. He slashed at them as they came within range, but there were too many. They came at him from all sides.

Something bit his leg, stinging him with poison. Another one stuck him from behind, ripping his skin open. The smell of his blood drove them into a frenzy. His sword was ripped away and hard, strong hands took control of his arms. He lashed out with his booted feet, but no matter how many he sent flying, there were more to take their place.

Tiny, serrated teeth sank into his flesh. He felt their poison setting in fast, weakening him.

Logan searched for sight of Hope. He knew he wasn't strong enough to survive this much poison.

He'd failed her.

Chapter 30

Inside, Hope was screaming, struggling for control of her body. But it didn't listen to her. It did exactly what Krag wanted. And right now, he wanted her to watch Logan die.

"Enough!" he shouted, parting the sea of black nothingness surrounding Logan. "Secure him over there."

Krag stroked her back, and she wasn't even in control of herself enough to shiver in revulsion at his touch. Somehow, he'd bypassed her free will and she had no idea how to get it back.

Logan was taped to a steel beam. His shirt had been slashed in so many places, it hung in tatters on his body. His blood leaked from dozens of bite and claw wounds; the honeysuckle scent cleansed the stench of this place.

Hope sucked in a deep breath, and somehow it helped reconnect her mind and body for an instant. Her hand twitched, clenching into a fist. She hid it quickly, refusing to let Krag know he wasn't in complete control.

He left her side and grabbed up a cup from the arm of his throne. It was silver, the stem formed by a trio of women holding the cup in their outstretched arms. He pulled a dagger from his belt and handed it to her.

"Take it," he ordered.

Hope did. Her hand moved toward the handle and there was nothing she could do to stop it. She knew what came next. She could see it in the evil plumes of excited anticipation swirling in his aura. He was going to make her use that dagger on Logan.

I won't hurt him, her mind screamed. Her mouth said nothing.

The metal was cold. She gripped it so hard it bit into her skin. The point was wickedly sharp, and a long groove ran down the length of the blade.

Krag dragged her over to Logan. She tried to fight, but whatever he'd done to her was strong—too strong for her to resist.

One reptilian finger pointed to a spot on his neck halfway between Logan's ear and his shoulder. "There, I think. Not too deep, now. We don't want him bleeding out right away."

Hope's hand lifted. The dagger shone in the candle-light, trembling with her frantic efforts to fight Krag's will. The tip moved to Logan's neck, hovering above the skin.

"Fight him," said Logan as his pale eyes met hers. "You're stronger than he is."

She wasn't. Her hand kept inching closer, that wicked blade moving closer to his skin.

"She's mine now," said Krag. "We had a deal and now she's a good, obedient toy."

No. Hope wasn't. She could never do anything to hurt Logan. She loved him.

"I love you," whispered Logan, his voice growing weaker by the second.

His confession of love swelled inside her, giving her the strength to fight. The blade's progress stopped. She was shaking hard enough she wasn't sure how she stayed on her feet, but at least she wasn't hurting Logan.

Krag leaned down next to Logan's ear. "She's mine now. Her blood is rich—rich enough I bet she'll be able to bear my children. I want you to imagine that while you die. Imagine me fucking the woman you love."

Hope's stomach heaved. Like hell that would happen. She'd die before she let him touch her like that.

Krag turned to her and let out a bellow of rage. "Do it!" he commanded.

A grating whine screeched through her mind and she felt the weight of the promise she'd given him bearing down on her again. Her head pounded. The room spun. She couldn't breathe.

"Do it!" came Krag's imperious voice again.

Her hand moved. She screamed inside, but no sound came out. The tip of the blade touched Logan's skin. He sucked in a breath, but didn't look away from her. Not even when she pushed harder and cut him open.

"Don't blame yourself. Not your fault," whispered Logan.

But it was. She'd made a deal with the devil, and now Logan was the one to pay the price for her stupidity.

Krag let out a satisfied laugh and pressed his cup under the wound. Blood flowed freely into the cup for a few seconds before the wound shut.

Hope watched it close before her eyes and let out a relieved breath. He was still strong enough to heal himself.

Krag raised his cup to Logan. "Heal yourself all you like. The longer you last, the more fun we'll have." He stroked Hope's hair. "Isn't that right, my pet?"

He wanted her to answer. She could feel that answer bubbling up inside her, but she clenched her teeth around it, refusing to let it free.

Krag sipped from the cup casually, as if it weren't Logan's life filling it. "I asked you a question. I demand an answer."

"Fuck . . . you," she shoved out past the grating compulsion in her head. He would *not* control her. She needed to be free to act and get both herself and Logan out of here.

Krag slapped her across the face, sending her flying to the floor. Logan's feet were in her field of vision. She was close enough to touch him. Maybe even undo his bonds. But where would he go? The sun was up. She could feel it rising, giving her strength to fight Krag's hold on her. She didn't understand how she knew it—the whole building was dark, all the windows blacked out with thick layers of paint—but she did.

She tasted blood and realized her teeth had cut her lip. She wiped it away and heard a faint groan coming from Logan. She looked up and saw his eyes focused on her hand, a hungry light spilling down across her skin.

Her blood. If she could give him her blood, he'd be strong enough to free them both.

Hope sat there on the cold floor, her mind spinning with some way to trick Krag into letting her get close enough to feed Logan.

She reached up and grabbed Logan's legs, using his body to pull herself up to her feet. She pressed against him, feeling the heat of his skin. His tattered shirt was stained with blood, and this close, she could see the poisonous effects of the bites they'd inflicted on him. Red streaks spread out from the wounds, just beneath his skin.

This was all her fault. If she hadn't been captured and forced Logan to come here to save her, he'd still be safe and sound. She couldn't regret loving him. She couldn't even regret meeting him. He'd turned her world upside down, but without him, she'd still be living a lie, pretending the world was no more than what she saw on the surface.

Most of what she'd seen was ugly and cruel, but not Logan. He was beautiful and selfless and noble. He spent his life helping others find the kind of happiness he himself could never have. It was sad, but there was a beauty in what he did—what he was forced to do to manage inside such an ugly world. Rather than stealing life, he helped create it.

Krag's hold on her mind urged her to move away. She heard his command ringing in her head, pounding at her skull to obey.

She refused.

She brought her wrist to Logan's mouth. She didn't need to tell him what to do and he wasted no time in biting through her skin.

Pleasure streaked up her arm and settled in her chest. She could no longer feel Krag's pull on her. She was free of his presence, for a few brief, peaceful seconds.

Her body flew backward. She landed inside a pile of women. One of them cried out in pain.

Krag had ripped her away from Logan and was now stalking toward her, his black eyes wide with fury. "You feed only me. Your blood is mine."

He reached down and grabbed her by the throat, jerking her up to her feet. He shook her, making her body flail in the air.

Pain shot down her spine until her legs went numb. He picked up the dagger and dragged her over the floor until she was at Logan's feet.

He ripped open Logan's tattered shirt and plunged the dagger into his chest.

Logan's cry of pain echoed off the high ceiling. His body tensed and the tendons in his neck stood out in his agony.

Hope stared in shock, unable to process what had just happened. Logan wasn't even supposed to be here. How could this be happening?

Krag yanked out the knife, and a bright river of blood ran down Logan's chest.

Panic crushed the breath from her lungs. Logan was dying. Because she'd tried to save him.

A wounded sound rose from her lips, full of anguish and grief. "No."

"You shouldn't have defied me," said Krag, pulling her up by her hair.

She couldn't stand. She couldn't even feel her legs. Everything had gone numb.

"Now take back what you gave him," the monster ordered her, then shoved her face against Logan's chest.

Blood wet her cheeks, her lips. The sweet, calming

scent of it rose up, comforting her and ridding her of her shock.

She was going to kill Krag for taking Logan away from her. She was going to make him suffer and feed him to the demons.

From the shadows, she heard a chorus of hungry growls. Eerie green eyes lit up.

"Drink," he demanded, jerking on her hair.

A heavy wheezing sound echoed inside Logan's chest. His lung had been punctured.

Krag grabbed her face with his reptilian hand and pried her jaws apart. Logan's blood hit her tongue, but instead of being repulsed by it, she felt something else.

It was like the pieces of a giant puzzle had suddenly clicked into place. Something within her—something hidden and asleep—woke up and pulled in a deep breath. It stretched and unfurled itself inside her, growing until she was sure she'd burst under the strain.

Power soaked into her cells, changing them. The numbness in her legs disappeared. The crack in one of her vertebra that she hadn't even known was there healed up. The wound on her neck closed; the infection that had begun to spread was eradicated. She could see it happening in her mind even as she felt it in her body.

And then the wall around her memories began to crumble. Things she'd never been able to touch were there, waiting for her to remember.

She saw strange places and faces. The sky burned a bright orange and there were two suns blazing on the horizon. There were no buildings here, no roads. A cluster of rough cabins stood under a canopy of giant trees. The leaves were bluish and so shiny they looked almost metallic. She looked down and found a nut lying on the ground. It was different from any she'd ever seen before, but she somehow still recognized it. An instant later, an old woman with a smooth face that hid her years handed that nut back to Hope. Her name had been burned into it—a token of remembrance so she wouldn't feel so empty in her new life. If she had a name, she had people who loved her enough to give her one.

Hope had held on to that thought as she'd allowed that woman to build the wall and hide all those memories from her.

She didn't know what any of this meant—whether it was real or some kind of hallucination caused by Logan's blood. What she did know was that she was going to get them out of this. She wasn't going to find her past now only to lose it to some asshole demon.

Hope lifted her head. She pressed her hand to Logan's wound, following instincts she hadn't even known she had.

His flesh closed up under her touch. His eyes flared in surprise he quickly hid. She could hear his heartbeat now, faint but steady. He kept his head down, but she could hear a slight tearing sound behind him as he freed himself from the tape.

Krag stared at her, eyes narrowed in suspicion. "What did you do?" he demanded.

His power over her dissipated like smoke on the wind. Her mind was her own and he couldn't touch it. Not anymore.

Krag's demons closed in around them, forming a circle of fangs and teeth and claws. She didn't know how she was going to fight them all off.

Logan broke free and flew at Krag, knocking the demon to the floor. He was thin, his ribs showing clearly beneath his skin. And he was still wounded—covered in festering bite marks. There was no way he was strong enough to defeat Krag.

"Run!" shouted Logan.

Hope couldn't. She knew it would be a death sentence for Logan if she did. He needed her help.

Frantically, she searched for a way to fight off the encroaching monsters. They were only a few feet away now, and she had the distinct impression that once Krag was dead, no one would control them.

Hope grabbed Logan's shirt and used a candle to light it on fire. She tossed it toward one hideous beast that was getting too close for comfort, and then picked up the dagger.

Krag roared, letting out an inhuman sound of pain. Logan stumbled back, holding a black, slimy mass in his fist. Krag's heart.

The demon twitched, bleeding onto the floor.

The group of women who had sat still and silent through this whole ordeal began to cry and scream.

The circle of Synestryn tightened.

Hope grabbed Logan's arm to hold him up. "We need to get out of here."

"I'll hold them off," panted Logan. "You run."

"I'm not leaving you behind."

"I can't fight them off. I can only slow them down. And I can't go in the sun with you. Another Warden will come and kill everything in sight."

Hope looked up at the painted windows.

Logan saw her do it and said, "We might not make it."

"I don't see a choice."

A demon lunged at Logan and he kicked it back into the group. "Do it. Fast."

Hope gathered up all the strength she could and hurled the dagger at one of the high windows. It shattered, letting sunlight and fresh air spill in.

Demons hissed, cringing back from the light.

A shaft of light hit the concrete directly to their left. Logan stepped into it and pulled Hope in for a tight hug.

The air vibrated until she could feel it in her chest. Searing brightness filled the room, blinding her for a moment.

She held on to Logan's body, hiding her face in the crook of his neck.

The sound of wind chimes and breaking glass exploded around them. Demons screamed.

Something warm and soft surrounded her. She opened her eyes to see the bluish light of one of Logan's shields. It spread out over them and the sobbing women who were staring in shock at the slaughter.

The Warden's swords slashed through the air, hitting something with every strike. Black blood rained down over them only to roll off of Logan's shield.

Hope felt his body shaking as he grew weaker. The urge to feed him swelled inside her, forcing her to act. She pulled his head down to her throat, knowing he wouldn't be able to resist.

He didn't. One arm tightened around her while he pierced her skin and drank.

The fight no longer mattered. The abused, broken women winked out of existence. The Warden and the demons and the rain of black blood became inconsequential. All she cared about, all she could feel was Logan's mouth tugging on her throat, his tongue stroking her skin and his body growing stronger as he held her.

It ended too soon. His mouth pulled away and she sagged in his hold, unwilling to step back away from him.

"You're safe now," he whispered into her ear.

Safe? Hope looked up. The Warden had made quick work of the demons, and what it hadn't killed, the sun had left smoking in ashy piles. The women were huddled together nearby, safely inside Logan's shield. At some point, he'd moved her into the shadows, leaving that glowing beam of sunshine.

One of the steel walls of the building was buckled in. A truck had rammed into it, breaking it open from the outside. A tall woman in black leather stood next to a man with a sword. Her hand was raised, and a few feet away, floating inside a giant, translucent bubble was the Warden.

"Cover your ears," shouted the woman.

Logan's hands came down over her ears an instant before an enormous boom shattered the Warden into pretty shards of crystal.

"Clear," yelled the woman.

"Friends," said Logan a bit too loudly, as though he couldn't hear himself.

"Handy friends."

The woman tossed Logan a metallic survival blanket folded into a neat rectangle. "Cover up. Nicholas is waiting outside with the pink-haired girl."

Rory.

Relief weakened Hope for a moment, but she suffered through that weakness, thankful that her friend had been spared.

Unlike Sister Olive.

The nun's body was where Krag had dropped it, staring up into the sunlight. Grief choked Hope and she had to swallow twice to ease the tightness in her throat. "I have to take care of her."

"We will. We won't leave her here."

"You go ahead and get out of the sun. I'll take care of her," said Hope. It was only fitting, since Sister Olive had taken care of her all these years.

Logan touched her face, so gently it brought tears to her eyes. "You're not alone. My friends will care for you." His tone sounded suspiciously like a farewell.

"Will you come find me after sunset?"

He shook his head. "I cannot. One of the others will take you to Eric. He'll make you happy."

She grabbed his arm to keep him from walking away. "I don't want Eric. I want you."

His gaze roamed her face as if memorizing it. "Don't," he whispered. "Just . . . don't." And then he turned and walked away, huddling inside the metallic blanket and out of sight.

Hope stood there, letting the chaos pass around her. He'd said he loved her. It hadn't been a lie. She would have seen that kind of deception flare in his aura.

Sadly, love wasn't as important to him as duty. And because she loved him, she had to let him do what was going to make him happy. Being with her wasn't it.

Chapter 31

Not even the heavy lethargy of midday could lull Logan to sleep. It had been three days since he'd slept, three days since he'd last seen Hope.

Tynan had taken over her care, ensuring she didn't ovulate while Logan's blood was still pumping through her system. Tynan had also seen to her placement in Project Lullaby. He and Alexander had arranged for her meeting with Eric.

Reportedly, she'd tried to kill him with a butter knife.

Tynan said he had another man in mind for her—one a bit more refined and less barbaric. Whomever the man was, Logan hoped he knew how lucky he was.

Logan rose from his bed, washed, dressed, and went upstairs to find something to occupy his thoughts.

Hope was probably already with this man, starting her new life with him. Forgetting all about Logan and the time they'd shared.

Jealousy twisted inside him, grating against his already raw nerves. It was unfortunate that jealousy would get them no closer to discovering why the power in Hope's blood seemed to cling to Logan's cells. None of the other Sanguinar had been able to extract any power from the blood he'd offered them, and they needed to determine if this was a new development.

If so, their job of finding rich blood sources was going to become much more difficult, since no one Sanguinar could dependably identify a source.

He went to Tynan's lab, hoping to offer his services in some way. The need to be of use and end his heartache gave him a sense of urgency he couldn't contain, but he couldn't stand the thought of being around people right now. His mood was too bleak and grating. With all the tragedy that had struck them recently, Logan dared not spread around his negative thoughts for fear of the consequences on the humans here at Dabyr.

The humans who'd been Krag's captives had been sorted out and dealt with appropriately. Those who were not Dorjan and had not been with him long had their memories erased. Those whose minds couldn't be cleansed were residing here at Dabyr, picking up the pieces of their shattered lives.

The few Dorjan whose minds were too infected to ever be free again were housed below Dabyr in the prison cells where they would live out the rest of their artificially brief lives. Most of them would be mad within a month. He'd never known a captured Dorjan to last more than a year before their bodies simply gave out. For them, death was a blessing that couldn't come too soon.

Jodi was safe, living with her parents while the photography studio was rebuilt. Rory had disappeared, probably back onto the streets.

Now that the homeless shelter was gone, Logan wondered where she'd sleep.

An idea began to form in his mind, taking wing and offering him a small blanket of solace. He may never again be able to see Hope, but he knew exactly how to honor her memory.

Tynan let him into the lab, set out some samples of blood for him to study, and left.

It was Hope's blood on those slides. Logan could smell her fragile scent filling his head. He tried to convince himself that never seeing her again was the best. For both of them. The lie left him feeling restless and edgy.

He couldn't concentrate on his work. He kept staring into the microscope, searching Hope's blood for something that wasn't there—a way he could have her in his life. Forever.

Tynan came back into the lab, and instantly, Logan knew he'd been with her. Hope's scent clung to him. She'd been afraid.

Logan shoved his chair back and faced Tynan, teeth bared. "What did you do to her?"

"Who?"

"Hope."

"Nothing. She's fine."

"She's afraid."

Tynan let out a heavy sigh. "I found another match for her. He's here at Dabyr. She wasn't sure things would work out as I promised, so she was a bit apprehensive. It's perfectly natural—nothing for you to worry about."

But he would. He knew he would. He'd worry about her welfare every second of every day for the rest of his life.

How could he not when he loved her so desperately? And how could he remain here, under this roof, knowing she was here as well? With another man.

Logan's body was an angry, alien beast. He lurched up from his seat, knocking the microscope to the floor.

"Either let me remove your memories of the woman or go home," ordered Tynan, his tone final. "I can't work around you when you're like this."

Rage made his limbs shake. "You will never take my memories of her away. They are all I have left."

"Then leave. I cannot tolerate your destructive tendencies."

"I need to keep busy."

"Read a book. Watch TV. Just please leave me to work in peace."

Tynan was right. As fevered as Logan's emotions were right now, he feared what he might do. If he didn't keep to himself, someone might get hurt. It was best he stayed isolated until he had better control over himself. Assuming he ever would.

He went back to his suite to pack. He had to leave this place, hole up in a Gerai house for a while.

He stopped in the hall at his doorway. Hope's scent lingered in the air, as if she'd passed this way.

His heart raced and he hardened in a fast rush. He never should have lain with her. While it had been exquisite, he now knew exactly what he was missing—what some other man would now share with her. He'd never again feel the silky glide of her skin, or hear the soft sighs of her pleasure. He'd never again smell the mingling of their scents, melding together so perfectly. He'd never again taste her kisses or the heated salt of her skin. Never again taste her blood or feel the heady rush of power she gave him.

It was too much to bear. He'd lost too much to ever recover fully. Time would ease the pain, but the hole she'd left inside him would forever bleed at her loss.

Logan swiped his key card and went inside his suite.

Hope was there, sitting on his couch. She froze when she saw him, her eyes going wide with surprise.

"What are you doing here?" he asked. This was some kind of cruel joke. Someone had let her in so he'd have to suffer her loss all over again. Whoever that was would pay dearly.

"Tynan said my choices were to stay here with my memories or leave without them. He said I could share this suite with a roommate. I was waiting to meet her."

"Her? He told me he'd found someone for you."

She stood slowly, her movements graceful and sinuous. She was so beautiful his gaze was fixed, soaking in her loveliness.

Logan remembered every curve of her body. He remembered how she felt under his hand, the way she sucked in a breath and bit her bottom lip when he found her most sensitive spots, like the one at her nape and the small of her back.

His blood heated and he took a few steps to his left so that the recliner hid his erection. It was his shame that he couldn't control himself around her, but it seemed beyond his ability.

She cocked her head to the side, unknowingly drawing attention to her neck. Her pulse beat there, strong and sure, and for the first time in three days, a knot of anxiety loosened up inside Logan's chest. She was safe. Whole. At his side, where he wanted her most.

"Are you saying he was trying to fix me up with another guy?" she asked, irritation plain in her tone. "After that chauvinistic asshole Eric, I'm never trusting a Sanguinar's opinion in men again."

"I . . ." He trailed off, at a loss for how to respond. Of course Tynan would try to find her another mate. Whether he'd told her that was another story. "This is my suite."

"You live here?" she asked, taking a small step toward him.

"Yes."

A smile tugged at one corner of her mouth. "Did you know Tynan told me I could live here?"

"No."

"And what do you think about the idea?"

"Idea?"

She came closer, skirting around the chair that he was using to shield his erection from her. "The idea of me staying here. Sleeping here."

"Sleeping? Here?" His mind couldn't quite grasp the concept. Why would Tynan have sent her here? He said he'd found a good match for her. That match couldn't be Logan. He couldn't give her children.

"Yes. Do you mind?"

Lack of oxygen made it hard to think. She'd been asking him something that he was sure was going to lead to Hope in his bed.

Ah, yes. Her staying here in his suite. Tynan had told her to stay here.

Did he mind? He'd never wanted anything more in his life. "No. Of course you're welcome in my home." That answer was going to cost him dearly as soon as she left. And she would. Logan could not allow himself any fantasies to the contrary. Hope's blood was powerful and his people needed her and her children, even if it took them ten years to find a man she accepted as suitable.

The other corner of her mouth turned up, her smile becoming victorious. She reached up and looped her arms around his neck. After so many days without it, her touch was a balm to his skin.

He shivered against the sheer pleasure of her skin on his, closing his eyes to revel in the moment.

Logan's phone rang. He fumbled for it like a lifeline, knowing that ringing had kept him from doing something disgraceful.

"She's there, I presume," said Tynan, his tone smug.

"Yes. Why? Why would you do this to me?"

"Because we both know that the root of a good match is happiness. You love her. Make her happy."

"But I can't—"

"Give her children. I know. We'll make do. For now, enjoy her. Make her happy. You both deserve it. Besides, I can't have her trying to kill anyone else. It's not good for business."

Logan didn't know what to say. He'd never expected to be freed from his duty, free to love Hope the way he wanted to.

"You're welcome," said Tynan in the face of Logan's silence. Then he hung up.

Hope took his phone, powered it off, and tossed it onto the chair. "We have some things to discuss."

"As you wish."

"You left me. I didn't like it."

"I'm sorry. Truly."

"You said you loved me. Did you mean it?"

He touched her face. He couldn't stand not to feel her

skin against his fingertips for even one more second. "I did. I do. With all of my heart, such as it is."

She pressed her hand to his chest. "I like your heart, such as it is."

"It's yours."

"I know your duty is important to you, and I respect that. But Tynan said it doesn't have to get in the way of us. Is that true? Because if it's not, I'll walk away right now and never bother you again."

"No," he hurried to say. "Don't go. My duty is to my people, but perhaps that duty is best served by showing them that they, too, can find happiness like I have."

"Are you sure?"

"Positive."

Hope nodded. "Good, because there's something I want to show you—something Tynan doesn't know."

"What?"

She pulled his head down until his forehead touched hers. She placed his fingertips on her temples and covered them with her own hands. "My amnesia. It's gone. I know who I am now and where I came from."

Logan's head flooded with images of a beautiful, alien place. Twin suns burned bright and the air was thick with moisture, making lush plants bloom all around. This wasn't Earth. It wasn't Athanasia. It was someplace new.

"Temprocia," she whispered against his thoughts. "I was born here. Raised here."

The image of a stunningly beautiful woman filled his head. She was ancient, but he wasn't sure how he knew that. There were no signs of her age on her face, just a wisdom in her eyes and a confidence in her carriage.

"She sent me here. To save you, to save the humans. She knows the Solarc cursed you and that you're dying. She knows your kind can never feel the sun, so she sent me to be your sunshine."

"What are you?" he asked, unsure if he'd said the words aloud or not.

"Like you. Or at least like you should have been if the

Solarc hadn't cursed you. She said it wasn't your fault, and that no child should have to pay for a decision their parents made."

"You know about that?" he asked.

"I know that your father raped your mother and the Solarc banished you and cursed you to live in eternal darkness because of it. That's why a Warden comes every time sunlight touches your skin. It's the Solarc's way of punishing you."

"It wasn't just my father. It was the fathers of all Sanguinar—powerful human men who invaded Athanasia, abducted women, and raped them. It was a premeditated act—one for which my grandfather the Solarc never forgave them."

"He should have punished them, not you."

"What better way to punish a father than to harm his child?" said Logan.

"And you're still suffering for that mistake. Hundreds of years later."

Not anymore. He wasn't going to let the sins of his father ruin even one more day of his life. He had Hope now, and that was all the sunshine he'd ever need.

"How did you get here?" he asked.

"The Tyler building. There's a Sentinel Stone in the basement. I was sent through that, alone."

A Sentinel Stone left unattended? That could not stand. "We must go there and retrieve it, bring it to Dabyr where it can be guarded."

"We will. Later. It's been there a long time. It can wait there a while longer."

"Are there more like you?" asked Logan.

"Maybe. If there are, they won't know who they are. Their memories would have been stripped away to protect them from attack, the way mine were."

"So you did allow your memories to be taken?"

"Yes. It was the only way to come here and fulfill my duty."

"And what duty is that?"

"The same as yours," she said. "Fighting the Synestryn. Protecting the humans."

For the first time in a long time, Logan did not feel nearly so alone. He had Hope, which was more than he deserved.

He had to find a way to give his brothers the same gift she'd given him—the hope that his life would not always be one of pain and hunger. Surely, if there were others like her, there had to be some way to locate them.

"Is there any way we can identify these people?" he asked.

Hope shrugged. "I see auras—colors surrounding people that tell me about them. Maybe others like me see them, too."

That explained the halos of color he'd seen while in her mind. "I don't know how that's going to help us find them."

"I don't, either. But I remember growing up with others like me—all different ages."

"Maybe the Sentinel Stone in the Tyler building holds the key. We should go and investigate."

"We will. Tomorrow. Tonight, there's something I need to say."

"What?"

"I love you, Logan." She went up on tiptoe and kissed him, her lips soft and warm against his.

All thought of duty or responsibility fled, leaving Hope and her love for him burning bright at the center of his world. She was his refuge, his heart, and for as long as he held her in his arms, his life would be complete and perfect.

Read on for a sneak preview of
Shannon K. Butcher's next novel,

RAZOR'S EDGE

Coming from Signet Eclipse in November 2011

Catching a thief was easy. Catching a thief in the act was more of a challenge—one that made Roxanne Haught's skin sizzle with eager anticipation.

The lavish retirement party was her idea, despite the fact that she'd never met the guest of honor. It was the perfect trap, complete with juicy bait her target would be unable to resist.

She mingled among the well-dressed partygoers, smiling and making small talk as she passed from one cluster of people to the next, waiting for the right time to strike.

Her client, Mr. Chord, had graciously opened his home for his friend's party—something the middle-aged reclusive genius had never done before. Because of that, dozens of people had come here tonight, curious to get a peek into the executive's estate.

Roxanne cared little about the details of the hand-carved woodwork or the intricacies of the mosaic tile floor inlaid with semiprecious stones that seemed to delight many of the people here. She'd seen it all before. She was more interested in the number of exits on each floor and the location of the information she'd been hired to guard.

The stage was set. The party was in full swing. Mr. Chord had made sure that his newest employee, Mary Smith, knew that the plans for Chord Industries' latest invention were being kept safe on his hard drive at home, away from any possible thieves at the office. That machine had no Internet or network connection, making hacking it from a remote location impossible. No copies were being stored elsewhere, not since the last fiasco. If someone wanted that information, the only way to get it was by breaking into his home office.

He was being extra careful this time. Too bad for Mary Smith that her boss suspected her of the theft and had hired Roxanne to catch her in the act.

The Kevlar stitched into the bodice of Roxanne's beaded evening gown gave her little comfort. Mary looked more like the kind of woman who would prefer knives—up close, personal, and silent.

She was a small, innocent-looking woman. She had delicate, softly rounded features, like a porcelain doll. Her bright, cherry red hair was styled in an old-fashioned manner that reminded Roxanne of glamorous actresses from the forties. Her dress matched her flamboyant hair color and skimmed the kinds of curves that made men forget their own names. If it weren't for the fact that her boss was a freaking genius, Mary probably would have continued to get away with stealing his intellectual property.

But Mr. Chord *was* a genius, and after a bit of surveillance, Roxanne was sure he was right. Mary Smith was a thief.

Roxanne stood on the grand staircase that led to the second floor, where several people mingled. She watched Mary laugh at something Mr. Chord said, placing her delicate hand on his chest while she batted her fake eyelashes. The redhead stared up at him in rapt attention, hanging on his every word. Her hands were quick, but Roxanne was watching carefully, expecting the woman to make a move.

Mary didn't disappoint. With a quick, graceful motion, she swiped Mr. Chord's key card from his breast pocket, palming it until it was safely in her red beaded evening bag.

Busted, but not good enough yet. Mary had to be

caught stealing the information or no one would believe Little Miss Innocent was guilty of anything more than stunning good looks.

Mary excused herself, heading toward the staircase. Roxanne turned to the nearest group of people and chatted with them as the other woman passed behind her, moving up the stairs and to the right, toward Mr. Chord's office.

Roxanne caught Mr. Chord's gaze and gave him a slight nod. Tonight, she was going to plug her client's information leak once and for all.

A smile stretched Roxanne's lips as she waited until the last flash of red dress was gone before following Mary down the hallway. The floor plan to Mr. Chord's home was firmly in her mind. There was only one reason Mary would be headed down this hall: to reach Mr. Chord's office.

Roxanne waited a few brief seconds outside the solid wood door, giving Mary time to power up the PC and begin her illegal hacking.

The high-tech keypad controlling the office door indicated the door was securely locked. Roxanne used her key to open it. By the time she swung the door open, Mary was already standing, her eyes wide with innocence.

"What are you doing in here?" asked Roxanne.

"Mr. Chord asked me to look over some of his papers." She held up a key card. "See? He gave me his key."

"Liar," said Roxanne, her grin widening. "But then everything from your dyed hair to your name to that résumé you used to get hired is a lie."

Mary did a good job of sputtering in indignation and picked up her cell phone from the desk. "How dare you? I'm calling Mr. Chord right now to have security escort you out."

"Go ahead," said Roxanne, shrugging. Mary was caught, and if the sweat beading along her hairline was any indication, she knew it. The only way out was through the door behind Roxanne or out the window, which was easily twenty feet down, thanks to the high ceilings on Mr. Chord's first floor. It was too high up to jump out the window, and there was no place in that outfit for her to hide rappelling gear.

Mary Smith was well and truly caught.

"I've been made," said Mary into the cell phone. "Heads up. Window."

Roxanne's confusion lasted for a millisecond, but even that was too long. Mary had a partner—something Roxanne had failed to uncover.

Roxanne lunged across the room to stop the woman, but before she could cross the space, Mary hurled a stapler through the window, jerked a USB drive out of the PC, and tossed it through the broken glass. Roxanne slammed into Mary, pinning her to the window frame. Outside, she saw a man below pick up the drive and sprint across Mr. Chord's manicured lawn.

Sure, the data on the drive was fake, but that wasn't the point. Roxanne had been charged with catching a thief, and she'd failed to realize there were two of them.

Fury boiled up inside her as she grabbed the dainty woman's arm to spin her around and tie her wrists with the flex cuffs she'd brought with her. Mary had other ideas.

She lashed out, slamming her pointy elbow into Roxanne's stomach. Pain flew out from that spot, driving the air from her lungs. Mary shoved away from Roxanne, but moved only two feet before Roxanne snagged her arm and jerked her to a halt.

"You're not getting away," Roxanne snarled.

Mary's hand snapped out, striking Roxanne's forearm hard enough to break her grip, likely leaving a bruise. She reached beneath her short skirt and pulled out a slim knife. "Like hell I'm not."

Sometimes it sucked being right.

Roxanne hated knives. She really did. She would have much rather been at the receiving end of a nice fat shotgun. There was something inherently wicked about knives, something far more sinister than the effective simplicity of a revolver, or the efficiency of a semiautomatic pistol. Guns were designed to kill; knives were designed to hurt. It took a long time to die from stab wounds unless you were lucky enough to have an artery severed. And while Roxanne had been trained to deal with the threat, facing a shiny blade still had the power to make her break out in a nervous sweat.

Mary stabbed toward her, slicing at Roxanne's arm. The blade didn't cut her, but she was sure some of the hair on her forearm had been shaved clean. Good thing she'd brought a gun to a knife fight. It was in her evening bag, which she'd dropped on the floor by the door when Mary had shattered the window. All Roxanne had to do was get to it and the fight would be over. One way or another.

Mary kept swiping, holding Roxanne at bay as she backed up to make her exit. Roxanne made sure not to glance at her beaded bag, not wanting to give away the fact that it was important to her. A woman cruel enough to carry a blade as her weapon of choice would not hesitate to use anything against her she could find.

"I'm leaving. Keep quiet and I won't hurt anyone on my way out," said Mary. The wicked gleam in her dark eyes didn't instill confidence in her words.

"Bullshit. We both know that's a lie."

A slow, amused smile spread across Mary's mouth as she backed up a bit more. Roxanne followed her. As she passed the desk, she picked up a heavy crystal paperweight and flung it at Mary's head.

The woman dodged it, and Roxanne took the opening. She charged forward, gripping Mary's wrist and shoving it high to keep the knife away from her. She used her momentum to slam the woman into the hardwood door. Mary's head hit hard. She blinked several times as if dazed.

Roxanne didn't wait to see if it was an act. She

smashed the knife hand against the wood over and over until the gleaming metal fell to the floor.

Mary screamed in outrage and head-butted Roxanne right in the nose.

Pain flashed red behind her eyes and made them water like crazy.

Roxanne grabbed the front of the woman's dress and flung her to the floor, face-first. Mary's skin squeaked against the gleaming hardwood floor. Roxanne crashed down on top of her, driving her knee into Mary's back hard enough to make her cry out in pain. Something along Mary's back popped, but Roxanne didn't care what it was. She wrenched Mary's hands behind her and pinned them there while she fished another set of flex cuffs from her evening bag.

Mary was secured, moaning, and no longer fighting.

Time to go after the other thief.

Roxanne picked up the knife so Mary couldn't use it to free herself, and dropped it into her purse. She took out her cell and dialed Mr. Chord as she raced out of the office and down to the exit nearest to where Mary's partner had been. "Mary is in your office. She might need an ambulance."

"What the hell did you do to her?"

"Not as much as I would have liked. She had a partner. I'm going after him."

Roxanne didn't wait to hear what he had to say. She raced across the lawn, but the second thief was nowhere to be seen. Behind a screen of manicured bushes, several bars had been recently cut away from one section of the iron fence surrounding Mr. Chord's property, and on the other side of that, there were dark tire marks on the street.

Roxanne had failed to catch him, which meant it was only a matter of time before a new Mary showed up to finish what the last one couldn't.

Mr. Chord was not going to be pleased.

*   *   *

"Mr. Chord is pissed," said Roxanne's boss, Bella Bayne, the next morning.

Bella was the owner of the Edge—the growing private-security company in Dallas where Roxanne worked. They handled all kinds of needs, from threat assessment to protective details to U.S. troop support to ridding foreign countries of any number of pesky criminals. For the right price.

Roxanne's specialty was stealth security for corporate espionage cases. She made sure the bad guys didn't know who she was until it was too late and she caught them with their hands in the cookie jar. At least that *had been* her specialty. Based on Bella's scowl, she might have been demoted to cleaning the locker room toilets if she wasn't simply fired.

Roxanne really didn't want to walk away from the job she'd come to love. She had to find a way to make things right.

Bella stood to her full, impressive height. She was easily six feet tall in her combat boots, and every inch of her was sleek, sculpted muscle. Her stormy gray eyes narrowed in fury. "Where shall we start, Razor? With the fact that your client's information was stolen? Or maybe with the part where the guy who stole it got away?"

"The data was fake. I planted it. Whoever has it isn't getting anything of value."

"And now they know that, too. Mr. Chord told me how hard it was to orchestrate that setup. Your chance to catch the thieves is gone, and he still has no idea who Mary works for or with."

Roxanne looked down and toyed with her wide cuff bracelet. "Were the police able to get her to talk?"

"Not a word. Not even to a lawyer. And now whoever is doing this knows we're onto them."

What was worse was the fact that the police were now involved—something Mr. Chord had wanted to avoid from the beginning, which was why he'd hired the Edge to deal with the problem. If word got out that his designs were being stolen, his company's stock price could plummet. He might lose investors.

Roxanne had no idea about the specifics of the devices that had been stolen from him. She didn't need to know any secret information to do her job. But what she did know was that Chord Industries had contributed to several advances in the field of medicine. His machines helped people. Saved lives.

Because of her, he was losing his ability to do good in the world, and that pissed Roxanne off more than her own failure.

"I'm sorry, Bella. I should have realized Mary could have a partner."

"Yes. You should have. So the question is, Why didn't you?"

Roxanne considered giving her boss some lame excuse. She could come up with a half dozen that might help her cover her ass, but she couldn't do that to Bella. They were friends. Bella trusted her, and she wasn't going to screw that up by lying.

Roxanne took a deep breath and admitted what she'd hoped she wouldn't have to. "I've been distracted."

Bella crossed her arms over her chest and lifted a dark eyebrow. "Distracted? Care to elaborate on that?"

"My ex, Kurt—he's been sending guys after me, having them follow me. I thought he'd stopped a few weeks ago, but I guess I was wrong. He's not done with his games. A new man showed up yesterday, and I spent so much time losing him before I went in to do the job, I was rushed. I wasn't completely focused."

Bella's face darkened with rage and her voice became lethally calm. "What, exactly, are these guys doing to you?"

"Nothing. They just watch me. Kurt was the jealous type, and even though we split three months ago, he apparently still hasn't managed to accept the fact that we're over."

"Give me Kurt's address. I'll go speak to him."

"No, Bella. You'd only make things worse if you confront him. I already did, and he denies everything. I know he's lying, and I told him I'd have him brought in for stalking if it happened again. I thought I'd gotten through, but either way, this is my mess. I'll be the one to clean it up."

Bella glanced at Roxanne's arm, where the bruise from last night's combat darkened her skin. "Did he hurt you, Razor?" she asked, her hands clenching to fists at her sides.

"No. It was nothing like that. He's not a bad guy; he just didn't want to let go."

"I could make him."

Roxanne had seen Bella angry. She'd seen the woman take down three armed men by herself. And she'd heard stories about that building Bella destroyed in Mexico a few months ago. But Roxanne had never seen this kind of steely, quiet rage, so intense it vibrated through her entire body. She'd heard rumors that Bella had a dark past—one she never discussed with her employees—but seeing this kind of reaction made Roxanne wonder just what that past had been.

"I've got it covered," said Roxanne. "I'll go see him today and make sure he quits playing these games."

Bella swallowed several times before her hands unclenched and the redness in her face abated. "I won't have anyone hurting my people."

"Kurt isn't hurting me. He's just jerking me around."

"Are you protecting him?"

"No. He's an asshole for screwing with me like this, and I plan to tell him that to his face."

"I don't like the way he's treating you."

"Neither do I."

"He interfered with your work, and I can't let that slide."

"I know." Roxanne let out a long, resigned breath. She loved her job, but she knew the score. A mistake like this was too big to simply ignore. "Are you going to fire me?"

Bella pulled back her lips in frustration. "I should. That would certainly appease Mr. Chord. But no, you're not fired. However, I'm not handing out any more chances, either. You blow it again, you're out. Our work is too dangerous for distractions. You need to get your personal shit straightened out before I can assign you any more jobs."

"What about finding the guy who got away?"

"The cops are involved now. They're looking into it."

"So . . . what? We just leave Mr. Chord hanging?"

"No. I'm going to offer him our services for free to calm him down, but he already said he didn't want you back. I'm sorry."

The rejection stung, but not nearly as much as her failure did. Mr. Chord was right to be mad. She had let her personal life get in the way of her professional life, which was a big no-no. She knew better.

"I understand. I'll go see Kurt on his lunch break and make sure he understands that his games are over. I should be back by one."

"No. I don't want you back until you're sure you've fixed the problem for good."

Roxanne took a deep breath to keep herself from shouting at her boss. "How long is long enough to convince you?"

"As long as it takes. No less than a week."

A week? If Mr. Chord's thief had left any trail, it would definitely be cold by then. "That's more time than I'll need."

"This isn't negotiable, Razor," said Bella. "If his buddies stay away for a few days, chances are they won't come back. And there's something else, too."

"What?"

"Assholes have a tendency to escalate things when confronted. I'm not letting anything happen to you, so I'm assigning the new guy to you. Wherever you go, he goes. Got it?"

"You're giving me a babysitter?" Roxanne did shout this time, and jumped to her feet in anger.

Bella strode around her glass desk and got right in Roxanne's face. "I'm giving you a badass former special operations babysitter—one I want on our team. Don't fuck that up."

Great. Now she wasn't going to be able to look into possible leads on the thief. Her babysitter would no doubt rat her out. "I don't need him, Bella."

"I think you do. And he needs you, too. While he's babysitting, you're going to explain how things work at the Edge. He's already passed all our tests and breezed through training, but he hasn't taken on any real jobs yet. Think of this as his orientation." Bella pressed a button on her phone. "Lila, please send Tanner in."

"This isn't a good idea. I'm a horrible teacher. You need to get Riley to do the training. He's good at that kind of thing."

"Riley's good at everything, which is why he's too busy for this. You, on the other hand, happen to have some free time on your hands. Deal with it, Razor. This is happening."

Fine. Roxanne had screwed up. If this was her punishment, she'd take it like a woman, get through the next few days, and be back to her real job in no time. "Let's get this over with."

"Nice to meet you, too," said Tanner as he came in on the heels of her statement.

Bella made the introductions. "Razor, this is Tanner O'Connell."

Tanner was not what she'd expected. She'd been so upset about being saddled with a babysitter that she hadn't even considered that he might be a hot one. And he was. Smokin'. Taller than Bella, Tanner stood with a posture that screamed complete confidence. His shoulders were wide, his back straight, and his blue eyes stayed fixed on her, unblinking. An amused grin lifted one side of his mouth and formed little crinkles at his eyes. His jeans clung to thick, long legs, and on his feet were the worn cowboy boots of a true Texan.

"Tanner, this is your new partner, Roxanne Haught. We call her Razor."

Tanner's dark eyebrows went up at that. "Razor? Is that because you have a sharp tongue?"

"The sharpest," she replied. "You'd better beg Bella for a new trainer or I'll skin you alive."

His gaze dropped to her mouth. "Might be worth it."

Bella grabbed each of them by one arm and pushed them toward her office door. "I see you two have a lot to talk about. Outside my office. I have work to do."

"This is a bad idea," said Roxanne, praying for a last-minute reprieve.

Bella ignored her. "And don't think you can come back here in a few hours claiming you tried to make it work. There will be no trying today. Just doing. Got it?"

"Yes, ma'am," said Tanner. "We won't let you down."

Bella gave Tanner a stern look. "She's going to try to ditch you. Don't let it happen. Some asshole is giving her trouble, and if she gets hurt, you're fired."

All hints of amusement fled Tanner's rugged face, making his eyes turn cold. He seemed to grow a couple of inches taller and took a step closer to Roxanne. It reminded her of her best friend, Jake, who had a tendency to be a bit overprotective.

Tanner nodded. "I understand."

"Good. I'm glad that's settled. Now get out." Bella shooed them through the door and shut it behind them.

It was time to let the new kid know how things worked around here. "If I'm going to be your trainer, we have a couple of things to get straight."

"Such as?"

"I'm in charge. You do what I say, when I say."

The slightest creases formed at his eyes, but he didn't refute her order. "That it?"

"No. I don't want or need a babysitter. I'm going to

deal with my personal problems on my own, without your interference."

"Anything else?"

Wow. He was taking that remarkably well.

"I think that covers the basics. But I reserve the right to change my mind."

He moved, somehow maneuvering her so that her back was against the wall. He nudged closer, breaking the edge of her personal space. His voice dropped to a quiet rumble that Bella's secretary, Lila, would have had trouble overhearing from her desk a few feet away. "Then it's my turn to talk. I don't work for you. I work for Bella, which means she's the one who gets to hand out the orders, not you. So, while I'm happy to learn whatever it is you have to teach me, I'm sure as hell not going to stand around like a good little boy while you deal with your personal asshole problems when Bella specifically told me not to."

Roxanne wasn't sure what she'd expected from the seemingly good-natured man, but it wasn't that. She pulled in a breath to put him in his place, but an instant later, his thick, hot finger pressed against her lips, quieting her.

She was so shocked by the touch, she forgot all about the fact that she should have been upset by it.

A touch of vertigo spun inside her head, and she realized she'd forgotten to breathe. The roughness of his work-hardened finger grazed across her mouth as her lips parted slightly so she could pull in enough oxygen.

"I'm not done," he told her. "You and I are going to be working together, and I'm not going to let you do anything to screw up my chances of keeping this job. I need the work. So you and I are going to get along real nice-like and make Bella proud. Got it?"

As close as he was, she could see deep blue streaks radiating out from his pupils. The creases around his eyes were pale, as if he'd spent a lot of time in the sun, squinting. His scent reminded her of a summer drive in a convertible—warm and exhilarating, with just a hint of an incoming storm.

She felt her skin heat and attributed it to her sudden flash of irritation at his high-handed ways.

Roxanne pressed her hands against his chest to push him back, but as soon as she felt the hard contours of his muscles beneath her hands, her mind stuttered for a moment before she remembered herself and finished pushing.

Tanner stepped back, his finger shiny from her lip gloss.

Roxanne pressed her lips together to fix the damage he'd done to her makeup and swore she could taste him. Salt and earth and something else that made her wish for another taste just so she could figure it out.

Not that she would do that. Bella generally frowned on her coworkers tasting one another.

Roxanne cleared her throat to cover her discomfort. "I can see already that you and I are going to have problems."

"Nope," he said. "Not a single one. We're both going to do what the boss says."

No way was she letting a stranger into her personal life to help her make an ex-boyfriend back off. But he didn't have to know that. "Fine. You win. We'll meet back here after lunch and get started on your training."

By that time, she'd have dealt with Kurt and no longer have anything to hide. She'd throw herself into training Tanner, and in a few days everything would be back to normal.

ALSO AVAILABLE FROM

Shannon K. Butcher

LIVING NIGHTMARE
The Sentinel Wars

For nine years, the Sentinel Nika has had one goal:
to save her younger sister from the Synestryn who
hold her captive. Now, the psychic bond Nika forged
with her sibling on that terrible night is fading, and
time is running out. But the one man who can
unlock the power inside her may be the greatest
danger to her.

**Available wherever books are sold or at
penguin.com**

ALSO AVAILABLE FROM

Shannon K. Butcher

RUNNING SCARED
The Sentinel Wars

Lexi Johns has one purpose: to free her best friend
from the hands of the Sentinels. And the Sentinel
she has been running from for months, Zach, has
one goal: to convince her that their destinies are
entwined. For the magic that Zach has absorbed
could destroy him if he doesn't find the woman
to channel it for him.

And he knows Lexi is the one...

Available wherever books are sold or at
penguin.com

Shannon K. Butcher

BURNING ALIVE
The Sentinel Wars

Three races descended from ancient guardians of mankind, each possessing unique abilities in their battle to protect humanity against their eternal foes—the Synestryn. Now, one warrior must fight his own desire if he is to discover the power that lies within his one true love...

Helen Day is haunted by visions of herself surrounded by flames, as a dark-haired man watches her burn. So when she sees the man of her nightmares staring at her from across a diner, she attempts to flee—but instead ends up in the man's arms. There, she awakens a force more powerful and enticing than she could ever imagine. For the man is actually Theronai warrior Drake, whose own pain is driven away by Helen's presence.

Together, they are more than lovers—they may become a weapon of light that could tip the balance of the war and save Drake's people...

Available wherever books are sold or at
penguin.com

S0046

FIRST IN A BRAND-NEW SERIES FROM

Shannon K. Butcher

LIVING ON THE EDGE
An Edge Novel

After a devastating injury, Lucas Ramsay knows he's finished as
a soldier. But when the general who saved his life asks him for a
favor, he says yes. All Lucas has to do is keep the general's
daughter from getting on a plane to Colombia—which is easier
said than done...

Independent to the core, Sloane Gideon is a member of the
Edge—a group of mercenaries for hire. But she's not on the
clock for this mission. Her best friend is being held by a vicious
drug lord, and Sloane must rescue her—no matter how many
handsome ex-soldiers her father sends to dissuade her.

With little choice, Lucas tracks Sloane to Colombia—where she
reluctantly allows him to aid her in her search. But as they grow
closer to the target, they grow closer to each other. And before
the battle is over, both will have to decide just what they are
willing to fight for...

**Available wherever books are sold or at
penguin.com**

S0208